ALL IS SILENCE

A DESERTED LANDS NOVEL

ROBERT L. SLATER

ROCKET TEARS PRESS

Bellingham, WA

To all my students; yesterday, today and tomorrow. Thanks for teaching me so much and sharing your lives with me.

This book is one small attempt to pay some of that forward.

One generation passes away,
and another generation comes;
But the earth abides forever.
Ecclesiastes 1:4

PART I

The End of the World as We Know It

1

"I HOPE YOU ALL DIE!"

Those weren't the last words Lizzie had told her family, but they might as well have been. She couldn't remember what she said when Mama took Jayce and Jerkwad to the hospital, but it didn't matter anyway. They were gone, and all she could remember were the screaming fights and hateful words.

Lizzie stared out through the gap in the dust-encrusted living room blinds. The streets were empty. At first patrol cars had come by several times a day blaring, "STAY INDOORS. NO PHYSICAL CONTACT."

Now all was silent. Lizzie couldn't remember when she had last seen a patrol car.

The clock showed mid-afternoon, but the gray excuse for a day in the Pacific Northwest was fading. Lizzie hauled herself out of the threadbare recliner and trudged to Mama's bedroom. She snuggled under the covers wondering what she should eat for dinner. Mama had filled the freezer with pizzas before she left, but the same menu for a week was getting old.

Holes in the sheetrock beside the nightstand and the wires hanging out reminded her of the dead land-line. The day they went to St. Joseph's Hospital, Mama called to say Jason, Jayce to Lizzie, was in room 314. The next day the phone didn't work. At some point, fixing it became tearing it out of the wall in frustration.

Cell systems had been overloaded since state officials declared the pandemic four weeks before. With the phones down and spotty Internet, Lizzie was alone and disconnected from what was happening. She wanted to go outside. Screw the quarantine.

AC/DC's "Highway to Hell" jerked Lizzie back to her surroundings. Her cell phone? When had it started working? She threw off the covers and followed the sound to the couch in the living room. A picture of Mama that Lizzie loved and Mama hated glowed on the screen.

"Mama?" Lizzie sat on the couch cradling the phone to her ear.

"Honey… I've been trying to call on both lines." Mama's voice teetered on the brink of hysteria.

Lizzie stopped breathing.

Mama sniffed. "Doug's dead."

Lizzie sighed, her shoulders relaxed. Not Jayce. Just Jerkwad, Mama's boyfriend. "I'm sorry, Mama." She hoped it sounded sincere for her mother's sake.

"Are you okay? How's Jayce?"

"Jason's a trooper."

Mama hated Lizzie's nicknames for her little brother.

"I'm in his room," Mama's voice softened. "They didn't have enough empty beds. You have food? You're staying inside?"

"Yes, Mama." Lizzie gritted her teeth; she wasn't going to cry. "How are you?"

A cough exploded into the ear piece. "Other than too many years of smoking? Lizzie, burn the bedding. In Doug's barrel in the yard. Then come back in. Promise?"

"Okay. I will. I promise. Is *Jason* awake?" Jayce was eleven. Was he as freaked out as Lizzie?

"No. He's asleep, snoring. Can you hear?"

"Yeah." Lizzie laughed. Jayce could sleep through anything. She took a deep breath. "Mama. I'm sorry for all the things I said. All the times I was a bitch."

"Lizzie-girl. It's okay. I was your age once."

Lizzie didn't remember having a conversation where Mama forgave her for anything. "Mama?"

"Get some rest. We'll call you tomorrow. Sweet dreams, Lizzie."

"Mama, don't go. I—" She heard the phone click. "I love you, Mama," she whispered.

Jayce is doing good and Jerkwad is dead. Jerkwad always said she'd be out of the house at 18. *Well, I'm here, you're gone, and I'm not 18 for two months.* Was Lizzie a bad person for being happy?

Mama sounded horrible. What if they didn't come home? The cat lady next door never did.

She fidgeted with her cell. It still had the picture of Lizzie and her ex-boyfriend Chad at the water slides. They had stayed friends when she broke up with him at the beginning of the summer. And in September after school started, he was the first person she knew to die. Then the names of the dead started to flow from the school loudspeaker and down her Facebook feed, one by one, until classes were cancelled and the world finished falling to pieces.

She crossed to the liquor cabinet and pulled out Jerkwad's favorite whiskey, the glass Canadian Club Reserve bottle he kept refilling from plastic ones. Lizzie pulled out the sticky cork, "Here's to you, Jerkwad." She tipped it back, her lips on the bottle. The whiskey burned going down, but there wasn't a lot in the bottle, so she took another swig.

If cell phones worked again, were things getting better? Lizzie spun through her contact list and stabbed a name at random. Jennifer. It rang and went to voicemail. "You know who I am. You know who you are. You know what to do."

"Jen. It's Lizzie. Call me."

Another stab; another message. The sound of voices, even if the people were gone, was like music.

Jayce's screaming-bird alarm clock woke her the next morning. Lizzie's head throbbed, her mouth so dry her tongue felt like sandpaper.

She rolled off the living room couch with thoughts of murdering her brother and his wake-the-dead clock. "Jason Ronald. Turn that thing—" Reality slammed back into place. Her brother was in the hospital with Mama. "Shit." She stumbled to her feet, clothes twisted from sleeping in them. Lizzie stalked the alarm clock to its nightstand, wrenched the cord out of the wall and dropped it on the floor.

Lizzie wobbled back to the couch. The whiskey bottle on the floor made her heart jump. Jerkwad's best. But he was dead. He would not be slapping her, or anyone else, for it.

Mama had rotten taste in men. She'd kicked Lizzie's father out when Lizzie was three, blaming drugs and the army. The only thing left was the CD and movie collection Mama kept. When she was old enough Lizzie claimed them and Mama hadn't objected.

Lizzie raised the whiskey bottle to swig the dregs, gagging as it hit her dry tongue. Her stomach threatened to empty its contents. She went to the bathroom, turned on the cold water, and splashed her face. Her head pounded and she knew from experience it would only get worse. She grabbed some ibuprofen from the medicine cabinet and swallowed a few.

She returned to the living room and flopped back on the couch. Her phone flashed. MISSED CALL. "Damn." She thumbed the 'return call' and held it up to her ear. "Mama?"

"Lizzie?" Mama's voice was feather-light and tired.

"Yeah, Mama. Sorry, I missed your call. I was sleeping." Lizzie's explanation felt lame.

"Liz." Her voice broke off.

Lizzie could hear her crying. Her gut twisted and her throat tightened; she felt like she was going to throw up. "Jayce?"

Mama sobbed harder in response.

"No, Mama. I'm coming over there."

"NO!" Her mother's voice was steel. The sobs stopped. "You will not. You are not sick. I am. Doug is gone. Now Jason's gone. Dammit, I'm dying! Please. Lizzie, promise me you'll stay inside." Another sob escaped. "Promise."

"Okay, Mama." Tears fell. Lizzie heard a voice in the background.

"The nurse is here to give me meds, Lizzie. I'll call you, okay?"

"Yeah, Mama. Okay." The phone clicked.

Why hadn't she said *I love you*? Was it too much like goodbye? Or was she just withholding her love like her mother had done? Lizzie grabbed a plate, the closest thing to her, and hurled it against the wall. It left a dent, fell to the floor and shattered. She screamed. It gave her no release.

She headed to Mama's room, keeping her phone close. She collapsed onto the bed and pulled Mama's pillow into her arms. It smelled like her: spicy sweet perfume and a hint of her cigarettes. It had been a week, but Mama's scent had not faded.

Lizzie thought of little Jayce, his short blonde hair she'd dyed red for his first day of school, all the ketchup he put on everything, his annoying habit of having the right answer for everything and never getting into trouble for anything. Jerkwad loved to point out that Jayce was only her half-brother. But losing Jayce wasn't half the hurt; blood was blood. Sobs wracked her body. She lay there for a long time until the sobs faded.

Her head throbbed again. She slid from the warmth of the covers and stepped into slippers. She walked into the bathroom and opened the medicine cabinet, going straight for Mama's pills. She ignored the bottles with her own name, prescriptions meant to help her "get along better" in the "normal" world. Not much point in that anymore.

Mama's codeine would kick her headache quick. She opened the container, dropped one in her hand and put the container back on the shelf.

The pale face staring at her in the mirror reminded her of Mama. She'd never seen it before, but in the black circles and the sad, red eyes, she looked like Mama. Except for the piercings and the hair. Lizzie's buzz-cut had grown out to a boyish length. The frizzy pale pink at the tips faded to bleach blonde and dark at the roots. *I need more sleep.* The alarm woke her way too early.

Maybe she would sleep better in her own bed. She trudged past the sign that said "This way to the asylum" on her way upstairs. The house was bigger than most of the mobile homes and trailers she spent her childhood in, but still small for a family of four. A previous owner had converted the attic into a bedroom with enough space to stand upright if you were short. That's why it was Lizzie's room.

An eerily quiet noon day sun streaming in her window Lizzie woke from her dreamless sleep. No noise—alarms, angry voices, or TV —blared through the thin walls.

She grabbed the cell, checking the screen. The phone was working but Mama hadn't called. Jayce was gone. Dead. Her chest felt hollow, her eyes beaded with tears. "Jayce."

Lizzie wanted to call Mama, but it probably wouldn't do any good. *Trust the nurse, Lizzie.* Mama said she'd call. "But what if she forgets? Shit."

Her head no longer pounded. She felt more herself and even more alone. No people. Not even her cat, Gordito. He'd disappeared last summer—probably had gone away to die.

Out of habit her hand found her cigarettes—one left. She searched for a jacket to go outside and smoke. Mama and Jerkwad had tried to get her to quit, but had done a pretty half-assed job. They both smoked, but they insisted she do it outside by Jerkwad's illegal burn-barrel and use her own allowance. Screw it. She lit up and smoked on her bed.

The cigarette helped, but her restless nerves needed activity. Lizzie could clean up, but the amount of cleaning overwhelmed her. There were piles of laundry, candy wrappers, old CDs and cases strewn all over the floor. Sheets of paper lay in stacks and on top of journals, most scribbled with song lyrics or tattooed with intricate pencil and pen art of abstract shapes, calligraphic characters and rudimentary nudes. Some of the art had made it to the walls. She'd intended to plaster over the ugly blue and green paisley wallpaper, but had only gotten partway done.

Lizzie tucked the cigarette between her lips and pulled out a small burgundy velvet journal, Jayce's birthday gift for her. She held a pen over a blank page, not knowing what to write—how to honor her brother. Her mind flitted from memory to memory.

With pen in hand and only tears on the empty pages, Lizzie gave up. The cigarette she had forgotten to smoke had burned down. She ground the butt out onto one of Jerkwad's CDs she had adopted as an ashtray, wondering if her own cigarettes were more like second-hand smoke.

She could hear Jayce's voice offering to help her organize her room. She'd thrown Dante's *Inferno* at him. If she couldn't write for him, Lizzie could at least clean up a little. She shoved the journal and pen in her pocket and started in on the mess on the floor, piling clothes and stacking similar things. Everything called up thoughts of the past. She picked up a multi-colored shoe done in permanent marker and threw it at the closet. Enough cleaning.

Lizzie ran downstairs. Her hand caught the asylum sign, tearing it off the wall. She wadded it up, wishing she could go back to the past as easily as it came back to her.

2

LIZZIE LEANED IN THE DOORWAY to Jayce's room. His clothes were all put away, and his books were in alphabetical order. He'd had the same shitty fatherless life she'd had, but he couldn't have been more different, escaping from it all with fantasy novels and precise conformity. Now the alarm clock in the middle of his floor marred that conformity. Lizzie stooped to pick it up, and set it on his bedside table next to his calculator watch. She'd teased him mercilessly about the geekiness of it, but he'd never given up thinking it was cool. She smiled sadly, slid the watch onto her wrist, and went in search of some coffee.

Coffee had always been there for her when Lizzie wanted it—cold, but brewed. Now she found the carafe empty. She had seen it made all her life. How hard could it be? She flipped open the lid and found a moldy filter and grounds. She made a face and dumped it in the garbage. Filter, coffee, and water—simple. Three of the big scoops of ground coffee looked about right.

After she turned on the pot, Lizzie sat down at the computer. If the cell phones were working again maybe the Internet was back too. The old dinosaur took forever to boot up. Mama had picked it up for Jayce at a yard sale.

As the hard drive churned away, she flipped the radio on and tuned it to her favorite oldies station. The radio had never quit working. For a few days all the stations had played non-stop record-ed emergency bulletins, "This is the Emergency Alert System, this is NOT a test," interrupted occasionally with a song or two. But, after a while, the stations switched to digital playlists on repeat with alerts on the hour. She'd listened long enough to hear the same songs in the same order.

"...Can't you hear the thunder, you better run, you better take cover..." blasted out of the speaker. This part of the playlist was some DJ's twisted end of the world humor. "... on a heavy trail-head full of Zombies..." She had never figured out the lyrics. She turned it off and plugged in her player instead. She put it on the Dad's Music playlist.

The computer was still loading. She swiveled in the chair, trying to chill. Lizzie heard the final hiss and burble of the coffee maker and grabbed a cup. Not as dark as it should be. She dumped in sugar and settled back into the chair as the browser window popped up. Yes! She had Internet. A new message winked from Jess on the screen. Lizzie clicked to open it.

Jess, Lizzie's best friend from grade school, had moved to Texas in eighth grade. Away from the "bad influences" her father claimed. He had never liked Lizzie. West Texas might as well be on another planet.

Lizzie's father had family in Texas, somewhere. The Guerreros and the Salazars. She couldn't ever remember meeting any of them, though Mama said her grandparents had come up once when Lizzie was two.

Jess's message finally opened. **You out there?**

Lizzie typed: **Im here. How u doing?** Lame, but what could she say? She scanned through the posts in the Facebook newsfeed as she waited for a response, but they were all spam, nothing from real people.

Where is everybody? Lizzie typed a post on her wall:
Roll call. Check in if u r alive.

Then she headed out to the freezer and found some rocky road ice cream. She ate it out of the carton as she clicked into a Google News search. All the articles were variations on the same theme: "PANDEMIC. End of humanity!" None of them were recent. Last one was a couple days old, from the CBC, a Canadian news site. She scanned the article:

"...Can't find the source of the plague...

...long incubation period...

...swift death...

...predictions of 95-98% succumbing..."

She almost choked on her ice cream at the numbers. She swallowed more than she intended and then squeezed her eyes shut as the brain freeze hit.

I'm finally one of the One Percent. She flipped back to see if Jess had replied.

At the bottom of the article in big bold letters was the same warning she had heard so often in the last few days: "STAY IN-DOORS. NO CONTACT." Lot of good that plan was.

Her AC/DC ringtone was barely audible over the stereo. Her phone was charging in Mama's room. She scrambled out of the chair, knocking it to the floor. Lizzie ran, diving onto Mama's bed. She grabbed the phone, and jammed the answer tab with her thumb.

"Mama?"

"Lizzie," an unfamiliar voice said, and Lizzie's heart stopped. "Your mom's here. She's feeling pretty weak."

"Can I talk to her?"

"Sure." The nurse coughed. She didn't sound so hot herself. "Here she is."

"Mama, I love you," Lizzie blurted.

"Love you, too, honey. I'm doin' oooo-kay..." Mama drawled out her words and then trailed off; she sounded totally baked. "Nurse is nice. She's got the good stuff."

"I'm glad, Mama."

Silence on the other end. Then: "Sing to me, Lizzie. Sing the songs I used to sing to you."

"Ok, Mama." For once Lizzie didn't refuse the request. The songs that Lizzie liked to sing now were not the ones Mama wanted to hear. She started with Mama's favorite, "The Rose." When she was done, she paused. "Mama, can you hear me?"

"Uh huh. Sounds. Lovely. More."

Lizzie lay down on Mama's bed and sang through her tears.

When she ran out of Mama's oldies she sang lullabies.

"Hush little... mama, don't say a word, baby's gonna buy you a mockingbird." She made up lines the way she had heard her father had done, keeping the song going and going. Even when her voice cracked and faded to a hoarse whisper.

"Lizzie?" the nurse again.

Lizzie stopped, swallowing to dampen her dry throat.

"Your mom- she's gone."

Lizzie knew—had known. "Can you put the phone by her ear? I want to sing to her some more."

"That was a wonderful thing you did." The nurse took a ragged breath. "I don't think I'm going to see my daughter again."

Lizzie didn't know what to say, so she sang some more. Muffled weeping told her the nurse must be listening. Some countless hours later she realized her phone was dead.

She felt sedated, like her first few days in the psych ward after she'd cut her wrists sophomore year. She stood and tried to shake the cobwebs off. She had to do something. Mama said burn things to kill the germs.

Lizzie grabbed a pile of Jerkwad's crap, plenty of germs there. She kicked open the back door, and hauled it outside into the gloomy evening. She held her breath to keep from breathing in the foul odor of his alcohol-sweat-stained pillow. She dumped everything into the burn barrel. Jerkwad ignored the law, too cheap to pay for garbage more than once a month. Now she would happily burn his garbage in it.

Barking and howling echoed in the distance. Dogs keened, mourning in a cacophonous chorus. She shivered, tugged her shirt tight, and dumped lighter fluid over everything in the barrel, adding a pile of junk mail and advertising for good measure. Rolling up a Target store flyer, she lit one end with her lighter and then held it over the barrel. She held it until the heat hurt her hand, before dropping it and ducking so she wouldn't singe her eyebrows.

The fire burst upward as the lighter fluid caught, flames consuming what was left of Jerkwad's worldly possessions. All except the whiskey she would keep to burn her throat and help her forget. She tossed a few sticks of wood in and thought of getting some marshmallows and toasting them. The thought brought a memory of a blazing beach bonfire, Mama smiling, Jayce making S'mores. It was a bad idea; the marshmallows would taste like Jerkwad's shit.

Lizzie woke to a dark house. She panicked for a moment, fumbling for her lamp. It turned on. Barely 7 o'clock. The sky was socked in with dark clouds. And she was awake. Weird.

She rolled out of bed and went through the house turning lights on as she went. It was probably only a matter of time before they stopped working. She found the defrosted ice cream on the desk, poured it into a glass and added a shot of Mama's favorite liqueur —Gran Marnier. She plugged the charger into the cell and huddled on the rolling office chair at the computer. A response from Jess blinked on the screen.

Roll call. Jess. Texas.

"Sounds like a porn star," Lizzie muttered, smiling despite herself.

Then another. **Lizzie? Are you there? I'm scared. And lonely.**

Lizzie's hand cradled her drink as she one-finger typed a response. **mamas dead. jayces dead. phones dead or id call.** She grimaced at her lame joke, sipping the cold concoction. Mama would have liked it. **what do i do now?**

There was no answer for a long time. Finally: **OMG. My family too. So sorry.**

Lizzie raised the glass to finish the drink, but it was already gone. **me 2. r u alone?**

She wished the dinosaur of a computer would work well enough to do video chat, but last time Jayce had tried, it had taken three reboots to start it up again.

Yes. Wish you were here.

me 2. Her phone had enough juice to turn on now. **im calling.** She left it plugged in as she dialed.

"Jess?"

"Lizzie. Good to hear your voice."

Lizzie set down the drink, as if she could hold Jess through the phone. "Yeah. What're you gonna do?"

Jess' response was a long time coming. "Don't know. I need to bury them."

"They're in the house with you?"

"In their beds. Didn't know what else to do. They kept getting sicker. And I didn't get it. One by one, they just…" Jess' voice faded to silence.

Lizzie whispered into the phone, "I don't want to be alone."

"Don't do anything crazy. Don't even try."

"Hey, I'm Crazy Lizzie. Supposed to do crazy, stupid things."

"LIZ! Don't! Okay?"

Lizzie swallowed; her throat felt raw. *Maybe I'm getting sick.* "I can't promise."

"Dammit, Lizzie, you're my best friend since forever. You don't get to be a cop out. Go outside once it gets light. See if you can find anyone left. Then call me. You hear? If you kill yourself, I'm going to kill myself too."

They'd had this conversation before. "Okay. I won't. I promise." Lizzie sighed. "Not without telling you. But I don't see much to live for."

"Free candy? There aren't any store clerks anymore, right?"

They both laughed and then there was silence.

"I'm exhausted." Jess yawned. "Call me tomorrow, Lizzie. I love you."

"Thanks, Jess."

Lizzie went back to the medicine cabinet and picked through Mama's collection. She took two Sonata sleeping pills and washed the green capsules down with a glass of water, refilled it and drank another one. Then she put on music from the Mama's Sad Songs playlist. She lay down on the couch and wrapped a blanket from Mama's bed tight around her. She wanted to keep that scent around as long as possible, even if it meant she might catch this thing and die. She would never burn Mama's things, even though she had promised.

Breakfast was a bowl of Apple Jacks and the last of the milk. Lizzie mechanically shoveled it into her mouth. Then she drank the pink milk at the bottom of the bowl.

"I go outside, or I never leave, and I die here," Lizzie said aloud, as if Mama was listening. Seemed like she was always breaking her promises.

She went upstairs to her room to get dressed: jeans, Doc Martens with extra socks, one of Mama's threadbare flannel shirts over a baby blue t-shirt with her band logo in permanent marker: *Cut Glass.* She dumped her school backpack and its contents of done and undone homework. The Dante paperback slid across the floor.

Jerkwad had said she'd never graduate high school. Lizzie was seventeen and still needed almost two years of credits, but she had planned on proving him wrong.

"Fuck you," she said and kicked the schoolwork away from her.

She opened her shallow sock drawer feeling for the old cigar box Mama hid from Jerkwad. Cash for emergencies. If this wasn't an emergency, Lizzie didn't know what was. She didn't know if she'd need money, but it would be good to have it. She pulled out the box Mama had disguised with pretty contact paper.

Inside were Mama's class ring, grandpa's hankie, baby photos of her and Jayce. One slipped out she didn't remember: Mama and a very handsome soldier in uniform, and a little baby in a yellow dress with shocking dark hair. Her jaw clamped to keep from crying. She took the photo and all but one of the crisp twenties. She closed the lid and returned it to the drawer.

3

OUTSIDE THE SOUNDS OF BIRDS greeted her. Canada geese squawked overhead, drowning out the more melodious calls of the smaller birds. The drizzle had lifted and the clouds had cleared away for one of those frigid, but glorious winter days.

The goose honks faded into the distance and Lizzie realized what was missing—the sound of traffic on I-5 that helped her sleep at night. Now there was nothing. Over the warm flannel she zipped up a winter coat she dug out of a storage bin under Mama's bed.

She headed down Lincoln Street, putting in her ear buds. The upbeat sound of *4 Non Blondes* brought her a bit of a warm glow as she shuffled through the mushy piles of damp leaves blown up on the sidewalk. When the song said "…screamed at the top of my lungs, 'What's going on?'" she screamed it, too. Nobody complained.

The air smelled crisp and wintery, but as she crossed under the freeway a repugnant smell invaded her nose—the smell of death. It reminded her of when she'd done community service at the Alternative Humane Society. They had gone to a dog farm accused of abuse and neglect to save the animals still alive. She breathed through her mouth and turned the music up.

Someone, or something, was watching her. Lizzie could feel it. She couldn't help thinking… —*Zombies*. She spun around and jerked her ear buds out. She felt stupid, but how many years had her generation waited for zombies?

She spotted something on a porch swing—something slumped over. Her first dead body—an old man, definitely not one of the living dead. His head lolled back at an impossible angle. Lizzie's stomach churned and her eyes darted, searching for something else to look at. The last few leaves falling from the trees held her attention as she continued walking.

As she passed a cute little cottage, a frantic little head popped up and down in the front window, yipping. Poor puppy. She knocked and tried the front door—locked. The dog had heard her and the yipping increased in frequency and volume. She jogged around to the back of the house. A chain link fence wrapped around to the other side of the yard. She reached across and lifted the latch. She tried the back door. It opened into a kitchen, the stench of death and dog shit hit her nostrils. The pup's nails clicked on the wooden floor. His tail wagged as he brushed past her into the back yard.

Lizzie filled the water bowl and found the food in the cabinet over the dish. She dumped the bag on the floor.

A little red light on the counter caught her eye. A cell-phone charging. *What if some cell-phones work while others don't? Maybe I should get phones from different providers.* With a momentary twinge of guilt she grabbed the phone and its charger. As she left the house the pup ran back in and dug into the food. Lizzie shoved the door all the way open and pushed the garbage can against it. She jammed a garden hoe upside down in the dirt to keep the gate from closing.

How many other pets were trapped in the city? And what about the rest of the country? The world? How many people had thought of man's best friends in the end?

A few hours later Lizzie had gone six more blocks, accumulated a couple more cell phones with chargers, and "saved" six cats and four dogs.

She had gone no further into the pets' homes than she'd had to. She had seen no more bodies, living or dead, which was fine by her. But the smells in each house told her if she had pushed in much further, she would have. She had to stop. Sooner or later she would come across a house where the former residents were not tucked away in bed, out of sight.

Across from the Fred Meyer Lizzie paused out of habit for the "Don't Walk" sign, glancing both ways. She chuckled. Middle of the day and nothing was moving. The "City of Subdued Excitement" was dead. Lizzie glanced around, nervous. She tried to shake off the scents lingering in her nose and the feeling that someone was watching her.

The doors to Fred Meyer startled her by opening obediently. Fluorescent lights buzzed overhead in the strange silence of the empty store. The deli reeked and the produce swarmed with fruit flies. She found a couple of decent apples, wiping them on her pants. The refrigerators hummed along. Lizzie picked up a frozen pack of burritos and stuffed it in her backpack.

All the good-for-you wheat breads were green and white in their packages. Lizzie selected one of the suspiciously well-preserved loaves of white bread. The milk all expired on the 8th, but she opened one and smelled it. It didn't stink, so she tipped it back and touched it to her tongue. Not curdled yet. She grabbed some mac and cheese—the spendy Kraft kind—a 2-liter of Coke and some waffles.

She approached the checkout lane, glancing around. She thought about paying, but dismissed the thought with a laugh. Jess was right. Free candy. And nobody to bust her for shoplifting. She shoved handfuls of chocolate bars into her backpack and pockets, then opened a pack of M&M's to munch on as she exited the store.

Outside, she decided to take a different way home. The fading daylight made her quicken her steps; dark rain clouds gathered on the horizon. On the other side of the empty overpass she hurried past the old St. Luke's branch of the hospital, an outpatient drug rehab and nutrition clinic that had been converted into a makeshift triage hospital. The sign out front said, "Danger! Quarantine! Do NOT enter!"

Lizzie thought she saw movement down Holly Street. Probably another dog. She passed through downtown. Am I really alone? Bellingham was a medium-sized city, half an hour from the Canadian border. She tried to recall how many people lived in the city— 100,000 sounded right. But there was no sign of them.

Most of the lights still advertised empty storefronts. Nothing looked disturbed. Just empty.

Jess had told her to find someone, all she had found were pets— how typically "Lizzie." Animals were easier to deal with than people. She wasn't even sure what she'd do if she did see someone. Run, probably.

The second body she found was at a small mom and pop store. It lay face down. A dark raincoat covered the corpse, but a pool of dark blood-saturated water lay around it. The store window had been smashed. A bat lay amongst the chunks of glass. Lizzie backed away. That one hadn't died of the plague. She started running, but stopped at the end of the block. Was there anyone alive to chase her?

Lizzie walked to Bellingham High School on the off chance that someone she knew was there. One of the clear-windowed, garage-style roll down doors was open. She walked into the building. A few birds circled inside. Lizzie yelled, "HELLO?"

A white board had the words "School Closed" written across it, along with various locations for hospitals and triage centers and the ever-present "Stay inside" warning. She erased it and wrote a new note: "If you can read this and you're not infected, come visit me. Lizzie G. 2224 Lincoln St." The address didn't exist, except some-where under the freeway, but she could see anyone looking for it from her house.

She left out the back door onto Kentucky Street. A shape sham-bled in the distance, odd but unmistakably human. Her brain told her to run, but she told herself there was no such thing as zombies and shouted: "Hello?"

It turned and moved toward her—a man in his mid to late-thirties. He had a patchy beard with a few white hairs, a leather jacket set off with studs, and a spiked dog collar around his neck. His eyes looked wild as he drew nearer.

"Hi." It was all she could think of. Lizzie could see his mouth working, but no sound came out. She thought maybe he was drunk or stoned, or both.

"Are you infected?"

Nothing registered in his eyes.

Maybe this wasn't such a good idea. "Wait! Please, stay there." She warded him off with her hands.

He looked confused, but he did stop, staring at her as she stared back at him.

"Are you hungry?"

That got a response. He lurched forward. His eyes were alive and his mouth looked like he was salivating. She pulled out a Snickers bar and tore it open with her teeth. He ran toward her. Lizzie screamed and backed away. He stopped again. She tossed the candy bar at his feet. He collapsed cross-legged and wolfed it down—she was pretty sure with the wrapper.

She continued to back away. She pulled the candy bars out of her pockets and dropped them in the path. As soon as she was around the building she broke into a run. She ran all the way home —the milk and 2-liter bouncing painfully against her back.

Inside, Lizzie locked the deadbolt behind her and slid to the floor. How long had it been since she'd run that far that fast? Years. But her little feet had carried her quick and sure. Her little feet. Mama's joke about boobs and Dolly Parton's feet came back to her. 'Things don't grow well in the shade.' Nothing but shade in Bellingham.

When her heart stopped racing, she noticed it had gotten dark. She flipped the light switch on and opened the closet, reaching back to where Jerkwad's shotgun lived. She pulled it out and spun the numbers on the trigger lock. Her hiking pack leaned against the back wall. She pulled it out, too. The first aid kit, freeze-dried food and warm clothes might come in handy.

Lizzie checked that the shotgun was loaded and set it on the kitchen table. She slipped off the backpack and put away her haul, adding it to the minimal contents of the fridge: Jerkwad's cheap beer, a bit of lunch meat, salsa and salad dressings. She grabbed one of the beers, popped it open and took a swig. It tasted like carbonated piss. She set it back on the shelf and shut the door.

She cracked open the pack of frozen burritos, threw a couple in the microwave on a paper towel, then nudged the mouse at the computer. Maybe Jess had left a message.

Sure enough. **Lizzie! Call me.**

Lizzie pulled her phone out and hit the redial button. It rang and rang.

Jess picked up, breathing hard. "Thank God, Lizzie. You had me all worked up. I called your number, but you didn't pick up. I thought maybe you…"

"Jess! I'm here. I promised." She glanced at her phone. "Stupid ringer button was off. I went out today, like you said. You know how I used to say Bellingham was a dead city, now it really is." She laughed.

"Lizzie? You fucking scared me."

"Jeez, Jess. You dropped an F-bomb. You don't talk like that. I went out like I said I would."

"Yeah. I thought you killed yourself."

"I'm sorry," Lizzie said. "I met someone…"

"Alive?"

"Yeah. Mostly. Kinda weird. He couldn't talk. Seemed kinda dumb. Reminded me of the dogs I was saving today." Lizzie recounted her adventures of the day, but stopped when she realized that Jess was too quiet. "You okay, Jess?"

"No." Jess sniffled. "I tried to dig a grave. But I didn't have the strength. I gave up. I thought about burning the house down."

"Oh, Jess." Lizzie wished she could hug her through the phone.

"We have an old root cellar, sunken, near the house. I wrapped them in blankets," Jess said, weeping. "Carried them in a wheelbarrow." A sob punctuated her pain. "I lay them on the shelves. I don't think I can stay in the house, Lizzie."

"No. You can't. Go into town. Is there anyone else you're in touch with?"

"An aunt. In Maine. And it's been a few days." Jess's voice turned angry again. "Why'd God do this? Why are we still alive?"

"I don't know that God did this." Lizzie sighed. "I wish I was there or you were here."

"I'd rather be there. With you." Jess sniffed. "Tomorrow I'll go into town. Not sure where from there."

"Me neither. It's weird. The worst part is the silence. Outside, the quiet gets to me." The microwave chimed reminding Lizzie her food was heated. "Hey, I'm gonna put you down while I get my burritos, 'kay?"

"I'm wasted tired. I just need to sleep. How 'bout I call you tomorrow night."

"'kay. Night, Jess. Love you."

"Love you, too. Night, Lizzie."

Lizzie snuggled into her Mama's bed, eating her burritos and salsa. She settled in to watch a movie marathon from her dad's collection: *Pretty in Pink*, *Sixteen Candles*, and *Some Kind of Wonderful*. End with the best: Watts, the feisty drummer, was her favorite character ever.

The endless repeating menu music of *Some Kind of Wonderful* woke Lizzie about three a.m. She turned it off and got up to brush her teeth.

Back in bed the quiet would not let her rest. Her mind raced. So much had happened today, she didn't know what to make of it all. She knew one thing for certain. She was alone.

4

LIZZIE WOKE SWEATING. *GOD, AM I feverish?* She put her hand to her forehead. *You're being paranoid.* It was the covers; she kicked them off.

The clock read 5:35 AM, but she was wide awake. She felt tired, but didn't want to go back to sleep. She sat up and looked out the window. It was a dark, damp November morning. The crescent moon shone through a gap in the clouds.

Lizzie felt jealous of the moon as she got out of bed and headed for the kitchen. The moon always returned, even after her darkest hour. Lizzie had no idea how she was going to come back from all that had happened. She poured a cup of yesterday's coffee and put it in the microwave. Then she fixed herself instant oatmeal.

After breakfast she stepped outside into the pre-dawn air. It was cold, but not freezing. She shivered and zipped her coat. Yesterday she looked for food, and someone left alive. Today she had a different goal.

Destinacione: El hospital. Though her father spoke Spanish and her original last name was Guerrero, the only Spanish she knew was from Dora the Explorer and song lyrics: "Uno, dos, tres, catorce" and "Si no me quieres, librame." *Lo siento, Papa.* Lizzie hit the street, and headed up the opposite direction beside the freeway.

At the end of the street she took the trail leading to her old elementary school, Sunnyland. The clouds had cleared away and the sliver of a moon appeared stark in the growing daylight. She slipped through the shadows of the trees until she came to the one Jayce said looked like an old man's face. It stared at her with mournful eyes.

She came out at the War Memorial and walked toward the school. It was strange to see the play equipment, with its faded primary colors, silent and empty.

Lizzie left the school behind and crossed James Street. She felt a tingling on her neck again like someone was watching her. This time she stepped behind a car and ducked down. Sure enough, her hungry acquaintance from yesterday was following her.

"Shit," she whispered. She should have brought the gun. Lizzie looked through the semi-tinted windows of the car. He'd seen her and was walking straight toward her.

"Hey, dog-collar man, you hungry?" She took out another Snickers bar, peeled back the wrapper and held it up for him to see, laid it on the hood of the car, and backed away.

A big, dumb smile lit up his face when he saw her. While he devoured his treat, Lizzie hopped a fence and cut across a couple backyards to lose him. She reached the end of the row of houses. Exposed to the street again, she ran.

She reached the hospital, her nerves live-wired, LIzzie hopped in an unlocked car, closed the door, and watched the way she had come. Her fingers found their way to her mouth. *Don't chew your nails.* It was always Mama's voice saying that.

She'd picked up a tail. He acted like a dog, a dog-man.

After a while, she decided she was safe, safe. *Safe from Spike, the dog-man.* Lizzie smiled to herself—Spike suited him. She headed to the hospital doors. Like at St. Luke's, a sign in front said, "Danger! DO NOT enter! Quarantine!" She kicked the sign over as she passed.

The automatic doors opened as she neared. "Abandon all hope, ye who enter here," she muttered, quoting Dante. Air whooshed out like she had unsealed a tomb, carrying the reek of death and bleach. Her stomach heaved and she clamped her hand over her mouth.

A body slumped over the information desk. Others lay at odd angles on and off the seats and stretchers in the waiting room. As she pushed further in she had to pull her shirt up over her face against the smell. Everything screamed at her to run away. Her imagination went into hyper drive. She envisioned the dead bodies rising around her. *This is real life, not the movies,* she told herself, trying to shake the images.

At the directory on the wall she looked for the elevator. She hit the up button. Out of the corner of her eye, she thought she saw an arm move. She hurried in and punched Floor #3.

The elevator doors sealed together with a bang. Her heart lurched. What if they didn't open again? What if the elevator plummeted down and smashed her to bits? But it glided upward like it should. As it came to a slow stop at the third floor, Lizzie tugged the doors open.

There was a morbid orderliness here: bodies stacked neatly against the wall. This time Lizzie's stomach upended and most of her breakfast landed in a potted plant. She rinsed her mouth in a water fountain and got a handle on herself, scanning door numbers for 314.

A shuffle sounded behind her. She froze. *Get a grip, Lizzie. Stop freaking out. It's your imagination.* It had to be. But no. Something moved again. She swiveled slowly. A hand reached out for her and she screamed.

Her scream trailed off as a middle-aged man wearing scrubs and a stethoscope strained to speak. "You shouldn't be here," he mumbled, barely able to put the words together.

"My mom and brother. They came here after they got sick." She didn't know what else to say. Was she in trouble?

His name tag read: Dr. Reynolds, Pediatrician. He eyed her strangely, trying to keep his balance. He didn't look like he was in any shape to enforce the quarantine.

"You—you're immune." His words came with more difficulty and he stumbled to the floor.

"What?" She knelt beside him, not sure she understood. *I'm immune?*

"Not sick. Natural immunity." His speech was slurring and running together, becoming less and less coherent. "Find others. Have babies. Keep on. Strong."

Then, as if he'd burnt the last of his candle, he smiled a half smile and slid to the floor.

Was he dead? Lizzie pulled away from him in horror, skittering backwards like a crab, bumping into a medical cart. She used it to scramble to her feet and then pushed it so it blocked him into the other end of the hallway. He snored, letting her know he still lived.

The doctor's freakish plan to have her survive and repopulate the planet had a fatal flaw. She was sterile. Her family doctor had told her she would never have kids after some asshole gave her chlamydia.

Room 314 beckoned her like a haven from the nightmare behind her. She closed her eyes as she opened the door, not wanting to see yet another awful scene. She breathed deep and opened her eyes. There lay Mama with Jayce nestled in her arms. They looked asleep, peaceful. Had Mama refused to let Jayce go? Or had there been nowhere left to put him?

On the floor, curled into the fetal position, was the nurse with a bottle of pills in her hand. Lizzie gently extracted the bottle from her stiffened grasp. Oxy's. Empty. A way out of the nightmare, an emergency exit. Without the bottle the nurse appeared to be praying.

Lizzie kissed her mother's cold forehead. Straightened her hair and tousled her little brother's. "I stole your watch, little man. I miss you," she said through sobs. "I love you both." She lay her head down on them, but they weren't there.

She had come to find out—to make sure. It was real. She thought about burying them, but if Jess couldn't do it, how could she? The thought of leaving them there pissed her off. She screamed, letting the rage keep the tears away. All the profanity and swear words she knew boiled out in a torrent.

When she was done, she pulled a sheet up to cover Mama and Jayce, and stumbled from the room. She couldn't go back past the doctor so she pushed open a door at the end of the hall that said "Emergency Exit Only," ignoring the shrill alarm that sounded behind her.

She couldn't remember the walk home. It was like she'd lost that time. The shot glass in her hand, the pink frilly one Mama got in Vegas, was filled to the top with amber liquid, Mama's brandy. She raised it, pondering what to toast.

"A better place!" she said and downed it.

The brandy burned down her throat and out her nostrils. She filled the glass again. Pain was an old friend. It told her she was still alive. She stared again at the ladder of cuts on her arm. Her fingers traced the scars, soft white lines that had started as a vivid red ruin. She hadn't cut since she moved the blade to her wrist. Blood and pain had always seemed like the only true reality.

There were no messages on Facebook, no texts, no calls. There were 37 saved messages in her voicemail from before the end of the world. Lizzie listened to them one by one: Jayce's voice. Mama's voice. Jess. Even one from her ex, Chad. All normal, dull and wonderfully "real." It should have made her sad. But the brandy flowed in and no tears came out. She jabbed delete at the various drunken and angry messages from Jerkwad, and saved the rest.

Lizzie tried calling Jess. She let it ring. No answer.

She tried the family cells. No answer.

Finally she texted: **Call me. Please. Lizzie.**

She plugged in her player and set it to random. The bottle of brandy was getting low. She recognized the darkness coming. She'd hated her life, high school, her mother's endless string of boyfriends. Well, she got her wish and everyone had left her alone, but it felt more like they left her behind.

Why did I have to be immune? It could already be over for her if she had gotten sick and died like everyone else. She sent Jess another text: **Dont know if i can take it much longer.** She'd made a promise to Jess, but what if Jess was already dead?

She sat heavily on the computer chair nearly upending it. She grabbed the desk to steady herself and pulled up Facebook. She tapped the letters on the keyboard with a dramatic flair: **Goodbye cruel world.**

Lizzie glanced at the shotgun sitting on the kitchen table. She stood and stumbled toward it, picking it up, hefting the weight in her hands. A vision of blood spreading over the ground popped unbidden into her head, like the body at the convenience store. No sense leaving a mess.

She walked into the bathroom, lay down in the tub, and put the barrel of the gun in her mouth. The metal tasted acrid and oily. She checked that she could still reach the trigger. Then she lay there, hugging the shotgun like it was her last friend in the world.

"NO!" Lizzie shoved the shotgun away. It hit the wall with a clatter and slid behind the tub. She couldn't do it. She couldn't pull the trigger and blow her brains out.

She dragged herself out of the tub, holding onto the toilet. The medicine cabinet. Her eyes wouldn't focus to read the labels, but she figured there was no need to be choosy if she took enough. Her hands struggled with the lids, but soon she had a double handful of various pills.

She started swallowing, chasing the pills with water. *I don't want to die in the bathroom.* She stumbled to Mama's bed and took the last handful.

By the time she got to the last two pills, her hands could barely lift them to her mouth. Her eyelids were just as heavy. She managed to pop them in as the world got dim, but they caught in her throat. The last thing she remembered was coughing, and her body wracking with spasms.

5

THE NEXT SENSATION LIZZIE FELT was her body being lifted and carried. She didn't want to open her eyes; she was in a warm and safe place. It felt like the times a long ago when she would fall asleep and wake up to find someone carrying her to bed. *Daddy?* She wanted to stay in this place.

"Lizzie?" A male voice asked.

"Daddy?" She opened her eyes reluctantly. Light stabbed at them and she brought her hand to her head with a groan.

"No. It's Zach."

"Zach?"

"Zach Riley. From high school. Sophomore year? I saw your post."

She was mortified. Did she say "daddy" out loud? "I wasn't expecting you. Is this Hell then?" She giggled. Zach had been a pest, forever pledging his love for her.

"No. But I bet it feels like it. You threw up all over yourself. You need a shower."

Lizzie smelled the puke and squinted down at the crusted mess on her Queen t-shirt. She gagged at the sight.

"I'm going to sit you on the toilet seat," Zach said, setting her down gently.

"'kay." She felt her body make contact with the hard seat and felt a twinge of regret at being separated from Zach's warmth. One strong hand stayed on her shoulder though as he turned on the tap in the tub. The connection felt good. Even if it *was* just Zach.

It had been a couple years since she'd seen him. This strong young man with the John Deere ball cap was very different from the short, pimply punk kid she remembered. "Where'd you come from?"

"Sedro. Drove up as soon as I saw your post."

"My post?"

"You said you were gonna off yourself. On Facebook."

"Oh, I don't remember that at all." Her face flushed, and she turned away from Zach.

"How are you feeling?" he asked.

"Hungover." She leaned her face against the ceramic sink, solid and cold. Someone had found her. "Not dead."

"Good." Zach said looking concerned.

Nobody had looked at her like that in a long time. "Fuck you, Zach," she said, trying to push him away and stay upright on her own. Was it the look of concern that made her angry or the fact that she wanted it. "I didn't want a hero."

His eyes dropped. Her anger threatened to melt. She always had a hard time staying mad at him. Damn puppy dog-eyes thing. Lizzie wrapped her arms around him and squeezed. Her head only made it up to his chest where his heart pounded. Here was a peaceful place. She hadn't touched anyone alive since hugging her mother and brother goodbye. The tears welled up in her eyes. "Sorry, Zach. You didn't deserve that."

"I didn't save your life, you know." he said soft in her ear. "I found you. Disgusting, but definitely alive."

"Oh."

"You still want to die?"

"I can't decide." Lizzie sat back. "I think I can stand." Her feet were wooden, but the world didn't feel quite so spinny anymore. "I gotta shower."

"You think it's safe?" Funny how the anxious red-headed kid still stared out of the now adult-sized face.

"You mean am I going to fall down, or am I going to try to kill myself again?" She could see from his face that was what he meant. "Look. I tried to kill myself." She took a deep breath to calm herself and then punched his gut to get the dopey concern right off his face. "I thought I would never see anyone again. But here you are."

Lizzie continued forcing her voice to a softer tone. "I'm not going to do it again. Not now anyway. And besides, I don't seem to be very good at it, right?"

That got a hint of a smile from him. And that pissed her off. "So, leave me the hell alone so I can get this puke off me!"

As soon as she found someone, all she wanted was to be alone again. What was wrong with her?

He continued to appraise her. His look said he wasn't going anywhere and she realized she needed to try a new tactic.

"I'm hungry. Can you fix us something to eat?" She pulled off the vomit-covered shirt and stepped out of her sweats. The bathroom was cold and she felt goosebumps spread across her skin.

He stumbled for words, his eyes dropping to her bra, then lurching back up to her face. "Yeah, sure..."

"Go." Lizzie pointed. He scurried out as she slipped off her bra. Boobs and butts: Quickest way to turn an intelligent male into a bumbling idiot.

She slipped out of her underwear and jerked the tap all the way to hot. Not waiting for it to warm up, she pulled the shower knob out and climbed shaking into the freezing water. The cold water poured down drenching her hair, it was longer than she was used to; there was actually something to shampoo.

The water got hot, but not too hot. Damn Jerkwad—more like tightwad. Tomorrow she'd turn up the temperature on the water heater. For that matter she should crank up the furnace too; make the house livably warm.

Damn she had gotten skinny—a month of hardly eating and stress had made her as bony as those anorexic supermodels she so loved to hate. If Chad could see her now would he even recognize her? LIzzie ignored the hair in her armpits and on her legs. It had gone from stubble to dark hair. Fuck it. End of the world rules apply.

Tears flowed. They mingled with the water. She tried to let the shower wash them away like they didn't exist, but her body shook with sobs as she sank down into the tub. She wrapped her arms around her legs and sat in the spray bawling her eyes out.

She hadn't cried like this since she was a kid. Weakness got you pushed around like Mama. Lizzie never wanted to need a man like that. Not even if she was the last girl on earth and the world needed to be repopulated. She sobbed harder. But here she was at the end of the world, and she felt like she needed Zach desperately.

The water went cold. She gritted her teeth, slammed the knob in, and stood up, grabbing a fluffy towel. One of the good 'guest' towels. It felt good. Not scratchy like the old ones Mama made them use. *Like they ever had guests.*

She hoped Zach hadn't heard her crying. Just because she needed him a little, didn't mean he had to know it. She wiped the fog from the long mirror on the back of the door and checked to see if her eyes were puffy. She'd looked like shit in general, so he probably wouldn't notice. Still, she ran a washcloth under cold water and pressed it to her eyes. One of Mama's tricks of maintaining dignity.

All the bedrooms were on the other side of the kitchen from the bathroom. She had no clothes other than the vomit covered ones, so she had no choice but to wrap herself in a towel and walk past him.

She opened the door and hustled down the hall, something smelled good in the kitchen; she slowed enough to glance in. He looked up from cooking and his eyes got bigger. She hurried past and took the stairs to her room two at a time, shouting, "Back down in a minute."

Her clothes strewn on the floor in various piles still looked like a mess. Lizzie yanked a black knit skirt her friend Nev called cute from her "mostly clean" darks pile. No. The last thing she wanted was cute. She tossed the skirt aside and grabbed some jeans, holes worn in, not cut for effect. She needed a bra, or did she? Mama's voice nagged in her head: "You don't want to sag faster than gravity requires." She picked a bra and then pulled on a t-shirt, from one of the light "clean" piles. Its writing looked like Asian Kanji characters, but said "Fuck you" if you looked at it sideways. She remembered with a smile how long it had taken Mama to catch on; her teachers never noticed.

She shrugged at herself in the mirror; her boobs were too obvious so she put on an army fatigue shirt to complete the outfit. That was better. She didn't want to give Zach any ideas.

The smell of whatever was cooking wafted up the stairs to her room. Bacon? Her empty stomach tugged her downstairs. She padded gently into the kitchen wanting an element of surprise. Zach had his back to her, stirring something in a skillet.

"Smells delicious."

He spun around wielding the spatula like a knife.

"On guard," she said. She was glad to see he was nervous too, but she felt a little guilty—she knew that what she had been through put her on edge.

"You look less dead," Zach said, lowering his spatula.

"Thanks. You're pretty handy with that spatula. Should be useful if we get into a deadly food fight."

He smiled at her with the same goofy, lopsided grin Lizzie remembered.

"What's for dinner?" Lizzie asked, peeking at the sizzling skillet.

"Breakfast. Found some bacon in the back of the freezer and you had a few eggs. Hope you like 'em scrambled."

"You mean we had something that wasn't frozen or in a box?" She lifted down the last clean plates; the sink overflowed with dirty dishes. Jerkwad always hounded her about the dishes and she was pleased not to do that particular chore anymore. "How'd you learn how to cook?"

"Contemporary Living class and cooking shows on YouTube." He shrugged.

She raised an eyebrow.

"Dad and I moved in with Grandpa after mom kicked him out. None of us could cook. So I had to learn a few things."

Lizzie took the open beer out of the fridge.

Zach snatched it out of her hand and replaced it with a glass of orange juice. "How about O.J. instead?"

It was the perfect accompaniment for breakfast dinner. She thought about adding vodka, but Zach seemed pretty determined to clean her up. She wasn't sure she wanted to let Zach think he could tell her what to do. But the thought of more alcohol did make her queasy, so she let it slide. She chugged down half the glass; it was cold and sweet. "Mmm, where did you get it?" She knew it hadn't come from her fridge.

"Raided your neighbor's freezer."

Lizzie laughed, realizing how unnecessary her trek to the Fred Meyer had been. Plenty of stocked fridges and freezers all around.

They sat at the kitchen table. Other than adding a little pepper, the eggs were perfect and the bacon was that barely crispy, firm texture.

For a while they didn't talk. Food shoveled in. Lizzie watched Zach. From time to time he glanced at her again with that serious 'being-an-adult' expression.

"You can smile, you know," Lizzie suggested. Zach did. It was a nice smile; but it didn't quite reach his eyes. He was still worried.

"That was amazing." Lizzie set down her fork. "Thanks, Zach. For the food. For coming up here. Is your family...?" She wanted to ask what had happened to his dad and grandpa, but she couldn't find the right words.

"Hey, we go back a long way, Lizzie. Remember that time you, Nevaeh and I played strip poker, but you guys got towels." He laughed, but it sounded forced.

Lizzie could take a hint. She laughed. "Yeah. I was a pretty bad influence on you two, wasn't I?"

"Yeah, you were." Zach scraping the last few bits from his plate was the only sound in the room for a long time. Then he used his fork and knife to perform a mock drum solo on the table and plates.

Lizzie watched him skeptically. He could still be as annoying as a middle-schooler.

He finished with a crash. "You want me to do the dishes?"

"Hell, no. We'll throw 'em out back. Lots of clean dishes in the neighbor's houses." Lizzie laughed. "Besides, you cooked; I'll clean." She walked out the back door with the dishes and dumped them in the garbage.

Zach stared at her. "You're—"

"Crazy," Lizzie finished for him. "Yeah. Watch this." Lizzie snagged a plate from the sink and hurled it out the back door. "Frisbee!"

After she 'did the dishes' Lizzie headed to her mom's bedroom. "I gotta run a load of laundry."

Zach followed her. "Really? You throw out the dishes, but you're going to wash the sheets?"

The bed was gross. The remains of the pills she had taken were all over—a few untouched and still recognizable. She recognized them in shock. Multivitamins her mom had gotten prescribed so she could get them for free. *Shit. She really did suck at suicide.*

She wadded up the sheets and the mattress pad; the comforter had escaped the deluge. There was only a little that had soaked through to the mattress. She grabbed a sock off the floor and scrubbed at the mattress then tossed the sock in with the rest of the bedding.

Lizzie sighed. Over the last year she had finally gotten to the point where she could recognize the ebb and flow of her mood. The meds her doctor prescribed had been mostly useless, but pouring her energy into something always helped.

Zach watched her from the door as she marched the pile of bedding to the washing machine. She grabbed him around the waist once the wash was going and hugged him. "I'm glad you're here."

He smiled down at her.

Lizzie felt self-conscious. It must seem like she was getting the bed ready—because of him. Her cheeks got hot. She slapped him on the back hard and said, "Man hug!"

"Thanks." He winced. "Let's watch a movie."

"You want to watch a movie?" Lizzie grabbed the John Deere cap off his head and stuck it on hers.

"A chick flick? Something light."

"Really? You're not too big of a man for that?"

"Nope. Thinking one of those feel-good movies you and Nev used to make me watch. I always hoped one of you would get all mushy and I would end up getting a kiss out of it."

"Poor Zach," Lizzie teased. "Never going to happen."

"No?"

"How about one of the Brat pack films? Something John Hughes? I tried to watch a marathon the other night, but fell asleep during *Some Kind of Wonderful*."

"Is that the one with the tomboy who plays drums?"

"Yeah."

"Well, how am I supposed to get a kiss at the end if you're gonna fall asleep?"

She punched him in the gut. "No funny business. We're friends. Even if it is the end of the world, and everybody else on the planet is dead." That hit a little close to home. She saw tears in his eyes, but carefully didn't notice.

6

A FEW HOURS LATER ZACH nestled Lizzie in his arms, happy in her warmth. She hadn't made it through the movie this time either. He squeezed her gently and kissed her soft cheek. His left arm tingled from being under her so he shifted. Her arms tightened around his waist.

He had been so certain on the drive that he would be too late. Finding her alive meant that everything might turn out. He had forgotten how difficult she was to deal with. They were friends since elementary school. Back then she was one of the boys. She and Neveah, both were. Two of the three Musketeers had survived the end of the world. Zach's chest tightened as he thought of Nev. Why hadn't he thought of her?

He remembered spending Saturdays with the two of them crashed out on couches watching Lizzie's movie collection, their very own *Breakfast Club*.

As he tensed and relaxed his arm trying to get some blood flow back, he marveled at how little Lizzie had changed since he'd seen her. She had hardly recognized him, but other than longer hair, she looked exactly how he remembered her. There were a few more scars on her arms, a couple more holes in her ears, probably tattoos somewhere. She still smelled good, too. Not in a perfume kind of way, but like her. He sat and watched the rise and fall of her back as she breathed.

Lizzie's body tensed. Spasms shook her arms and legs. Was she fighting someone? "Lizzie?" He squeezed her arm. "You havin' a bad dream?"

"Huh? What the f—" Lizzie's head spun toward him. She pushed him away. Her eyes stared at him confused, panicked.

"Lizzie. It's Zach. You're safe."

The haze seemed to clear. "Zach." She blinked the sleep from her eyes. "Right." She sighed and collapsed, suddenly seeming even smaller. "Sorry, I fell asleep."

Zach nodded. "Right before the dice scene."

"'Mess with the bull, get the horns.'"

Zach knew the response. "'Whatta we gotta do to win big? Lose big. Whatta we doin'?'"

"'Losing big,'" they finished together.

Zach shifted his body. "I gotta pee."

Lizzie pushed herself up and away from him. "Me first."

He saw the dark cloud had returned to her eyes. She shuffled off.

Zach called after her. "You got two bathrooms?"

"No. I'll be quick. 'Sides, guys have bigger bladders."

That was Lizzie—self-centered and always right. At least from her point of view.

Lizzie fixed breakfast. Sort of. Zach stared at the bowl of cereal.

"Not up to your cooking, I know. Milk's still good. Got it yesterday. Pop Tarts in the toaster. You want orange juice?"

"Thanks." Zach ate cereal. "It feels weird, like we're playing house. Like we're still ten or something."

Lizzie shook her head. "You must be thinking of someone else. I never played house."

And I never convinced you to play doctor. He smiled. *Not from lack of trying.* "How come you stopped answering my e-mails?"

"You don't know?" Lizzie glared at him.

Zach shook his head. "No."

"What's the last thing that happened before you left for Skagit?"

Zach searched his memory. What had he done? She acted like he'd raped her. "No idea."

Lizzie looked exasperated. "Why do I always have to explain? The cops? Shoplifting? You said you did it. You lied."

Zach's brain raced to make sense of her anger. "I took the fall so you and Nev wouldn't get in trouble. Everybody expected me to be a thief and a no-count. I just fulfilled their expectations."

"Yes, and?" Lizzie said, expecting an answer.

Zach had no idea what to say. He raised his hands in defeat.

"I deal with my own shit." She stalked away.

Zach sat and puzzled. So that was it? He'd done the right thing, hadn't he?

The toaster popped up with the Pop Tarts.

Lizzie came back in and grabbed one. "Hey, I accepted your friend request on Facebook. Good thing, huh?"

Zach nodded. "You still feel like killing yourself?"

"Not so much. I'm over it, the shoplifting."

Zach started to ask, "Really?" but she cut him off.

"It's been two years. Besides, you never post. And I'm not good at answering e-mails. Sorry." Her eyes were intent, probing him. But still, it felt good to hear a live voice again.

How long had it been since he'd talked with anyone? Since Gramps and Dad—. Too much time alone. "What do we do now?"

"Maybe we can go out salvaging." Lizzie jumped up and headed out of the kitchen. "We can free some cats and dogs."

Zach chuckled. "Sounds like a blast. We can get some more food." He followed her.

"You complaining about my cooking? Maybe we'll see Spike."

"Spike?" Zach climbed the stairs, caught himself staring at her butt and looked at her art on the wall instead.

"My dog-man friend." Lizzie dug through the piles on her floor.

Zach sat on her bed as she explained about the weird guy with the dog collar.

"Didn't your mom warn you about strange men? He might be dangerous."

"He seems pretty safe. Just hungry." She found her block-heeled black Kiss boots, duct-taped together. Held them up for Zach to see. "Remember these?"

Zach grinned. "I remember you leaning on me when the heel broke. Hobbling around until we found duct tape in the Drama room."

"Yeah. I was so insecure about being short." She tossed them aside. "A-ha!" She raised her combat boots over her head. "Win!" She sat down on the floor and slipped her feet into them. "Second hand at Goodwill, they're actual combat boots, not some Hot Topic knock-off."

"Cool." Her energy always infected him.

"Sorry I fell asleep." She finished tying her boots and turned toward him. "You're still sweet." She placed her hands on his knees to stand up.

Her face dove in and startled Zach with her incredibly soft lips on his. Then they were gone.

He closed his eyes, trying to nail the memory into his head. "Damn, Lizzie." He shook his head. "What the hell was that? You said you thought of me like a brother."

"Yeah. Mostly." She hopped up, boots laced. "You're here. I don't feel so alone. Somebody I know on this side of the country." Lizzie stopped and spun on her combat heel. "Shit!" She flew down the stairs.

By the time Zach caught up, she was at the computer. "What's wrong?"

"Lizzie, you're the most self-centered bitch alive." She pounded on the keyboard, ignoring him. "You don't deserve friends."

Zach put his hand on her back, trying to soothe her.

She shoved his hand away with fresh tears in her eyes. "It's Jess! I can't believe I forgot her. She was going to kill herself if I did it!"

Zach watched as Lizzie spun back to the computer.

"I need to post something or Jess is gonna think I killed myself." She flipped the mouse back and forth like it might help. "My phone's in Mama's bedroom."

"You want me to get it?" Zach hustled for the phone.

"Yes." The screen came alive. "Damn. She hasn't answered me."

"Got it." Zach yelled. "No missed calls."

When he returned, Lizzie stood running her hands through her hair. She stood and whirled around.

"What're you looking for?" Zach put a hand on her shoulder.

"Don't know." She jerked out from under his touch. "Shit. I was so happy. Didn't even think."

"Hey. Chill. I'm sure she's fine." Zach reached out to pull her into a hug. She pushed him away.

"No, dammit. Give me the phone." Lizzie yanked it out of his hand and spun away.

Her fingers twisted like they had a mind but no eyes and were trying to grab something out of the air.

"Jess, answer, dammit." She stuck her thumb in her mouth and chewed at the nail.

Zach stared at Lizzie. Nev had told him she'd been medicated, but he hadn't ever seen her this freaked out. "Lizzie."

"Answer the phone!" Her free hand at her tugged at her hair. "Jess. It's Lizzie. Call me now. I'm sorry. I didn't mean to kill myself without you. Call me, please. Now. Please. I didn't— I'm still here." She tossed the phone at the couch.

"Careful." Zach kept his voice low and calm. "She can't call you back if your phone's broke."

"That's why I aimed it at the couch, stupid."

"Fine." Zach felt his anger rising. "I'm going outside. When you want my help or want to treat me some other way than shitty, come find me." He took the other Pop Tart and headed for the door.

"Zach. Wait." She stepped toward him, tears in her eyes. "I'm sorry. I'm a shitty friend."

"No. No, Lizzie. You're not." He sighed and let her come to him. He wrapped his arms around her and felt her warmth as she shook with tears. "Jess is probably out of cell range or the power is out or something."

"Yeah. Maybe," she mumbled. "Thanks." Eventually her arms gave him a squeeze and released. "You got a cigarette?"

Zach let her go. "No. I thought you quit."

"I did. Mostly." Her thumb went back in her mouth. She looked down at her feet.

"I did. Completely. Even with Dad smoking."

"Well, goody for you. I gotta go to the store. Come with me, please." Lizzie grabbed his hands and pulled him down the stairs.

Zach let her take the lead. She needed the distraction.

Outside, the sun shone off the droplets of water on the mat of leaves covering the still and quiet streets and sidewalks.

Stay chill. She'll come out of it. Zach kicked a beer can.

Lizzie jogged away from him. "Come on," she said.

He increased his stride to keep up with her.

At the Chevron station, Zach tugged on the doors, but they were locked. "No good. Don't really feel like setting the alarm off. Might attract attention."

"Maybe we want attention. I want a cigarette," Lizzie said.

"Okay. There are other doors, 'kay?" Zach trotted around the side and tried the door into the garage half. It opened. "Over here." He stepped inside and walked softly. It was spooky quiet, like everywhere else. Like any minute the owner would jump out of a closet.

Lizzie shoved the door aside, banging it against the cabinet.

Zach spun around. "Was that necessary?"

"I want a cigarette."

"You already said that." Zach stepped inside the store. "What kind?"

"Virginia Slims."

"You're kidding, right?" He reached down a pack of V's from behind the counter and tossed them to her. The pack of Marlboros caught his eye. He had always figured if he was gonna kill himself slowly it might as well be for the Marlboro Man. But the more his dad smoked the less he wanted to, not that it was easy to quit.

"I used to steal my mom's. Nothing else tastes quite as bad!" She opened the pack automatically. "Saw a dead guy two, three days ago, looter, I guess, shot on the sidewalk." Her eyes were searching.

I don't want to die on the sidewalk. "Light?" Zach grabbed a football-shaped lighter from a bin. "Not many people left to shoot us." He flicked it and she inhaled.

"Coffee. Hey, they've got one of those instant espresso makers." She was bouncing, barely in control. "You want one?"

"Sure. They got caramel?" Zach wandered the store stuffing candy bars and jerky in his pockets; he tore a beef stick and cheese combo open. "Spose this stuff'll kill me, but not like cigarettes." He took bit some of both. "Damn that salt and fat tastes good."

"Here's your coffee." Lizzie balanced the coffee and a lid in one hand, the cigarette in the other.

Her phone crooned Shelby Lynne's "Things are Tough All Over." The coffee flew toward him. Zach tried to snag it but only ended up keeping what stayed in the cup from falling. The hot coffee burned through his jeans. "Dammit, Lizzie!"

"Jess? You're alive?" Lizzie answered the phone, focused. "She's alive, Zach." She spun him around.

"Lizzie! Watch the fricken' cig. You're gonna burn me again!"

"Sorry," Lizzie said over her shoulder as she barreled into the door. It didn't move. She turned, looking stunned. Her hand went to her head and she grimaced, then broke up laughing. "Door's locked."

"Jesus, Lizzie." Zach tried to stay angry, then shook his head and joined in her laughter. "Jess," he hollered at the phone. "Glad you're okay. Lizzie was pretty freaked." Then in a quieter voice to Lizzie. "I'm going outside to scout around."

7

LIZZIE HELPED ZACH MAKE SPAGHETTI for dinner. Zach had her chop onions and garlic to go with the ground beef they liberated from the neighbor's freezer. *How much longer are we going to be able to get relatively fresh meat?* She watched the burger sizzle in the skillet.

"Maybe we should have shoved the rest of the meat in the stores in freezers before it went bad. What happens when the power goes out?" Lizzie asked.

"The dark ages begin again?" Zach laughed.

Lizzie didn't. "They haven't already?"

"Yeah. I guess." Zach looked thoughtful. "We're probably better off than some places. We're on hydroelectric power. The rivers won't stop. I bet power will run for quite a while. What happened to all the nuclear power plants? I hope to hell they're shut down."

"Can they just shut them down? If they don't have people monitoring them—" She made an explosion sound and her hands flew apart.

"Not a lot we can do about mushroom clouds," Zach said. "But I'm pretty sure they just melt down and spew radiation."

"That makes me feel lots better." Lizzie took the spatula from Zach and stirred the blend of meat and veggies. "Mmm. Smells good." The aroma was a hundred times better than any frozen pizza or burritos.

After dinner, they settled in to watch another movie. She picked

Highlander from her dad's collection, put it on and leaned back into Zach's warmth.

Part way through a sex scene in the movie, she felt a hard lump in the small of her back. Zach shifted uncomfortably.

Zach had always been her 'buddy guy,' like a brother, despite his ridiculous crush. But watching the actors make love on the screen and feeling the heat of him in her back, a warm tingle spread through her body and her breathing deepened. "Uh, I forgot about this scene. You want me to change it?"

"No. It's just… Yeah. Maybe——"

She paused it.

"Liz?" His voice came out somewhere between a croak and a gasp. "You know I've been in love with you since we were like ten?'

"As soon as you met me." She couldn't help teasing him; her face hovered inches in front of his.

Zach stared into her eyes. "I want to kiss you."

"Then shut up and do it." Her voice came out husky, every part of her ached for him—for a human connection.

He leaned in. His breath, tempered by the spices of dinner, was warm on his lips. His eyes were closed. For a moment she wondered what her breath smelled like—smoke, an ashtray. But she let her eyes close, too.

As their lips touched, she convulsed in laughter. An image of him peeing on the wall and writing his name flashed in her mind.

"Lizzie." He stared at her with those sad, puppy dog eyes.

"Sorry." She took a deep breath. Zach wanted her. Desperately. The warmth in her own jeans flared; she wanted to have him. Not just another man hug.

"Please," he whispered, his hands grasped her hips and pulled him toward her.

His eyes begged her for more. She wanted to give him what he wanted, her. She slipped her hand under his shirt. He shivered at her touch. "You want to come upstairs with me?"

His breath stopped and he nodded.

She clasped his hand and led him up the stairs and into her bedroom. Streetlight lit the mattress; she tossed a pile of clothes off the bed.

"Don't kiss me on the lips and don't say a word." She lay down and slid her jeans off.

He lay next to her.

She tugged the covers over them as she slid toward him. She pulled off her shirt. Her breasts pressed against him through her bra.

Zach wrapped his arms around her.

Her hands moved down and loosened his cramped jeans.

His mouth opened, his breath escaped, as the jeans came off.

She felt his hands range across her bare back, his touch tingled.

Lizzie tugged at his shirt.

Zach sat up and pulled it over his head, his muscular chest silhouetted in the street lamps' glow.

Her breath sighed out.

Soon there were no clothes between them. He slid back under the covers and she guided him where she wanted him. Then they moved together.

Zach's breath caught. "Oh, god."

Lizzie smiled. "Yes." She recognized the uncontrolled response as her body followed his.

A few minutes later he pulled away from her and lay beside her, one hand scrunched up underneath, caressing her shoulder and the other hand resting on her stomach as her breathing returned to normal.

Lizzie lay awake listening to Zach's soft breath in her ear, his arms around her nude body. *SHIT! What the hell was I thinking?* She'd been lonely. And he'd been princely. *But how am I getting out of this? He'll want more, and after all the years I kept him firmly in the friend zone.*

She had to end it. Fast. Mama said to kill a snake you do it quick or risk getting bit. She had to kill the snake. But for now she lay there relishing the heat of another human body. *Just another minute,* she thought as she closed her eyes.

The next thing she knew she was alone, covers wrapped warmly around her, and the smell of cooking teasing her nose.

Lizzie snagged her clothes off the floor and pulled them under the covers to dress. Then she sat on the bed with her head in her hands. "Shit."

She heard steps and glanced up to see Zach at the top of the stairs.

He knocked on the door, but didn't come in. "Pancakes'll be ready in a few. You want to go out, free some more cats and dogs and maybe get me a new truck?"

"Sure," she said. *Was last night just a dream?*

He didn't mention anything at all during breakfast. Like it hadn't even happened. *What the fuck? Wham, bam, thank you, ma'am?* He got what he wanted and that was it? Lizzie nibbled at a piece of toast, trying to calm down. It was silly for her to be angry at him. He hadn't led her upstairs.

They went out after breakfast.

"Let's stop at Trader Joe's. I want to leave some food out for Spike," Lizzie said, pulling herself into the cab of Zach's old pickup.

"You think he's still around?" Zach pulled away from the curb.

Spike was nowhere to be seen at Trader Joe's. Lizzie left him a Snickers bar anyway. By the look on his face, Zach thought Spike was a figment of her imagination or something.

They went to the Toyota dealership; Zach had a plan. He wandered up and down the rows while Lizzie lounged in the comfortable leather seat of a Toyota Avalon. Finally, he picked out a black Highlander. He grinned at her. "'There can be only one!'"

In the showroom, Lizzie spotted a big black cabinet. I'll bet you it's locked." It was. It had a code panel, so all you had to do to open it, was know the code. It looked like it was wired to an alarm and nothing short of plastic explosives was likely to open it. And then only in the movies.

"Damn." Zach looked like he'd lost his puppy.

"Let's try someplace a little lower tech."

At a used car lot down the street, they had to break into the office. Nobody was there to protest as the glass tinkled to the ground, nobody holding people accountable to the law. They found a key rack with all the keys labeled and accessible.

Zach found a solid-looking Ford Expedition. "At least it's not the Eddie Bauer edition." He climbed in and it fired right up with a growl. "Good thing gas is cheap and plentiful. These things get crappy mileage."

"Let's go scavenging." Lizzie glanced back in the giant vehicle. They would really be able to get a haul in this thing.

"Gotta fill up the tank," Zach said.

"The Tank?" Lizzie grinned. "I like it."

"I meant the gas tank." He grinned back. "Let's go get some stuff. Christmas comes early this year."

"Right. First we check and see if there are animals to free." Her brain created a list of procedures in her head. "We need something to break windows."

"Just a sec'." Zach stuck his head inside the Tank. "Here." He held one of those car safety hammers. It broke windows cleanly.

"Then we look for cell phones with chargers."

"Why?"

"If one cell phone quits," Lizzie explained, "if there's an unpaid bill, a network goes down, whatever—we have back-ups."

Zach looked skeptical, but looked like he would humor her. "After that we get anything useful."

Lizzie grinned, "Or things we want."

They loaded bags with food from cupboards, tools from garages. Zach grabbed a nice laptop. Lizzie snagged a killer camera, one of those SLR Digitals with a monster lens like someone was compensating.

Zach presented her with a Crown Royal bottle, full and still in the velvety purple bag. They took their time in the houses that didn't smell and did a quick in and out for pets in the ones that did.

Lizzie drank a slug of the whiskey and filled the bag with jewelry and cell phones. She shrugged off the morbidness and morality.

When Lizzie got to the Sunset overpass, she headed back on the other side of the street. Zach hustled across. She noted with amusement that he checked to make sure no cars were coming.

They went up to the Church of the Latter Day Saints. The door opened. Inside it was even more creepy and deadly quiet than the houses. Lizzie watched Zach stop a few steps in. Then he shook his head. He turned his face white.

"What?" Lizzie asked, stepping forward.

Zach held his hand up. "Don't."

"Okay. Not sure God's here anyway." Being inside a church set her skin on edge, even before Zach saw something. "Let's skip the churches after this."

"Yeah." At the next house, Zach stepped out of the garage with a chainsaw. "Always wanted one of these electric start ones." He fired it up and grinned.

Lizzie paused at the door of the little cottage next door.

Zach let it idle and stop.

"Cause we need that?" she yelled.

"I guess you're right. But I might want to come back for it. How am I going to remember which house it's at?"

"I don't know. Cut a tree down?"

"Great idea."

"Jesus, Zach. I was joking." But he was doing it. Poor spindly little tree was big around as her thigh. The chainsaw roared and spit saw dust. Zach grinned at her as it fell.

"Zach Riley, sometimes I wonder why people think I'm crazy."

"Yeah. Me, too." He stuck out his tongue

The Tank got full as they hit house after house. They were going to have to go home soon. Zach came toward her with a guitar case. He could hardly contain himself. "Wait for it. Close your eyes."

She did, smiling.

"Okay, open 'em. It's an SG. Dark red." It lay nestled in its black, soft bed.

"I know, stupid." Lizzie reached out to touch it. "Like Angus Young's. Way cool. I always wanted to learn to play guitar, but the band needed a bass player." Supposedly her dad played. She took the guitar from the case surprised at the weight. "It's as heavy as my bass."

He gave her a lopsided smile as he gently removed it from her hands and sat on the cement wall. He played the opening few bars of "Stairway to Heaven."

"No 'Stairway,'" Lizzie said, sitting beside him.

"Denied!" He played the first parts of "Hell's Bells."

"Cool."

"I only know the beginnings." Zach stopped playing. "Hurts my fingers after a bit."

"Yeah. Keep it. Maybe we can learn to play something together." She stood up. Her fingers rubbed where her own callouses should have been. It had been too long. "I've written some lyrics. A couple bass lines."

"You're probably way too good for me."

"I definitely am," she said.

He laughed.

"You gonna try and catch up? I got eight cats, three dogs and two cell phones with chargers. Uh… thirteen. You?"

"Four cats, six dogs and one cell phone. No charger, but it's the same as mine so it counts. Everything's worth one point?"

"Eleven." Lizzie left Zach to put away his guitar. "I get the next one." She jogged across the empty lot to the back. A sound stopped her as she came up to the back door. Strange how cats voices and cries sometimes sound so human. She tried the handle—locked. She pulled out her car-hammer, turned away and pounded the window with the pointy part. The glass shattered and she reached in to turn the knob. The yowling had stopped. She stepped in carefully.

This house smelled like shit and death. There was a bag of cat food dumped out on the floor. Formulated for mature cats. She heard movement. "Here, kitty."

Small feet sounded on linoleum. A small human voice answered. "Da da?" A little boy, diaper-less and rashy trundled slowly toward her. His eyes were wide and red.

8

"OH, MY GOD!" SHE WANTED to hold the little boy and comfort him, but his smell repulsed her. He started to hyperventilate. *Here comes the howl.* Sure enough, like Jayce at that age, he opened his lungs and bellowed, his cry ragged. The piercing yowl of a child in need rose in volume by the second.

"Hey, Sissie's here." Lizzie touched him on the shoulder, where he was mostly clean. His little body stiffened and his squall paused, but he continued to breathe hard, sucking air in and out, like a lawnmower trying to start. She pulled him into a hug. Despite his filth, she couldn't bear his distress. She bounced him, humming the same song she'd sung to her mama. "Hush little baby..." His tense body began softening in her arms.

In the bathroom, Lizzie found what must have been the boy's mother lying on the floor curled around the toilet. She backed out of the room turning the baby so he wouldn't see her. His cry had returned to a gentle sobbing. She stole a glance at his face hoping that wouldn't start him back up. No tears.

"You're dehydrated." The mother couldn't have been dead long. How long could someone, especially a toddler, go without water?

She put on a happy face and said in a happy voice, "Let's see if we can find some formula, huh?" He should be eating solid food, but fluids first. She returned to the kitchen and found cans of premixed formula—the expensive stuff. She opened the dishwasher and pulled out a bottle, nipples and rings in a little basket.

Her hands automatically put the bottle together while bouncing the baby. The little boy went quiet, and as soon as the bottle got near his face he pulled it into his mouth.

"There, there." She stroked his arms and his back as he sucked. His tiny hands were balled up in fists pressed against the bottle. As he began to relax they opened and she saw something in his grasp. She teased his hand opened the rest of the way and found little pellets. Cat food. She smiled. At least he had enough protein.

"We need to get you cleaned up. Then we can get you some food for little boys." She looked around but there was no sign of the cat whose food had probably saved the little boy's life.

She walked down the hall, closing the bathroom door as she passed. Here was the baby's room—all baby-blued, rainbowed and teddy-beared.

"Lizzie?!" Zach called her name somewhere outside.

She'd totally forgotten Zach. Lizzie crossed to the window and slid it back. "Zach?" she called gently to not scare the baby. "In here. I've found something you gotta see to believe."

Opening windows was a good idea, she realized, as she breathed in the freshness from outside. She opened the rest of them.

"Damn, it stinks," Zach said as he entered the baby's room. "Holy shit." He stopped short, staring in disbelief at the little boy Lizzie had laying on his back on the diaper changing table.

"Not very holy, but shit it is. You're very observant." It was dried and caked on. There were weeping sores in spots. She dabbed as gently as possible with a wipe. Lizzie had been Jason's main caregiver when her mom went through rehab. She knew what to do.

Zach stood frozen like a deer in headlights. "What the hell do we do with a baby?"

"Take care of him. He needs a bath, but we need to get out of this stinking house first." She slipped a clean diaper expertly under him, coated the red spots with some ointment and pulled it up.

Zach stared, his mouth opened and closed. "Where the Hell did the baby come from?"

She teased. "Having sex has consequences."

"Very funny."

She grinned, picking the baby up and wiggling her nose against his tiny one. The baby was fascinated, but still serious.

"You were always good with kids."

Lizzie thought of Jayce and regretted making the joke.

"I'll get him packed. You see if you can find out what his name is." She shooed Zach out of the room before he could say anything else. She stuffed the diaper bag with a couple handfuls of diapers, then piled all the ointments and powders on top. She pulled a cute blue pair of pajamas out of the dresser and pulled them on him, zipping them up, her finger inside next to the skin. *Nothing quite so butt-puckering as zipping a baby's skin.*

A sucking noise told her he'd finished the bottle. She hugged him close and headed for the kitchen, her hand patting his back hard enough to burp him.

"Let's find you some num nums." Lizzie found the baby food in the cupboard. She packed the jars into the diaper bag, along with some formula. She tore open a new bag of teething biscuits and offered him one. It ought to taste like manna from heaven after cat food. His hand shot in and tore it from her grasp, his sharp little teeth grinding on it with zeal.

"Sebastian. Sebastian Jones." Zach called from another room.

"Sebastian?" She found a binky in the dish drying rack and added that to the diaper bag.

Zach came in carrying a framed certificate with footprints. "I like Sebastian."

"How do you make it short? Seb? Bast? Bastian?" Lizzie balanced both baby and diaper bag, one in each arm. She was ready to get out of this place. "Has he got a middle name?"

"Antonio."

"Tony. Does he look like a Tony to you?"

"I think you're overthinking this."

"Sebastian Antonio Jones. SAJ."

Zach give her a 'what the hell are you talking about' look. "Sadge?" He said, sounding it out.

"S. A. J. Saj." Lizzie grinned as the baby smiled back. "I like it."

"Fine," Zach agreed. "Saj it is. Let's get Saj out of here."

"Two more things. I'm going to find him something from his parents, and we need a car seat. Can you find it?"

Zach shrugged. "All right. Then we go."

She found a photo on the mantel of two young parents, well-dressed, like they were at a wedding. She tucked it into the diaper bag and went down the hall.

The room on the opposite side of the wall was the parents' bedroom—relatively neat, but cluttered. Lots of little knick knacks covered the shelves. In the nightstand drawer she found a Bible inscribed to Josephine Marie Lamb. It had a lovely golden bookmark with a stylized *Claddagh*, hands and heart like the Irish wedding ring. She slid the Bible in next to the photo.

Saj had gone quiet in her arms.

"We'll come back later, Saj," she said, hoisting the bag onto her shoulder again.

Lizzie wiped away the moist remains of the biscuit from his mouth. "It's gonna be all right. Sissie's got you."

"Sss...sss."

"Yes. Sissie Lizzie." She held him close. "You lucky little boy."

Outside the house she found Zach fighting with a car seat. "I can't figure out how to get the fucking thing attached."

Lizzie chuckled. "I'll get it." She handed Saj to Zach.

Zach looked skeptical, but took the little boy. "Hey, little guy."

Lizzie had the car seat installed in moments, but getting Saj in his car seat was a bit of a fight. "Come on, Saj," Lizzie pleaded. "It's only a few blocks."

"You could just hold him in your lap," Zach said.

"No. You need to be firm with kids." Her mom had always caved, or resorted to bribery and threats. She wasn't her mom. "Here we go, Saj." She pressed him gently in and pulled the t-straps over his head. He finally stopped arching his back and she snapped the clasp between his legs. "All right. Let's go home."

A bath with a bag of oatmeal, a liberal covering of ointment, and another bottle later Saj was starting to perk up. He wasn't quite so solemn and serious and had even started to smile and laugh like a baby should. Lizzie lay down with him on her mom's unmade bed and Zach brought her a sandwich.

"He seems fine," Zach said.

"Yeah. He's got food and warmth, friends."

"Counts for a lot."

"Yeah. How many others might be out there? I feel powerless." Saj stopped sucking when the anger came into her voice. "Sorry, little guy."

Zach sighed. "Can't save everybody. Nobody expects you to."

"What are we still here for anyway?" A song tickled at her memory "We're all here." she sang softly to Saj. Then she spoke with a shiver. "'cause we're not all there.'"

"I can't understand why we haven't found more people. How many people are still alive?" He counted on his fingers. "You, me, Saj, Jess, and your 'Spike'. Are we it?"

"And the Doctor." Lizzie yawned. "Think I'll sleep down here."

A frown shadowed across Zach's face. "Uh... Lizzie?"

"Spit it out, Zach. You wanna sleep here, too? Okay." *Kill the snake.* "But not like last night."

He shrugged. "But, I-"

"No. I'm sorry, Zach." Lizzie watched his eyes go puppy-dog. *Dammit.* "I shouldn't have slept with you."

Zach nodded, his eyes didn't mask the hurt.

"I should have followed my own rules."

"It's okay," he said.

"It's not okay. I can tell from your voice and see it in your eyes. But it has to be." She felt bad, but she hadn't done it by herself. "How many times did you tell me we could fool around and not get serious. Now we have and..." Her voice trailed off.

"Yeah," Zach said, picking up the glass of milk and the plate. He strode out of the room. "Really ought to do the dishes," he hollered back.

"Dump 'em out back. We can always get more tomorrow." She pulled the comforter up around herself and the little boy in her arms. She wasn't his mama, and he wasn't Jayce. But she would love him and care for him, for all those who would never be found.

A few minutes after she heard the crash of dishes, Zach slipped in behind her. His hands wrapped around her and Saj. She patted his hand. *Sorry, my friend.*

The silence again woke Lizzie. It felt like an alien world without noise. When would this be normal? She reached down to the little bundle in her arms. Wet diaper, wet mattress. *At least he's hydrated.*

She rolled out of bed, Saj stayed asleep as she lifted him off the mattress and kissed the fuzzy soft spot on the top of his head.

Playing house wasn't all fun and games with a real baby. She'd learned that with Jayce. Lizzie had always been the kid who couldn't sit still. She wanted to explore, to discover, to live, not have kids and an endless string of partners who didn't live up to their end. Being more a mother to Jayce than Mama was enough.

As Lizzie stripped the soaked diaper, Saj woke, staring at her with eyes too serious for a baby. Exposing him to the air triggered the usual response; a stream of urine rose over the baby's shoulder and onto Zach. He stirred in his sleep, but did not wake.

Lizzie cracked up. "Zach. Probably want to wake up." She shook his shoulder until his groggy eyes opened. "Don't be pissed off, but you've been pissed on."

"Damn." He scooted away and climbed out of bed.

"Besides you could use a regular shower." She added more ointment to sore spots. Saj stayed wide-eyed and quiet.

After Zach showered, he joined them in the living room. He focused on Saj and didn't meet Lizzie's eyes.

So it's going to be the silent treatment. It could be worse.

Lizzie left him in charge of feeding Saj a plastic tub of baby peas while she took a shower. When she closed the bathroom door she could hear them both giggling.

In the shower Lizzie reveled in the heat, she'd turned up the temperature in the water heater—her house, her rules. She felt a calmness she hadn't felt in days as the water washed over her. Then the door burst open.

"LIZZIE!" Zach yelled.

"What the Hell, Zach. Get out!"

"Lizzie," he said, "I'm not looking." His arms covered his face.

The tone in Zach's voice made her forget modesty and with a belly full of dread she asked, "What's the matter?"

"Nev's alive!"

"Jeez, Zach, you scared the shit out of me! Is it too much to ask not to feel like the sky is falling for half a second?"

Zach stammered an apology.

"Never mind, where is she?"

"Tumwater. She started at Evergreen State in September."

"Can she get up here?"

"I don't know. I just got her message online."

"So what are you waiting for? Get the hell out of the bathroom and call her!"

"Okay." Zach left, closing the door behind him.

9

LIZZIE TURNED OFF THE WATER. Her mind raced. What were the odds? She'd totally failed statistics, but the math didn't matter. It was crazy that she knew someone else still alive. She chuckled out loud. Nev was another one of Zach's crushes. Maybe things were getting better.

Lizzie walked past Zach wrapped in nothing but a towel for the second time since he'd arrived. How was she supposed to set boundaries like this? Screw it. He would have to deal.

"Nev doesn't drive either." Zach's eyes widened, but she could see him trying to play it cool. "What is it with you people?"

"Bite me." Lizzie glared. "Anyway. What did you find out?"

"Some people took her in, but they're ultra-religious nuts and it's freaking her out."

"So we could go get her. ROAD TRIP!" Then she remembered the baby. "Shit." Kids complicated things.

As if on cue Saj toddled in. His eyes lit up when he saw her.

Lizzie swung him up into her arms. "Zach, you go. I should stay with Saj. His butt isn't up for a day in the car seat."

"Okay, I should be back tonight—tomorrow at the latest. Don't know if the freeway is clear all the way down."

She could see his excitement. "Okay. Get food. Get gas. Get going."

Zach headed out the door. "I'll hit a 7-11 when I get hungry."

"Be safe," Lizzie said. "Don't do anything crazy."

"I won't, if you won't."

Zach waved. The Tank spun out as he gunned it down the street on the wrong side, squirreling back and forth.

Lizzie shook her head. She wrapped Saj in a blanket over his pajamas. *He needs more layers than I do.* She hadn't gotten any heavier clothes. Zach had his mission. Her mission would be getting Saj warmer clothes, and setting up someplace for him to sleep.

She needed a car. Easy to drive would be good, with her rudimentary driving skills. Mama's car was at the hospital, and it was a stick shift. At least the street was empty. She'd tried to learn with Jerkwad; Mama didn't have the patience. Jerkwad wanted to quit 'wasting' so much time taking Lizzie places. It ended badly. The silver lining was that he left her alone for weeks.

The cat lady had a Honda CRV. Maybe the keys were in the house. Lizzie put Saj in his car seat. It was a fight, but less than yesterday. "Sissy'll be back in a minute."

The house did not smell of death. It smelled of old lady potpourri and medicine. She had gone to the hospital first and never returned. Her kids took the cats. The musty scent of old books and doilies collected over decades permeated the air. *Where would I put extra keys?* She examined the area near the front door. No luck.

She wandered back into the kitchen. The calendar was still on September and covered with scrawled cursive. Under it, a gray Honda valet key hung on a key rack, amid a collection of rusty skeleton keys and a modern house key with a leopard print. Lizzie grabbed the Honda key and headed out the door.

The CRV smelled like old lady, too. Lizzie stuck the key in and turned it. The engine coughed a bit and sputtered, but started. She left the door open and got Saj and his car seat. She buckled it in and returned to the front seat. She sat. *I'm waiting for what?*

"What the hell. Let's go, Saj." She'd seen it done enough. She pulled it from P to D and stepped on the gas. The vehicle lurched forward and she slammed on the brake.

The little snake sounds, Saj's attempt to say Sissie, came from the back seat.

"Yeah, Sissie's working on it."

Setting her jaw tight, she tried again. More gently this time; it slipped forward. She tried to give it more gas. The car lurched again, and she ran over the curb. Swearing, she jammed the brake —*again*. If at first you don't suck seeds... She could feel herself sweating. "Just breathe, Lizzie."

Gradually they made it the six or eight blocks to Saj's house. She pulled up in the driveway. "Sissie's gonna leave you in here, okay, Saj?" She turned on the radio, then flipped it to CD, and a 'Doo wop a doo' came from the speakers. "Ugh. 50's music. Probably drive me crazy, but maybe you'll like it." She blew Saj a kiss and hopped out of the car.

She went around the back and entered the tomb-like house. What should she do with Saj's mom? Someday he might want to come here and see more of where he was from. Well, maybe she could get help from Zach when he and Nev got back. The three musketeers back together again—stealing from the rich was going to be a lot easier. Or was it the three stooges? Probably depended on the day and the stupid or brilliant things they'd done.

Lizzie scoured the house for baby clothes, diapers, wipes, things Saj needed. She snagged the mobile above his crib and carried it all out to the car through the front door. He seemed satisfied to sit and listen to music, but she didn't want to leave him long with that diaper rash.

The crib, one of those fold up ones, was portable if she could figure out how the damn thing folded up. Jason's had been like a bear trap, virtually impossible to open and way too easy to get painfully pinched, it was a miracle she still had all her fingers.

Lizzie surprised herself by getting it on the first try. It became a compact, bulky box. Saj watched her as she stuffed it in the CRV. She handed him a teething biscuit and chucked him under the chin, noting how tight his clothes looked. They wouldn't fit him long. Back inside she uncovered a stash of clothes, but they all looked big. She took them anyway and climbed into the driver's seat.

She returned to the car. "Need to get some better music in here, Saj." She put the CRV into reverse and it started rolling backwards into the street. She kept her foot poised over the brake and gradually turned the steering wheel. When she was pointed mostly in the right direction she stepped on the brake. The CRV lurched to a quick halt. She shoved it into N-neutral.

Lizzie took her foot off the brake, shaking her head. "Sorry, Saj, Sissie's not a very good driver yet." She let the car roll slowly down the hill. Probably safer not to even use the gas.

Saj wasn't so sure and he began to whimper. His cries built

steadily toward a wail.

"What's wrong, Saj?" She turned in her seat. He'd dropped what was left of the slimy teething biscuit. She could see it; she stretched but could not reach it. "I'll get you some good food when we get home, "kay?"

She turned back to the front as a young man stepped in front of the car, waving. She stomped on the brake, but realized too late it wasn't the brake. She spun the wheel as the car gunned forward, she jammed both feet on both pedals, not wanting to make another mistake.

The young man jumped behind a car as she swerved to a stop, engine racing. She shoved it in park, threw the door open and hopped out. The adrenaline had her wired. "I nearly killed you. What the Hell were you doing?"

"Lizzie? Is that you?" He came out from the parked car. He had longish hair, a Led Zeppelin T-shirt over a beer belly and black, white and gray camo fatigues.

"Do I know you?" She bent over shaking. Her brain twisted in her head. She knelt down trying to stabilize it.

"I was a senior when you were a freshman." He offered his hand. "Curtis Madison? Went by C.J. back then."

"C.J.? What the hell?" Lizzie stared at his hand. No contact. She grabbed the handle on the door and stood back up. "I'm trying to get back to my house. You want to drive? Might be safer." She grimaced. "My first day driving."

He got in the driver's seat and she took shotgun.

"Oh, C.J. meet Saj."

"Curtis." His eyes followed hers to the baby. "Sure. Lincoln Street, right?"

"You know where I live?"

"Your note. At BHS? 2224?"

"Oh, yeah." Now that she knew there were more survivors she should go erase the whiteboard.

"Wrote my number down there, too. Your kid?"

"No. Saj is another survivor Zach and I found."

"Zach? Zach Riley?"

Lizzie nodded.

"That red-headed kid?" He slapped his thigh. "I used to sell him pot and shit."

"Yeah, that's him. He's picking up Nevaeh. You remember her?"

"Oh, yeah. Zach had a crush on her, right?" C.J. made a right onto her street.

Lizzie laughed. "Zach had crushes on everybody." That niggling thought about survivors was back. "You were on the trip with us to Honduras. The water purifying trip? You were the sick one, right?"

"Yeah, that was me. Ended up making everybody miss an extra week of school." He pulled to a stop in front of her house. "Why?"

"A bunch of the survivors are from B.H.S. We were all on that trip." She hopped out of the car and extricated Saj from the car seat. "Maybe that's why we're immune."

"Maybe you guys owe me." C.J. carried the crib in from the car.

She walked behind him carrying bags. He set it inside the front door and turned to face her leaning his arm on the door jamb. He was uncomfortably close.

She ducked under his arm and brought the bags into the living room.

"Mind if I hang out until Zach gets back." He plopped on her couch. "That cool?"

"Sure. Thanks for the help." She preferred not to be alone, even if it meant hanging with the annoying C.J. "You hungry?"

"Always."

Zach accelerated up the onramp to I-5. "Let's see what you can do." He glanced back automatically to merge. No one coming. *Duh.* His foot pressed harder toward the floor. The engine whined, but kicked in, bursting forward. Ignoring the center line he straightened the curves. On the curvy hills above Lake Samish he decided that more than 90 m.p.h. was probably what he would have termed crazy before the whole world went there, but when the speed limit jumped to 70 he opened it up and hit three digits on the straightaways.

A moment of misgiving crossed his mind when he saw the remains of a car seat in the median. Should he have left Lizzie and Saj? He'd be back soon enough.

He kept up his speed. It was a lovely November day, the trees swayed in a light breeze as he passed the exit to Gramp's place off Cook Road. The Skagit Valley flats were devoid of human beings, but snow geese dotted the fields along with the big white marsh-mallow rolls of hay. Crossing the bridge into Mount Vernon, he remembered when a span of it had fallen into the Skagit River. It was before he drove, but he remembered hearing how bad most of the bridges were. If it went down now, no one would fix it.

He pulled off to forage for food at Safeway. Garbage cans propped open the doors, but they slid aside as he approached then clanged back into the cans. He grabbed some frozen chicken fried steaks and found a microwave in the break room.

After lunch he continued south, his mind mulling the same questions over and over. Why had he and Lizzie and Nev survived? What was next? And what the hell was he supposed to do about his feelings for her?

How many times had he said they could *sleep together and still just be friends?* It had been lovely. He remembered bits and pieces, delicious moments, a flash of flesh in the moonlight, the touches of skin on skin. So much had already escaped his brain.

He pretended to be asleep when she woke in his arms, pretend-ed not to feel her stiffen, pretended not to hear the deep sigh that sounded like anything but contentment. When it got light he waited until he was sure she was asleep again. Then he snuck out from under the covers, backing away from her, letting her be alone. He remembered the last glance he'd taken as he left her room, her calm, pleasant face and the softness of the skin he had touched in the dark.

Zach sighed, flipped on the radio and hit search. When it stopped on a 99.9, The Rock, playing Alice in Chains, he cranked it. The growling voices and guitars provided the mood he wanted. "It's all right," He sang, "Had a bad day."

He took the exit to Tumwater. He had nearly fallen asleep, jerking awake every few miles. The sun had gone down, but the light had not left the sky. He hit redial, calling Nev's number.

"Zach?" Nev answered before he even heard it ring.

"I'll be there soon."

"I'll come find you. There are a bunch of streets with similar names. I'll meet you by the gate. It says Silver Ridge."

"Okay. If that's what you want to do." He followed the G.P.S. and stopped at the entrance to the Silver Ridge development.

The wind whipped Zach's face as he stepped out of the Tank. "Zach!"

Zach spun. Nev sprinted at him, her arms wide open. He stepped forward spreading his arms wide. She careened into him, dropping her backpack and wrapping her arms around him. He hugged her. "Nev, I'm so glad you're alive."

"Zach." Nev pushed him back and appraised him. "You're…" Her words stumbled. "Uh, me too." She finally said as she released him and retrieved her duffle bag. "Let's go."

"You're all ready to go?"

"Yeah. I said my goodbyes. Things are weird here."

"Okay. Sooner we hit the road, sooner we're back in Bellingham." He took the duffle and tossed it in the back seat.

When they got back to the freeway he noticed her still staring at him. "What? Have I grown a third eye?"

"No," she giggled. "You're a lot bigger than you were. It's only been a couple years."

"Oh, yeah. Grew six inches in three months my Junior year. Went from short to above average like that." He snapped his fingers. "So fast I got stretch marks on my shoulders."

"Wow. And not just up. You've been working out?"

"Well, some at school but mostly from 'working out' on the farm. Gramps-" He couldn't talk about Gramps, yet.

Nev nodded soberly. "Is he?"

Zach knew the implied question and the answers to the rest. "Yeah. Everybody in the family."

"Mine too." He saw her jaw tighten, but she turned her face into a smile. "I didn't think anybody I knew was still alive. Now you and Lizzie. And I'm heading home to Bellingham."

"Bellingham is dead. Except hippies and dog people. That's what Lizzie calls the folks who aren't all there anymore."

Nev nodded. "One of the reverend's kids is like that. Charley stares out the window all day. They said he got sick, got better, but something's off. He'll eat if you give him food."

A siren went off behind him. Zach saw flashing lights spinning in his rear view. "What the hell? Didn't anyone tell him it's the end of the world?" Zach stepped on the gas and felt the Tank rumble underneath him as it surged ahead.

10

LIZZIE MADE FROZEN PIZZAS AND opened a plastic carton of mixed fruit for Saj.

C.J. chuckled over her yearbooks in the living room.

"Hey, C.J.? What do you want to drink? Milk? O.J.? Crappy beer?"

"What kind of beer?"

"Coors Light?" She snorted. "Jerkwad, my mom's boyfriend was watching his weight."

"Sure. Coors is cool."

"Okay. Sorry about the cuisine. Zach's a decent cook. I'm not." She sat down at the kitchen table. A high chair would've been a good thing to grab. Saj toddled toward her.

"Hey, you cooked. I appreciate it. When Zach and Nev get back you should come out to our place. We got a farm out Deming way, me, my brother, my dad and some others. I'll return the favor. If you're lucky, somebody else will cook though. One of the guys is a farmer, excellent cook. Got the best beef. And we got us some venison, too. Got kind of a commune out there. We need more hands to get work done on the place."

Lizzie smiled and nodded. C.J., aka Motormouth in high school, was still as talkative as ever. "Dinner for sure. Not sure we want to sign on with anyone."

"That's cool. Take care of your own, my Dad always says." He laughed, still flipping through an old yearbook. "Can you pass me another beer? Your pictures in here are pretty hilarious."

"Yeah. I used to have hair. Brown, I think it was." She handed him the beer. Lizzie got herself a glass and poured a shot of Kahlua.

"Hey, you got any whiskey? I'd take a shot."

"'Beer and whiskey, always risky.' After this I'm off-duty as your server." She poured him the shot and set it down next to him on the end table.

"Thanks. I'll get you your tip later."

She sat at the computer and sent a few messages to Jess.

Saj came up next to her and plopped down on the floor. "Sss-sss."

"Yeah, I'm gonna tell her about you, Saj. She's never gonna believe it. Me with a kid."

The cop kicked in his overdrive; his lights flashing as he accelerated toward them. Adrenaline pumped through Zach; he forced himself to think straight. *What's the worst thing that can happen?* His foot stayed jammed to the floor as the Tank built up speed. But it was no match for the police cruiser. It had flanked him and the cop jabbed his finger at the side of the road.

The siren wailed as the cop pulled past and slowed down in front of him.

"Shit." Zach tapped his own brakes. "I guess we stop?"

Nev nodded. "I don't want to die in a car crash."

Zach took his foot off the accelerator and pushed in the brake. He'd broken 100 mph again. Now he was shaking. What the hell was so important?

The police car continued to slow in front of him finally whipping to the right and straddling the road. Zach jammed the brake the rest of the way in and the seatbelts tugged as the force pulled them forward.

The policeman exited the car with a shotgun.

"Jeez," Zach muttered, "watch enough cop flicks?" He raised his hands.

The officer motioned for him to roll down his window. Zach pushed the button and it slid down. "What's the deal? Sir." he added as an afterthought.

"Nobody goes north. There's a new outbreak in Oregon. We've got all roads north blocked off."

He acted like a cop. Zach read the tag on his uniform. "You're really Officer Williams?"

The cop nodded.

"The pandemic is over," Zach said. "The scientists say if you haven't gotten it you won't."

"Nobody knows that for sure, kid." Williams moved along the Tank looking in the windows. "You'll have to come to the Quarantine Center."

"With people who might already be sick?" Nev's eyes were wide. "That's crazy."

"You looked around much, young lady? Crazy is the new normal. Now, turn this rig around and follow me."

"Wait. Can we go back to where I picked her up? Tumwater? She'd got people there."

"Call them," Nev begged, "They're from the Mountain View Church."

"Mountain View? I used to take my kids there." His face twitched. "Above my pay grade. You need to follow me to the Q.C."

So his kids were dead. Zach turned to Nev. *Convince him.* She looked like she was going to start crying.

"Please," Nev said. "Officer Williams, all my family's dead. I don't want to go around sick people. Please let me go back to the Reverends'."

The officer swallowed. "Is Josie alive?"

Nev nodded, her eyes pleading. "And John. Can we call them? I'll go back there."

Zach saw Officer Williams consider, as he glanced back and then back to Nev. Then he smiled.

The cops face softened to a more pleasant human expression. "All right. I'll escort you back to the exit."

"Thanks," Nev said. "God bless you."

"I'll follow you." Zach said to Williams retreating back. He punched the window button up and then they were safe again. "So are we really going back?"

"Not for long," Nev replied through her tight jaw. "We'll have to take back roads north after dark."

"Suits me," Zach said, "better text Lizzie we're going to be late. At least I'm not feeling sleepy anymore." When the adrenaline wore off he'd have to stop or he'd literally crash.

A text had popped up on Lizzie's phone. Nevaeh. **Ran into trouble getting out of town.** Her cell buzzed, another one. **Won't be there till morning. Can't wait to see you, banana.** *Banana? Oh, mañana.*

After a brief exchange, Lizzie decided to call it a night. Saj had fallen asleep, beat from the day's activities, and her eyes were starting to droop. She lifted the baby to her chest and carried him toward Mama's room. "Gonna put the kid to bed," she said over her shoulder to C.J. "Thanks again for your help with the crib and stuff."

"Yer welcome. Gonna get me some more of this, s'all right with you?" He tipped his beer can toward her sloshing some of it onto the floor. "Shit."

Lizzie hesitated, looking at the puddle. "Don't throw up in the house?"

"I can handle my booze, baby."

"Whatever, C.J." What would she find in the morning? She got Saj into the crib. *C.J. was still as obnoxious as he was in high school.* She pulled on her mom's old flannel pajamas and snuggled into bed. The clean sheets felt nice. It had been one hell of a week. At least, she was no longer lonely.

Lizzie came aware to a weight pushing down on the bed and the covers lift up. "Zach, it's not gonna happen again." She rolled over groaning. "Go away."

A hand went up her pajama top and cupped her breast.

"Shit! Zach get out!"

"It's not little Zach. It's big Curtis." C.J.'s voice was slurred.

"Jesus, C.J." She shoved him away. "Get the fuck out of my bed."

"No." His breath heaved and stunk of whiskey and cigarettes.

He tossed off the covers. His strong arms jerked her onto her back. The heavy weight of his body rested on her thighs as he straddled her.

"Please, C.J.."

"Need to repopulate the planet."

Shit, this is not happening again. She couldn't see his face in the dark. "I can't have kids, C.J. Please don't do this."

"Then we're just gonna practice." C.J. wheezed, he wasn't as fat or heavy as Jerkwad, but he wanted more from her than Jerkwad ever had.

"Zach and Nev are going to be here any minute."

"Nope. Not till tomorrow. Saw the post." His hands reached down between her legs.

His hard hands fumbled with the drawstring on her pajamas. He grunted and yanked. She heard tearing fabric. *Shit. Change of tactic.* "Curtis. Please. I gotta pee." She wiggled her legs together. "You don't want me to pee."

A ragged chuckle escaped his throat. "No, I ain't a pervert."

His weight lifted off of her. Lizzie pulled what was left of her pajama bottoms up and stumbled into the hall. The lights were still on. He hadn't even bothered to turn them off.

"But I'm coming with you."

She glanced back. His pants were already off and he was ready for the deed he was trying to inflict on her. *Not if you were the last person alive.* She backed away toward the bathroom. "I can't go when you're watching. Thought you weren't one of those perverts."

"All right, but I'm gonna be right outside the door here listening. Don't try nothing."

Lizzie closed the door. A string of profanity ran through her head. She clicked the lock. She flipped the lid of the toilet up as she glanced around for something, anything that would get her out of this. "It might take me a minute, I'm all stressed out."

"Take your time, I'm waiting."

The bathroom had no windows, but rows of glass brick to let in light and a skinny slider to get some air circulation. She couldn't get more than her arm out. *Keep playing* "Okay, C.J., it'll be just a minute."

The metallic hose on the shower hung down. No way she could choke him, he was too strong. She stepped in the bathtub and slid the window open. "Help."

"Nobody's gonna hear you," C.J. said. "They're all dead."

"HELP ME," she screamed.

"Quit hollering or I'm breaking down the door." The knob jiggled. "You know these doors are no better than cardboard."

Lizzie looked down. Behind the bathtub. Jerkwad's shotgun. She reached down the other side, her shaking hand tightened around the gun. Now she would have control.

"C.J.?" she called surprised at the steadiness in her voice. "I've got a shotgun in here."

His drunken nasty laugh repeated. "Sure, ya do, honey. And I got a big gun out here for you."

"I'm serious."

"Look, Lizzie, don't play this shit with me. I want you."

"I don't want you." She sat down in the bathtub as far from the door as she could get. "Please, C.J. Go away. Leave me alone."

BAM! He bashed against the door. She heard it splinter.

"C.J. Don't."

Another crash and the door bowed inward. "I'm coming in, Lizzie." A pause and then the door burst, the frame splintering away from the wall. C.J., half naked, his face screwed up in anger, stood there breathing heavily.

Lizzie steadied the shotgun.

C.J. stared in disbelief. "Well, fuck. You do have a shotgun." His eyes flitted from the shotgun to her face. "But you ain't gonna use it or you already woulda."

"Curtis! Please, don't come any closer." In the other room Saj started to cry.

"You're even prettier when you're angry and scared." He stepped toward her.

Another step forward and he could touch the shotgun. Then he would have control again. "No," Lizzie whispered. She could feel the metal of the trigger pressed into the flesh of her finger. "C.J., please." She aimed the gun at his crotch.

His hand reached for the barrel. "You ain't gonna hurt me, Crazy Lizzie."

"Don't!" She screamed. *I never want to feel that dirty again.* Lizzie let the barrel drop.

He grabbed and pulled on the gun.

"No." Lizzie closed her eyes. *Never again.* She pulled the trigger.

The shotgun exploded in her hands, bouncing back toward her.

The massive explosion in the small room silenced all other sound.

Sound returned: Saj's panicked baby cries. C.J. howling. Lizzie opened her eyes.

He wobbled in front of her, his bloody hand pressing against his thigh. Blood pumped in spurts from under his hand.

Femoral artery, some logical part of Lizzie's brain relayed. She wanted him to stop. She didn't want to kill him.

C.J. lifted his eyes to hers. His face contorted, pale. "I wanted you." He collapsed in a heap on the cream colored bathmat, now soaked black with blood. Blood pumped from his thigh, but not so fast. His body shook. His breath hissed, and he was still.

If he's not dead, he will be soon. "C.J., you stupid fucker. Why'd you make me do that?" Lizzie had no idea the human body could hold so much blood.

Saj wailed.

She stepped out of the end of the bathtub as far from the body as she could. She did not let go of her death-grip on the gun.

"Saj, I'm coming." Her pajama pants fell around her legs. She kicked them off and tossed them on the floor where blood flowed under the tub. "Shit, what a mess."

Saj stood in the crib crying, pulling himself back and forth against the wall of the crib. "Saj, honey, it's all right. Sissie's okay." *Like Hell she is.* She leaned the shotgun against the crib. "Sissie had trouble."

She lifted him out of the crib and held his little shaking body to hers. Her sobs echoed his, her tears flowed to mingle with the hot wet streaks on his cheeks. Her voice joined his in a wail of fear and anguish. Eventually their keening subsided.

Lizzie sniffed, wiping her nose. "Sissie should check your diaper."

"Sis sis," he agreed.

She took one last deep shaking breath. Saj's diaper needed changing. She could do that. She did. Then she mixed him up a bottle with formula, testing the water from the microwave on her wrist to make certain it wouldn't burn him. For a moment she lost herself in the routine. Then she laid Saj in his crib with the bottle. He sucked hungrily, everything again right in his world. She envied him. His eyelids drooped. She picked up the shotgun and shut the light off.

Lizzie pulled on her mom's gardening jeans and a flannel shirt from the closet, leaning the shotgun inside. She returned to the carnage of the bathroom. Curtis's body lay as she had left him. His empty eyes stared at the ceiling. Part of her wanted to close the lids, so she didn't have to see those eyes. But if that would offer his soul some level of peace, she wasn't ready to grant him that, not yet. She remembered trying to read Dante. This sick bastard needed to spend a long time in purgatory at least. Not that she believed in souls or an afterlife.

She noticed her blood spattered hands, flipped the hot water to high, took the rubbing alcohol out of the medicine cabinet and poured it over her hands. When the water was steaming she stuck her hands under and rubbed at the red spots. The water burned, but she wanted to be clean, and it helped her focus, to feel alive. She scrubbed her hands dry on the "Guest" hand towel and tossed it toward the clothes hamper. Then she put on some latex gloves from the first aid kit.

The blood-soaked bathmat was large, and had most of the mess on it. She grabbed the corners and tugged it out of the room. His left leg caught on the remnants of the door. She flipped it over her arm and continued pulling.

Dammit, he's heavy. "C.J., you fucking asshole." The smell of blood, death and beer threatened to make her vomit. She looked away, down the hall. Blood was smeared all over the carpet. *Well, it had been ugly before.*

When she got to the front door her breaths heaved and her shoulders ached. She stood and shook herself out. She opened the door. His body seemed stiffer. How long did it take for rigor mortis to set in? She had no idea.

At the base of the steps, outside the front door, she let his legs fall. His body leaned on the steps; his unseeing eyes stared at the sky. She started crying again. Silently this time. Through her tears, she stabbed her latex-covered finger in the blood and wrote one word on his white t-shirt: *Fucker.* She stared at blood on her hand. She'd done this. C.J. was dead. They'd been friends. Sort of. She reached up and slid his eyelids shut. *I'm sorry.* His body was already too cold.

Lizzie wiped her finger on the grass. Then rage overtook the sadness and regret. *Never again. You're never gonna rape anyone again. Never. Never. Never.* She punctuated each thought with a kick. Her body shook, she dropped to her knees, and puked all over his legs.

She sidled away from the body and hugged herself, arms around her legs in the pre-dawn light.

After a while, cold brought her back to herself. She stumbled inside, shutting and locking the door behind her, She retrieved the shotgun and cleaned herself up in the kitchen sink. In the other room Saj began to cry.

"I'm coming, Saj." She went to him carrying the shotgun. "Come on, little man." His cries changed to a whimper at her voice. "Sissie'll hold you." She picked up the binky and put it in his mouth. She took him into the front room and sat down in the recliner, spinning it to face the door.

She balanced the shotgun on her lap and pulled Saj onto her chest, his head nestled under her chin.

He snuggled against her—his breath calm and his eyes closed as he sucked the binky. Lizzie watched his back rise and fall. She faded into sleep, but kept jerking awake. Each time, her heart racing, she expected to see the bloody apparition of C.J. coming through the door. Too many damn zombie movies.

11

A SOUND JERKED LIZZIE AWAKE. Someone was pounding on the door. *Jesus, C.J. is on the porch and coming in.*

"Lizzie!?"

The knob turned. She pulled the trigger and the shotgun blasted in her arms. The force spun the chair and slammed the door, leaving holes where the morning light streamed in.

"Jesus fuck, Lizzie! You shot me! It's Zach, for fuck's sake."

Zach. Lizzie dropped the shotgun on the floor. Saj's eyes were wide awake, and his mouth worked, but no sound came out.

"Zach. Sorry. It's safe. The gun is on the floor."

"Unlock the door."

Lizzie stumbled to the door, twisted the deadbolt and swung it open. Zach's head poked in as Saj's cry took shape.

"What the Hell happened, Liz?"

"Shh, shush, Saj. Sissie's better now. No more loud noises." He settled down when she stuck her thumb in his mouth, his mouth got suction and his sharp tiny teeth bit down.

"C.J. a.k.a. Big Curtis. That's what happened." She couldn't say anymore or she would be a quivering mass on the floor.

Zach stared at her, immobile.

"I shot you?" Lizzie asked.

That distracted him. "Just a little. Don't think anything got inside." He held up his right hand, a couple spots oozed a little blood. "Nev, you can come in."

Nev's slim blue jean and sweatshirt clad form slipped inside the door. "Jesus, Lizzie. What happened?"

As soon as Nev came through the door, Lizzie rose and rushed to her. She hugged her friend close with one arm still cradling Saj.

"Where the hell were you guys?" Lizzie couldn't say anything more. In Nev's hold, her body shook.

Zach pulled the fussing Saj from her arms, Lizzie reached for him, but Zach 'flew' him up in the air and made goofy faces. Saj stopped whining and giggled.

Nev led her upstairs, helped her change out of her bloody clothes. Lizzie dressed mechanically then collapsed onto the bed, pulling herself into a little ball, while her friend tucked her in.

Lizzie shook while Nev ran her fingers through her hair. After a time the shaking subsided.

Nev rubbed her back. "You can talk when you want to, Liz. But you don't have to."

Lizzie lay there a long time. "Why me? Do I have a fucking 'Rape Me' sign on my back?"

"Oh, my god." Nev hugged Lizzie's back. "He was always a jerk, but, I didn't think he'd—"

"Me neither. Why did he have to do it here? In this house? It's all I have left of Mama and Jason."

"I'm so sorry, Lizzie."

Lizzie saw sympathetic tears on Nev's pale cheeks. She sat up. "I need to get out. I need a shower. I can't be here; I need to go someplace that doesn't smell like death."

"We'll figure it out." Nev held her hands out, Lizzie let herself be pulled into that warm safety again.

But she couldn't stay still. "I need a drink and a cigarette."

"Maybe eat something first?"

"Maybe."

Lizzie sat at the picnic table in the back yard with a cigarette and a bottle of whiskey. She didn't touch the whiskey, but for once she smoked the whole cigarette. She felt calmer as she inhaled. The wind blew the lame tire swing back and forth. Lizzie remembered pushing Jayce on it, and on other swings in parks. He always wanted to go higher and higher. Until the time he'd flipped upside down and face-planted on a tree root sticking out of the ground. There had been so much blood. Lizzie shook herself.

Nev brought Saj out. "Can you take him?"

Lizzie nodded, sucking on the last of the cigarette and dropping on the ground to twist it under her foot.

"You thought of where you want to go?"

Lizzie shook her head and blew out the last of the smoke. She reached for Saj and laid his sleeping form in her lap. "Only away."

Nev kissed her forehead, warming up Lizzie's insides a bit. "All right. You think and we'll get you packed." Nev turned and Lizzie watched her lithe runner's body as she jogged back into the house.

Saj slept on her lap while she stared off at the clouds. *Where? Was there anywhere she wanted to be?* Saj's eyes opened. "Sissy."

"I'm here, baby." Her hands stroked his silky hair. His eyes fell closed again. She thought about taking a drink, but the effort necessary exceeded her desire. She stared at Saj's little chest rising and falling. Her racing thoughts calmed as she watched his little face, his eyes twitching behind his lids. "What are you dreaming about, Saj?" She felt her own breathing relax. The clouds were moving in the distance.

The door opened behind her. She spun her head—Nev and Zach. They were talking quietly and intently. Something about the body. They stopped talking as they approached.

Christ, they probably think I'm really going crazy now.

Zach had a plate of sandwiches. He placed one in her hand. "Here, eat something." He mussed up her hair.

Nev's arms wrapped around her. "We got you all packed, girl. I got clothes and toiletries. Zach got your notebooks and journals."

"Everything's loaded." Zach glanced around the yard as he munched his sandwich. "Any last requests? Anything you can't bear to leave behind?"

How about everything? Lizzie shook her head. "I don't want to leave my music collection, but we can come back. Not like someone's going to steal it."

Zach sat across from her and tapped his fingers on the table. "Where do you want to go? We could go down to my Gramp's place. It's in the middle of the sticks."

"Do you want to go there, Lizzie?" Nevaeh asked.

She shrugged. *Where do I want to go?* Not to some stranger's house.

Lizzie set down the sandwich. She wasn't hungry, but she'd eaten half of it. "No, but if Zach wants to…"

"I don't, not really," Zach said. "Probably stop by at some point. Besides we've got our choice of rich neighborhoods."

Lizzie's mind leaped. "There's a house out on Lake Whatcom. My ex, Chad, lived there when his dad was home. Chad hated his dad. The house is really nice in a stuck up, rich-businessman kind of way. We sometimes *used* it when his dad was out of town." She laughed wryly. "Sometimes I think he dated me to piss off his uptight father. If we're lucky he was away when the virus hit."

They didn't bother cleaning up the lunch leftovers.

Lizzie looked up the address in her phone and told Zach where to go. Mama had made her text her where she was going to be. Chad had always driven, so she wasn't sure she could find it without help. She plugged her player in the auxiliary jack. Lynyrd Skynyrd came on.

"Unluckiest band in history, "Zach said. "Seems like a good soundtrack for the day." He sang along. "'Hell, yeah. Ooh that smell, can't you smell that smell?'"

Lizzie tried to laugh at his off-key singing, but the subject of the song twisted her gut. "Zach, I'm gonna skip this song." He shrugged as "Lady Luck" by The Black Crowes came on.

"Could we listen to something from this century?" Nev asked. "Maybe after this song?"

Lizzie shook her head. "Nothing on my player younger than me, except U2."

Nev rolled her eyes. "You need to get new music. It's all gonna be old soon enough."

Lizzie lit another cigarette and rolled the window all the way down, paying attention to the streets. She figured she should be able to find it again if she had to. It was down a long driveway through trees and invisible from the road. "Solar power." Zach nodded, scanning the house. "Cool. Good choice, Lizzie."

"Let me go by myself. In case his dad is there. Okay?"

"Good idea," Nev said, "You sure we should be breaking in?"

Lizzie smiled. "You never made a good criminal." She jumped down from the Tank, ground out her cigarette on the ground and put it in the soda can in the door. If this was going to be home, she could at least keep it nice. The stray leaves and branches covering the always clean and neat multi-texture driveway suggested no one had been here this season.

She knocked on the door, rang the doorbell and waited. Then she glanced back at the Tank and shrugged. After a few minutes, she stepped into the rock 'garden.' They hadn't grown at all since the last time she'd seen them. She picked up one of the larger red volcanic rocks. Her fingers squeezed inside the hole in the bottom and loosened a key. She held it up and waved her friends over.

As she slid the key into the lock she had a momentary twinge of guilt. Like she was using Chad. And he was dead. But Chad always wanted to give her all she wanted. If only she knew what she wanted. She took a deep breath, noticing how fresh the air smelled out here, turned the key and pushed the door open. A loud warning beep repeated.

"Shit." The alarm. Hopefully he hadn't changed the code. She punched in the numbers—hoping she remembered. The beeping stopped and she breathed again.

Lizzie walked through the clean, empty house and out to the back deck. Something smelled. She followed her nose and found the emaciated body of a big mastiff out back stuck in its chain-link fence enclosure. Lizzie saw where it had tried to dig itself out under the fence, but it was strong with poles embedded in a wall of cement. Another perfect prison for one of man's best friends.

Zach came up behind her. "Awww, shit."

"What a shame," Nev said, cradling Saj and blocking his eyes. "Saj, look at the lake. Big lake."

Zach found a shovel and dug a grave on the slope by the lake while Nev and Lizzie explored the house and got some dinner going.

After dinner, as the sun set, they all went down to the newly covered grave. No one said anything. Lizzie wanted to, but nothing seemed profound enough. She held Saj tight, kneeling to smooth the dirt. Zach and Nev wrapped her in their arms as she held Saj. He clung to her, eyes wide. For once he did not cry. Powerlessness overwhelmed her. She let herself be comforted by the warmth of her friends.

When the cool night wind came and the sobs stilled, Lizzie sniffed and let them help her to her feet. The sun had passed behind the dark hills and in between the scattered clouds a few evening stars sprinkled the sky.

Lizzie pulled her shoulders back. Saj was heavy, asleep in her arms. "I'm gonna crash. Zach, you can have Chad's room. It's down the hall, second door on the left. Nev, let's take the giant bed in the master suite. There's room for you, me and Saj."

"You okay, Liz?" Nev asked.

"Okay as I'm gonna be for a while. I need sleep and Saj here's my sleeping pill." Lizzie figured they'd be talking about her and how screwed up she was, but tonight she didn't care. She took Saj and collapsed into bed.

The following morning after a quiet breakfast, Lizzie did the dishes.

"Why not throw them out?" Zach asked.

"We'll keep this place nice; might become home."

"Okay. I think we should hit Fred Meyer." Zach stood up. "Clean out the non-perishable stuff since we got so much space."

"You go ahead," Lizzie said. She needed to get away from people. Needed some freedom or she would explode. "But first take me back to my house. I wanna drive my car." Her skin tingled and she felt sweat. *Kill the snakes.* She had to face the horror head on, not slink away. C.J. wasn't going to control her.

Zach laughed. "Your car?"

"Yeah."

Nev and Zach glanced at each other.

"Jesus, guys. Yeah, I'm fucked up, but I'm a big girl."

Nev nodded. "I'm worried about you."

"Thanks, Nev."

"And I don't know if you're safe to drive on your own." Zach frowned.

She knew what he really meant was safe to be by herself. "Fuck you, Zach."

Zach closed his mouth. Then opened it. "Whatever. Let's go."

On the drive Lizzie sat on her hands and tried to pay attention to her breathing. Bellingham looked normal for a quiet Sunday maybe. She sat in the back by Saj, avoiding any more interaction with Zach and Nev.

At the house, Lizzie bent over Saj in the car seat and kissed him on the top of his head. He looked up at her. *What do you think of this crazy girl who found you?* "Nev-nev is gonna take care of you, Saj. Sissy'll see you in a bit."

He flapped his hands on the crossbar of the car seat. "Sissy."

Lizzie turned away before she started to cry.

Zach said. "If you get lost or stuck, call me. If you don't make it back by dinner time, I'm coming after you."

Lizzie shook her head, not looking back. "I'll be fine. I'll call if I need help."

After they left Lizzie started up the CRV, but she couldn't leave yet. She wasn't fine, tears pooled in her eyelids. *Dammit, I won't cry.* She sat there afraid to go in. *Kinda funny after all the weeks I was scared to leave.*

Lizzie pulled the car around to the back alley with fewer lurches than last time she'd driven. She could miss walking by the bathroom this way. She shut the car off.

Her brain spun as she took in the empty alley, the house that had been as close to a home as any she'd lived in. She wanted something. *But what?* The CDs seemed silly today. She had all those songs on her phone and her player. Time to let go of Daddy like she would have to let go of Mama. Then it came to her. Mama's memorabilia box. She wanted it like she wanted Saj to have something from his mom. She got out of the CRV and went in the back way.

The door swung open, bouncing loosely against the wall in the brisk wind. She went straight up to her room and grabbed the cigar box out of the back of the bottom drawer. She opened it and pulled out the little hankie her grandmother had embroidered her grandpa's initials on. She loved hearing her mom talk about them, maybe the only time Mama had been happy.

She took a few of her drawings off the wall and tucked them under her arm. Glancing around she saw the tiny fake-diamond stud earrings Mama had bought her when she'd turned 16. They'd never been bizarre enough for Lizzie's sense of style. She sat on the bed and put them in, taking the balls out of her nostril and her left tragus hole.

She picked up an empty journal and started writing.

> Spam me, jam me, tell me lies.
> Tell me that you're old and wise
> And all that I don't realize.
> Spam me, jam me, tell me lies

Rape me, make me take the blame
Tell me it's always the same
Till I don't even know my name
Rape me, make me take the blame
Feel my heat, my anger, tell me everyone's a liar
Let it cauterize my feelings, let it burn a wall of fire

There was a knock at the front door. Lizzie tucked the hankie inside and left the bedroom, heading downstairs. "Zach? You didn't need to come back here after me." She reached the door and opened it.

It wasn't Zach. A dark-haired man in jeans and a Carhartt jacket spun on the bottom step and backed down as the door opened.

As she swung the door open she stopped breathing. It wasn't a knock. It had come from a hunting knife embedded in the door. Pinned under the tip was the bloody scrap of C.J.s' T-shirt that said *Fucker*.

He stepped toward her. "You killed my brother."

12

LIZZIE SCREAMED AND SHOVED THE door closed. "Leave me alone!"

"Lizzie, right?"

His voice was calm, but Lizzie heard menace. How'd he know her name? *Shit. The stupid sign at the school.* The doorknob turned. Lizzie grabbed it, trying to shove the deadbolt. The door shoved her back and the deadbolt popped out.

He stepped in.

Lizzie heaved herself at the door, slamming it with her shoulder.

It caught on his foot. She shoved again as he pulled his foot back. The door closed to where the deadbolt stuck out. She got the safety chain hooked, but he rammed his shoulder into the door and she couldn't get the deadbolt retracted. She gave up and ran toward the back of the house.

She heard heavy thuds and then tearing. The chain gave way.

He crashed through the front door, and shouted after her. She didn't hear his words over the string of curse words she was screaming at him.

She slipped on the kitchen floor and landed on her mother's box. It broke. Her pictures flew. She shoveled the contents back in and stumbled through the back door as he came toward her.

He grabbed her around the waist as she tried to get out to the back deck. She swung backwards with her hand trying to claw his face. Her feet kicked out.

"Hold it!" He yelled as they fell into the screen door.

She scrambled up and got out the door. He dove, catching her around the legs. Then someone was between them, snarling, punching, kicking—Spike.

Lizzie jerked her legs from her attacker's grasp and she struggled to her feet clutching Mama's box. Spike was big, but clumsy. He was losing ground to C.J.'s brother. She ran for the car, slamming the gate behind her.

Lizzie flung the door open, tossed the box in the passenger seat, and twisted the key. It started; she threw it into drive and stepped on the gas. The tires spit gravel. To her amazement she drove in a straight line down the alley and didn't hit anything.

He appeared running alongside the car. Lizzie screamed and jammed the lock button. She slammed the gas to the floor, and swerved sideways into him. He jumped out of the way.

"Almost hit your damn brother, too. Should have!" She gripped the steering wheel tightly as the CRV careened forward. In the rear view mirror she could see him coming, still running. "I can lose you in town." She swerved sharply onto Iowa Street, fighting to keep the car from barreling out of control into a storefront.

Her pursuer followed her around the corner and then stopped, watching as Lizzie pulled away. "You're stupid, Lizzie. What'd you tell everyone your address for?"

He turned around and walked back the way he'd come.

She needed to be on the other side of the freeway, but didn't want to be followed. Turning another sharp corner onto Franklin Street, she held the steering wheel tight and slowed. Visions of her mangled body in a wreck flashed in her head. Behind her, she couldn't see anyone. But he must have a vehicle.

"Shit, shit, shit." She let the car glide forward.

When she reached James Street, she rolled down all the windows, listening for any sign of pursuit. She coasted through the intersection, her eyes darting in every direction. No sign.

In front of the Trader Joe's building she saw Spike hunched over and limping. Her foot slammed the brake and she pitched forward into the steering wheel. *Should she pick him up?*

It was the right thing to do. She drove into the parking lot. He saw her approach. His face had been bloodied, his large nose redder than usual, but he didn't look very hurt. She jumped out and opened the back door. "Come on, Spike. Get in the car.

Lizzie's gonna try and help you now."

Spike obediently climbed into the back seat.

Lizzie jumped back in the front seat. "Breathe, Lizzie."

She popped it into drive and turned around, then drove across the freeway. She was amazed at how much control she had driving when she didn't stop to be afraid of it. She kept off main streets, zig-zagging forward, like she remembered from ninth grade English what Theseus had done in the Labyrinth.

Spike cowered. "We'll clean you up in a bit, Spike." His head popped up. "How much can you understand?"

His head tilted to one side, staring in confusion.

When she reached the house she honked like a maniac.

Zach came running out. "What happened?"

She jumped out, wired. "C.J.'s brother. I think he wants to kill me," she babbled and collapsed in Zach's arms.

He held her. "It's ok. You're safe."

Nev hurried out carrying Saj. She looked Lizzie up and down.

Lizzie saw her relax when she didn't see any injuries.

"What happened?"

"C.J.'s brother. You were right, Nev. We should have done something with the body."

"Spike saved me. I brought him home." Lizzie managed a smile. "Can we keep him?"

"Spike?" Zach stared at her. Then his eyes bugged out as he saw the passenger in her backseat.

Lizzie let Zach help Spike out of the car. He was shifty and nervous with so many faces peering at him. "It's okay, Spike. These are friends." She put her hand on his shoulder. "He needs a bath."

"The hot tub?" Nev said.

Zach shook his head. "What if we want to use it? Let's try the shower next to it.

Lizzie coaxed Spike into the shower with dinosaur-shaped chicken nuggets. It wasn't too long before he was naked and somewhat clean. Nev brought a big towel, they wrapped him up in it and took him inside by the gas fireplace.

"Okay, now what do we dress him in?" Lizzie asked. "He's like a six-foot baby."

No one came up with any answers so she went and found a man-sized bathrobe. She continued feeding him chicken nuggets until he fell asleep. Then she escaped to the bedroom, while Zach and Nev watched a movie.

Sitting on the bed, Lizzie reopened her mom's box of memories, now squashed on one side. The old cigar box under the pretty contact paper showed through.

Lizzie picked at the paper, trying to figure out if she could fix it. As she pulled it back she saw her father's name: Manuel Guerrero. She peeled it further back. And found an address: P.O. Box in Del Rio, Texas and a phone number with an 830 prefix. *I can call my dad? Mama!?*

She dialed the number quickly before she lost her nerve. It rang for a very long time. Then she got a voicemail box. Lizzie took a deep breath. "Mr... Manuel, uh, it's Lizzie. Elizabeth. Your daughter. If you get this please call." She said her phone number twice, slowly. "If you ever get this..., Daddy."

The word sounded weird coming out of her mouth. She hadn't seen him since she was too young to remember. But she loved the idea of him—his music, his movies.

She set the phone down. *Don't get your hopes up, Lizzie.* He didn't care enough to look her up when everyone was alive. Even if he was alive, would he want to see her?

Zach awoke early, his body still on farm time—time to get up and feed Gramp's livestock. He didn't want to wear the same dirty clothes he'd had on for days, but hadn't thought to pack when he had made his rescue run up to Bellingham. Chad's closet was full of clothes, ski gear, hiking gear, a wetsuit. But none of them fit. He found an unopened pack of boxers, pulled on a pair and decided the joy clean underwear brought was priceless.

After dressing he stuck his head in at the master bedroom. Lizzie snored softly with Saj cradled in her arms. Nevaeh was already up; her side of the bed was pulled together as much as could be without disturbing the others.

Maybe the dad's clothes would fit Zach better. The mirrored closet doors slid silently on their rails. Zach grabbed a pair of flannel-lined hiking pants off a shelf.

With a quick glance to make sure Lizzie still slept, he shucked off his pants and pulled on the new pair. They were baggy, the way he liked them. He snagged a comfy-looking flannel, retrieved his belt and decided to go out for some fresh air. Nev had probably gone outside.

He slipped out the door into the cold, gray morning. The sun had risen, showing bright through clouds over the hills. He walked down to the lake past the once-manicured lawn that now looked a ragged. Fog floated out over the water.

At the lake's edge, he tossed a rock out into the glassy surface, then knelt to splash water on his face. The cold was bracing; he felt alive as a breeze swept past. He heard feet on gravel and turned to see Nev, oblivious to his presence as she jogged toward him. She wore neon green running shorts and a black running bra. Looking at her made Zach shiver and not just from the cold.

Canada Geese honked across the lake, forming a perfect V in the dawn's light. At least they had one solid path to follow. He was torn, north or south? He'd go North—away from Nev. With her dressed like that, he wasn't sure what he might say. He liked her, but he had just been with Lizzie. They were all supposed to be friends. *What a mess.* He strode at a good pace along the shore path.

"Zach? Wait up."

He stopped. Nev ran toward him like an Olympian, her arms and legs pumped with fine precision, her body moving only to propel her forward.

When she got close she slowed, breathing puffs of white fog. She made her mouth into an O and puffed a few at him.

"Morning. Cold and frosty," Zach said.

"Who you calling cold and frosty? It's pretty," Nev said. "I couldn't sleep anymore. Seems all I've done the last few weeks. When I dream, everyone is still alive. I get worried about stupid shit like track and school and work, but..." she faded off.

"But you always have to wake up." Zach finished for her.

"Yeah." Nevaeh glanced back at the house.

Zach stared out over the lake. The wind had picked up; the fog slid across the water, leaving behind pretty white caps. "What are we gonna do for Lizzie?"

"Wait." Nevaeh sighed. "She's gotta work through it."

He knelt to pick up some rocks to toss in the lake. "Saj is probably a good thing to distract her." Thinking about the little rug-rat warmed his heart. "Spike? I'm not so sure. He makes me nervous." He threw the stones, skipping them despite the choppy surface.

"Yeah. I love the way she looks at Saj. I remember times she'd look that way at Jayce when he was little." Her body shook with cold. "Gotta keep moving."

Zach watched Nev as she began to jog, but slower. His eyes followed the curve of her body where it slipped underneath her clothing.

"You watching my butt, Zach Riley?" She laughing. "The world might end, but some things never change."

Zach blushed. Then with a sudden burst of courage he blurted, "Yup. You mind?"

"Not as much as I used too." She turned and faced him. Hands on her hips. "Race you to the next dock?"

"You're on. I'll give you this much head start," he said, indicating the space between them.

"I don't need it. On your mark, set? Go!" Nevaeh sprinted.

Zach exploded from his kneeling stance, his arms flying in rhythm. He gained on her, but only barely. Another hundred yards. He focused on the trail under his feet and poured on all he had. He watched her butt now as a competitor.

He closed the distance as she slapped the piling. He slowed, still several strides away, running at her in full tackle mode. She sidestepped like he knew she would, but clotheslined him as he passed. He managed to grab her arm and drag her down with him, rolling into the heavy grass.

They laughed. Icy dampness from the long grass seeped into his clothes. It was like old times, for a moment all their troubles were gone. He took the chance, and leaned in for a kiss.

Her lips curved upward but she turned her mouth away and attacked his ribs, tickling him ruthlessly. He laughed uncontrollably until he finally turned the tables on her. He had her wrists pinned tight while he tickled her.

She contracted in hysterical laughter.

"Please. Zach. Stop!"

He continued to tickle.

"I give." She twisted her hands and slid from his grasp.

"Hey, how'd you do that with your hands?" he asked, fending off her return attack.

"Wrists actually. All in the wrist. People call it double-jointed. It's not really, just stretchy tendons, I think. Check this out." She stopped trying to tickle him and pushed her fingers all the way back until they pointed toward her elbow.

"Jesus, doesn't that hurt?"

"No. A girl needs to be able to defend herself." Her grin turned serious.

He was thinking it, too. What kind of a world were they living in?

She gave him a goofy grin. "All this tickling has worked up my appetite. I'll make breakfast." She rolled toward him, hugged him quickly and jumped up. "Race you back."

She ran off; he didn't join the race, but jogged after her. That was Nev, always trying to stay positive. But he knew she was worried. He was worried, too. He knew one thing that would help him feel better. Safety.

No one besides Nev was awake inside. Zach searched inside the house and garage. Even with all the scavenging they had done, there was one thing they still needed. Guns. More than Lizzie's shotgun. With people like C.J. and his brother out there, they needed to protect themselves.

He found nothing but a classic wooden bow and some wooden arrows. They were pretty, but not what he needed. He slipped into the master bedroom and checked the closet. If there was a gun in the house, it was too well hidden. He returned to the kitchen and sat down.

"Breakfast is ready." Nev put a big bowl of oatmeal in front of him. "Any luck?"

"No." He put brown sugar, cinnamon and raisins in the mush.

Nev smiled at him, eating hers plain. "What're you looking for?"

"Guns."

"Oh." Nev ate.

"You want to go out with me?"

"Oh, Zach, I thought you'd never ask," Nev said in a syrupy southern accent.

Zach grinned. "For guns."

"Yeah, I suppose."

When Lizzie got up they explained the plan to her. She seemed relieved to stay at the quiet calm of the lake place with Saj and Spike.

13

ZACH CLIMBED INTO THE TANK. He started the engine and revved it. The big V8 rumbled and the hood of the truck see-sawed as the engine torqued. "Sure you don't want to learn to drive?"

Nev grimaced. "This beast? No way."

"It's an automatic." The Tank lurched forward as Zach stepped on the gas. "Not too fast, but it is powerful."

They drove up driveways. Zach wasn't certain what he was looking for. How can you tell from the outside of a house that there are guns inside? "Maybe we should go to Wal Mart."

Nev laughed. "Yeah. We can pick up a flame-thrower while we're at it."

"I'm serious." He pulled back onto the main road and headed for town. "You can get major firepower at Wal Mart."

"Okay. Anything else we need? Maybe a mega-pack of diapers."

Zach contemplated the new world order while he drove. *Where they really in danger?* Nev flipped through the radio stations, but gave up. Oldies and three-week-old recorded Emergency bulletins weren't good listening.

When they got to Wal Mart they found a truck-sized hole in the glass front. Zach rolled down the windows and they sat outside for a while listening, in case anyone was still in there.

After five minutes Zach opened the door and jumped down. "Should have brought Lizzie's shotgun."

"Yeah," Nev hissed, following him. "Brilliant. So you can get your head shot off."

Zach stepped in onto the broken glass. It crunched under his feet. The lights were all on. He sidled around the store sticking close to the walls. At the sporting goods counter he realized some-one else had had the same idea. The cabinet glass was broken, shelving units sat askew. Anything that could shoot a bullet or a pellet was gone. "Damn." He kicked through the garbage, glad he had on his heavy steel-toed boots. He found a couple boxes of ammo, two of .22 and one of 9mm. Probably the thieves were nervous and in a hurry. He stuffed them in his jacket pocket.

"Let's go, Zach." Nev glanced around.

She looked jittery. A compound bow box on the top of a shelv-ing unit caught his eye. He climbed the shelves and knocked it off with a bang.

"Zach." Her tone was sharp and her voice a whisper. "Come on."

"Okay." He picked up the box. He glanced around, but could see no arrows. The box said there were two included. "Let's go." He worked his way back the way they had come. Nev had him wound up. He peeked around each corner before stepping into view. Nev stayed close behind.

As they neared the front of the store, Zach thought he saw movement out of the corner of his eye. He froze and, then spun. Nev rammed into him. He knocked a bunch of vases on the floor. They shattered in the stillness. A box fell from a high shelf with a flutter of black wings. Half a dozen angry, cawing crows scolded them.

"Hell, Zach." Nev's face was white, her eyes wide. "I nearly peed my pants. I hate crows. Can we leave?"

The birds returned to their roost, still chittering at them.

"Yeah." Zach laughed. "Hey, everybody. We're here. If you somehow missed that." He smiled at Nev and waited a few seconds; there were no more sounds.

Back in the car, Zach headed south from the shopping area. "Let's try Yeager's."

"That old place with all those old record player things hanging from the ceilings?"

Zach nodded. They drove past a pack of dogs, mutts of various sizes. Clustered together, they chased the Tank.

When he got to Yeager's, Zach drove around back. The door had a piece of plywood covering it with a dumpster rolled up against it. So, whoever had done it was probably back outside. "You wanna stay in the Tank?"

Nev shook her head, "No way."

Zach pushed the dumpster aside and lifted the plywood away from the door to the side. "Always loved this place," Zach whispered.

Someone had filled a cart with camping gear and freeze dried food. It was quiet. The lights were off, but there was a decent amount of light to see by.

Inside he did not find the mass destruction he expected. "Somebody else loved it, too. It's clean." He grasped Nev's hand and they walked together through the aisles. He motioned toward the front of the store. "Would you go that way and keep an eye on the street?"

Nev nodded and headed for the windows, seeming less nervous here. Zach was glad she had come along. Though she didn't have Lizzie's toughness, she also didn't have the bad attitude.

Zach picked out a Bushmaster AR-15 and a smaller, simple bolt-action .22 caliber. He grabbed ammo for both and Lizzie's shotgun and left the box of 9mm from Wal Mart. "Okay. We can go."

Nev hustled toward him.

"This one's for you. It's a beginner. .22. Mostly to scare people."

Nev stared like it was a live snake. "No. I don't want one."

Zach acknowledged her discomfort. "Okay. Maybe later."

"Not likely." She shook her head. "Let's go."

They didn't talk much on the way back.

When they got to the lake, Lizzie ran out to greet them. Zach could see another manic mood.

Lizzie said. "Let's go to Western."

"The university," Zach said. "Why?"

"Maybe there are more people," Lizzie replied. "Maybe young people, college students, are more likely to survive."

"Most of the kids at Evergreen went home right away," Nev said.

Zach saw her jaw clench. *Why hadn't she gone?*

"Well," Zach said, "we haven't been down that way, so we can go. But we go out safe. Every gun is loaded.

"Jeez, Zach," Lizzie said. "You sound as paranoid as me."

Zach ignored her comment and continued. "We watch ourselves. We gotta assume people are dangerous. If they don't have guns and a grudge, they might be infectious."

Lizzie scoffed. "The scientists say if we're alive we're okay."

"The same thing he'd said to the cop. "Better safe than sorry," Zach said. He sounded like Gramps.

Lizzie didn't seem to hear. "Remember the ceremony in the rock circle at Western, Nev?" she chattered. "We wanted to communicate with Jess by a sending."

"Yeah. I was okay." Nev laughed, "as long as we didn't have to be naked."

"Shit." Lizzie's laugh was hollow. "Stupid little girls. But how're you gonna learn?"

Zach remembered Lizzie's Wicca phase; messing with magic made him nervous. Maybe he believed enough in higher powers to be scared. He parked in the main University parking lot next to Fairhaven College.

Lizzie continued. "If I was going to go to college it would have been at Fairhaven. Rumor has it their community garden has pot plants interspersed with the vegetables."

Lizzie had been talkative since he brought Nev north, but Zach knew it was more than being excited to see her. He remembered hunting with Gramps, when he'd got his first kill, a buck. Afterwards he couldn't stop talking. His father and uncle had teased him about babbling like a little girl; Gramps had only nodded. The blood and the warmth of the body had been nauseating, but he'd been wired, couldn't sleep. *First kill.* His mouth went dry as he realized his hadn't been human and saying 'first' implied there would be a second and a third.

They wandered through the campus—big gray monolithic buildings hidden among the trees.

It felt different here than the rest of the city, more alive. Zach couldn't quite put his finger on why. Then he realized. There were faint sounds, a murmur of people close by.

As they rounded a corner Zach spotted an older guy in a straw hat pushing a cart loaded with boxes. He wore a Hickory shirt like Gramps when he worked on the farm. The man waved at them and continued on. As if a group of strangers wandering in was an everyday thing. Zach looked at his companions. "People?"

"Let's catch up to him."

Zach hoofed it, but couldn't see where he'd gone.

They could hear the people before they got to the communal gardens. Zach was elated. People, dozens of them, were cleaning and picking produce: carrots, onions, cauliflower and broccoli. They looked up and nodded, but continued their work.

"Well, I'll be—" Zach wasn't sure what he'd expected from other survivors, not a brass band or anything, but he expected them to at least be interested.

"Hey, look." Lizzie pointed.

The man, his cart now empty, shuffled toward them with a grin on his face. He set aside the cart and came forward, taking his straw hat off and scratching his balding scalp. "Welcome." He offered his hand.

Zach hesitated, shrugged off his nerves about infection and shook the firm, calloused hand. "Thanks. You're the first people we've seen other than us."

"I'm Vern. We get a few folks trickling in. Yesterday some folks came down from Canada." Vern didn't seem to be able to stay still.

"I'm Zach. This is Nev, Lizzie… And the kids."

"Welcome. We can use more hands. Besides this—" He motioned to the garden, "we've got the Joe's Garden greenhouses over the hill."

"We aren't really into gardening," Lizzie said as if she could answer for them all.

Vern's smile fell a little.

Zach held his hand up. "Hold it, Lizzie. I'd be interested in helping out." He couldn't help but like the man. Lizzie glared at him.

"You help, you get fresh produce." Vern grinned. "The first batch is free."

Lizzie plastered on a smile. "We're trying to get uh, adjusted. Figure out what's up."

She stared at Zach like she wanted him to back her up. He shrugged. "Yeah."

Vern nodded. "Okay, I get it. Well, lots of work to do and the weather won't let it wait. Follow me if you want. I'll get you some food and you can 'figure out what's up.'" He set off at a brisk pace.

Zach pulled Lizzie close as she walked past him. "What the hell was that about, Lizzie?"

"He's weird. I don't trust him." She jerked her arm out of his and followed Vern.

"You don't trust anyone." Zach glanced back at Nev. She rolled her eyes.

Vern held the door open and they stepped inside a cement building. "I taught History at Fairhaven before this all went down." He said it as if he expected them to say something about themselves. The first question adults always asked each other was "What do you do?" The guy was odd, but Lizzie, as usual, had overreacted.

Vern handed Zach a bag and a loaf of bread. It was rustic and warm.

"Thanks." Zach dug through it to find carrots, string beans, broccoli, garlic, onions and cauliflower. "This is awesome. Thank you."

"You're welcome." Vern beamed. "There's a gathering at Sehome High School gym tomorrow. We're trying to figure things out here, too. Come. Bring your friends. Good to meet you folks. Lots to do. " And he was off again.

Zach turned to Lizzie. "What's the plan?"

"Why are you asking me?" Lizzie spun away and stomped out the doorway. "Hell if I know."

Zach counted to ten. *Act like the boss until you don't want to make a decision.* Nev put her hand on his shoulder. He saw sympathy, but not much help. She had never been one for confrontation. He followed Lizzie out the door. "Lizzie, wait."

"What?" She spun around.

"Look, I just asked a question—"

"Never mind." Lizzie strode away again.

Zach's stomach rumbled, inspired by the smell of the fresh bread. "Let's head home."

Back at the lake, Zach pulled marinating steak out of the fridge. "Ta Da!"

"Yah, Zach!" Nev clapped. She started flipping open cupboards. "We need a nice bottle of red wine."

Nev was such a nice counterpoint to Lizzie's negativity. He remembered Nev helping his mom cook, back in the days when everything was fine.

"Come on. It's out in the garage." Lizzie's eyes focused on the steak. "I don't know anything about wine. But I'll help you pick a pretty bottle."

Zach loved the attention his food and cooking skills got. It made up some for all the crap he took. He grilled the steaks on the barbecue while Lizzie got the wine open.

Nev made a salad of grated carrots, chopped greens, broccoli tips, onions, black olives, then tossed it with a raspberry vinaigrette she'd found in the pantry.

Lizzie set the table with some nice china she'd found in the cupboard and added candles. "This is more like it," Zach said, slicing into his still pink-in-the-middle steak. "Ah."

"It's like perfect for training," Nev said. She wiped dressing off her mouth with the back of her hand. "When I was getting ready for a half marathon, I'd eat protein and veggies. Never could get into the vegan thing, but I do love veggies."

Spike seemed to sit up a little straighter. He tried to use the knife and fork, but Lizzie helped him cut the meat.

Zach decided his first judgment of a dumb dog was not fair. Spike was more like a smart dog, giant and bumbling. Maybe even a dumb kid, but it was hard to get over the six- foot height if he ever stood up. Acted like a kid at the dinner table, too. Only wanted steak and bread. His hair hung down over his eyes. Somebody better cut it soon. *And that somebody is probably me.*

After dinner, Nevaeh helped him clean up. They filled the dishwasher and ran it. When the water pump kicked in, the lights flickered. Zach wondered how well solar power would work in Bellingham, Washington in the winter. Was there anyone left even thinking about it?

Zach glanced around at the group sitting around the fake gas fire, considering where they'd all been a week or so ago. Lizzie's dark mood had lifted a bit and she was singing *Row Your Boat* to Saj. Spike squatted, leaning his head on the soft leather arm of the chair and staring into the fire. Nev surfed what was left of the net on the expensive laptop he'd retrieved with Lizzie.

He closed his eyes; the sounds were soothing. Zach wished it was real wood popping and sputtering in a fireplace. *But this is nice.* It reminded him of the best of times, when Mom and Dad were together and happy and they were at Gramps when Granny Mae was still alive. In the summer, after working in the fields or hunting, they'd all sit by the fire, laughing and singing.

The thought of hunting made him think of the guns. Maybe they were just being paranoid. There weren't really enough people to worry about. But they needed to stay away from C.J.'s brother.

14

SUDDEN HARD RAIN ON THE skylight overhead jerked Zach awake. His first thought was gunfire, but then he recognized the heavy rain. The room was dim, the fire still unchanged. The gas fire was okay for a while, but the repetition paled in comparison to real red-hot, flickering coals.

Spike was nestled into the love seat with a blanket tucked around him. The girls were gone. Zach stood, stretching stiff limbs, and walked toward the master bedroom.

He knocked on the door gently and heard some sort of murmur that sounded like an affirmative. Turning the knob cautiously he pushed the door open. Nev stared at the laptop. Lizzie lay on the bed next to her with Saj sleeping in her arms.

"Have a nice nap?" Lizzie asked.

"Not bad. A chair's not as comfortable as a bed," Zach said. "Why'd we bring the crib if you're not going to use it?"

"I didn't want to wake him up."

"Oh." Zach flopped down next to Nev. "What're you doing on the laptop?"

Nev raised an eyebrow at him. "Trying to see if there is anything approaching an organized recovery."

Zach snuck a hand up to tickle her but a glare stopped him. "Any luck?" He lay on his back with his hands under his head, enjoying at least touching the warmth of her hip with his.

"Not yet." Nev shut the laptop lid. "Seems like someone should have their shit together. More than us anyway." She dug her elbow in his rib.

"Ouch, Nev." Zach squirmed away from the pain. "That didn't tickle."

Lizzie looked up. "Most of 'em are probably partying." She glanced around. "Like us."

Zach snorted. "Partying, yeah, that describes it. Or surviving and trying to find other people."

Lizzie got a distant look in her eyes as she said, "Like Jess."

"Why not join the hippie-dippies?" Zach asked. He liked Vern. And the vegetables.

"You want to be told what to do by a bunch of old people?" The disdain in Lizzie's voice was clear. "We're fine. We've got each other. You can't tell me this isn't cool."

"Yeah, it's cool, but—" With Lizzie almost all adult men and most adult women were the enemy. *Keeping us from being free.* "Sheez, Lizzie. They've got food. They're not exactly 'The Man.'"

"Maybe. Maybe not. Besides I don't know if I even want to stay in Bellingham."

"You don't know?" Zach wondered if he would ever figure out other people. "Whatever. I'm going to the gathering tomorrow. I want to help."

"Gathering?" she asked. "'There can be only one!'"

Zach recognized the quote from the movie they had watched the night she had taken him up to her bedroom. They said it right before they chopped someone's head off. "Uh, Lizzie, it might be a good idea if you and Spike both kept away. In case C.J.'s brother shows up."

Lizzie scoffed. "Why would I go anyway? But you can go. I'm not your boss or anything. You can give me the highlights later."

"I will. It would be good to have more people around. Even if they are a bunch of hippies."

Lizzie shook her head and turned away. "G'night, Zach."

"G'night, Zach," Nev echoed.

"Dismissed, huh?" He stood up, mocking hurt. Lizzie's comment stung, but Nev's burned. *What the hell?* "Thank you very much. I'll take my big man ass to the boy's room while you princesses occupy the suite."

"We already have our little Prince." Lizzie smiled down at sleeping Saj.

"Well, you enjoy his affections, ladies. I'm outta here."

He closed the door and returned to the living room. Spike had left his comfortable perch. Zach spied him hunkered down in the darkest part of the room. "'sup Dogman?" There was no response.

Zach crossed to the big man. Something stunk. "Dammit, Spike." He grasped Spike's arm and pulled him across to the mess on the loveseat, then walked him the ten or so feet to the bathroom. When Gramps died he had thought he was done being a nurse.

"This," he picked up the blanket, "goes in the toilet." He flipped the light switch and dumped what he could into the bowl and flushed it. "Sit and shit," he growled.

Spike's arms flew over his head, wounded eyes stared at Zach. *Now I scared him.* "God help me." He pulled his own pants down and sat on the toilet, miming the activity and adding grunts for effect.

The girls had definitely gotten the better end of the stick tonight.

Once Zach got Spike's mess cleaned up he went to bed. But sleep was not in the cards. Zach lay there awake, restless. Yards away in a bed together were the two girls he had been in love with, girls who thought of him as a little brother. *It's not fair. But life never is. It could be worse. I could be alone.* That held little comfort as he pulled the covers up around himself.

Zach still hadn't cried. He tried to release himself to tears. *I should be sad. Or I should be happy or angry. I should feel something, dammit!* And still he lay there unable to sleep, unable to cry, unable to take the steps into the other room and ask for comfort, companionship.

The sun's heat through the greenhouse glass steamed the dirt. Lizzie dripped sweat. She threw the weeds aside with a growl. Spike ducked and scuttled out of the way. "At least you could help instead of staring at me with those puppy-dog eyes." His head cocked at an angle, very dog-like, and he watched her warily.

She had agreed to help out at Joe's Garden while Nev and Zach went to the gathering, so she wouldn't be seen if C.J.'s brother came. Nevaeh offered to take Saj, and Lizzie thought it would be some quiet time away from everyone. She hadn't realized her break was babysitting Spike while working her ass off at a business. She remembered hearing about the Joe's Garden franchise before everyone got sick, but her family could never afford the fresh veggies. Some black beetles in the compost pile distracted him.

"Hey, Spike?"

He glanced up at the sound of his name and shambled over.

She shook off a skinny little carrot and scrubbed it on her pant leg. It was sweet and crunchy. She offered one to Spike. He took a bite and then another. "Maybe you could dig up a row yourself and then I could shake off the weeds and keep the carrots." His head cocked again. "Come on, Spike."

Standing over the furrow, she motioned digging up the carrots. She tugged him gently into place and helped his hands go into the dirt. Then she moved slightly further on and made a flurry of digging. She spun to watch Spike. "Come on. I know you're not a dog, but please?" She patted her thighs. "Spike, dig!"

He dug his hands in and tossed the dirt backward, weeds and carrots and all. Lizzie cheered. Spike grinned. He did a few more feet. She clapped her hands together. "Go, Spike, go." He went. She followed along, shaking the carrots off to one side and kicking the weeds to the other.

Lizzie was thirsty, so she carried an armful of carrots to the table by the door and poured herself a cup of water. She pulled off her winter jacket and refilled the water cup, wondering if Spike had the sense that God gave dogs to know he was thirsty too. "Spike, you thirsty?"

She slapped some lunch meat and bread together; handed the water cup to Spike and bit into her sandwich. She made another for Spike.

He scarfed it down happily and loudly. She rubbed his head since he was squatting; if he stood straight up she'd be lucky to touch his shoulder.

Lizzie steamed inside, too. Why did Zach want to go hang out with the hippies? Settling in with even more people was the last thing she wanted. But what if Nev and Zach both wanted to join the stupid little commune? She and Saj and Spike could stay at the lake. *Why can't I stand to be with people—or alone?* She took a deep breath.

The heat and scent of the fertile earth comforted her somehow. She'd never had a green thumb, but then again she'd never really had any opportunity. She randomly pulled up leafy things, finding radishes, but sometimes just leaves, colored and green. Zach would probably know what to do with them. She ate the radish, zingy, but not too hot, and went back for another. She placed the rest of the plants by the door.

Vern had said to harvest a row of carrots and then weed the additional rows. She knew Spike couldn't get the hang of weeding and Lizzie was tired of the carrots. Vern would have to deal with it. She pulled Spike away and headed him for the door. She grabbed her jacket and put it on as the cold outside the greenhouse doors hit her sweaty skin.

It would be a good idea to get Spike to go to the bathroom. She was glad Saj used diapers. She took him up to the nearest house in the stupid, generic neighborhood.

Lizzie helped Spike get his pants down and sit on the toilet. Nothing happened. "Don't worry Spike, you'll get there." He sat. After a wait, she took him back outside.

"Let's case some of the houses, Spike. Whattaya think?"

Spike looked eager to move. "Go, Spike. You pick which direction. Go." He shuffled off behind the next house, more monkey than dog-like. *Can we teach him? How much can he learn?*

She sighed and sucked in air; it stung her lungs, but the cold seemed to temper the level of the stench from the dead and dying.

A low growl came from around the house. Lizzie ran and found Spike facing down a Doberman guarding a spilled garbage can. "Spike. Come." The Doberman was ready to strike. "Spike. Now." He backed away from the dog until he was next to her.

"Good job, Spike." Lizzie patted his back as she pulled him. The Doberman took a step past the spilled garbage. "Stay," Lizzie said in her lowest tone and took another step back, still standing up straight and glaring at the dog. The Doberman growled, but made no move.

They backed further away. The Doberman would let them be if they didn't mess with his lunch. He didn't see them as lunch yet. A couple mutts rounded the corner. They spied the Doberman and he spun to defend his treasure from the new interlopers. They circled snapping, each of them grabbing some of the garbage, barking and posturing at the others. The former pets had not figured out their pack hierarchy. Lizzie could see that as food got scarce, they needed to be more careful around man's best friends.

She tugged Spike back, his muscles tense, ready to spring. His wild eyes darted, nervous, trying to see in all directions. They got back to the greenhouse without the dogs following them, and she breathed a sigh of relief.

How soon are Zach and Nev coming back? She pulled out her cell to check the time and send a text. Missed call flashed in red. The Texas number. Her breath sucked in.

Oh, my god. Daddy? Or was it someone who lived in the house with him? She slid the screen to voicemail. A new envelope flashed with the number on it. Her hands shook as she tried to access the call. "Oh, my god, oh my god." It played; she shoved the phone to her ear.

A male voice said. "Lizzie?" Then a pause. "Elizabeth. It's...It's Mannie, uh, Manuel, your father. Sorry I missed you. I'm glad you're alive. I..." *Daddy?* A jolt shot through her body. *You're alive.* She had always assumed he was dead. He should've been dead. Where had he been on her birthdays? On her first days of school? On the day she needed someone to teach her to drive... "Call me, please." He ended the message with a sigh.

"Fuck you!" She hurled the phone. It landed in the grass. She ran to pick it up and texted Zach. **Need you now**. She slid the phone back to voice mail and listened to the call again, sitting in the cold grass. Spike slid down next to her. His head nudged at her side.

"What the hell am I supposed to do?" she asked Spike. He stared at her with sad eyes.

She scrolled through other messages, back to the last one from her mom. She listened to it, but it only intensified her pain. "Mama. What do I do? You taught me to hate him. Or at least forget him. I created a better him in my mind." Her lungs fought for air; she was hyperventilating.

She heard the low rumble of vehicle before she saw it. The Tank slid to a stop when Zach saw her. He jumped out, leaving the door open and the vehicle running. He ran over. Nev was only steps behind him.

Zach knelt by her, pulling her toward him. "What the hell's wrong? We saw C.J.'s brother at the gathering, I think."

Nev nodded. "Then he disappeared. We thought he'd found you. Are you hurt? Show me."

Lizzie shook her head, but she couldn't speak. She tugged at Zach's shirt and sobbed into it.

"Lizzie, Lizzie. What is it?" Nev begged.

In between breaths Lizzie managed to spit out, "My dad called. My dad's alive."

Zach pushed her back, but didn't let her go. "Your dad's alive? And that's an emergency?"

Lizzie wouldn't meet his eyes. She pulled away from him. *God, he could be an ass sometimes.*

"Zach, come on." Nev furrowed her brow at him. "Did you call him back, Lizzie?"

Lizzie shook her head, trying to slow her breathing.

Zach made an exasperated sound. "Why not?"

Lizzie sniffed back snot. "I'm a mess."

"Yeah," Zach said. "What say we head back home? Discuss this on the way. C.J.'s brother is somewhere in the area."

They got into the Tank and Nev climbed in the back with Lizzie, snuggling her. Lizzie snuffled. "My god, Nev. Why am I such a basket case? I've lost everyone and now one of them comes back from the dead and I'm pissed off?"

"He's not the one you want back," Nev said, her voice soft and soothing.

"I guess." Lizzie's breath returned to a slower state. "What if he really is the bastard my mom said he was?"

"Maybe he is, or was, but he's older, too. And wiser, maybe."

"Maybe." Lizzie pulled Nev into a hug, tearing Nev's shirt. "Sorry 'bout your shirt."

"Hey, there are a million shirts. Only one you." She laughed loudly. "You wanna go shopping? We could go places we can't, uh, couldn't afford." She handed Lizzie her phone back.

"Like R.E.I." Lizzie said. "Outdoor gear for the apocalypse?"

"What?" Nev smiled at her. "No, you're such a boy. I don't mean hiking boots and multi-tools. I mean clothing stores. Velvet, animal print, voluptuwear!"

"Okay, Nev. I'll let you take me to girly stores."

"Sissie." Saj grinned as he pounded on his car seat.

Lizzie's anxiety melted away. "Sebastian, you make me smile."

"Thought his name was Saj," Zach said over his shoulder.

"The more names the better. I'll call him Sebastian Antonio Jones when he's in trouble, right, Sebbie?"

She stuck her thumb into his tiny hand. The perfect fingers gripped it tight and pulled toward his mouth. He sucked for a moment then bit. "Ouch. Sebastian Antonio."

After that she sank into silence. *What the hell am I supposed to do about my father—the sperm donor?* She would call him back; she needed to.

He hadn't really said anything. She could tell he'd wanted to say Dad. Or Papa or something. At least he had the decency not to. Nobody called her Elizabeth, but Mama always told her he had picked the name. She'd always thought she'd go by Elizabeth when she got a job and career.

Jobs. College. Careers. All gone. Survival school is all that remains.

And her dad was alive. *The father I dreamed of, the one I'd imagined he might have been, is not him.* But we have things in common. Music and movies. *What was that worth? Was it worth the missed birthdays? He hadn't sent a card. How hard was that?* "Okay," she said, finally making a decision.

"Okay what?" Nev asked.

"I'm going to call him. Don't know what I'm going to say."

"He probably doesn't know what to say either," Nev said. "What'd he say in the message?"

"Nothing. I want to tell him the fuck off, for all the years he wasn't there. All those years of nothing."

"Well," Zach said, "that's one way to do it."

"You might ask him why?" Nevaeh suggested. "Why he wasn't there. Maybe later…" She pulled Lizzie's eyes to hers. "Lizzie, when you call him…. Do you want us there?"

"I don't know. But let's do that shopping trip first."

"Some old-fashioned consumer therapy without the cost." Nev grinned at her. "So really, it's just a dress-up day."

15

LIZZIE PUSHED THE MALL DOOR open at the entrance to the food court by the movie theatre. Her nose scrunched; the big open seating area smelled like rancid grease and old pizza. Gone was the heavenly scent of cinnamon rolls. She heard skittering noises and saw a flash of dark fur as they came in. "God, I hope that was a cat."

Spike wouldn't come in. Something about all the glass seemed to set him off.

The short ride had put Saj to sleep in the car seat. Zach carried him in and set the car seat down outside the entrance to the theatres. Then he raced in and vaulted the concessions counter. "Soda? Popcorn? Only a hundred dollars." He dumped popcorn kernels into the popper.

Lizzie laughed. "We'll take like two mega-super-gigantimous sodas." She grabbed Nev's hand. "It's like our first date."

Nev squeezed her hand back. "We haven't decided what to see, yet."

"What about Star Wars Episode IX?" Zach offered thoughtfully. "Or something romantic, what do you think, young lady?"

Zach leaned over the counter conspiratorially and whispered in Nev's ear. "You wanna get a kiss at the end of the date? I'd suggest the new Nicholas Sparks film."

"Oh, I'd love that," gushed Nev.

Lizzie broke character. "The kiss or the movie?" She felt warm inside. "Do you know how to run a movie, Zach?"

"Don't know. Never tried." He grabbed soda cups. "What kind do you want, girls?"

Lizzie answered, "Coke. Classic. Or Vanilla." The smell of popcorn got her mouth-watering. "We should try."

"Try what?" Zach handed her the giant cup.

"Starting a movie."

"I want a diet Coke," Nev said, "I know it's weird; I like the flavor. No ice. I might chew it."

"You know what they say about girls—" Zach grinned and raised an eyebrow as he poured the soda. "Maybe I could—"

Zach was the same old Zach again. His pissy attitude had degenerated into teenage lust.

"Zachster." Nev took the diet Coke and sucked loudly on the straw. "Keep dreamin', buddy."

Lizzie rolled her eyes. "Besides, she's my date." She pulled Nev into a hug. "We came here to shop."

"Okay," Zach said. "You girls go shopping; I'll see if I can get a movie going."

"You sure?" Lizzie asked. "The baby? Saj?"

"Leave him here." He nodded toward the sleeping baby in the car seat. "If he wakes up with a messy diaper, I'm calling you."

"Keep him with you." Lizzie thought of the dogs and the shape she'd seen. "Keep him with you, okay?"

Zach caught her drift and his face turned serious. "I will." He picked up the car seat and a drink and headed into the theatre.

Lizzie turned to Nev. "Okay. Let's go."

"What's the most expensive place here?" Nev sipped her soda as they walked out of the theatre.

"You're asking me? I don't shop here." They rounded the corner past a jewelry store—one of the few with closed doors, it looked like someone had tried to force it, but, unlike most of the other stores, it had withstood the assault.

"Okay, well. Let's find one. Race you." Nev put her soda down on the floor and ran.

Lizzie glared at Nev as she raced away. Nev had always been slim and had never filled out like Lizzie. "Bite me." She hadn't beat Nev in a foot race since they were twelve.

Nev ran back towards her. "Come get me."

"What the hell." Lizzie set her soda down by Nev's and took off after her. Nev let her catch up as they entered Macy's at the end of the mall.

Nev piled a cart full of clothes. She kept squealing and holding things up against Lizzie. "Perfect," she would say. Or, "This is exactly what you need to set off your eyes." Lizzie wondered what she had gotten herself into. They went into the handicapped changing room with the entire cart.

Half an hour later, Lizzie and Nev both had new clothes—perfect fits, clean underwear. Lizzie had to admit she looked nice in the clothes Nev had picked. And Nev looked even better. Even if the clothes were terrifyingly normal. Nev had classy taste and trying on clothes for her gave Lizzie a warm, safe feeling.

Lizzie pushed the cart out of Macy's; alarms went off as they passed the doorway.

Nev took the cart. "Better get those stupid plastic thingies off so we don't have to cut them later." She pulled the cart up to the checkout counter and tossed everything up there. With a practiced motion she pulled the clothes through and removed the security tags.

"Wow," Lizzie marveled. "You're good."

"I worked last summer at Wet Seal in the Capital Mall. Helped pay for books and fees." Nev tossed the clothes in the cart and they passed through the security sensors without any alarms.

They'd found outrageously expensive and sexy bras at Victoria's Secret with the threat to torture Zach later. Lizzie grinned at Nev. Only at the end of the world would Lizzie be found shopping at a mall instead of a thrift store.

They got sweats and slip off pants they thought would fit Spike and grabbed a pile of jeans and work gear for themselves and Zach. They got bigger clothes for Saj at Gapkids.

"We should get winter stuff: gloves, hats, mittens." Nev grabbed knitted stuff off a rack. "Last winter I didn't make it the one time I tried to go home. Icy roads."

Lizzie saw a darkness in Nev's eyes when she said 'home.' "Nev. I've been a horrible friend. I haven't asked you about your family, your life. What happened?"

"Shit, Lizzie. Your family died, you almost got raped, you killed a guy. You've been a little preoccupied. 'sides. I don't wanna talk about it. My family is dead. I wasn't there."

Nev was the one who took care of people. It was easy to forget she sometimes needed taking care of, too. Lizzie hugged her, squeezing extra tight. She didn't know what else to do.

Nev held her for a moment and then let go. "And I've got my two oldest friends back. It might be a tiny silver lining, but it's pretty amazing to me."

"Yeah. It is."

They found Zach playing with Saj on the carpet near the video games. Lizzie tried to sneak up on them, but Zach spotted her.

"Look, Saj, it's Sissie and Nev," Zach said.

The little munchkin toddled toward Lizzie as fast as his legs could carry him. She knelt, grabbed him by the armpits and spun him up in the air in a broad arc. His breath sucked in and his eyes glowed. When she set him down, he jumped up without his feet leaving the ground.

Zach broke up laughing.

Nev smiled, too. "Pretty much the cutest thing I've ever seen."

"Again?" Lizzie asked. "Again?"

Saj bounced with all his energy. He could fly if his body would obey.

"Okay. Sissie make you fly again." Someone had made her fly when she was small. She grabbed him and spun him around sideways, rising and falling, spinning dizzy until his little shape threatened to pull out of her grip. Then she sat him down and stumbled to the floor herself, collapsing, her center of balance off. He fell into her arms and she held him tight.

Zach had deciphered the film projector, admitting that all you had to do was get things turned on and push play—like Internet streaming. They got refills on popcorn, frozen ice cream bars and chocolate-covered raisins.

The newest saga about the children of Han and Leia failed to distract Lizzie. Her mind kept going back over her life without her father. She had nothing to pull up. She should have remembered something, but she'd walked herself through this forever. All that she had was an image of him from his music and movies. It was the image of a Hispanic version of Judd Nelson. Not very original. She fantasized he would come back and take her away. She'd only wished for him in the worst times, and he'd never come. Or called. Until now. And that was because she had called him first. Well, these were the worst of times.

Lizzie sat alone on the bed in the master bedroom. She'd decided to make the call alone. She battled herself about what to say. "Why the hell did you never call me?" or "Fuck you."

"Come save me, Father," she said aloud, then laughed at herself and flopped back onto the bed. The ceiling fan spun. She let her eyes follow it for a minute. Then she sat up and deliberately pressed the numbers.

The phone rang on the other end, several times. Then "Lizzie?"

"Yes. It's me, Daddy." There, that was that. She didn't even know she would call him Daddy. But it slipped out and felt right.

"Yes." There was a pause. "I'm sorry."

Not ready to forgive him, yet, she listened to him breathe, wondering if he was doing the same. Finally she said, "I'm glad you're alive." Her voice came out as a shaky whisper.

"Oh, god, Lizzie. It's so amazing to hear your voice." His voice cracked. "I wanted..."

"Yah, me too." She heard the touch of anger in her voice and breathed deep; it came out ragged. "Mama and Jayce are gone."

"I'm so sorry. She loved you very much. Jayce's your little brother?"

"Yeah. Jason. I basically raised him."

"Ah."

"Where are you?"

He cleared his throat. "Del Rio, Texas, near Mexico."

"Near your family?"

"Yeah. They were here."

There were questions Lizzie wanted to ask, "I have some people here with me. Two of my best friends... We all survived."

"Wow. That's amazing."

"It is. I feel lucky. It's strange. A bunch of us survived; we were all on a trip to Honduras a few years ago. Did you ever go there?"

She heard him chuckle, but it sounded sad.

"No. I didn't travel except places the military sent me. And away from people I shouldn't have." He paused and gave a long sigh. "Oh, Lizzie. I am so sorry. For everything. I missed everything. There is no excuse. And I know you must hate me...."

"Yeah. But, not always. I prayed you would come take me away."

"And now?" he asked.

It was an impossible question. How did she feel about him now? Even she wasn't sure of the answer, so she didn't give one.

They sat, silence stretching the phone connection.

Change the subject. Lizzie began again. "I don't know what you do. Did do."

"I worked at the Amistad Reservoir for the Park Service after... After I left you." He went silent.

"You don't have to explain." It was a lie. But she wanted it to be true. She wanted a relationship with a dad with no baggage, a clean slate. *Too bad. Want in one hand...* Lizzie had heard the explanation all her life. "Mom said it was drugs and drinking. You left because you couldn't leave the war behind and have a normal family life."

There was another long silence before her father answered. "Is that what she told you?"

"Yeah. Not what happened?" Lizzie asked.

"There are always at least two points of view in any relationship," he said, evading the question. "Someday, I'll tell you my side. But not today. And not on the phone. Doesn't really matter now. At Amistad I'm— I was a fish & game guy, kind of like I was in Washington before you were born. But here I was a manager, kept fish stocked for sports fishermen. Not a lot of need anymore."

"Dad?" The word Dad still sounded strange in her mouth. "Do you want me to call you something else?"

"No. Dad is lovely."

Lizzie wondered how she could sit here, talking on the phone as if they had a relationship. She wanted one. And he was the only real family she had left. "How long does it take to get to Texas?"

"If you've got two drivers and you drive through the night only about two days, but really, with one driver, probably at least a week."

I could be talking to him in person in a week! Then old tapes reasserted themselves. "I don't know. Maybe it's a bad idea."

"There is some mighty pretty country between here and there."

His voice sounded positive.

Lizzie sat up. "We could meet in the middle. I'd like a road trip."

"Whoa. No. You stay in Bellingham. I'll come to you."

"I need to get out of Bellingham." Lizzie wanted to tell him about everything that had happened. But not tonight.

"We have no idea how safe the roads are, what conditions. How long have you been driving?"

"I'm learning. I'll bring my friends. Zach's a great driver."

"You don't know how to drive?" His tone of voice had darkened. "The roads might not be—"

"But everybody's dead. It's a great time to learn to drive. What's half-way?"

"Salt Lake City, but honey. Eliza— Uh, Lizzie—"

"Honey is fine. Or Lizzie. But you can call me Elizabeth, too. If you want to."

"I'd like that. Elizabeth, a cross-country trip under normal conditions is no picnic."

"Please, Daddy?" Lizzie heard her voice. *What am I asking his permission for?*

"Can we talk about this tomorrow?"

"As long as you help me figure out how to do it."

His breath escaped like he'd given up fighting about it. "Okay. We need to have a plan."

"Oh, and Daddy, I have a friend, Jess, in San Angelo. Used to live in Bellingham. Can you bring her up here? Her family's all dead."

"Yes. We still need a plan."

"We'll have one. Thanks, Daddy. G'night."

"Goodnight, Elizabeth."

Lizzie sat there in the dark. She hadn't noticed the room getting darker. Through the skylight, she could see the first stars of the night coming out. An evening star, one of the planets, sparkled brighter than the others. In the big picture window, the waxing moon peeked over the mountains over the lake. It looked like a cold night. She lay there, basking in the warmth of a direction, a new focus in life, a reason to be.

She pulled out her phone and punched in Jess' number.

It rang once and then Jess picked up, "Lizzie? What time is it?"

"I don't know. Did you make it into town?"

"Yeah," Jess sighed. "Found some people. It's okay."

"You want to come to Bellingham?"

"Hell, yes."

"Well, listen to you Miss Suddenly Profane."

"Ef you," Jess laughed. "How?"

"My dad. He's alive. In Texas. He's going to pick you up."

"Oh, my god. You're not kidding?"

Lizzie smiled listening to Jess gush, a rare occurrence in all their years together. "No. I'm not."

"Yes. Please. When?"

"Soon. I'll give him your number."

"Oh, Lizzie. I can't wait to see you."

"Me, too. See you, that is. I'll call you tomorrow, okay?"

"Yeah. Aren't you glad you didn't kill yourself?"

"Yeah. Good night, Jess." There was a tap on the door. "Yes?" The phone connection ended.

"It's Zach. Can I come in?"

"Yeah." The huskiness in her voice startled her.

Zach came in, shutting the door softly behind him. "Hey."

"Hey." Lizzie could see a thousand questions in his eyes. She didn't have that many answers. "We're going on a road trip."

PART II

You Can Sleep While I Drive

16

MANNIE REPLACED THE HANDSET IN its cradle. His heart was higher than he ever remembered. Even higher than the day she had been born. He jumped out of his chair, opened the front door and hollered out into the starry Texas night, "My daughter's alive!"

He pulled out the old road maps from the glove box of his truck and carried them into the kitchen table. Mannie needed Rubi, the Jeep Rubicon he drove for his work with the Forest Service. He trusted her in any conditions. And if he headed to Salt Lake City, there'd be a variety of conditions. He would have to go back to the Ranger Station.

His zombified existence since Isabel died, eating, sleeping and reading, was over. She'd been dead for less than a month, but it seemed like half a lifetime already. Now Mannie was awake again. And ready to go.

He spread out the maps. The Internet had been down for weeks in Del Rio, so he would have to rely on the paper version. He realized he was lucky his cell phone still worked. *What if I had missed her call?*

Rubi had GPS, but it was fritzy. It hadn't taken to the automatic updates for a year and sometimes went dead. The route to Salt Lake wasn't complicated: head northwest and drive. First he need- ed to get to San Angelo, three hours from Del Rio, to pick up Lizzie's friend, Jess. It was a university town and a military intelligence training center during the Gulf Wars. Mannie had never been there, but figured it wouldn't add much time to the trip. And it would make Lizzie happy.

After San Angelo it was I-87 through Big Spring and up to Brownfield, across to Roswell, then Albuquerque. He wondered how many of Albuquerque's million people were left.

Near Durango there might be snow. Mannie had been up in those mountains before. Might get tricky. He should hit the road tomorrow to get through the pass before weather got worse.

Elizabeth hadn't sent her friend Jess' number yet. He needed to make sure she was in San Angelo, not just somewhere near. Why had he agreed to let her come south? And that he'd go pick up her friend? Guilt. And a genuine desire. He wanted to try to help her be happy.

His stomach growled. He often skipped dinner with no one else around and now it was time to hit the sack, a long day, but worth staying up for.

Mannie found a can of baked beans in the fridge, though he didn't remember when he'd opened it. No mold and it didn't smell. Mannie heated it in a pan on the gas range. The can said, "Best if used by 2023." He suspected it should be edible for some time after that. He smiled, yesterday he wasn't thinking about the future.

He felt like celebrating. He eyed the box high on a shelf, tucked away for a rainy day. It wasn't good to keep a bottle of whiskey around when you were a recovering alcoholic. It was damn tempting every day, especially on a day like today when he had something to celebrate. Part of him kept it because it was old and expensive and he couldn't stand to waste it. Another part of him kept it to challenge himself. *I dare you to drink it, you worthless shit,* he would think whenever he caught himself looking at it. *Go on. Show everyone what a loser you really are.* It was a way to keep himself honest. If he wasn't strong enough to say no...." He stood on a chair and lifted the box down.

The antiqued wooden box had been a gift from an old friend. "Keep something good in it, that's all I ask." *Well, this was good.* He opened the clasp and withdrew the russet golden bottle and set it back up on the shelf. He would put something else 'good' in it when he packed. He popped the top on a cold Coke, enjoying the fizz and then first taste as it burned his throat.

Mannie dumped his dresser drawers out on the bed and packed

the essentials, planning for cold weather. Living in Texas, he didn't have a lot of cold weather gear. Maybe he'd do some shopping once he reached Albuquerque.

Isabel's photo stared at him from the dresser. He counted on her for stability, her love had seen him through some desperate times. He should have married her like she wanted, but now she was gone.

The past was dead now. No need to keep souvenirs, but he grabbed it anyway and stuffed it in his rucksack with the clothes. In the years since he'd left Washington State, he'd learned to travel light and leave things behind.

He set his bags by the door and went for a walk outside to clear his head. The night was crystal clear and shirt-sleeve weather. He focused on the first star that caught his eye. "Star light, star bright, first star I see tonight." It was a silly children's rhyme, but it was one of the things he remembered doing with Elizabeth as a child. He sometimes thought about her looking at the same sky—doubly foolish since Bellingham was two hours behind him and under a thick blanket of clouds most of the time.

Mannie scanned the sky. He had seen no airplanes for the last month, but he spotted a satellite. At least those would keep going for a while, maybe longer than the cell towers. But how much good would it do the survivors, and how long could satellites last without humans operating them? More importantly, who was in control of those satellites now? Or military facilities or missile silos? Before he knew his daughter was out there he had been content to let the world go to Hell. Now he couldn't.

Lizzie woke wired. Last night she talked Zach into the trip. He didn't want to go, he wanted to stay and join the hippies. But Lizzie knew if she convinced him she was going, he wouldn't let her go alone. Nev insisted on coming, too. They discussed leaving Spike, but he'd become a member of the family and the potty-training was going well. The warning pops of flatulence preceded an explosion. And they still changed Saj's diapers, so it hardly seemed fair.

Despite her complaints about gigantic vehicles like Ford Expeditions, Hummers and Escalades, Lizzie let Zach talk her into taking the Tank. Her biggest issue was the damn thing got like five gallons to the mile in fuel economy. But there had to be a hell of a lot of gas out there with no cars on the road. All the other things she hated about them: high ride, over-powered, huge, four-wheel drive, were actually benefits for a cross-country route that would take them over mountains, desert and who knew what else. But she was still going to tease him about compensating.

Zach had found a trailer with a locking tool chest and a few empty gas cans. That along with the topper should allow them to scavenge as they went. He filled the tool chest with the new guns, ammo and a bunch of tools from the lake house garage.

"All right." Lizzie was restless. "Let's go." She locked the house and took the keys. It felt a little weird. What argument would they have if they came home and found it occupied by some other set of squatters? But now it was as much of a home as she had.

On the way into town Zach stopped for gas. He came to the window as the pump churned. "I want to stop by the hippie commune before we leave." Zach made eye contact with Lizzie. "Tell Vern our plans."

He looked at her like he wanted her to ask why.

"Sure." Lizzie rolled her eyes. If it made him happy, today she didn't really care. She wanted to get on the road.

Lizzie said. "I'm taking you guys to R.E.I. for some real shopping. Hiking gear."

"Since when are you a hiker?" Nev asked.

"It was a phase with Chad. Spent most of my babysitting money on good used gear at thrift stores."

"Why do we need hiking gear?" Zach asked. "We can break into houses."

"Here on the west side maybe, but Eastern Washington?" Lizzie asked, "Idaho? Say we get in a wreck or something else happens to the Tank. Might be a long hike to some place to break into."

"Okay. That makes sense. I need…" He stopped.

Lizzie watched his face as a strange expression passed across it.

"I want to stop at Gramp's place," Zach said, "It's not far out of the way." He glanced at the sky and held out his hand, then climbed in. "I need to deal with some things."

"Near Sedro, right?" Lizzie stuck her hand out the window and felt rain beginning to fall. The sky to the south was an ominous gray.

They found Vern loading heads of cabbage into a truck. He had a surgical mask over his mouth and nose. He held up his hands. *Don't come any closer.*

Zach rolled down the window and slid the Tank into Park. "What's up, Vern?"

"A new arrival from last week is sick. So are the people that hung around with him."

"Shit." Lizzie muttered. "Bad news."

Zach glanced at Nev, "So the cop was right."

Nev nodded. "Another good reason to head east."

'We're heading over the pass—east," Zach called to Vern. "Any new dead?"

"No," Vern said, shaking his head. "You're young. Hope you make it. Good luck." He tipped his straw hat and headed back to the garden.

Zach slid the gearshift into reverse and hit the window up button.

"Hey, wait." Vern had turned back and was running and waving at them.

Zach rolled the window back down. "Yeah?"

"A kid was looking for Lizzie." Vern voice puffed out with steam. "Said he was friends from high school."

Zach glanced at Lizzie, her face had drained of color. "What did you tell him?"

"Said I'd seen her around with some folks in a truck. Might've said your name. Bad news?"

Zach nodded. "Yeah. You see him again? Tell him we headed north."

Vern nodded, his happy face troubled by a frown. "Okay. Good luck."

"Thanks," Zach said and pulled the Tank around. "Good thing we're leaving town."

"Yeah," Lizzie said. "Let's do it." She felt like she'd seen a ghost.

They stopped at R.E.I. for hiking/camping gear and Ace Hardware for a skinny garden hose to use as siphon. They broke into a register there to have cash for gas stations if and when the credit cards stopped working.

When they pulled into a long gravel road with Riley on the mailbox, Lizzie realized how long it had been since any of them had spoken.

Zach's hands were tight on the wheel and his jaw matched. Lizzie saw a backhoe and a pile of cement slabs stacked in a pyramid near a series of garages and sheds. Zach still hadn't said anything about his family.

The Tank rolled to a stop and Zach killed the engine. Saj woke up fussing.

"Dammit." Lizzie fumbled through the baby bag for some food. "I bet you're hungry, Saj. Sissie isn't doin' so hot taking care of you today."

In the back seat Spike whined in harmony with Saj.

"Zach," Lizzie said softly, "I think we better eat something."

"Fine." He glared and headed into the house.

"What the hell did I say?"

Nev shrugged.

Lizzie chose to leave it alone. She would probably make it worse if she forced it out into the open.

"I can help," Nev called after Zach and followed him inside.

Lizzie stayed in the Tank alternating bites of baby food between Spike and Saj.

Zach came back outside and fired up the gas grill on the porch.

The barbecue was smoking and Zach brought out a small cooler of beer, knock off-brand soda pop and some meat patties. "Ground venison. Waste if that ends up freezer-burned."

Saj played in the dirt with a stick. Spike sat all folded up with his arms around his legs, watching everything and everyone.

When the meat hit the grill, the scent made Lizzie's mouth water. She picked through the beer to get a crème soda and popped the top, sipping the carbonated sugar.

When the meat came out it was amazing, wild and peppery. "I don't know if I've ever tasted any meat this good," Lizzie said. "Even better than the steak you made the other night."

Zach nodded, eating quickly and silently. Then he disappeared, muttering something about things to do.

Lizzie wiped up the last of the burger juices, wishing she had some decent bread to sop it up with.

Noises of power tools came from the shop.

Nev stood. "I'm going to go check on him."

"Okay." Lizzie zoomed in on Saj as the stick headed toward his mouth. She had a sudden vision of him falling over and the stick tearing through his baby skin. She pulled the stick away as he began to howl. "Sorry, Saj. I shouldn't have let you play with it anyway."

A few minutes later, Zach reappeared with a wooden cross almost as tall as Lizzie. It looked like two cedar fence posts held together by a giant bolt and then wrapped in rope. Nev followed him with a sledgehammer, axe tool. Lizzie picked up Saj and followed. Spike watched them all, with his head cocked slightly to the side.

When they reached the pyramid of cement, Zach laid the cross down and took the axe thing from Nev. He swung it high and straight into the ground. It sunk in up to the handle. He extracted the tool and placed the pointed end of the cross in the ground. Nev held it vertical while he tapped the top with the sledgehammer side.

The cross slid into the soil. From the little signs that said beans and corn, Lizzie decided this must have been the garden.

When it didn't go in any deeper, Zach swung the tool high; it smacked hard into the wood and the sound echoed of the outbuildings. Then he dropped the tool and stood for a moment staring at the pile.

Lizzie wanted to go to him, comfort him, but Nev was already there. Her hand on his arm. He pulled himself away and strode back toward the backhoe. He fired it up with a puff of dark smoke and drove it into one of the garages. He pulled the door closed with a bang and hollered, "Let's go."

Nev looked at Lizzie, pleading for an answer, advice. Lizzie had nothing to offer. "Let's go."

By the time they reached I-5, the dark rain clouds Lizzie had been watching opened in a downpour. As the sun went down the raindrops flew and the wind buffeted the giant truck.

"It's about 5 o'clock," Zach said. "Let's spend the night in Cle Elum. There's a nice resort there."

Overhead a flock of trumpeters hooted southward.

Lizzie plugged in her player to the USB and the sound came through the speakers. Screaming Trees came on. "I nearly lost you..." she sang. "Nice system."

On the deserted highway near Marysville a doe and two fawns that had outgrown their spots ate grass in the median.

"Want more venison?" Zach asked. "Not like we're gonna run out of food anytime soon." He shook his head in annoyance. "'Anyone wanna help me field dress a deer?"

"Ew," Nev said from the back.

Lizzie pictured the lovely creatures riddled and bloody. "My shotgun's for protecting us."

"He's not coming after us," Zach snapped.

"I killed his brother, stupid. Some people take that kind of thing personal, apocalypse or not." Lizzie crossed her arms—the music played on. *What the hell?*

When they neared the I-405 cutoff, Nev spoke, "That's new."

Liz looked up from her reverie. The message on the giant safety sign said, 'ALL SURVIVORS REPORT TO THE CONVENTION CENTER ABOVE I-5!'

"When we came through last time," Nev chuckled. "They had the 'EXPRESS LANES CLOSED' warnings on."

Zach nodded. "Maybe they're getting things together. Should we go into Seattle?"

"NO!" Liz felt her heart begin to pound; her lungs felt tight. "Please."

A whine came from Spike in the back.

"Okay." Zach's voice was calm. "When we get back."

Lizzie chest felt tight. "I don't mean to freak— Once we decided... I can't."

Nev reached across the back seat and hugged her. "Lizzie, no worries. It's all good. Even if it's not."

Lizzie's heart slowed. "Thanks." She enjoyed the warmth of Nev's arms around her.

"Girl, you got a direction, something to do." Nev whispered in her ear. Then louder she continued, "Zach and I are along for the ride, right?"

Zach reached across and squeezed her knee. "Yeah. We're gonna go meet your dad and Jess and then we decide on other stuff."

The rain fell as the sky faded. With no traffic, they made good time. Stopping in North Bend to refill the gas tank and empty their bladders, they snagged ice cream, coffee and junk food, then drove on into the darkening evening.

Lizzie watched the wipers hypnotically splash away the giant raindrops. Tom Petty sang "Hard on Me;" the raindrops split into little lumps.

"Snow." Zach turned the wipers up a notch. "Pretty wet, though. We should be fine."

"Looks like God spit," Nev joked.

"Slain," Lizzie said, "slush and rain."

The Tank's lights cut through the darkness. The snow thickened until it reminded Lizzie of the movie two days ago. "Prepare for jump to hyperspace?" she said.

"I've got a bad feeling about this." Nev laughed.

"Trust the force." Zach growled in low tones.

They all laughed. Spike joined in with an awkward breathy guffaw. *Did he understand?*

They climbed toward the pass as the flakes grew and everyone slipped back into their own thoughts.

"Glad we have this beast of a truck." Zach's knuckles were white on the steering wheel.

"It doesn't look deep." Nev said. "I love how pretty the trees are. Feels like Christmas."

"No. it's not deep. We'll stay in the middle of the highway and keep on going." Zach grinned. "Four-wheel drive hasn't even kicked in yet."

"We gonna make it over the pass?" Lizzie ran her fingers over her old scars.

"Yeah."

But Lizzie saw his jaw strain as tight as his fingers. Suddenly she felt the truck turn, but Zach's hands hadn't moved on the wheel. His eyes widened.

The Tank slid. The automatic 4X4 light flashed. The vehicle shook sideways. They slipped toward the edge of the road. Her seatbelt dug into her shoulder. *Saj is in his car-seat.*

"Shit!" Zach spun the wheel. It didn't make any difference in their direction.

Zach turned the wheel toward the cliff.

"Zach!" Lizzie yelled.

"Trust me!" Zach yelled back.

Time slowed. She pictured them rolling down into the trees, the Tank exploding in a blast of fire in the pure white snow. The snowbank didn't look high enough to stop them. The stereo pounded bass.

17

LIZZIE FROZE AS NEV SCREAMED. Saj howled. Metal screeched behind them.

The Tank crunched into gravel on the edge of the shoulder. It slid into the snowbank.

Lizzie saw nothing on the other side but emptiness.

Chill. She clutched the '*Oh, shit*' handle. She shoved her feet against the floor like she could jump out. She couldn't do anything. Tune out the screams and chaos and wait. Snow shot up as they hit the bank.

Then it all stopped. And they were all still alive. Lizzie breathed.

Zach punched the stereo off and killed the engine. "Mother-fuckin' shit!"

Saj and Spike howled in unison. Spike bounced up and down in the back seat.

Zach shook, staring at his hands.

Only Nev's mouth moved, "Oh my god, oh my god, oh my god."

Lizzie turned to console the boys. "Saj, Spike, it's okay. Everything's okay."

"Everybody quiet!" Zach slammed his fists on the dashboard. Saj and Spike continued their cries. He jerked the door open, hopped down into the snow and shoved the door shut.

Lizzie tried to calm herself as the Tank shook. She glanced out her window. "ZACH!"

He spun toward her and pulled the door open. "What?"

Lizzie's voice was icy calm. "If I step out my door I will fall hundreds of feet. Please, get in and drive the Tank back away from the edge."

Zach's eyes grew. He climbed in, started the engine and turned the front wheels toward the road. "First gear," he said, is if it would provide comfort, "All wheel drive." The engine revved and the beast slipped forward. A screech of metal came from behind. The 4X4 light blinked as the screech turned into a clunk, clunk sound. When they were back on the freeway Zach stepped on the brakes and the Tank slid to a stop. He put it in park and stepped on the emergency brake. "Better?"

"Yeah." Lizzie nodded. *I guess I really don't want to die.* "Thanks."

Lizzie listened to her breath, her air sucking in and out. Her mind spun though the Tank was still.

"Now I better figure out what the hell that noise was." Zach slammed the driver's door again.

Lizzie shifted in her seat. "Nev, get Saj out of the car seat. Probably needs his diaper changed and something to eat. What time is it? Let Spike out, too. Zach can deal with him."

Nev handed Saj to Lizzie, flipped the door open and pulled the back seat up for Spike.

"Spike. Get out," Lizzie said. "You can play."

Spike scrambled out. Nev pulled the door shut as snowflakes flew in. Spike bounced around like a child, while Zach pounded on the hood of the truck.

"Too much testosterone." Lizzie bounced Saj. "TMT, way more dangerous than TNT. You're not gonna be like that are you, Saj?"

"Of course he is, Lizzie. Not a whole hell of a lot you can do about it."

"S'pose not." Lizzie knew Nev was right. Jason had started getting to be like that. "Get me some formula?"

Saj had calmed down. As Lizzie changed his diaper; the cold brought his penis erect. "Look at that cute little *wingwer.*"

"Probably why all men feel inadequate." Nev poured water from the thermos into a bottle. "Their mother's always told them they have cute *little* thingies!"

"That'd be weird." Lizzie laughed. "My, what a big penis you have, young man." She grinned at Nev. "Think that'll help?"

"Maybe. Not having a deluge of pop culture will probably help."

Nev shook the bottle. "This isn't warm."

"Better than too hot. I expect he won't mind as long as it doesn't scald or freeze his tummy."

Nev handed her the bottle.

"Hungry, little man?" As Lizzie brought the bottle close, his hands grasped it and pulled it toward his face. "Not in your eye, Saj." Lizzie redirected it. "That's better."

Dealing with Saj calmed her. "That was pretty freaky."

"Yeah." Nev shook her head. "Figured we all survived the plague to die on the mountain in the snow. On fire."

Zach opened the door. "Everybody all right?" Snow blew in.

"Yeah." Nev answered. "Still alive. How are you doing?"

"I'm okay. Thought we bought it." Zach climbed into the cab and pulled the door shut. "The trailer's hella twisted sideways and the tongue is bent." Snowflakes inched down his face. His several-day stubble had little crystals stuck in it. "I unhitched it and got the gas cans on the top racks and tied them down." He wiped his face with his hands. "I don't think it's a good idea to head further up the pass. Snow's not thick, but there's a sheet of ice an inch down."

"We can try again tomorrow," Lizzie agreed.

"I don't think so, Lizzie. Maybe with chains, which we didn't think to get." He watched her, his jaw firm and his eyes intense. "We're not crossing the pass this winter."

"Zach." The recent warmth of safety disappeared and ice replaced it in Lizzie's stomach. "I need to get to Salt Lake."

"Lizzie—" Zach warned.

"Please?" Lizzie watched him shove down an angry explosion.

"I'm not ready to die," Zach said through gritted teeth.

"Guys, we'll figure it out." Nev hugged Lizzie over the seat, smoothed her hair back. "We'll get you and your dad together."

Zach exhaled. "This pass is not the only way to Salt Lake City. We'll go down I-5 and cross over by the Columbia."

Lizzie nodded, her face flushed. She didn't trust herself to speak.

"I'll get Spike." Zach climbed out into the swirling snow.

Spike danced in the headlights, his mouth open.

"Spike is hilarious." Nev laughed. "Like he's never seen snow."

"I wonder if he remembers before the virus?" Lizzie said.

"Don't know. We better get him in before he catches pneumonia."

Spike didn't want to come along. Zach pulled at him, but Spike was taller and heavier. After a couple attempts, Zach climbed back in. "We're going. I can't fight him into the truck. Maybe if we go, he'll want to go with us." He started the truck; its throaty rumble roared.

"Wait!" Lizzie growled. She handed Saj back over the seat to Nev. "Don't ever drive without the kid in the car seat." Jerkwad had backed out of the driveway and knocked Jayce's head against the window once. "Give me your coat, mine's in the way back."

Zach shrugged out of it; Lizzie slipped into its warmth. She zipped it up and pulled the hood over her head. "Be right back." She opened the door and jumped down into the snow, shoving the door shut behind her. "Spike?"

Spike giggled, trying to catch snowflakes on his tongue. Ice covered his scraggly salt and pepper beard.

"Spike." He turned to her, smiling a delighted grin. Lizzie had never seen him this happy. "Come on, big man." She opened her mouth and caught some snow. "It's fun." And it was. She smiled back at him and caught a few more, letting their icy chill turn down the heat of her anger. "Spike, we gotta get back in the Tank. You're gonna freeze out here." The door opened and shut behind her. Spike wasn't listening or understanding.

"Not really working, huh?" Nev asked. She picked up some snow and made a snowball, tossing it at Spike.

Spike turned a bemused grin on his face.

"Good idea, Nev." Lizzie knelt and picked up a double handful of snow. She pressed it into a ball and held it up for Spike. "Here, Spike. Here's a big one." He came toward her.

She held it out in front of her as an offering. "Come on, Spike. Here's a big snowflake." She pulled off a chunk with her now freezing fingers. She held it up for him to eat. When his mouth opened she popped it in.

Spike's face glowed like a kid. Jayce had loved the snow when it came, but in Western Washington it always went away too soon. Lizzie wrapped her arms around Spike and hugged. Something hit her in the back. Snow. She turned to see Nev grinning at her, another snowball ready to fly.

Zach burst out of the truck and Nev threw it at him. Lizzie hurled what was left in her hands at Zach, too. She scooped more and threw one at Nev for retribution. Snow flew. Loud laughter sounded strange in the deadening soundscape of snow. Spike guffawed, sounding more hyena than human. Zach took refuge behind the truck near the snowbank.

Nev looked at Lizzie and gestured toward Zach.

Lizzie knew what she intended; they raced together, knocking into Zach and pushing him down into the snow. He came up stuttering and flinging snow wildly.

They all three sat for a moment watching. Spike capered and laughed. Zach pulled both of the girls toward him for a quick hug, but dumped snow on their heads.

Lizzie and Nev retaliated until Zach, laughing, held his hands up. "Stop. I give."

Lizzie pushed herself to her feet off Zach.

"We better get warm and dry," Nev suggested.

"Worry wart." Lizzie tossed the last of the slush ball at Nev. She dug another ball of snow. "Come on, Spike."

He turned, grinning. She jumped back toward the truck, holding the snow near the door. He lumbered toward her and bit at the snow, his drooling mouth barely missed her fingers. Nev climbed into the Tank. Lizzie tossed the snowball to her. "Come on, Spike. In the Tank. Get the snow." She slapped her legs and he hopped up. Nev gave him the rest of the snow and Lizzie slammed the door.

"Nice work." Zach hopped in, shifted the Tank into drive and it lurched forward. "Buckle up, buttercup."

When they were off the cliff side, Zach sped up. The Tank skated into the ditch. "Shit!" It wasn't deep and they didn't tip. He swore and shoved it in park. "I'm done for tonight. We'll sleep here. Glad we got sleeping bags. Tomorrow, when it's light, I'll try again."

Lizzie sighed and climbed out and pulled the bags out of the topper. In a few minutes she was in a bag with Saj cradled in her arms. She listened to her voicemails and stared at the pictures and videos on her cell phone. *I miss you Mama. You, too, Jayce.* When she had finished, Nev and Zach were both asleep.

Zach woke chilled; he had grabbed the best bags, comfortable down to 0 degrees. But in the middle of the night he had shoved the sleeping bag down because it made him sweat. He pulled the zipper up toward his face and rubbed his arms with his hands. The windshield was covered with snow and everything was quiet. The Tank smelled of body odor, baby smells and Spike.

He took stock of the crew as he hunkered into the downy comfort of his sleeping bag. Everyone still slept. Nobody froze to death. *Frozen plague survivors found dead from stupidity.* Quite the headline. Except there were no more headlines, and not a lot of odds on people finding the dead. He shivered, remembering the near miss on the icy snow.

Last night he woke several times with his feet shoved down hard into the sleeping bag trying to find the brakes as he drove them off the cliff. Well, despite their stupidity they weren't dead. Not yet.

Zach didn't want to wake everyone, but he had to pee. He extricated himself from the sleeping bag and pulled on his new wet and cold hiking boots. He opened the door as quietly as possible, but Lizzie's eyes opened. She looked at him, confused. "Gotta find a wood-pile," he said and smiled a goofy smile. She nodded and closed her eyes.

He avoided frostbite on his extremities, but certainly got chilled. By the time he returned to the Tank everyone was awake.

After everyone had taken care of their business he drove the Tank to North Bend. He promised to cook a big hot breakfast at one of the mom and pop diners if everyone was quiet and let him focus on the road.

An hour later he set plates down in front of them at a '50s style place. One of the few clear memories of his grandmother had happened here. He remember a cheeseburger served in a cardboard '57 Chevy followed by a giant banana split that he shared with her and then everyone else at the table: Mom, Dad and Gramps.

His friends scarfed down the food with compliments to the chef. Zach basked in the praise.

Spike ate fries with a fork, stabbing them and shoving them into his mouth. Zach thought about telling him fries were for fingers, but it was good practice.

Zach found a gigantic carton of vanilla ice cream, freezer-burned, but only on top. He scraped it off and brought it to share, dishing up some to everyone.

Lizzie accepted the ice cream with a nod as she focused on the road atlas they'd picked up in Sedro.

When Zach looked at Nev she was watching him. A hint of humor played across her face. He smiled back.

He filled a bowl for himself and sat. Saj slapped his hands, now slippery white with ice cream, on the table. Zach chuckled. Saj had gotten rounder since the day they'd found him.

"So." Lizzie spun the atlas around toward him. "We go south to Vancouver then across. Shouldn't hit any high mountains until right before Salt Lake. By then we can figure how to handle the snow."

Zach nodded. "We'll find some chains."

"Okay." Lizzie closed the atlas. "Let's head for the Columbia River."

"All right. I'm going clean up back there. Anybody wanna help?"

"Why clean up?" Lizzie stood, ready to hit the road.

"Cause it's a little bit of home." He headed back to the kitchen. *And I can keep it like it is in my memories.*

"I'll help." Nev followed him.

"Hey," Lizzie called after them, "I'm not against it. Just asking." She headed outside with Saj toddling behind and Spike bringing up the rear.

"Thanks, Zach." Nev put her hand on his arm. "For breakfast. For driving last night."

"For not killing you, you mean?" He laughed.

"Yeah. Thanks for not killing me. Us." Nev leaned up and kissed him gently on the lips. Her lips were firmer than Lizzie's, but still soft and warm. For a moment all his troubles melted, dripping away like the ice cream on Saj's face. His hands moved to her hips, his heart racing.

Nev pulled away, looking as surprised as he felt. She turned in a circle and then started washing dishes. Zach picked up the metal spatula and messed with scraping the flat steel grill, trying to figure out what the kiss meant. Was it a friend-kiss or a girlfriend-kiss? Things with Lizzie had gone too fast and ended badly. He was pretty sure he had a chance for something better with Nev, but he didn't want to make a wrong move.

18

MANNIE WOKE THE NEXT MORNING uncertain if he had dreamed. Outside it was still pitch dark, but the habit of getting up early for work or war didn't change even if the world had. He jumped into a hot, hot shower.

Coffee and yogurt with Grape Nuts stood in for breakfast while he went through the series of texts from Lizzie. They included extra phone numbers for Lizzie, a paranoid tactic after his own heart, and her friend Jess' number. He copied them down on a piece of paper and put it in his wallet. Then he copied them down again and tucked the paper inside the lining of his Smokey the Bear hat. He put on his olive drab work pants and the heavy gray khaki shirt. Something about being in uniform made him feel more solid. And if he was going to requisition a government Jeep, he better look like he was supposed to be driving it.

He refolded the maps and replaced them in the glove box. He picked up the double burner camp stove and a three-pack of camping gas, then put them back down. A sleeping bag went in the back of the truck in case he ended up sleeping in-between towns. But he would always be near towns. The cautious camper took over. He put the stove and gas in and added his one-man tent. He packed the rest of the Coke, a frozen loaf of bread, a pack of lunch meat, a baggie of fast food condiments, and a handful of water bottles from the fridge. The coffee went in a to-go mug.

Mannie found himself whistling; he couldn't remember doing

that in years. A new life. A new shot anyway. A shudder rippled through him as he thought about leaving Bellingham and his daughter. He'd made it to the next bar, drinking himself into a stupor and waking up in the drunk tank. After he got out he managed to hold off of the drink while he drove home. To his parents' here in Texas. This trip might reverse some of those years. Maybe.

He was ready to say goodbye. His heart felt a jab of pain as he took a last look around the living room. There was the worn place on the couch he and Isabel had spent weekends reading, napping, watching movies and the other things couples did together. At its foot was the dark spot on the rug where Isabel's black cat, Sheba, used to sleep. The cat had run off after Isabel died. Probably become coyote food. He shook off the ghosts.

What if Lizzie couldn't stand him? Wouldn't forgive him? He leaned against the wall and closed his eyes. *No. I can't think that.* Isabel would have said something about letting fear have control. *Elizabeth is counting on me.* He opened his eyes and went out, closing the door without locking it.

The old truck grumbled to life. The sun rose beautiful over the distant horizon, dawning a new day. The morning star had not yet winked out as he left the rocky gravel of the driveway and the wheels quieted on the pavement to town. First, the ranger station, then provisions in Del Rio and head north.

The station looked like a normal morning. He could almost expect everyone would be in later. Since he'd stopped drinking he'd become *that morning guy*, always the first one there to unlock things. If he was in uniform he didn't drink, so getting dressed for work helped him stay sober.

His right knee ached as he stepped down. He'd blown it out in the mountains a few years ago and though it worked, it ached when the weather changed or when he abused it. The pain served as a nagging reminder of his lack of invincibility.

He lifted the keys to 'his' vehicle, Rubi, off the rack. It bugged him when the station bought the big Jeep Rubicon. It was a big expense on the taxpayers dime, and overkill for the job needed. But over a decade she became a partner to him. She was showing her age and would've sold at auction last year if he hadn't fussed.

In the garage he crossed to Rubi, tossed his backpack into the passenger seat and transferred the rest of his gear to the way back. He heaved a case of MREs, Meals Ready to Eat, and a first aid kit for 'just in case' cases in the back seat. From the gun safe, he took out a Sig p220 pistol and holster, a Remington 870 shotgun and shoulder case, a couple boxes of ammo and a cleaning kit. He wrote a sticky note listing what he'd taken and their serial numbers before signing it. He closed and locked the safe. The world might really be headed to Hell in a hand basket this time, but he would follow protocol—the one thing the military had taught him. He printed his full name, Department of Defense ID and cell numbers, then signed it.

Mannie headed into Del Rio. The ache in his knee subsided as usual, though he knew the long drive would be problematic. He'd need stops to walk and stretch.

On the ride to Seattle, Zach's brain flitted from thought to thought: the kiss with Nev, the one with Lizzie, the responsibility of Saj and Spike. Nev had switched seats with Liz. She smiled sideways at him, flipping through stations to find tunes she wanted to hear: Fitz and the Tantrums, Muse and the Foo Fighters.

They crossed Lake Washington on I-90 and headed toward the Space Needle.

Lizzie popped her head over the front seat. "I don't want to go into the city."

"What the hell, Lizzie," Zach asked. But she had that look on her face. "You agreed."

"Under duress."

"Shit, Lizzie. You been watching reruns of Law and Order? Under duress?"

"Stop the Tank, Zach."

"What?"

Lizzie shoved her door open. "Stop. I'm getting out."

Zach engaged the brakes and the giant SUV slowed. When the ground wasn't moving too fast Lizzie jumped out and back, stumbling to catch her footing. Then she strode past where the Tank had come to rest.

Zach hopped down and slammed the door. "Lizzie?" he called after her.

Ahead Seattle lay partially enshrouded in fog. Lizzie kept walking down the freeway.

Zach opened the driver's door and stuck his head in. "You want to talk to her?"

Nev shook her head.

Zach sighed and shut the door more gently this time. "Hey, Lizzie. Wait for me." So he was going to try to convince the crazy girl not to be crazy. He jogged after her. "Can we talk about it?"

"Take the exit. Go see what's going on. You'll catch up."

"Do you realize how crazy that sounds?" He hustled ahead and walked backwards in front of her. "Lizzie, we're not moving in. We want to know what's going on. Maybe we need something these people have. What if the pandemic has returned?"

"What if, what if, what if." Lizzie glared at him and pushed him aside. "There's no what if. My dad's alive and I'm going to get where he's at."

Zach walked beside her. "Yes, Lizzie. And we're going into the city for a little while. Scouting, call it. I don't think it's a good idea to leave you walking through Seattle."

"Why? What's going to get me? Everybody's dead."

"Not everybody."

There was a rumble behind them. Lizzie spun, but not as fast as Zach.

"Oh, shit, Nev," Zach muttered, "Thought you couldn't drive."

"She's going pretty slow."

The Tank rolled toward them. "Come on, Lizzie," Zach pleaded, "An hour? Give us an hour?" He grabbed her arm and pulled her toward him. He stared into her eyes. *For once let me be more stubborn than you.*

Lizzie jerked her arm out of his grasp. "You better go help Nev drive that beast."

"Lizzie?"

"Yeah. An hour." She walked toward the Tank. "Then we hit the road."

"Thanks." Zach ran on ahead. The Tank ground to a halt.

"Not bad," he told Nev as she slid across to the passenger seat.

"I got tired of waiting for you to quit fighting again."

Lizzie hopped in the back, but stared out over Seattle.

So be it. Zach took the Convention Center exit and followed the signs.

Inside they found an exhausted city councilman sitting at a table as people filtered by. He didn't know anything. Zach wasn't sure if the city badge on the man's jacket was to keep people calm or impress them. Keep them calm, Zach decided. There was no glory in this job. The people milling around the check-in station seemed to cling to this evidence that structure remained like a drowning man clings to a life vest.

"Please, sign your names, give us your addresses." The councilman glanced at the newcomers, his voice scratchy and monotonous. "Any special skills? Knowledge of medi—"

"Whoa." Lizzie stopped him. "We're on our way to Salt Lake."

Zach watched Lizzie go into puffer fish mode—spiny all over. "Lizzie." He put his hand on her arm; she shoved it off. *Whatever.*

"We just stopped for information."

"Miss, please." The councilman sighed deeply and drank a slug of coffee out of a ceramic Starbucks cup. He continued, his voice still pleasant, "I'm Devin Miller. We're not trying to keep you. We want to know who's alive and get contact information—to try to make some order out of this mess. We need to help each other if we are going to survive this tragic occurrence." He recited it like a prepared speech.

"And how could you help us?" Lizzie arched an eyebrow.

Finally Mr. Miller broke from his politeness, "Frankly, Miss. I don't know if I can. Either fill it out or don't." He handed them each a quarter sheet of paper with contact information for the City of Seattle.

Lizzie deflated. When she spoke again, her voice sounded small like a scared girl, "How many people survived?"

Her tone shook Zac. He preferred the puffer fish. Lizzie had always been the tough one. Now he realized how much he relied on that toughness to keep himself stable.

"About 40,000 in the greater Seattle area. But we don't know how many of those are healthy and mentally stable. A lot of the people who got sick and recovered can't seem to care for themselves. We're temporarily housing them in the Key Arena. So far we've been able to keep them fed, but clean... that's another thing."

"Yeah, it's a challenge." Lizzie motioned to Spike standing awkward next to Nev. "This is Spike. Our Dog-man"

Zach watched in amazement as Lizzie shifted into helpful-adult-mode. That was a new one for Lizzie.

"We've been working with him and, well, it's like training a dog." Lizzie patted Spike's shoulder. "But he's learning a lot."

"Hhhmmm… Dog-man." Miller looked at Spike, clean and docile today, with hope in his eyes. "So, do you want to sign in? If you decide to stay, we have student housing open over at U.W."

Zach took the pen. "I'll sign. I don't bring a lot of skills to the table. I can shovel manure!"

"And you cook," Liz added.

"My food ain't half bad when you're starving."

"It's good. And I'm not starving." Nev squeezed his shoulder, and signed one herself. "If we stayed I could finally get into U.W."

"Yeah," Lizzie said, "but we aren't staying. Still a lot of miles between here and Salt Lake."

The councilman's eyes narrowed. "You're headed south? Watch out in Tacoma."

"You heard anything about any new outbreaks?" Zach asked.

Miller shook his head. "What's left of U.W. Medical Center says we're safe."

"Rumors going round about a second wave," Zach said.

Miller shrugged. "Lots of rumors."

Lizzie's phone rang. A sinister guitar riff ringtone echoed.

Zach knew the song. "Secret Agent Man." He sang along.

Lizzie grinned at Zach, "My dad's new ringtone." She shushed him and answered.

A few seconds later her voice raised, "You're shitting me?" Her fingers raced to her hair, twisting and pulling, face like she'd seen a ghost.

"What's wrong?" Zach asked.

"Find a doctor." Lizzie begged Zach. "Or nurse or something. Please."

Zach turned to the councilman. Miller flipped through his sheets. He withdrew one and pointed at a cell number next to a name and the letters: ARNP. Nev had her phone out and dialed the number.

At the grocery store the stench of rotting food greeted Mannie like a garbage dump. A wild looking stray dog ran out the door as he came in. He stocked a cooler with ice and pre-formed burgers. Flash frozen and stuck together they should keep for days. He grabbed a case of Coke Classic and some singles, laying them on top of the ice. He carried the case toward the car and added on some cans of soup and chili on the way.

Lugging the full cooler was too much. He got it out the door, but finally, set in on the grass outside. If he blew out his knee now, that was the end. He wouldn't be driving anywhere. No sick leave in the apocalypse. *Better learn to take it a bit easier, or I'm not going to get to reintroduce myself to my daughter.* He emptied half the cooler and made two trips. Around the corner of the building a flash of color caught his eye.

A woman, her slim form clothed in strips of sparkly bright clothing, looked like a girl until he got close. When he got closer he recognized her, Mary. She had been a little crazy before the disease, a local artist always getting in trouble with the Sheriff for harassing people with her portrait paintings. Isabel complained her morning hair was like Medusa's, but Mary's really was. Her wild eyes matched her hair.

She ducked down behind a dumpster. "Hey, there. You hungry?" Mannie went back in the store and found jerky and a chocolate bar.

He tore the bag of jerky open with his teeth as he approached the dumpster. "Here's some jerky." He lay it down on the ground. Then he opened the chocolate. "You've got to be hungry." He inched closer, holding out the candy.

She darted out grasping at the candy bar with her teeth gnashing. She missed the chocolate and bit his right hand. The candy bar fell to the pavement.

"Shit! Let go." Her jaw clamped and chewed; saliva dripped, blood oozed. He tried to shake her off, but she wouldn't let go.

He shoved at her forehead with his left hand. Her teeth ground down. Mannie cried out. He kneed her in the gut and hit her hard with the heel of his hand.

Mary grunted and her jaw released.

He shoved her away. She fell to the ground gasping for air. Blood ran from her mouth. "Jesus!"

She got up on her knees and came toward him. He turned and ran.

Mannie jumped in the Jeep and twisted the key; it slipped in his bloody fingers. "Damn."

He glanced in the rear view mirror. She had stopped to rip apart the beef jerky with her bloody teeth. He locked the doors and clambered between the seats for the first aid kit.

Was she rabid or just crazy from the end of the world? There had been reports of rabid dogs a month ago. *Did I survive the plague only to get rabies?* He wadded up gauze and shoved it on the gaping hole in his hand. It soaked with his red blood in seconds. He wrapped tape tight around the gauze to stop the bleeding.

Everything's going to be fine. Mannie fought to bring his breathing back under control. He peeled off more gauze and wiped blood from his fingers and keys. He started the engine and popped the Jeep into gear one-handed. The tires spun in the gravel. He accelerated toward the hospital. "Cool it, Mario." He eased off on the gas. He wanted to get there in one piece.

When he pulled into the hospital emergency bay he cradled his cell phone in his bloody bandages and hit redial.

Lizzie answered. "Hey, we're in Seattle already, how are you?"

"Lizzie!" His voice came out a growl. "I'm hurt. Bit by some crazy lady and I think she might have rabies."

"You're shitting me."

"Hell, no. I'm freaked out. I'm at the hospital, but it's deserted. I need to know what to do and I don't have access to the Internet. I was hoping you could help."

Lizzie said something cryptic about doing him one better and hung up. Mannie tucked the phone back in his pocket and limped like a wounded animal into the ER. To top everything off he had twisted his knee during his escape from Crazy Mary's vicious teeth.

He sat down in the waiting room with the first aid kit he'd brought with him. At least he knew where those supplies were. He stripped off the tape and bloody gauze. He opened one of the antiseptic wipes and swabbed at the jagged gashes. Human bites were worse than animals. He had better clean it.

His cell buzzed. He answered it, holding it carefully with his left hand. "Del Rio Texas Emergency Room."

Lizzie laughed, "My dad's got a sense of humor. There's a nurse here."

"Thanks." *How the hell did she find a nurse?*

A brusque male voice came on the line, "You're at the hospital?"

"Yes."

"And you've been bit by a dog?"

"No. A dog-lady. A woman. Wild woman. Survivor, but I was trying to feed her. She bit me hard enough I could use my hand to make her a set of dentures."

"And what make you think she's rabid?" The nurse asked, skepticism in his voice.

"There were a spate of cases a month or so ago. Real dogs. The woman was aggressive. Salivating. Reminded me of a dog. I don't think I should take any chances."

"Well, even if she has contracted rabies, human to human transmission is unlikely. There isn't usually enough virus in human saliva. But you're right, you need to get the vaccine. How big is Del Rio?"

Mannie chuckled, "Not very."

"Odds are there isn't any vaccine. But you can check. You'll need to get into the dispensary."

"And where might that be?"

"Relatively central."

Mannie hustled to the elevator. The map outside said the pharmacy was B1. "Headed there."

"Once you're inside, there should be a refrigerated cabinet. Look for a multi-pack, taped or rubber-banded."

The elevator moved. At least power hadn't gone out.

Mannie found the dispensary. "Okay." The doors were locked so he slid the phone into his pocket and smashed a potted plant through the glass window. He gingerly put his hand through and opened the door. "I'm in. What are the meds?"

"RabAvert or Imovax."

Mannie flipped through the meds in the refrigerator. "No. Nothing like that. Recommendations?"

"What's the nearest big city?"

"San Antonio."

"They'll have vaccine. I'll see if I can reach someone there and have your daughter let you know which hospital to go to."

19

THE ROAD ROLLED BY UNDERNEATH Mannie. The trip to San Antonio had long ago ceased to fascinate him; nothing changed—same flatlands, rocks and sagebrush.

Past, present, future all mingled in his mind. Baby Elizabeth, Afghanistan, the darkness, Isabel and the brighter days. And now baby Elizabeth was grown-up Lizzie. And if he could live long enough he would see her, talk to her, hold her. If she wanted.

Mannie hadn't prayed since he was a kid. Getting over the addictions had been a challenge without a belief in a higher power. His choices and their consequences were his and his alone. He hadn't been able to 'Let go, let God.' But now he prayed: *Please, if there is a higher power out there, let me see my daughter. Let me ask for forgiveness. Please.*

The road flew by. His head ached from the road glare. Near San Antonio he pulled over to check his phone. A text from Lizzie. **Military hospital. Theyll find you.** "What the hell?" He tried Lizzie, but a message said, "Network busy."

He drove on. When he crossed over Loop 410, the ring road, an ambulance with lights flashing and a camouflaged truck approached. Mannie slowed to a stop as they blocked the road in front of him. A small squad of armed men, a few middle-aged with ill-fitting uniforms got out of the back of the truck.

Mannie got out of the jeep and walked to the truck.

A creased, tan-faced Captain stepped down from the driver's

side and saluted. "Manuel Guerrero? Lieutenant, U.S. Army Reserves?" His uniform ID'd him as Wiser.

Mannie answered the salute. "Yes. I suppose."

"You need a rabies vaccine, correct?" Wiser demanded.

"Yes. Does everyone entering San Antonio get this reaction?"

A doctor came around the ambulance. She looked all business. "We ensure infected people don't enter the city. If you're coming in, you must be quarantined until we can verify your system is clean." She slipped on rubber gloves and a mask over her face.

"I don't want to come into San Antonio," Mannie said. "I'm heading north to meet my daughter in Salt Lake City."

"That could be useful to us, Lieutenant," the Captain said.

"What could?" Mannie asked. The use of his rank made him uncomfortable, as if he were being called to active duty by that word alone.

"Command is trying to get intel on various parts of the country," the Captain said, as the doctor raised her eyebrow.

"What has that got to do with me?"

"There has been limited communication with Utah," he continued. "We had contact with National Guard at Dugway Proving Ground. But then we lost them."

"Captain Wiser. Look. I am not in the Army anymore. I'm going to get my daughter. Nothing else. " Mannie adjusted his posture to *attention* and faced the officer. "They sent you with the vaccine?" *I don't like this game, but I'll play it. Lizzie is counting on me.*

Wiser nodded to the Doctor.

She asked Mannie a few questions, checked his vitals, and rebandaged his wound. "Nice job on the wound care." Then she gave him the first dose of rabies vaccine.

"Here's the remainder." She handed him two packets with vials shrink-wrapped inside each. "You need to keep it cold, but not frozen. You'll need two more injections, seven days and then 21 days later. Can you handle self-injections?"

Mannie nodded. "If I need to."

Wiser pulled one of the vials from Mannie's hands. "This is expensive stuff. Are you sure you can keep it at the right temperature for 28 days?" He handed the vial back to the doctor.

The doctor glared at Wiser, but accepted it, twisting on her heel and returning to the ambulance. The driver started the engine and drove away.

Mannie's teeth clamped together. It was these kind of games, this kind of 'old boy network' that had him hating the military. *Power corrupts.* But this was the only game in town. *I play; you give me answers.* "I'll see what's happening in Utah, *Captain.* What's going on nationally?"

"Not much out of Washington. Nothing from the president. Or the cabinet. A few senators and representatives have checked in. No one has invoked the presidential line of succession yet. Here in San Antonio we are the law and the government."

"Martial Law."

Wiser nodded, "Most survivors are military or former military. It makes sense, until things get stable. Here are contacts for the information." He handed him a piece of paper with phone numbers and e-mails. "Good luck, Lieutenant." The driver saluted him as he got back in the truck.

Mannie returned a perfect, forceful soldier's salute and tucked the paper in his wallet with the other numbers. He stared at the truck as it went away. "I guess fading away was out of the question," he muttered as he climbed back into Rubi.

In Sonora, city of a thousand single-wides, Mannie made a pit stop to give his knee a little stretch. There was a text from Lizzie. He called up to report in and got voice mail.

"Hey. It's Dad." He wandered as he talked, breaking into some calf raises and partial squats. "I'm doing fine. Probably about an hour from San Angelo. Gonna call Jess, give her some warning. Thanks for the help this morning. Maybe you can help me remember to give myself another shot in seven days. Need to figure out what day it is. Talk to you soon. I'll call when I get to Jess." He hit end call; then he pulled the slip of paper with Jess' number from his pocket and dialed.

"Hello?" The voice had a hint of the southern softness.

"Jess? It's Mannie. Lizzie's dad." A flash of lightning appeared off to the east under the dark blanketed sky. Thunderstorms were coming.

"Thanks for coming to get me." She sounded hesitant.

"No problem."

"Where are you?"

"In Sonora. An hour away, I think."

"You'll be in time for dinner."

"That'd be great. How do I find you?"

"Call back when you get in town. I've been sleeping at the Motel 6. I'm at Central High School with some survivors, but I'll meet you at the motel.

He ended the call and continued his stretches. The only time he ever did the damn exercises the physical therapist had taught him was after the aches started. He climbed back into the Jeep stiff and tired of driving. He rolled through town on 277 as it twisted and turned. It was desolate here before the end of days, scrub pines bordered the road, outcrops of low stone jutted out of the bleak desert. Every few miles a large sign proclaimed some cattle farmer's domain—Broadwell Ranch, B & D Acres, Deer Creek Ranch. Sometimes there was a fancy stone gate with its cattle grate. Red and yellow strata showed where they'd cut the road straight through a hill. He drove past boarded up buildings, roadside stores, an empty strip club. Too bad the Jeep didn't come with an autopilot; this country was going to put him to sleep. He opened another Coke.

San Angelo was a thriving metropolis comparatively; someone had whitewashed a billboard of a rodeo with 'Survivors Welcome! Follow the signs to Central High' painted in broad red strokes.

He stopped the Jeep under the sign and hit redial for Jess.

She picked up and told him how to get to the Motel 6.

He found it. A pretty girl with a cowboy hat in hand detached from the late afternoon shade of the building and walked toward him.

He pulled into the shade, the warmth of the day still oppressive for November. He pulled his stiff body from the cab and hopped down; shaking his leg and knee out. He put his right foot up on the tire and rubbed around the knee.

"Hi, Mister Guerrero." She put her hat on her head. Her cloudy grey eyes held a touch of sadness that made her more beautiful.

"Jess? Call me Mannie. Or Manuel." He stuck his hand out.

She looked at it for a second. "How's your hand doing." It was an excuse, he realized. This soon after the plague, shaking hands with strangers seemed risky.

He pulled it back. "Doctor cleaned it up outside San Antonio. Good to have somebody who knows what they're doing…"

She nodded. "You hungry?"

"Not too much, yet." He bent his gimpy leg a couple more times." I could use a walk."

"A walk sounds good. I can take you over to the school and introduce you around." She started ahead of him and then slowed down. "I remember meeting Lizzie in grade school. We were inseparable. Lizzie thought she loved horses." Jess told him the story of how Lizzie's first real encounter with a horse had not gone well.

Mannie nodded, listening. It seemed like a peace offering. Jess was giving him something about his daughter he didn't have, a memory. Or perhaps it was a warning—just because Lizzie liked the idea of a dad, didn't mean she would like the real thing. They walked in silence for a while.

After a couple blocks Jess said, "I missed her when my family moved down here."

Mannie nodded again. "I miss her, too."

The school looked like any other high school in America, faded Homecoming Dance signs, white patches of paint to cover graffiti, and an awful lot of blue and orange—school colors.

The people Mannie met seemed haggard, but pleasant. Jess introduced him to Tom, the baker. He handed her fresh baked rolls.

"How's San Antone?" Tom asked when he heard where Mannie had been.

"Seem to have things under control. Lots of military folks. Martial law."

Tom nodded. "Yep. Times like these. A bit of discipline keeps things together."

Mannie smiled, wondering if people really needed to be under control.

They walked back to the Motel 6 as the sun set. Jess heated up a large can of beef stew and the rolls. It was nice to see people sharing in a time of crisis. He had seen enough of neighbors turning against neighbors in Afghanistan.

The bread was melt-in-your-mouth tasty and Mannie ate like he hadn't eaten in a month. Having people around to talk to was something he didn't realize he missed. "Any idea how many people have come into town?" He sopped up the last of the stew with another chunk of bread.

"They've got a count going; 792 was the last number I saw."

"But nobody you know?"

"Oh, I know some of them. A couple of the jocks and cheer-leadery types. Nobody I liked. When I found out Lizzie was alive, then Zach and Nev..." She sniffed a little. "I was kind of jealous. When Lizzie phoned to say she was sending you, I was packing a bag before I hung up the phone."

Mannie stirred his coffee. The light outside had disappeared except for the street lamps shining through the curtains. Neither of them had bothered to get up and turn on the lights. "I'd given up on seeing Elizabeth." His voice was soft and he could feel his throat tightening. "I messed things up pretty bad. The PTSD and the alcohol led to drugs..." He shook his head. "I wasn't myself. Took me years to get back to figuring out who I was. By then I'd burned my bridges. When I got set up down here, I tried to call once. Somebody named Doug answered. Said he'd tell Lizzie. That was all I had in me. Figured she was better off."

Jess broke the long silence. "Doug was a jerk. Lizzie loved your music collection. We used to watch the '80s movies in your DVD collection."

Mannie wiped his eyes and crossed to the light switch. "Mind if I turn the light on?"

"No." Jess' eyes were red and damp.

He set his empty coffee cup by the sink. Then, remembering his manners, picked it back up and rinsed it. "Thanks for the food. Figured tomorrow we might make it to Albuquerque. About five, six hours on the road."

"Sounds good."

She stood awkwardly.

"Well, I'm gonna find myself a room."

"Oh, I got you a key to the room across the hall." Jess grinned. "Figured out the computer system all by myself." She handed him a keycard.

"Thanks." When he turned to leave Jess jumped forward and hugged him tight. Her body shook and the tears from earlier turned into sobs. He held her close and ran his fingers gently through her hair. "Go ahead; cry it out."

"I never cried. Not when Grampa died. Nor Papa. Or Mamma.

Her eyes were big and tear-filled. He found himself saying, "It's all right…" Even though the words meant little.

Eventually her body stopped shaking. She sniffed and gently shifted. Mannie released her and dug in his pockets for a handkerchief. But the hanky was bloody. He offered her the Dairy Queen napkin. She took it and noisily blew her nose.

"Thanks, Mr.— Mannie. Lizzie's lucky."

"Maybe. But I think I'm luckier. Didn't think I'd get a second chance." He held up the room key. "Thanks again. You got a time you want to leave?"

"Not really. Been waking up early. I used to sleep in. But now, I wake with the light."

"Me, too. Good night."

"Good night, Mannie."

"Jess. It's gonna be okay."

"I hope so."

He left the room and crossed the hallway. *It's gonna be okay.* How did such flimsy words have the strength to keep people hanging on when things went completely to shit?

Lizzie's head nodded as the truck hit the endless bumps on the freeway south of Seattle. The last thing she saw as her head dropped against the seat was the row of planes sitting idle at Boeing Field.

The squeal of brakes woke her abruptly.

"Holy crap. Would you look at that?" Zach stared straight ahead.

Lizzie followed his gaze. A couple of tigers, the size of small horses, padded patiently across the freeway. The Tank's approach and its skidding stop had not disturbed them.

Zach glanced back at Lizzie. "I guess that's what the guy meant about watch out for Tacoma."

Lizzie watched the graceful cats cross into the median. "You think someone let out the big animals like we let out the pets?"

"Looks like it." Nev said.

Lizzie yawned. "Let's take that as a sign not to stop in Tacoma."

"Suits me." Zach eased forward, passing the cats.

Lizzie's brain was still trying to wrap itself around how many people were left. "One percent," she muttered, doing mental calculations. "I think there were about 100,000 in Bellingham, but I have no clue about the rest of Whatcom County. Which means, what… 1000 survivors? Total? In Bellingham?"

Zach gave a low whistle.

Nev gaped. "At Bellingham High School we had 950 students. That's no more people left than fit in the gym."

Zach whistled and did his drum roll on the dashboard. "And how many are like our buddy, Spike, back there?" Spike's head popped up. "Hey, Spike. We're talking about you, aren't we?"

"I still don't know what it means," Lizzie said.

"What do you mean, 'what it means'?" Zach shook his head. "It means shit. It means the human race is pretty screwed."

"Or does it finally mean we're not? No more population problems, a lot less cars on the road…"

"I dunno," Zach drawled. "I'm a hick from Sedro-Woolley. But I know India had more honor students last year than we had students!" He smiled.

"You mean like, all of a sudden there is enough gas?" Nev smiled. "And enough water."

"And enough beer." Zach laughed.

Nev chuckled and dug a finger into his rib. "Course, I was hoping for a track scholarship and then a B.A. in B.S. There goes my chance to charm some rich guy into marrying me. Money isn't worth what it used to be."

"But now a guy can shower you with diamonds after a quick trip to a jewelry store." Zach winked at Nev and she blushed.

Lizzie intentionally ignored them and continued her calculations. "40,000 people left in the Seattle area. How many people in the whole world? Before this, I mean."

"Over seven billion, I think." Nev took up the calculation. "a billion is a one with nine zeroes, one percent of that is a one with seven zeroes, right? Ten million for every billion. Doesn't really seem like we're in that rough of a place. Not like extinction watch."

"What're we going to do," Zach asked, "once we connect with

your dad and Jess?"

Lizzie had no answer. "No idea. Where is it safe? Where do we find people we want to hang out with? Where do we want to go? Northwest Washington is a decent place. No tornados, hurricanes."

"We've got flooding," Zach said.

Lizzie nodded. "In the lowlands."

"And volcanos," Nev said.

Zach grinned. "In the highlands."

Lizzie pressed on. "But that didn't stop any of us from living there before, right?"

"We could drive across the country like nomads." Zach tapped the dashboard gently. "I like this big hulking, gas-guzzling vehicle."

20

MANNIE ROSE AND MADE COFFEE in the foolish little hotel coffee-maker still stocked with one decaf and one regular packet. Two cups later he had a driving plan from San Angelo to Roswell and then on to Albuquerque. He better find some chains. Rubi was pretty sure-footed under most conditions, but there was no more Triple-A. Might want to get an extra spare tire. He started a shopping list for Albuquerque: spare, clothes, chains, an extra sleeping bag... "What else?" What did Jess need? At least she didn't seem like a girly girl with two suitcases for an overnight.

A knock at the door. "Yeah?"

"Mannie? It's Jess."

He opened the door. She stood there, dressed to travel, a plaid shirt over a white blouse, and jeans tucked into her cowboy boots. She picked up the duffel bag on the floor next to her and walked in.

"Figured we could eat with the folks at the high school." She sat in the chair, then hopped back up. "We can go from there. I want to thank them."

"Sounds good." He glanced down at his bare feet, *Gotta get myself moving.* "Was going to snag a shower. Not sure when we'll have another opportunity and who knows about hot water and electricity."

"Already did. I'm gonna head over. See if there's anything I can do before breakfast."

His knee ached, but no worse than usual. His hand continued to throb. In fact, his whole body ached, but that wasn't really too surprising, considering the vaccine. Mannie drained the last drips of coffee, cobwebs wrapped around his brain. Hopefully they had more coffee at breakfast.

He blasted the hot water, though the pressure was pretty mediocre. It didn't matter; it washed away the sleep and eased the soreness of an abused body.

After the shower, he dressed in his uniform. It gave him a bit of comfort.

He found Jess with two trays of hot food: corn beef hash, scrambled eggs and giant glass of milk.

"You want coffee? Didn't know how you liked it."

"Black with sugar."

She disappeared and then reappeared with a large cup of steaming coffee and napkin with half a dozen sugar cubes.

The food was good, but bland; he wanted more spice. He glanced around for some tabasco for the hash and eggs, but settled for salt and pepper.

Jess had wolfed down all of hers by the time Mannie finished half of his. The coffee reminded him of the his army mess halls, burnt tasting and strong.

They finished their food and Jess said her goodbyes. Tom the Baker gave her a basket of muffins and wished her luck.

Mannie could see she had made connections. He wasn't sure she noticed how Tom's eyes teared up when he said goodbye.

Out on the road the miles flew by. After all these years he still missed real trees. Well, there'd be some near Salt Lake. For a while they rode in silence. Jess seemed pensive.

In Lamesa he stopped to fill up the tank and walk his knee around.

Jess got out and surveyed the town. Her face registered disappointment.

More of the same; dry, flat. Jess stretched her arms over her head, and he caught a flash of a pink jewel belly button piercing. He focused on the gas pump.

Her arms came down. "The trip from Washington was really the only traveling I've ever done. I bet you did a lot of travelling with the army."

"Some." Mannie shook the last drops of gas from the nozzle. He went inside the convenience store to scrounge for snacks, and Jess followed.

"Oh, sorry. They probably aren't really great memories, huh?" she said, took off her hat to run her fingers through her hair.

"Some good, some bad."

"The idea of travelling always felt exciting and fun—like an adventure. My dad's big adventure was going to Washington. He said we moved back because of 'bad influences' on me, but the economy had gotten rough, and Bellingham was expensive. Moving back to Texas was him giving up. He got crabby anytime I mentioned seeing the world." She talked like she was trying to make up for the last few hours of silence.

Mannie didn't mind. It didn't matter what she said; Jess had an energy, a positive spirit, that radiated from her. Listening to her was like lying in the warm sun on a cold day. He was surprised to find that he was enjoying having her along on the trip. He'd imagined that she would be childish and annoying—that the mission to collect her and bring her to Lizzie would be like babysitting.

They stopped for lunch at a Stripes convenience store in Brownfield: frozen, microwaved burritos. Not really food, but it did silence the rumbling in his stomach. They found a picnic bench nearby and sat down to eat.

"Next stop, Roswell." Mannie chuckled. "Home of the Aliens."

"Really?" Jess bit off half her burrito. The girl could eat. Her eyes lit up. Covering her mouth, she asked between chews, "Can we go to the UFO museum?"

He laughed. "I guess we need to stop somewhere."

They washed the burrito off their hands in a water fountain and then returned to the road.

As they got close to Roswell the sky grew darker. Mannie didn't feel good about the color. It didn't look like yesterday's thunderclouds.

"Is that smoke?" Jess asked, reading his mind.

"Shit. Wildfire."

"Is that where we're heading?" Her voice quavered.

"Yeah." Mannie tapped the GPS on. "We can probably get around it."

"Probably?" Jess eyes were big and round, she chewed her thumbnail.

"We're about to head north. As soon as we get in town." He

tried to keep his voice calm and confident for her sake.

Jess nodded, staring at the darkness. She noticed her thumb and pulled it self-consciously away from her mouth.

The fire seemed to be south of Roswell. But as Mannie drove out from between the red ridges and across the Pecos River, the sky grew darker, until it felt more like evening than midday.

"That feels close," Jess said. "Do you think it's in town?"

Mannie shook his head. "Don't know." They passed a pretty, white Victorian farmhouse framed by trees and a picket fence. "Shame to see that go up in smoke."

There were no signs of flames, but the smoky haze had gotten thicker. Mannie put the air on circulate and thumbed the air conditioner. Rubi sealed up pretty well; as long as it didn't get too bad, they would be fine. He gently increased the pressure on the accelerator.

"I don't need to see the Alien museum," Jess was panicking like a cornered cat.

Mannie needed to distract her. The way her hand clawed at the door handle, he wouldn't be surprised if she jumped out of the moving vehicle and ran back the way they came. "Jess, you know how to use a gun?"

She took her eyes off the fire to roll them at him. "I live in Texas."

"After we get some place safe we ought to get you something you're comfortable with." Farmer's supply places, empty storefronts and industrial buildings flashed by.

"To protect me from what?" The fear flooded back into her face.

Hell. Wrong tangent. "I don't know. Not that I'm expecting— You know. Not a lot of cops, so..."

"So, cougars? Zombies? Rapists? Shit like that?" Her voice had gone reedy and high. Her eyes spun back to the fire. "Mannie, shouldn't you slow down?"

Mannie glanced at the speedometer. Approaching 70 and they were entering Roswell. "Shit. Maybe." He released the accelerator a bit. "Guess I'm nervous about the fire, too."

Jess released the door handle. Her hands clenched and un-clenched. "I'm not nervous. I'm freaked. Had a burn once in the back forty. My jacket caught on fire. Daddy threw me down and got it out."

"Yeah." Mannie had seen plenty worse. "This isn't all that bad, we haven't seen flames yet." He slowed; the smoke rose in a plume due west.

"You're sure it's safe driving into that?"

"I'm pretty sure we can outrun the fire in this rig. I got plenty of fuel." It was two hours back to Brownsville, the last major cross-roads, and then hours of extra driving.

"Fuel and fire," she squeaked, "don't exactly mix well. Mannie, I'm scared. Really."

"Jess. I've been in tighter spots than this. Trust me. I am going to get us to Salt Lake and Lizzie. It's a little brush fire. No real trees to burn." He patted her knee. "Chin up. We'll make it." He smiled at her, but her eyes focused ahead.

Mannie turned back to the road. In the darkness ahead was a red glow; fire had swallowed the road. "Hell." He let off the gas and braked. "Not this way."

He spun the Jeep around and headed back. "Don't really want to head into the mountains. Let's see if we can get around it, okay, Jess?"

She nodded. Her hand hovered near her mouth.

"Gonna try to get to 285." Mannie tapped the GPS, driving slow. He turned onto North Grand street. It dead ended in a few blocks. The fire had engulfed the center of town. He pulled off into the dusty dirt and head across the railroad tracks.

"Is this a good idea?" Her eyes scanned. Her head swiveled, trying to see in every direction.

"We need to get north of the fire and hit 285." Rubi bounced across the old railroad tracks. *Don't pop a tire here, Mannie.*

He drove onto 10th street. There was smoke ahead, but he didn't see fire. Mannie pulled onto Main. "I think this is 285." The column of smoke to the south had grown. Jess' hands were in her lap, clasped together. Her eyes were closed.

Maria, madre de Dios. Keep us safe. Praying was becoming a regular habit. The smoke diminished. As he drove through it, a smaller, darker plume rose straight ahead to the west.

Keep your eyes closed, Jess. He continued, accelerating back to highway speed. The wind whipped the jeep. No wonder the fire was spreading. *Let me get past it.*

The smoke and open flames were jumping across the prairie brush. Tomorrow this would all be black. He pushed the accelerator to the floor.

Mannie looked over at Jess. Her eyes were open again, her body rigid. She stared at the flames ahead.

He glanced in the rearview mirror. What had only been smoke was now open flame racing upward as the town caught fire. *Don't look back. Straight ahead.*

Too late. Jess turned to see the flames. "Mannie?" her voice reached a high fevered pitch. "We can't go back?"

"No." Mannie focused on the road ahead, still only smoke, but a black wall of smoke floated toward the road on a river of fire. Jess' hand clenched on his arm. "We're gonna be fine. Come on, Rubi." His hands gripped the wheel. *Panic does no good.* He breathed.

Jess' eyes closed again and her lips moved. No sound came out. A gust of wind tugged at the Jeep, but he kept it straight ahead, racing the conflagration. How long could it take? He'd hit 111 and Rubi wasn't going any faster.

He gained on the darkness. They were going to make it. *Don't say anything yet.* He drove into the wall of black smoke. *Let us come out the other side.*

As he burst through, the smoke pushed ahead of the fire by the wind, sucked toward him in the tailwind. Ahead, clear and hazy air greeted him.

Mannie sighed in relief. "Jess. We're clear." He let up on the accelerator and let the Jeep get back to regular cruising speed.

"Really?" Her eyes opened and a weak smile lit her face.

"Sorry." Jess stared behind her as the terror retreated in the distance. "Silly little girl, I guess."

"Fear is… A little fear is a healthy thing." He'd started to say, *Fear is how you know you're alive.* Something his XO used say. He used to say it, too.

Mannie thought he'd passed all that machismo shit. He could have avoided the fire, spent several more hours taking the long way around, but when the stress kicked in the old tapes played.

Jess was quiet.

The sun was going down by the time they hit old Route 66, now I-40, at Cline's Corner. They picked up salisbury steak dinners from the mini-mart and cooked them in a double-wide mobile home next door. They needed the stove. Mannie walked in. The door was unlocked, no bodies, no scent of decay.

After dinner, Mannie finished his Coke. "Less than an hour to

Albuquerque? You wanna go on or sleep here?"

Jess' face twisted up a bit. "I'm okay either way, but I'd rather sleep in a motel. Seems weird sleeping in someone else's bed—like they might show up at any time. I know it's not reasonable, but…"

"No, I understand. Let's move on then." He tossed the can in the garbage on the way out the door.

As they hit the highway Jess pointed at a sign that said Historic Route 66, and started singing, "'Get your kicks on Route 66.'"

When she ran out of words. Mannie sang the first verse; she joined him on the chorus. By the time he ended the song he was grinning, his feelings of stress from the fire faded. "*Mi abuelo*, my grandpa, Luís, came out West from Chicago on Route 66."

"Cool." An embarrassed smile crossed Jess' face. "I only know it from *Cars*, that Pixar movie?"

"Might be hard to believe, but I'm not old enough to remember the original song either."

They rolled out of the Sandia mountains to a pink and orange sky. Mannie wasn't sure which was more glorious, the brilliant sunset or the sprinkling of electric lights in Albuquerque. "Okay, first big city. I don't know what to expect."

Her head swiveled, her eyes fearful again. "What do you mean?"

"Nothing." *Keep her calm, Mannie.* "I don't know. We're, uh, likely to see people. Every place isn't going to be as nice as San Angelo. Let's be cautious."

On the eastern edge of the city they found a bunch of hotels. "Super 8?" Mannie asked. "Beats a Motel 6. Or America's Best?"

"Just a sec. Let me check my phone." Her fingers flew. "There's a Hilton Garden Inn, a bit farther. Twice the price. And more stars."

"Not sure I can afford it." It felt good to smile again after a long intense day.

Jess directed him from her phone's GPS. The place looked like every other mass-produced hotel chain. "I hope it's more impressive inside." He pulled up to the valet parking sign.

"Me, too." Jess snatched her duffel bag and jogged into the well-lit lobby.

Mannie pulled his rucksack from the back and followed more slowly, stretching his legs and massaging his knee.

Jess stood behind the counter. "I got the computer and the key machine going."

"Think you could get us two rooms adjacent?" Mannie leaned over the counter. "If they're not too full."

Her fingers tapped the keyboard. "Better. Here's a room with two double beds, microwave and fridge. Computer says it has a view."

He hesitated. "I'm not sure—"

"Mannie. This is a big city. You said yourself that we should be more cautious. And after today I can't handle another second of being scared."

"Okay, if it'll make you feel better. I'm knocked out. Haven't driven that much in years. I need a bed to collapse into. Where's the room?"

"Third floor."

Mannie trudged toward the elevator. The lobby's fancy tile and woodwork caused him to chuckle, like they wanted you to think the hotel was old and prestigious. He punched the button for the elevator then changed his mind and took the stairs. They were a contrast to the rest of the hotel, painted cinderblocks and pipes. He was going to take better care of himself and get back in shape. How many doctors had survived?

"Boo!" Jess popped out of the elevator.

"Jesucristo!" Mannie had his rucksack halfway in the air to attack. She grinned at him and jogged down the hall.

Just let me sleep. The room was clean, everything perfectly in its place awaiting the next paying customer. Mannie took the first double. He sat on the bed, tossed the note about towels and room service in the garbage. He slid inside the bedding and debated taking off his pants. No. Who cares about messing up this bed?

Jess bounced on the other bed, then went to the balcony and pulled back the curtains. "The mountains are lovely. Sunrise should be nice. Do you mind if I leave them open?"

Mannie turned to look. The light from the setting sun etched the tips of the peaks against the darkening sky. "Nope. Not going to keep me awake." Evening stars were shining in the blue.

"I've never stayed in a hotel this nice." Jess slipped under the covers. "G'night, Mannie."

"Good night."

21

LIZZIE COULDN'T STOP THINKING ABOUT her dad, though he and the nurse both said there was nothing to worry about. The drive south had been quiet, but Saj was getting fussy. He squirmed, whining. She sniffed his diaper, nothing. Maybe he sensed her mood. Or maybe he was tired of riding in the car seat. She didn't blame him; her butt was sore, too.

"Zach?" Lizzie leaned forward. "Can I get some driving in?"

"Hey," Nev said, "Me, too."

Zach glanced back at her in the rear view mirror. "Sure." He pulled the Tank to the side of the road and hopped out.

"Nev," Lizzie asked, "you got Saj?"

"Yeah." Nev got in back. "How's my little buddy?"

Lizzie climbed up into the driver's seat, a lot farther from the ground than the CRV or anything else she'd ever tried to drive. "This thing is a monster."

Zach got into the passenger seat. "It's a gentle giant. You point it, give it a little gas and it goes where you tell it."

"Everybody belted in?" Lizzie adjusted the mirrors. She could see Saj focus on Nev, quiet for the moment. "Saji? Sissie's gonna drive!" She took a deep breath and depressed the accelerator. The motor revved, but nothing happened. She looked over at Zach in the passenger seat, a pained look on his face.

"You're in park and your e-brake's on."

Lizzie nodded, popped the emergency brake release and pulled the shift into drive. She pressed the gas pedal and they rolled forward.

Zach nodded. "Here we go."

Nev laughed. "I'm glad I went without a driver in the car. I did the same thing."

A few random cars sat on the side of the road; some had dates in neon orange paint on the windows, now faded in the sun. After a few miles Lizzie had the Tank up to the speed limit. She felt barely in control. The power steering was too loose and easy for such a big vehicle; with a slight delay, it had a sliding bounce. Once going the freeway driving was much easier than stop and go in a city.

Cars rolled north on the other side of the highway in long intervals. Like her group they were full of people. The first one was exciting, a miracle, like the tigers. It felt weird. In the old days the highway would have been full of cars with single people. Now folks were coming together, even if they were strangers. But wasn't everybody alive kind of family?

In her experience family wasn't what it should have been: Jerkwad, Mama and her father. Even her little brother was an annoying jerk most of the time. The friends she chose usually treated her better than family. And they didn't understand why she didn't trust anyone. Now everybody alive was part of a big dysfunctional family and keeping distance made sense. C.J. was an example of that dysfunction. She kept glancing in the rear view mirror, expecting to see his brother coming after her. But the highway behind was always empty.

Her shoulders were tense and eventually her hands were cramping. "Think I'm done. All tired and achy." She felt like she'd been driving for hours, but it looked like about 25 minutes. She pulled off I-5 near the Ft. Lewis exit and jumped down from the driver's seat.

"Relax next time," Zach said. "You did good. Nev? You wanna drive through Olympia?"

"Yeah, sure." She climbed into the driver's seat. She sat there for a minute and then spoke, not to Lizzie or Zach, but to the windshield. "I want to stop in Tumwater. Check in on the folks I stayed with. Tell them I'm okay. Lizzie? You all right with that?"

"Of course." Why did Nev think she would throw a fit? She understood Nev wanting to check on her temporary family. *I'm not that bad, am I?* Lizzie was too exhausted to give it more thought.

Nev switched the radio back on, some sort of techno dance station, but at least it didn't have many words.

She lay the seat back and tried to follow Saj's lead and take a nap, but every little jog of the Tank pulled her awake. Once her tired brain convinced her that Nev was driving them off a cliff. The next time C.J. and his brother were pulling her from her seat. So much for sleep. She played through her messages from Mama and the videos of Jayce.

Saj napped with the peaceful abandon of a toddler, his fist curled around her thumb. She smiled and watched his eyelids flutter at some pleasant dream. Instead of trying to find her own peace she immersed herself in his. She tuned out the passing scenery, the past, and all that lay behind them.

As she finally nodded off, the truck stopped. Lizzie sighed and pulled herself through the haze to reality. She pushed her head away from the window. Had she slept? They must have gotten through Olympia to Tumwater. Nev jumped out and jogged over to a nondescript, brown split-level house.

Lizzie wiped the fog her breath had formed on the window. A middle-aged couple answered the door, a stream of children poured out, bouncing around Nev. Lizzie watched the scene through the smeared wet glass, like something out of a movie—the perfect family reunion.

Then Nev turned and waved at the truck. She ran back and patted Zach's window. He rolled it down.

"They've invited us for dinner," Nev said, out of breath. "Did you know today is Thanksgiving? Whattaya say?"

Lizzie shrugged. "We gotta eat somewhere." Maybe this Turkey Day wouldn't end up with drunk people yelling at each other.

"You know me," Zach added, "I'm always hungry." He climbed out and let Spike out of the back seat. Spike squatted staring at all the people.

Lizzie caught Zach's eye as Nev ran back to the house. *Not too long,* she mouthed and tapped the back of Jayce's watch. "I'll wait out here until Saj wakes up, 'kay?" He gave her a thumbs-up and followed Nev.

Saj stirred. Lizzie cooed at him and rubbed the bridge of his nose to keep him asleep. Spike cocked his head sideways watching her. "You don't want to go in either, do you, Spike?" His head changed sides, still staring. Lizzie let Saj sleep. Zach came out with deviled eggs and rolls. She took an egg and swallowed it in two bites, the peppery paprika taste burned pleasantly. "Thanks."

"No problem." Zach fed Spike an egg. It disappeared in a bite and Spike's mouth was open again.

Zach placed a roll in his hand. "Dinner's ready in a few minutes."

"Great." Lizzie said. Saj stirred and whined as his eyes opened. "How is it in there?"

Zach gave a noncommittal, "Fine."

She unstrapped Saj and pulled him out. She tried to put him down to walk, but he clung to her. "Me, too, baby."

Zach waved another roll at Spike, "Come on, Spike, more food." Spike followed Zach and the food toward the house.

Lizzie followed Spike inside the house, Zach's "fine" was chaotic. There were people everywhere. And they were all watching her.

Nev introduced her to the ad hoc parents: Reverends Josie and John.

Were they a couple? Lizzie couldn't really tell. They seemed like two sweet, forgiving, churchy types. She nodded and smiled, awkward in the sudden overwhelming volume of people. "Nev, could you take Saj? I've got to use the restroom."

In the bathroom she splashed water on her face and ran her fingers through her hair. "Gotta eat sometime," she muttered and sat on the toilet seat. She took a deep breath. How offended would Nev be if Lizzie took a pass on Thanksgiving dinner? *If I was her I'd be very offended.*

"Supper's ready," a voice called from the other room.

With regret, Lizzie left the quiet bathroom and walked to the front room. There were two tables, a big one nearly full and a smaller table through an arch into the living room. The children clustered around the smaller one.

Lizzie went to Nev and held out her hands for Saj. "I'll eat with Spike and the kids."

Nev handed over Saj to Lizzie with a quizzical look. "Okay."

The adults were still staring and Lizzie didn't feel like talking about herself.

In spite of her mood, the kids brightened the meal. She asked them their names in between bites. Cristina and Consuela, twins, 12. Joshua, age 9; James, age 6; She could play the painful adult who asks questions. But she couldn't ask her first question, *How had all the siblings survived?* Genetic immunities maybe.

"I hate yams," Joshua said, pushing them onto his brother's plate.

James screwed up his face. "I don't like them neither."

"You eat 'em or I'll tell mom about you-know-what."

James sank down. Lizzie hadn't taken any yams, so she scooped half of them off James' plate. His face broke into a grin. She put her finger to her lips. *Don't tell.*

"When baby Jesse's eating solid food," Joshua said, as if it was the law of the universe. "you can make him eat your yams."

"This is delicious." Lizzie had never tasted a turkey with that much flavor.

One of the 12 year-old twins spoke up. "We raised that turkey with my brother Gerardo." Her sister glared and her mouth pursed. They both looked ready to burst into tears.

What questions are safe? "Well, you did a good job," Lizzie said, ladling more mashed potatoes in Saj's bowl. He loved them, but not with the gravy. Spike lapped up the gravy gratefully and ignored the potatoes.

The kids were energized, but subdued. If they got a little loud one of the older ones would shush them. Only one was not talking. A boy, brown-eyed, dark-haired kid about 10 years old, couldn't keep his deep eyes off her. "What's your name?" He reminded her of herself at big gatherings.

"He's Charley," said Cristina/Consuela in a snide, know-it-all voice. "Doesn't talk, though."

"Prob'bly can't." muttered a voice at the other end of the table.

Lizzie ignored the rest of the children and spoke to him directly, "Do you like yams?" His yams were nothing but an orange slime trail on his plate.

Charley busied himself with his food.

"My friends and I are going to meet my Dad. He's coming up from Texas. Where are you from, Charley?"

He continued staring at the food and shoveling it in.

Oh, well. Sometimes you lose.

Lizzie caught him staring during the meal and she smiled at him, but he always shied away. From the other room she heard talk of heading down toward Centralia; there was a church group down there that was sending people out to bring in the flock. *Even the chosen don't know where to go or what to do.*

As the kids finished, they took their plates, and politely excused themselves. Charley still stared at Lizzie.

She went around the table and sat down next to him. "Is there something you want to ask me?"

His head nodded. Barely whispering, "Yes."

She'd gotten a response. *Sometimes you win.* "Well," Lizzie said, "Just ask. I'm not going to hurt you."

He stared at his shoes. Then slightly louder than before, he asked, "Can I go with you?"

"What do you mean? Why would you want to come with us?"

His head came up. His eyes held tears threatening to fall. "My grandpa lives in New Mexico. He's the only family I've got left."

"Oh." Lizzie frowned. "Charley, we're not going that far. Only to Salt Lake City, Utah."

"But…" He gritted his teeth. His hands turned to fists. "Can you take me part way?"

"How old are you?"

"Twelve."

"Do you know how far it is from Salt Lake City to New Mexico. What city?"

"He lives on the Mescalero Rez."

Lizzie had no idea where Mescalero was or even how far it was from Salt Lake to New Mexico. "Are you native?"

"Yeah. I know I don't look it." His eyes fled again to his feet. "They always tease me at the powwows. I'm half. On my mom's side." His lip trembled and his jaw worked. "I talked to Grandpa a couple weeks ago, but he said the power had been flickering and now I can't reach him."

Lizzie saw his pain. And like hers, there was a possibility to relieve it. But what if Grandpa is already dead?

"I only have a backpack of stuff. And I'm ready to go."

Charley must have seen something slip inside her.

"No promises, Charley. We'll talk to your par—, the Reverends."

Charley's eyes glowed, his stolid silence broken. He pushed his seat back and ran off. *Oh my, Lizzie. What are you, the Pied Piper?* She stood, steeling herself for the conversation.

Charley had found the Reverends; he was animated, pleading his case. The "parents" looked bemused as they listened to him.

Reverend John said, "Charles, I don't think it's a good idea."

Charley's face fell. Lizzie watched him fighting back the tears.

She saw John see it, too. John took a deep breath. Josie stepped forward and put her hand on Charley's shoulder.

"Charley, we," John said, his head motioned to Josie and Lizzie, "the adults, will talk about it."

Charley nodded, his countenance serious.

Oh, God, I'm an adult now? Lizzie's eyes followed Charley as he trudged away.

Josie moved close in to Lizzie. "He seems to connect to you. That's more words than he's spoken here in the last three weeks."

Lizzie nodded, "Yeah. He just opened up."

"Neveah said you were meeting your father in Salt Lake City?" John asked. "That's not New Mexico."

"I know." Lizzie bit her tongue to keep the tang from her voice. "And his grandfather might not even be alive."

There was sadness in John and Josie's eyes. They meant well. She could see why Neveah wanted to leave and why she wanted to come back by. Her thought from earlier returned in a new context. *The shepherds don't know what to do for their flock.*

"My father is from Texas. Once we meet him we'll make sure Charles gets to his family." *What the hell am I promising?* "If we can't find them, he'll be part of ours."

She observed the interplay of unspoken words between the Reverends. Living with Jerkwad and Mama had given her skills at sensing others feelings and intentions.

John turned to her, smiling. "We will allow you to take him. If you promise to keep him safe and get him to his grandfather."

"And let us know where he is," Josie added. "Neveah knows how to reach us."

"Thank you," Lizzie said with sincerity. Taking Charley felt like relief for them. *Do they really have Charley's best interests in mind if they'll let him go with me?* She wondered if her intentions were any better. At least she wanted to help him get what he wanted.

"I'll tell Charley and help him pack." Josie hurried off.

Nev and Zach stepped into the room, looking happy and sedated by the turkey. Zach fixed his eyes on Lizzie. "What's up?"

"We've got another passenger south," Lizzie said.

Zach shrugged with the same look he'd given her when she found Saj and brought Spike home.

"Who?" Nev asked.

Charley burst into the room, nearly knocking Lizzie over with a hug. Then as quick, he pulled away. "Where do I put my stuff?"

Nev smiled. "Charley. You going with us?"

He nodded, grinning.

Lizzie felt her own smile growing. She knew she'd made the right choice. "You'll have to ride in the back with Spike, the dog-man."

"That'll be fine. I used to have a big dog myself. Got hit by a truck. We had to put him down." He hugged the Reverends.

"Go with God, Charles," John said.

But John was looking at Lizzie when he said it. A chill passed through her. *So help me, God.* She hoped she had the strength to follow through.

After all the goodbyes they headed out to the Tank with Charley and Spike following. The Reverend Josie handed Nev a box of food, leftovers for the trip.

They finished Thanksgiving driving toward Portland.

When they reached the Columbia River in Vancouver, Zach slammed his hands on the dashboard. "We weren't supposed to get to Portland. Must have missed the turn off."

"It's okay, Zach." Nev placed her hand on his shoulder. "We can't be far off track. You're tired. It's been a long day. Let's find someplace to sleep."

"Nev's right," Lizzie said. "Go until there's a hotel."

Zach took a deep breath. "Okay." Then he jerked the tank onto an off-ramp. "It says East, let's go until we hit 205 or a hotel." The off-ramp wound in a tight loop. The Tank tipped.

"Zach," Lizzie said, her voice tight, "You can slow down."

"Okay," he said again.

Lizzie could hear the stress in his voice. *Chill out, Zach.* She dared not say it out loud. Too much testosterone.

The Tank slowed through the turn and then Zach accelerated on the straightway.

Nev put her hand back on Zach's shoulder and squeezed it. "Relax, buddy. We're so glad you're driving, right Lizzie?"

"Yeah, Zach."

Zach released his hands one at a time flexing them get out the tightness.

In a couple minutes Zach pointed to a Holiday Inn Express sign. "How's that?"

"Looks great." Lizzie said.

Zach pulled into the parking lot, drove up to the front door, and came to a hard stop. The doors opened. "Your rest for the night, folks." He yawned, stretched his arms and got out.

"Thanks, Zach," Lizzie said. "Let's get inside. Nev and I will scope out rooms. Charley, can you help Zach and Spike bring stuff inside?"

"Hey, it's got a pool and a hot tub." Nev pointed at a sign with people cavorting in the water. "We should hit the hot tub."

Zach lugged in the duffel bags. "Sounds awesome."

"Go ahead," Lizzie said. "I'm beat."

They got into three rooms in a row, propped open for cleaning. The beds had already been made and the only setup was rolling the maid's cart out.

Lizzie ushered Charley and Spike into the first room. "You two," she motioned to them, "can sleep over there in the far double bed." She put Saj's car seat on the other double.

Charley led Spike to the bed and pulled the covers back. "Shoes off." He pulled Spike's big size 13 shoes off. "You sleep here. I'll be right next to you, Spike." Charley tucked Spike in, ran around the bed, snuggled in and pulled the blankets up.

Lizzie, Zach and Nev unloaded duffels.

Zach came up beside Lizzie and put his hand on her shoulder. "So cute. Gives new meaning to the term 'a boy and his dog.'"

"I thought Charley was a dog-person, too," Nev said. "He never spoke."

"Guess you can't judge a book…"

"Yeah." Nev hugged Lizzie, "You sure you don't want some time in the hot tub or pool?"

"Nah. I'm going to follow the boys' example."

"All right, we'll check on you before we head to our rooms," Zach said.

"Yeah," Nev said. "Night."

Lizzie's heart twisted as she watched Zach take Nev's hand. She threw her stuff on the other bed. *Well, they're both lovely people.* Logic said she had nothing to be upset about. Logic didn't help. Saj fussed and wiggled in his car seat. "Hey, don't cry."

22

THE SUN ROSE OVER THE Sandia Mountains as amazing as Jess had predicted. The black edge stood out against the yellow fire of the sun as it faded to rusty orange in the clouds. Mannie slipped out the door and down the hall, letting the door close firmly. She'd be up by the time he got back. He found the exercise area and was pleased that the key card Jess had made opened the door.

There was a pool and a hot tub. With a twinge of regret for not having swim trunks, he stripped down to his boxers and stepped into the pool. The water was cool, but not bracing cold. He dove horizontally away from the wall and pulled himself down toward the bottom before kicking gently forward. At the other end he did a kick turn and headed back. He focused on the breath, the stroke and kick. After a couple dozen strong laps he pulled himself out and walked, dripping to the hot tub. His knee didn't feel too bad this morning. *If I did my exercises, maybe it wouldn't be a problem.*

After a shower in the locker room, he pulled on his pants, leaving the boxers hanging on the faucet—going commando. He grimaced and adjusted as he walked down the tiled hall.

Mannie found the staff room and started coffee in the full-sized coffee maker. While it brewed he found the Business Center and got on the Internet to see if there was any new information about the disease and or recovery. What Lizzie had said about Seattle sounded good.

The news of the world hadn't changed. He tried ABC, CNN,

Reuters and finally BBC. BBC had a new headline. "Survivors Unite!" The subheading caught his eye. "If you are alive now the disease will not kill you." Something inside him relaxed. He and Lizzie had survived. He got up to get coffee. But why? Another reason to not believe in a god who would let him live and kill so many others.

With fresh coffee in hand, black with lots of sugar, he skimmed the rest of the article. A handful of surviving epidemiologists had been working together on-line. Certain species of animals—bonobos, orangutans and chimpanzees—had suffered similar fates. But the disease had done its work and the belief was that in doing so had killed itself off.

A week-old article suggested English districts send representatives to a new ad hoc Parliament. Mannie searched for similar information in the U.S. but found nothing. Maybe when Jess was up she'd have more luck. He wasn't bad for his age, but kids seemed to find what they were looking for faster.

When he returned to the room, Jess was sitting on the bed fully clothed and drying her hair. "You eaten?"

"Just coffee."

"Seems a little gritty for breakfast."

"The liquid version. There's more downstairs if you want."

Jess did have more luck on the Internet. "Two surviving members of Congress, Hilda Solis of California and Jack Schlossberg of New York."

Mannie chuckled. "East meets West."

"Does that make one the President and the other the Vice President?" Jess asked.

"Not a damn clue. Do they have a plan?" Mannie leaned over her shoulder, squinting. A grainy photo of an older woman and a young man accompanied the post. Without his reading glasses, he could only read the bold print. "He's a Kennedy. Breaking the curse?"

"They're suggesting people head for population centers."

"Well," Mannie said, "I guess we're doing that."

"New Mexico Governor says report to State Universities, including UNM in Albuquerque."

"I wondered why we saw no one in a city this size." He had no time or patience to deal with local bureaucracy. "I want to get to Lizzie."

Jess nodded. "Me, too."

They scrounged breakfast at a mini-mart and picked up all the items on Mannie's shopping list before hitting the road. The drive proved even less interesting than the previous day. The scrub brush and plateaus were lovely at first, but monotonous eventually. Odd formations jutted out from time to time, red rock cliffs and broken lands pushed up by some cataclysm.

In the afternoon they pulled into Mancos, Colorado. Mannie's knee needed a stretch and Jess wanted to explore in a new state. It was a small town; he could walk the whole length.

"All right, you go, but be back in 15?"

Jess' smile lit her face. "I will." She jogged away from him, her cowboy boots clunking on the pavement.

Mannie crossed the street to a natural foods store. He opened the door to an overwhelming wave of rotting food. He stepped in anyway.

The door opened behind him. He turned to see Jess, a sheepish smirk on her face. "Thought I'd wait to explore with you."

"Okay." In the produce section he found something not rotten yet. "Hey, Jess. Washington apples. He bit into one; it tasted bland, but great compared to the fruit he hadn't been eating. He tossed one to Jess and she did the same her smirk turning to a grin as she wiped juice off her face. The putrid stench drove them back outside, but he took the rest of the good apples in a basket. He left them in the Jeep while Jess continued up the dusty street.

The motorcycle shop across the street caught Mannie's eye. He hadn't liked motorcycles since burning his leg on the manifold of a dirt bike as a kid. Too dangerous, but he did like the idea of an escape pod if the jeep broke down. Maybe he should find a bicycle. Better than on foot, but in the snow? Brrr. A snowmobile would be good.

A crash pulled his attention off the bikes. "Jess?" he hollered. Another smash kicked in his adrenaline. He hobbled back to the Jeep and pulled the 870 shotgun from its case. More crashes echoed from the Mancos Liquors building. The front window shattered as a large bottle of wine exploded. A big, jacked-up 4X4 with giant tires and a gun rack was parked half on the curb outside.

"Jess?" Mannie stepped to the door and cocked the shotgun. "What's going on in there?"

"Nobody named Jess in here. Go away." Another crash. "'This

land is my land,'" Sang the drunken voice. "This land ain't your land. Get off of my land, go back to your land."

"Shit." If Jess was in there he needed to know. *Why mess with a drunk in a liquor store at the end of the world?* Then there was a scream. *That's why.* Mannie kicked the door open and stepped into the dim light of the store.

His eyes adjusted as a bottle burst at his feet, splattering his shoes with red wine. He could see two people at the back of the store. A large Native American—the singer—with a long dark braided ponytail stood over a dark-eyed woman on the ground glaring up at him. The taller shape had a bottle raised over his head prepared to throw. "Don't throw that." Mannie scanned the store for any sign of Jess.

"Well, I'll be a monkey's uncle." The big guy, tossed the bottle to the side. "If it ain't the Lone Ranger."

Mannie sighed. Maybe wearing the uniform was a bad choice. "Step away from the woman."

"She's my wife, Lone Ranger."

"Take it easy." Mannie used his calm, warm voice. "I'm not here to cause trouble. Ma'am. Could you step away from him?"

The big man spit in his direction. "This ain't your land, spic. Just 'cause you got a gun."

"Do I look like the people who stole your land?" Mannie's jaw tightened. "Jesus, we're both Native Americans; my tribe's just further south than yours."

"Fuck you. I ain't your Tonto, Lone Ranger."

Mannie's long fuse was burning shorter. "I'm not your enemy; that bottle is. Now, get away from the woman." He took a step forward, carefully staying on the doormat and off the wine-slick tile.

"Randy, I think you pissed him off." The woman tried to stand, but slipped in the puddle of booze on the floor.

She didn't look too stable, either. She grabbed a big plastic bottle of vodka and used it to regain her balance. She stumbled toward Mannie.

"Blackhawk's not bad when he ain't drunk." She stepped behind Mannie,

He turned to let her pass, watching her carefully. He remembered in domestic violence training, they said the cops often got hurt.

The big man picked up an open bottle and took another drink. He sat heavily. "Fuck you, Lone Ranger."

"Okay, Blackhawk? I'm going to leave and give your wife a ride someplace north a bit. Next town."

The big guy looked away.

"When you're sober enough to get there…"

Blackhawk grabbed another glass wine bottle, a big liter and a half. He held it up like he was going to throw it.

"Don't." Mannie heard the jeep start up outside. *Shit. If that woman is stealing my rig..* He grabbed the doorknob and ran out. He heard the wine bottle smash on the door behind. "Stupid drunk!"

Jess had the jeep rolling toward him and the door open. "Come on, Mannie, want a ride?" She grinned broadly.

Mannie glanced back at the building. No sign of pursuit . He turned to the giant 4X4 and shot a round into the front tire. It gasped and the truck sunk down. Mannie jogged to the jeep and swung himself up into the passenger seat. The woman from the liquor store was in the back seat giggling.

Mannie jerked the door shut as Rubi surged forward. Jess wasn't too good with the clutch. As they rounded the corner, he saw the door of the liquor store open and the big man stumbled out. He had a wine bottle in each hand and he threw them after the retreating Jeep. There was a crash behind them. Jess swung Rubi hard to the right; the tires screeched a bit, but in seconds she was it up to speed and headed north.

"Thanks, Jess." Mannie buckled his seatbelt. "Nice timing."

"Seemed like you needed some help. Mannie, this is BeeGee," Jess said, pointing to the woman in the back seat. "BeeGee. Mannie."

"BeeGee?"

"B dot G. Baby Girl. Mom had 13 kids, I's last. Lucky one I guess." She held her hand out.

Mannie looked at her hand, wet and sanitized with liquor. "I got a bite on my hand. Can't shake. Blackhawk's really your husband?"

"'fraid so. Not so bad when he's not drinkin'. Course all we been doin' is drinkin'."

Mannie felt under the seat for the towel he used to clean the dust off the windows. He handed it back to her. "You can wipe up with this some. I told Blackhawk I'd let you off at the next town. If you wanted. We're heading to Salt Lake. You're welcome to hitch a ride."

"I'll think about it." She twisted the cap off the vodka bottle from the store and offered Mannie the first drink.

The stressed and adrenalized part of him wanted the drink, the burn, then the buzz. He held his hand up. "No, thanks. I'm dry." He turned back to Jess. "You okay driving this thing?"

She nodded. "I'm okay for a while. I'd like to drive it in less stressful conditions." Her hands gripped tight on the wheel.

"Thanks for the ride. Be good for me to steer clear of him for a while." BeeGee's voice steadied. "You can drop me in Dolores, up the road a way."

"You don't have to stay in the next town," Mannie said. "We don't even have to stop."

"Yeah, we do," Jess said. "If we're driving much farther tonight, I want you behind the wheel."

"Okay. We'll stop," Mannie turned back to BeeGee, "and get some food. You can stay or you can come with us."

"Oh, yeah," Jess gushed. "Guess what? I forgot in the rush. Today's Thanksgiving."

"Really?" Mannie laughed. "Not sure we have a lot to be thankful for, but we're still here."

A dry chuckle came from the back seat. "A white woman, a Mexican and an Indian meet on Thanksgiving. Sounds like a joke."

But to Mannie, she didn't appear very amused. He changed the subject. "How long, you figure, before Blackhawk comes looking for you?"

"Tomorrow maybe." Even more sober, she stared out the window at the speeding scenery.

"I want a Thanksgiving dinner," Jess said. She turned her head to Mannie, "Please."

Once again he saw the little girl. "Sure." Mannie put his hand on her shoulder.

Twenty minutes later they pulled into the Naked Moose restaurant in Dolores, Colorado. The power was out and the sun nearly down. Mannie had Jess park behind the restaurant in case BeeGee was wrong and Blackhawk arrived sooner.

Inside in the walk-in freezer Jess found a whole ham still mostly frozen. Since the electric stove was out, Mannie fired the gas grill out on the deck. He wrapped aluminum foil around the ham and put it on the grill.

"I'm going to go see what other Thanksgiving kinds of food I can find," Jess said.

Mannie followed her outside. "Jess, thanks again for the cool head back there."

She nodded. "You're welcome. I'm off to explore."

"Be safe," Mannie said. He retrieved his maps from Rubi's glove box. When he got back inside BeeGee was staring at her phone, intent on playing a game.

Mannie familiarized himself with the next stretch of road: 70 miles before Monticello, then head north to Salt Lake City about 300 miles after that. If everything went well, he might see Lizzie tomorrow.

After about 20 minutes, Jess came back with cans of green beans, fruit cocktail, black olives and Coca-Cola. "The Coke's from your Jeep," she explained, opening the other cans. She tore off the wrapper and stuck the green bean can on the grill. When she lifted the lid smoke billowed out from the juice dripping through the aluminum.

"When we're done eating, we better move on," Jess suggested, setting the table with plates, cloth napkins and silverware. "I can smell that ham for blocks."

Mannie nodded. "Well, I'm pretty wired. I could drive for a while. BeeGee? You want to stay?" He cleared away the maps, folding them neatly.

"I dunno." BeeGee came over and sat down at the table. "Guess, I'll go on for a bit, 'til I decide what to do next. Randy's always been there. Don't really want to be alone."

Something relaxed in Mannie. He understood not wanting to be alone. There was power in numbers. Three's company. And he didn't feel good about leaving BeeGee.

Mannie stepped out onto the porch and turned the gas off on the grill. He wheeled it inside as he heard dogs barking nearby.

Jess wasn't kidding about the ham. By the time it was inside, a pack of dogs circled the yard. One of the dogs, a Shepherd mix, stared brazenly in through the front glass door.

The ham was juicy. He sliced off the burned outer skin and then big slabs fell to his fork. He laid the ham on their plates next to the green beans, olives and fruit cocktail. It wasn't the worst Thanksgiving meal he'd ever had.

Jess said a short blessing.

Mannie closed his eyes and held his tongue.

BeeGee said, "Amen."

They ate with gusto. No one spoke.

The dogs scratched at the door.

Finishing off the last bits of fruit, Mannie said, "Thanks, Jess. That was a great idea."

"Thanks, I..." Jess looked up from her plate; her eyes grew large. "Uh oh."

Mannie spun to the front door. The dogs whimpered and howled. But a larger shadow crossed the glass. A wild-eyed dog-man stared in. "Shit." The pack of dogs was larger than before.

Mannie didn't want to face another rabid attack. He raced to the door and flipped the deadbolt in place. "Okay. Let's throw the food out the front windows and then get out the back door." He took a butcher knife and hacked more of the ham into large hunks. The center was still frozen.

"BeeGee, get the back door open and see if it's clear." He handed the plate of ham to Jess. "Hand 'em to me when I get the window open."

"Only one dog, back here," BeeGee called.

"He'll come around front, I think." Mannie jerked the window aside and shoved the screen out. He tossed the ham past the furthest dog to attract the starved and vacant-eyed creatures. Jess followed suit. The dogs and the dog-man mobbed toward it.

"It's headed around front," BeeGee yelled. "I'm going."

Mannie pushed Jess toward the back door. "Run."

Jess tore toward the back of the restaurant with Mannie close behind. Mannie hopped in Rubi and cranked her up. They spun past the pack as they fought for their meals.

About 15 minutes later they turned onto US 491, BeeGee muttered something and Mannie thought he saw her cross herself in the rear view mirror.

"You okay, BeeGee?"

"Fine." She nodded. "Say your prayers."

"Why?"

"This highway used to be Route 666. It's the real Highway to Hell, The Devil's Road. Weird things happen."

Mannie smirked and Jess stifled a giggle.

"Laugh if you want. There's skinwalkers, dead girls, haunted semis."

"Well," Mannie said, watching BeeGee in the rear view mirror, "there probably are a lot of dead folks hereabouts, but I don't expect to see them."

"If you're lucky," BeeGee said and her focus returned to her phone.

Night darkened fully and with no city lights around the stars came out by the thousands. Mannie drove in silence, they were all lost in their own thoughts. The snow started to fall as he pulled the Jeep in at a motel in Dove Creek, Colorado. He had put as many miles behind them as he could for the day.

23

ON THE WAY BACK FROM the pool area, Zach let Nev lead him by the hand. He watched her towel-wrapped slight curves, walking in front of him, thankful she was in front and perhaps not noticing her effect on him.

"Which room do you want?" Zach asked.

Nev glanced back at him with a grin. She shrugged. "I don't know. Yours?"

Zach had a thousand things he wanted to say. His brain spun through them and nothing at all would come out. "Uh. Shouldn't we tell Lizzie where we'll be?"

"Why? She'll be fine. Or she can find us." Nev pulled him inside and shoved the door closed. "Now shut up and kiss me." Her smile dared him like it always had.

Zach grinned and leaned in. She did not laugh or move away when their lips met. The soft warmth of her lips pushed back against his. Her arms were strong; she'd rubbed his shoulders to try to get him to relax in the hot tub. She wrapped them around him, her hands slipping inside his towel, grabbing his buttocks. *Oh, my.* Then she fell backward, pulling him onto the bed as the towels fell. He kissed down her neck to the spot he'd tickled under her collarbone. The smell of chlorine reminded him of her quick disrobing and her lithe form slipping into the hot tub's bubbles.

He knelt in front of her; her body arched as his lips went lower. He knew she wanted him as much as he wanted her, but then he remembered the mess he and Lizzie had made. Nev's hands held his head to her chest. He could hear her heart pounding. *I don't want to mess this up.* His hold on her relaxed and his breath shuddered out. He wanted her, but he could wait. "Nev," he said, his soft voice hoarse, "Maybe we should just snuggle."

Her hands relaxed. "Yes," she said and exhaled. "Okay."

Zach climbed onto the bed, pulling the sheet over her in the light of the nightlight. She made room, nestling herself under his arm and laying her head on his chest. Her fingers found his, intertwining, squeezing her gentle answer. There would be time for them to make a decision they both might not regret.

Lizzie woke with a calm pleasant feeling she didn't recognize permeating her awareness. Saj's feet were on her stomach and he was pushed out at a right angle. His feet moved, pressing on her bladder. She extricated herself from the sheets. Spike and Charley were tangled in covers and no longer snuggled. As Lizzie padded to the bathroom a smile crept to her lips. *How many more hitchhikers am I going to pick up on the way?*

It was earlier than she was used to being up, so she stripped off her clothes and jumped in the shower. She realized it had been nearly two days since she'd had clean clothes. With clean clothes and her teeth brushed she felt brand new. She wandered next door, but stopped herself before she knocked on the door to Nev's room. *I'll let her sleep.*

Lizzie went back and repacked Saj's diaper bag. Sometime soon they'd either have to do laundry or get more clothes. Whichever was less work. If Nev helped, the shopping would be easier.

She sat down with her notebook and a pen and wrote herself a long diary entry. Partway through, a Creedence Clearwater Revival song insinuated itself into her head and their words turned into her lyrics.

> Cuz we're a travelin' band with our parts to play
> The music is fine when it all goes our way
> But the road it is long and the voices are strange
> That keep telling us all keep your eyes on the road
> Keep your eyes on the road

Whichever way you're going
Keep your eyes on the road
Without you it's still flowing
If you wanna come along, then you can join us
If you wanna wave us past, you don't need to know us
If you wanna little love, come and ride beside us
But keep telling us to keep our eyes on the road.

Her brain heard music. *Damn.* She wished she had a guitar or a bass. She sang the words over and over trying to nail it down. Maybe today they could stop at a music store. It had been a long time since her muse had sung a pleasant song to her. Saj stirred and Lizzie again thought about getting Nev or Zach up, but she could handle it.

A few minutes later there was a soft knock on the door. She opened it to Nev and Zach, both looking fresh and clean. And happy.

"We need to get a guitar today," she whispered, inviting them in, "or a bass. I started a new song."

"Cool," Zach said. "Let's get both? Acoustic maybe? We've got room."

"As long as we don't pick up any more strays," Lizzie said.

Nev smiled and hugged her. Lizzie stiffened as if her calm would go away if she shared it. "What's this for?" she asked, then she softened into the hug and held onto Nev.

"I always wanted to reach Charley." Her eyes strayed to the still sleeping boy. "But he wouldn't let me in. Now he's with us. It feels good."

"Yeah." Lizzie nodded, letting go, the warm calm still infusing everything.

"I'll check for music stores on our way this morning," Nev offered. "There's got to be places in Vancouver."

"The boys" started waking up as the "adults" voices got louder with the excitement and joy. Zach went off in search of continental breakfast; Nev and Lizzie pulled gear together. They were fed and on the road by nine o'clock.

Online, Nev located River City and Sound, a music store nearly on the way. Somebody had broken in before them, but Zach found a Martin Traveler guitar and a Kelly Travel bass. Lizzie carried the bass to the car and worked on translating the sounds in her head onto the fretboard.

Lizzie switched sides to behind Zach so she could turn in her seat and finger the bass without danger of hitting Saj. The bass's hum pulled Saj's attention like a magnet. Whenever she plucked a string his eyes grew and his hands went back and forth on his car seat like he was playing the bongos.

Everything stopped when Zach drove them across the Columbia on I-205. Mount Hood was impressive etched against the sky and the river was wide broken up by islands covered with greenery. To the west, Lizzie could see the airport tower south of the mighty Columbia.

Spike and Charley played some game in the back. She could hear Charley giggling and Spike doing his snorting guffaw from time to time. When her fingers ached and she'd written down the basic notes, she stuck her head over the back seat to check on them. Charley was feeding Spike bits of bacon left over from breakfast. "Whatcha doing, Charley?"

"Teaching Spike to talk." He said it as if she must have been stupid to not realize it.

"But you're not talking," Lizzie said. "Just laughing."

"Watch." Charley tapped the tips of his fingers and thumbs together and then scraped the fingers of his right hand in a circle on his chest. Spike made similar motions and Charley handed him a bacon bit that Spike swallowed. Charley touched his flat palm to his chin and pushed it toward Spike.

"Thank you," Lizzie said. "I know that one."

Spike copied him.

"My brother was mostly deaf. Too many ear infections. So I learned sign language. To talk to him." Charley paused, his lip pursed for a second then beamed. "Used up all the leftovers, but he can do it."

From the front seat Zach laughed. "Awesome. Can you teach him to say, 'I need to go to the bathroom?'"

"I'll work on it," Charley said. "But I'll need more food."

"That'll make sure he has to go!" Zach said. "Win-win."

"How do you say *good job?*" Lizzie asked.

Charley demonstrated: flat hand down into other flat hand and then double fists together.

"Like, *thank you* with a twist." Lizzie practiced.

Charley grinned proudly and told Spike, "Good job," with the signs.

Lizzie said, "Good job to both of you," and added the signs herself.

They both signed "good job" and "thanks" back to her.

"Charley, I think it will help Spike if you say it out loud, too." She turned back around in her seat. "Zach? Think we can stop for something to give Spike in bites?"

The rest of the drive Zach stopped at each rest stop and Charley patiently asked Spike in words and signs if he had to go to the bathroom. *God, I hope this works.*

Spike ate bags of chips and crackers, fruit snacks and cheese sticks, jerky and nuts.

At each stop, Lizzie worked on her new song.

Zach tried to play the chords on the guitar that she suggested, but his fingers were out of shape and the tips soon ached. He promised to play a little every day until they came back. Nev kissed his fingertips when he complained.

Nev danced with Saj, who stood on the ground and bounced. His hands alternated, flapping up and down like he was drumming. His whole face lit up. It was almost as much fun for Zach to watch Nev trying to copy him.

The afternoon culminated with success. Spike said yes, he had to go to the bathroom. They stopped and he did. They all cheered. Lizzie gave Spike a big hug.

Lizzie sidled up to Zach afterward and whispered, "You need to give him a shower."

Great. My favorite. He nodded, his jaw clenched. Something in Lizzie's tone set him off. She was pissed. He could tell. *What the hell had he done this time? Did she think he and Nev had sex last night? Even if nothing really happened?* A heavy sigh escaped his throat. "Somebody else needs to drive for a while. Lizzie?"

"Okay. Sure."

Nev started to get in the back.

"No," Zach said, surprised and instantly regretting the tone in his voice. He softened it. "Nev. You can sit in front. I'm going to sit back here and try to sleep." His hand brushed her hair as she turned away. *Damn it.* Now he'd probably pissed Nev off, too.

Lizzie had a way of making everything into some big drama. And he couldn't really explain to Nev. He could blame it on cleaning up after Spike, but it wasn't the whole truth. *What if Lizzie and Nev talked? Okay. Next chance, I'm coming clean. No bad stuff between me and Nev.* He tried to rest and sleep, but nothing came except more worries. He played the conversation over and over in his head. He could take his chances, but if it came out later? Then it would be really over. She couldn't blame him for being honest, right? He could hear Lizzie's voice. *Don't be naive, Zach.* Of course, Nev could and probably would be pissed even if he was honest. *Still better than this.*

He slept. When the car stopped, he came awake.

"Break time," Lizzie announced. She opened her door and jumped out, heading for the mini-mart at a jog.

"We need to talk," Nev said, getting out of the Tank and slamming the door behind her.

"Shit." Zach turned around. Charley and Spike were staring at him. "What? You heard Lizzie. Break. Everybody out." He shoved his door open and flipped the seat forward. Nev was striding away back down the street toward a rock formation. He didn't know where he was, but he knew he was in trouble. Had Lizzie said something while he was asleep?

He paced, keeping his eyes on Charley and Spike and listening for Saj until Lizzie came out. "I'm going to go talk to Nev."

Lizzie nodded.

Zach jogged in the direction Nev had gone.

"Thanks for not leaving the kids alone," Lizzie called after him.

He found a park with an outdoor pool and a skate park in the distance. The slim girl he sought, sat with her head down on a picnic table under a kite-shaped white shade. He slowed to a walk as he got close. He wanted to put his hands on her shoulders and rub the tension away, but he had no idea how she would react. He went around the other side and sat down. "Hey."

"Hey," Nev answered, not looking up.

"Let's talk."

"Go ahead, Zach."

He sat, his brain reeling through words he wanted to say and a lot that he didn't. He grabbed some and spit them out. "Lizzie and I slept together."

He didn't see any response from Nev. He felt all wound up, a ball of fear. He had to explain.

"Before I called you. When we thought we were like the only people left."

Nev raised her head up and looked at him, staring into his eyes.

Zach met her gaze. "It was weird. We're both pretending it didn't happen."

"And doing a pretty shitty job of that," Nev said.

"Yeah." Zach's heart beat fast. He wanted to hold her. Promise her... Promise her almost anything. Instead, he agreed. "I'm sorry."

"Me, too." Nev got up and walked toward the skate park.

"Can I come with you?"

"Only if you want to," Nev said, her voice soft.

He slid out from the picnic table and ran to catch up. Her hand dangled at her side. When they reached the trees, he grasped it gently.

She didn't pull away. "Is that why you didn't sleep with me last night?"

Zach walked along, thinking, feeling her hand holding his. "I didn't want to fuck it up."

"Good plan." Nev glanced over at him, tears in her eyes, but a bit of glow and a half smile. "What're you going to do about Lizzie?"

"I don't know. Talk to her, I guess."

"Good idea."

Behind them, the Tank pulled up near the slides and swings. Lizzie was calling to the boys, "Park. It's a park."

"Spike, let's play *Hide and Seek*," Charley hollered.

Nev and Zach walked away from the skate park and into the lightly wooded area.

"I'll get stuff out for lunch," Lizzie called after them. Nev waved and Zach copied her.

"Talk to her. We've hardly been on the road and it's already unbearable."

"It's not a picnic for me," Zach said. "But, yeah. I get it. Lizzie will be fine. I'm worried about you. And me. Us."

Nev turned to him, her lip twitched and the tears fell. She leaned toward him, her hand slid behind his head and tugged his face down toward her. Their lips met. "That's why I need you to talk to her."

Zach wrapped his arms around her and held her tight, letting their lips rest together, touching. Then she buried her face in his chest and squeezed him back.

They wandered, enjoying each other's company. Zach contemplated what he would say to Lizzie.

They wound back toward the playground on the trails, kissing once more before they came out in the open. Nev dropped his hand.

Lizzie had opened the care package box filled with food carefully placed in recycled yogurt and sour cream containers. There was sliced turkey and bread, olives and pickles, cranberry sauce and carrots. The three musketeers watched the boys play. Zach helped Saj get up onto the play pieces. Saj loved the bouncy bridge because when he jumped this time he went up and down. Nev and Lizzie didn't seem to be talking.

Zach watched Lizzie when it was her turn, spinning Saj up in the air. Nev was more sedate, patiently walking him up and down the stairs, swinging with him wrapped in her arms.

When Saj fussed and the wind picked up, Zach called to Charley, "Olly, olly all in free." Charley and Spike came rushing back, all red faced and laughing.

"I taught Spike," Charley blurted, "Run, Hide and Stay!"

"Good job," Zach said.

Lizzie echoed him and signed it.

They packed the Tank and Zach returned to the driver's seat. Nev took shotgun and Lizzie sat in back. There was no discussion; it just happened.

The sun set as Zach drove into La Grande. A big temporary traffic sign flashed. GO TO EOU. WE HELP U. "Hey, we need a place to spend the night…"

There was no audible response from either of the girls.

"The university seems as good a place as any—assuming it has dorms." Zach took the exit to the City Center.

As they got nearer, spray painted arrows repeated the directions. GO TO THE QUINN COLISEUM. 6th & G Streets. Zach followed the arrows and parked in the lot outside the Coliseum. Everyone got out of the car and stretched their legs. "I'm gonna go check out what's at the end of the arrows. Who wants to come with me?" He looked at Nev, hoping to get more alone time together.

But Nev jerked her head toward Lizzie. Zach groaned inwardly.

Nev was going to "fix" things with Lizzie by sticking them together.

He walked toward Nev, intent on dragging her with him. He pleaded with his eyes, trying for a puppy dog look. But before he got to her, she lifted up Saj like a barrier between them and said, "I'll stay with the kids. You and Lizzie go."

"Uh—sure," Zach said.

Lizzie rolled her eyes and set off ahead of him, following the arrows. He had to run to catch her.

"Lizzie, wait up," Zach called. He caught up with her inside the foyer. A bi-fold sign said, "This way" with an arrow. "Lizzie. Stop." Zach heard his father's angry voice in his words.

Lizzie spun around. "What, Zach? I know you didn't want to come with me. You want to be here with Nev." She shook her head and turned to walk away.

"Hold it." Zach didn't try to keep the anger out of his voice. "You said it didn't mean anything. You said, 'We can stay friends.' You spewed all the things I told you years ago right back at me. Now, when Nev and I might have something starting you go all jealous on me?"

Lizzie glared at him. He watched her mouth working. "Fuck you, Zach. I'm not jealous. I'm lonely and I'm scared and if you and Nev hook up, what am I? A baby sitter or a fifth wheel?" She ran down the hallway following the arrows on the floor.

"Well, shit." Zach strode after her. "It won't happen," Zach called. "You'll find somebody."

Lizzie stood staring at a spray painted X in the middle of a basketball court.

"I'm sorry," Zach said, quiet in this gymnasium. He stood behind her and scanned the empty seats.

"Maybe we're too late," Lizzie said.

"We're not too late. Nev's cool. We can make it work."

"Not that, dummy." She motioned to the empty room. "I mean too late for whatever the arrows mean. But where are the bodies?"

Loudspeakers boomed a deep male voice. "Welcome. How can I help you?"

24

THE MOTEL WAS COLD, BUT when Mannie turned the heaters on in the room, they rattled to life, spewing stale heat. The women each took one of the double beds and Mannie slept on the couch, not bothering to pull it out.

He woke around midnight to nature's call, pulled on his pants to answer and then went for a quick look around. Outside in the quiet street, the snow had started to fall. He stepped out into the silence. Holding out his hand he felt the tiny specks of cold hit and melt. The day had been long and eventful. "The damn planet's nearly empty and we're still fighting amongst ourselves." He sighed and let the snow swirling around the street lamps calm him. Eventually the cold bit through his clothes.

In the distance he could hear dogs barking, or were they coyotes? He saw shapes coming toward him in the storm. As they got closer he could see they were dogs, baring their teeth and growling. At least they weren't skinwalkers.

Mannie hustled back inside and crawled back into the now-cool bed.

But sleep would not overtake him yet. The strange dogs and the question of ghosts… What had happened with the virus? Where had is gone? How was it safe? He'd studied evolutionary biology when he got his eco-science degree at Huxley. The red queen had advanced. Could there really be a virus that would act so fast as to kill itself? Or was it simply waiting for a critical mass of uninfected, unexposed humans to reassert itself. Would the disease be coming after humanity for all time? Or could it really have killed itself off? It didn't seem like usual Darwinian behavior.

A chill raced across his skin. Had it been Mother Nature or pure human stupidity, pride, folly? The idea that humans could have taken the power of the gods into their own hands. Had this been a military weapon gone awry? He might never know. No one might ever know. But whomever, Mother Nature or human beings who had set this virus in motion, it had risen like a shooting star, burning itself out just to keep itself alive.

God grant me the serenity… His thoughts chased themselves around in his head until his brain was tired enough to fall asleep.

Zach wanted a gun. He wanted to run. It reminded him of too many movies with psychos. "This is too weird."

"We followed your frickin' signs. How can we help you?" Lizzie hollered.

"I can hear you with your normal voices," the baritone voice said. "Yes, this is weird. I'm not actually here, but I can see you."

"What the hell?" Zach pulled at Lizzie. She set her stubborn feet and glared.

"I can answer your questions. Please answer some of mine," the voice said.

"Okay," Lizzie agreed, "What do you want to know?"

"Tell me where you're from and why you're traveling through La Grande."

"Why?" Lizzie's voice rose.

Puffer fish coming. Zach scanned the huge room. It didn't make sense that no one was here. Where was the camera? The big screen hanging down lit up and he saw his own face. He looked scared.

"I am guarding something important. Not gold, not food, not jewels, but knowledge. I don't have anything to steal, but what I can give you is priceless. Please, trust me."

"Sounds pretentious." Lizzie laughed. "Oh, great Oz, what do you want in return?"

"More knowledge." The voice chuckled. "You're traveling. At

some point you might need my knowledge and you'll be able to relay new knowledge back to me—city situations, population, road conditions."

"What are we, your personal Map Car?"

"It's your choice. I am not forcing anyone. But I promise, if you agree to help me, I will help you."

"And if we don't?" Zach asked, straining to not yell.

"You go. I'm still safe. No one knows where I am or what I'm doing."

"Well, except we know what you're doing." Lizzie said.

"But you don't know where I am."

Zach took a breath and asked, "What do you want us to do if we agree?"

"Just a little toll to get the ball rolling. Information."

"About what?" Zach wished he could face the voice's owner.

"Where you're from, what you've seen, where you're going?"

Zach shook his head at Lizzie, mouthing the word, "No." Then felt a little foolish as he saw the bigger version of him doing the same on the screen.

Lizzie cleared her throat. "I'm willing to tell you our story in exchange for your services." She smiled.

Zach suspected the only reason she was cooperative was to piss him off.

There was an audible sigh on the loudspeaker. "Most of the people who've come through are too freaked out to deal with."

"We are headed to Salt Lake City. My Dad's coming from Texas to meet us there. Don't know what we'll do then. Maybe head down to New Mexico. We came from Bellingham, near the Canadian border."

The voice laughed. "I went to Western Washington University for a quarter. How are Bellingham and Seattle?"

"Bellingham's pretty subdued."

That got a laugh. Zach wondered if Lizzie was consciously testing the speaker. If he hadn't been at WWU he probably wouldn't have gotten the reference to the *City of Subdued Excitement*.

"But there's a big hippy contingent," Lizzie continued, "working on gardens in greenhouses and stuff."

"Sounds like Bellingham." There was another sigh and a pause. "Hey. You guys want to meet? I'm really tired of talking through these electronics."

Lizzie glanced at Zach, the question in her eyes.

You ask me now? He shrugged. "Whatever."

"Okay," Lizzie agreed. "It's kind of cold out here."

"Go back out the front door and turn to the right, follow the sidewalk and I'll meet you at the Hub."

"The hub?"

"Hoke Union Building. It looks like a giant Star Wars walker without legs. Follow the signs to the dining hall. I'll meet you there. There are vending machines, they still work, but there's no more Mountain Dew. Oh, I'm Glen. Glen Smith."

Zach followed Lizzie out of the building. The description of the Hub was perfect. *Glen is definitely a geek. But I knew what he meant. What does that make me?*

Lizzie turned and pulled him in a hug. "Man hug." Her hands pounded on his back and then released him. Then she punched him in the stomach and walked away.

Were they good now? Was it really that simple? Did Lizzie only need to know she wouldn't be abandoned?

They got everyone else out of the Tank. No use having them sit out there now that it was safe. Nev raised her eyebrow at Zach as if to say *Everything all right?*

Zach shrugged and nodded. "There's a guy here, says he can help us. There are snacks at least. Come on." He pulled out the illicit wad of bills from Bellingham.

Lizzie lifted Saj from Nev and headed toward the building.

Zach and Nev followed with Charley and Spike. Lizzie was pulling on doors, but nothing opened. Then a loud click sounded and a powered handicapped door opened. Glen probably had cameras watching them. He better not be the paranoid psycho Zach envisioned.

Inside they found the promised row of vending machines. Zach handed money to Charley and Nev and they all punched buttons until they had armfuls of chips, candy and packaged cookies. They followed Lizzie in. Saj cruised around the room.

When Nev ripped open the cookies to share with the boys, Saj's head shot up. He recognized the sound of food being opened. He toddled over to her.

Zach handed Lizzie a package of Grandma's Oatmeal Raisin Cookies.

She nodded her thanks.

Glen came in a side door. Zach sized him up: a big guy, balding, glasses, no pocket protector, but it wouldn't have looked out of place. His round, boyish face belied his size. No wonder he'd set up the theatrics, he didn't look like he would or could harm a spider. He approached with his hand out.

"I'm Glen," he said, pumping Zach's hand, then Lizzie's, then Nev's.

"I'm Zach. This is Lizzie, Nev, and the kids: Charley, Saj's the baby, and the big one's Spike." Zach watched Nev hustle off after Saj. Zach wanted to chase her.

Glen gave Spike a sad questioning look then turned to Zach. "Zach. Pleased to meet you. Who's the leader?"

Zach shook his head. "Not me. Lizzie is if anybody is." He hooked his thumb at her.

Lizzie glared at Zach. "We don't have a leader. They came along to help me."

Glen acknowledged Lizzie. "I've been trying to download everything of importance on the Internet since I got the first hint of the dispersion of this disease. I mean, who was going to do it? I was alive and somebody has to save the data. When the net goes down, can we rely on all those servers to maintain data? No, we— Shit, I'm geeking out on you." He grimaced. "Glen, watch the language."

"They've heard worse," Lizzie said.

"Why are you saving data?" Zach asked.

Lizzie walked away from them.

"I don't know. For me? For the future?" Glen chuckled. "Sounds silly saying it out loud. Guess I read too much science fiction."

"No, this is so cool. Saving data is brilliant." Zach called after Lizzie, "Hey, we need to get Glen connected with Seattle."

Lizzie came back over and pulled out the card the politician had given her in Seattle. "Here, Glen. Keep it. They want the same things you do. This ought to be worth lots of your help." She smiled.

Zach didn't think she was even being sarcastic.

"Hey, who wants to see the server rooms? There's a solar array on the roof. From a data standpoint the college rocks. The main power grid goes down? It switches to solar, turbine and battery."

Zach watched Lizzie tune out, but he wanted to see the techie stuff.

"You go ahead," Lizzie said. "Nev and I will hang out with the kids. Glen, there any place we can stay here? Dorms?"

"Yeah," Glen said. "There's family housing. I fixed up a place for myself, but usually end up sleeping on a couch upstairs."

"Great." Lizzie shoved Zach. "Go do the gadget guy thing." Saj pulled at Lizzie's pant leg. "We can get settled in later."

Glen's set-up was brilliant. He'd set each of the computer labs to run software he'd created to cull information, then it dumped into the school's extensive servers. He looked most proud when he talked about deleting all the student loan and personal data. The building was state of the art, a perfect oasis for a techie. Zach understood even more now why Glen would be paranoid.

Glen told him his dreams of saving the data and sharing with people who needed it. He'd been a teacher to pay for his post-grad, but as good as he was at it, what he really wanted to be was a student, learning forever.

After the tour Glen got them settled in Eocene Court, family student housing. The apartment smelled like old gym socks and bleach.

Zach volunteered to have a night with the big boys. Nev said she'd join him. Lizzie and Saj went next door after an exchange of hugs. Things were starting to feel back to normal between them, Zach thought. *Now, how can I get another night alone with Nev?*

The next morning Lizzie traded phone numbers with Glen over breakfast. "Any idea how long cell service will last?" she asked.

Glen shrugged. "Depends on power. Near as I can tell, back east, where the power comes from coal or nuke plants, cell service and Internet is already down. Out here in the west, we have more solar, wind and hydro power. Things'll work until the power goes down. That's why I'm here. When a circuit breaks, though, I don't know there's anybody anywhere fixing them."

"What about when bills don't get paid?" Lizzie had been worrying about that since Mama's land-line had gone off-line. An idea made her smile. "Can you use your techie skills to keep my bills paid?"

Glen's face exploded in a mighty grin. "Hell, yeah. I can do that for all of you. Are these all your numbers?"

Lizzie passed the sheet around to get Nev and Zach's and the extras. Then she added Jess' and her dad's. "That ought to do it. They're not all in our names. Some are uh, repurposed."

"You won't have to pay the bills ever again." Glen glanced through the list, verifying a couple numbers.

After breakfast they loaded up the Tank and headed south toward Idaho with Zach at the wheel, Nev riding shotgun, Spike and Charley in the back practicing sign language and Lizzie playing with Saj in the middle.

About an hour down the road, Lizzie's phone buzzed. Glen.

"Thought you'd want to know. I had a guy come through here. Asked if people had come through here from your neck of the woods—I got the feeling he was following you guys, but he wouldn't say what he wanted."

Lizzie shook, feeling clammy and hot.

"Wouldn't offer me any information, except his name. Duke. I told him I hadn't seen anyone from Northwest Washington, but I don't think he believed me."

Lizzie hugged herself, going inward. "Can you describe him?"

"Yeah. Young guy, mid-twenties. Camouflage clothing. Looks like a hunter."

"Thanks, Glen." She ended the call. "Shit. C.J.'s brother is on our trail." Lizzie tried to swallow, but felt choked. "His name is Duke."

"Should we stop and try and catch him?" Zach asked. "Sorry, I didn't believe you."

"And do what?" Lizzie felt exhausted, drained, the warm sweat now chilled her. "I don't want to kill him, too."

"We better get some additional protection," Zach said. "Keep an eye out for a sporting goods store. Shoulda grabbed Grandpa's rifle."

"Forget the rifle, Zach." Lizzie laid her hand on his shoulder.

"We'll need something anyway. We're heading into the wilderness. Two legged predators might not be the only ones." Zach slammed on the brakes. The Tank skidded to a stop. "Where'd I put the guns?" His hands twitched.

"I don't know," Nev answered.

"Mine's up inside the back seat," Lizzie said.

"Shit." He slapped on the dashboard. "The ones we got from

Yeager's are on Snoqualmie Pass, stuck in the tool chest on the trailer."

"Well, hell," Lizzie said.

"Who's C.J.?" from the back Charley's voice whistled softly, "Who's Duke? Why do we need guns?"

Spike whined.

"Bad men," Lizzie said. "We probably don't need guns, but—" Here came her Mama's words, "Better safe than sorry." The Snake River running alongside the freeway caught her eye. Idaho was on the other side. Lizzie wished they were already in Salt Lake City hanging out with her dad and Jess.

"Shit," Lizzie said. "Glen can help us find gun shops. He said he's got loads of data." She texted Glen the question.

He called her back in a few minutes. "I've got a bunch of addresses. Lock, Stock and Barrel is about five or six miles out of the way near the Idaho border."

Lizzie's insides twisted. She didn't want any more delays. "Anything closer to our path?"

"There's this one. Great name." Glen chuckled on the phone. "T-Bone's Buns and Guns. Sandwiches and gun shop."

Lizzie repeated it for the others in the SUV.

Zach nodded. "How close?"

"Twelve miles," Glen said.

He told Lizzie the address and she relayed it to Zach.

They found the shop manned. The sign flashed open and sitting outside was a big man with a long scraggly salt and pepper beard.

"Welcome to Idaho, folks. Guns or Buns?" He grinned as they climbed out of the tank.

"Some of both, I think." Lizzie smiled back, stepping inside as he opened the door for her. For a moment everything felt like the old days, before the disease. But the anxiety returned. They were here for guns to protect themselves. "Food first, we haven't had bread in weeks."

"Ours is fresh. Well, day old, but that's pretty damn fresh. Driven in from Boise yesterday." The big man turned and called back, "Jenny?"

"Yeah?" An annoyed female voice responded.

"We got more customers. Wash your hands."

"Awesome." She did not sound enthused.

They ordered sandwiches. The man at the counter might have

been T-Bone, but he never introduced himself. He chattered. *Where were they from? How was the weather? Had they been to Boise?* Sounded like Idaho was doing pretty well. Lizzie and the others answered the questions, but the friendliness didn't stop her from being suspicious.

The sandwiches were good. While they ate, the only sounds were T-Bone's running monologue and Spike's chewing. Lizzie tore off bits of her sandwich for Saj and Nev copied her. When the food was gone they bussed their own tables. As they were cleaning up, the man Lizzie decided was T-Bone opened the cabinets with the guns.

"What are you folks intending to pay with?" T-Bone rubbed his chubby hands together like he was getting ready to make a deal.

Lizzie looked to Zach. *What the hell was worth anything?* "Will you take cash?" She smiled at him.

"Well. That depends. How much do you have? I expect sooner or later, it'll be worth something. There's people in Boise forming a government and talking about using good old American dollars as currency. Of course, with all of it lying around, dollar's worth even less than it used to be. Also, depends on how much you're planning on buying. Jewelry's my usual currency."

Zach picked out an old-looking rifle. "This reminds me of my Grandpa's favorite."

"30 ought 6. Good choice. Probably the most common bore."

The wad of bills Zach had stolen for gas had hardly been used. He handed it to T-Bone, who took all but $20. Zach shrugged. "Easy come, easy go."

Lizzie's nerves, already on the edge, didn't like giving away all that cash. Even if it was only useful for vending and gas pay machines. And why would this guy even take it? *Don't be paranoid, Lizzie.*

Charley was sitting quiet, watching T-Bone with sharp eyes.

Lizzie wondered if Charley was suspicious, too.

"Don't want to leave you flat broke." T-Bone smiled. "Don't want to rip you off either. Now, you ladies want something?"

Nev shook her head.

Lizzie looked over the guns in the cabinet. She had the shotgun, but maybe something smaller. The jewelry she'd pilfered from the houses didn't mean anything to her and they could always get more. "Zach, pick me out a hand-gun, maybe one for you, too.

And a rifle for me. Not too much kick. I'll go get my rings and stuff." Zach's eyebrow arched, but he nodded and turned back to the case.

Nev followed Lizzie to the tank with Saj in her arms. "Lizzie, you're gonna give him your jewelry?"

Lizzie didn't look at Nev. "It's not really my jewelry. Just some things I picked up."

Nev didn't respond except to say, "I'll put Saj in his car seat and wait for you all out here."

T-Bone seemed like a nice guy, and how much choice did they have other than wild-goose chasing off the path. Charley came out of the store leading Spike as Lizzie headed back in with her Crown Royal bag of treasure.

"You boys, want to get in the car, too?" Lizzie asked.

Charley nodded, his face set in a frown.

"What's wrong?" Lizzie stopped him.

"I don't like that man."

Lizzie patted his shoulder. "Yeah, not sure I do either, but he has what we want. What we need. Get in the car so we can get going as soon as Zach and I are done.

"Okay." Charley tugged on Spike. "Come on, big guy. I'll teach you some more words." He dangled the rest of his sandwich in front of Spike's face.

Lizzie couldn't help but laugh. Charley was a good addition to the family.

As she turned away, her stomach twisted. Lunch came up in the bushes next to the building. The sandwich she'd eaten wasted on a shrubbery. *Shit. Don't freak out.* She wanted to feel safe. She spit to clean her mouth and went back inside.

Zach had picked out a snub-nosed .38 and a .22 rifle with a magazine for Lizzie.

"It won't stop anything big," he explained, "but it'll shoot every time you pull the trigger."

25

LIZZIE FELT BETTER ARMED AND back on the road. They continued south toward Boise. At a sign for Caldwell City Center, they came upon the most people they'd seen since Seattle. Emergency vehicles lined the road. Lizzie saw a Washington State Patrol car, a Border Patrol SUV, an ambulance and a local police car.

Zach slowed to a stop and a guy in an ill-fitting blue uniform with a gun on his hip and a badge on his chest came up to them. "What's up, officer?"

The man glanced around as if this wasn't his usual job. "Can I, uh, get you folks to step out of the car, please?"

"What's the problem?" Zach asked.

Lizzie watched as Zach pulled her little .38 handgun out of the Tank's side pocket. *Chill, Zach.* She leaned forward and touched his shoulder.

"We're trying to verify nobody sick comes into Idaho." The cop character looked shifty; he didn't really focus on them.

Zach shrugged. "We're only driving through."

Lizzie glanced at the other side of the road. More men with guns were coming toward them. "Zach. I think we better do as he says."

He turned and his eyes got wide. "Ah, shit!"

Everyone exited the car. Lizzie undid Saj's car seat and pulled him into her arms. Men inspected the Tank and the new guns from T-Bone were pulled, compared to a list, and the rest of the Expedition was searched. *Shit, I knew it was too easy. Bet he called ahead.* Lizzie counted it a small blessing they didn't find her shotgun. Whoever these guys were, they weren't very good at their new jobs. No one looked at them to take a temperature or anything.

Saj pointed at the ambulance and said, "Woo-woo."

Lizzie nodded. "Yeah. Some kind of emergency."

The original officer returned. He motioned to the men surrounding them. "Nadine, uh, the Commander, says bring 'em in."

Lizzie heard the way he said Nadine, like she-who-must-be-obeyed.

The gunmen guided them toward the police vehicles. Lizzie planted her feet. "I need the car seat."

The man pursed his lip, then nodded. "Okay. She and the kid can ride with us in their rig."

They got in with a driver and three armed guards. Lizzie watched Spike and Zach get shoved into the back of the cop car and Nev and Charley climbed into the ambulance.

A few miles from the road block there was new construction. People dragged cinder blocks onto pallets and lifted them onto a wall. The laborers had the same stunned look Lizzie remembered on Spike's face before they started teaching him.

She glanced back at him; his eyes were glued to the activity. Her nerves were on edge, her hands shaking.

They stopped where the wall was finished, eight feet tall and topped with barbed wire. A giant metal gate was being installed. They pulled through and stopped in front of an elementary school, but a new sign said Caldwell Independence Association.

A severe woman wearing well-tailored fatigues and a distinguished, graying man in a business suit came out of the door with more armed men. The woman shouted orders and guards separated Zach from Nev and took them off in different directions. They pulled Charley and Spike inside. They both stared at Lizzie as if she had the power to save them.

What the fuck? They let her take Saj; he was strangely silent. No fussing, just quiet and aware. *You must know I'm freaked out, Saj.*

An armed guard in uniform lead Lizzie to a room, the door still said counselor's office. *Oh joy, my favorite.* Colored poster paper covered the interior windows. Trips to the counselor's office had always felt like an interrogation. Why should it be any different now that the world had ended?

The gray-templed man came in after a few minutes. "I'm Bill. William Johnston. I'm going to ask you a few questions. If everything checks out we'll be inviting you to join us or allowing you to leave."

"Why would I want to? Why should I answer? Why can't we leave now?"

"I'll ask the questions." He was all business. He pulled out a tape recorder, a notepad, and then a handgun, which he laid on the table. He clicked the recorder on and restated his name. He flipped open the note-pad and flashed a tired, insincere smile. "Now. Tell me your name, where you are going and why?"

Lizzie gulped, eyeballing the gun. Bill seemed civilized. It was for show, but it made her nervous. "Okay. My name is Lizzie Gooden-Guerrero. I'm going to Salt Lake City to meet my father." Saj bleated and Lizzie bounced him on her knee facing her. "You're okay, Saj"

"Where is your father coming from?"

"Del Rio, Texas."

"Tell me where you were when the pandemic hit."

The questions continued and Lizzie answered all his questions. After telling him about Glen, including his location, her face got hot. Damn. She'd been talking without thinking. She didn't want to get caught hiding something and now she'd compromised someone else. Maybe these guys would trade information with Glen, too. Maybe it was okay. But it didn't feel like it.

Saj calmed down and slid from her lap to explore the room.

A guard came in with milk and chocolate chip cookies, like she was some kind of pet to be rewarded for good behavior. The cookies were still steaming and the milk was cold, so despite her principles Lizzie gulped them down, sharing half a cookie with Saj.

Finally Bill turned off the recorder and set down his notes. "Thank you, Lizzie. I think the others are probably done as well. Your cooperation is most appreciated." He put away his tools, including the gun. "Dinner should be coming soon. Hopefully the cookies didn't ruin your appetite."

Lizzie had caved. She knew it, and now he added insult to injury by patronizing her. She wanted to be angry but instead she felt dazed, like she had lost a part of who she was under his scrutiny. She was the one who never 'fessed up in the principal's office, never ratted anyone out. But there had never been a gun on the principal's desk.

The guards led her into the cafeteria. Her friends sat around the table eyeing her with the same dazed look. She felt immense relief at seeing them. But Spike was still missing. "Where's Spike?"

Zach shrugged. "Don't know. I assume he'll be here soon."

Men in uniforms stood by the door, no visible guns, but they were obviously guards. So much for being free to go after questioning.

A young woman brought in bread and more milk. She introduced herself as Rachael. She didn't know the answers to their questions. Lizzie thought she was telling the truth. Her eyes and manner were warm; her slacks and sweater were more sedate and adult than Lizzie's. Rachael seemed near the same age as Lizzie, but she seemed simple or at least sheltered.

Rachael brought in a giant pot of stew with the heavenly smell of onions, garlic and beef. She also brought a handful of baby carrots and some chunked up chicken. "Can I feed these to the baby?"

"He feeds himself mostly, but you can help him if you want." Lizzie nodded. Saj watched Rachael and he opened his mouth when she offered him a bite. He seemed to like her, but as she fed him, Lizzie saw her eyes get misty.

"What's wrong, Rachael?"

"Nothing. I—" Rachael's mouth twitched. "My baby... He got sick. Died. They want me to-" Her eyes flicked behind her, "Excuse me," she said and hurried from the room.

After a bit she came back, her tears dabbed. She had an old Fisher Price barnyard play set in a box and coaxed Saj onto the floor to play.

Bill Johnston came in accompanied by Nadine, the severe woman who had ordered them all questioned. "May the light welcome you." She put on a friendly face. She sat at one end of the table and Bill sat at the other. "I assume you will want to be moving on in the morning. We'll top off your gas. When you've reunited with Lizzie's father perhaps you'll want to come back this way."

Lizzie nodded, matching her fake smile. "We've come a long way." It was scary realizing that Nadine probably knew everything she'd told Bill. "Thank you for the food and the gas." *And fuck you for the interrogation and the treatment beforehand and we filled up already today.* Lizzie bit the inside of her cheek to help control her anger.

Don't piss these people off. "Where is Spike?"

The woman looked quizzical. "Spike?"

"Our dog-man."

"Dog-man? Oh, the drone? The special one."

Lizzie didn't like the way she said special like a disease. "Yeah. Big guy. Doesn't talk."

"He's with others like him. We're feeding and washing him. They tend to get pests."

"I want him here with us."

"I'm afraid that's not possible. We don't allow them in here."

"What?" Lizzie couldn't believe what she was hearing. "They're not stupid. At least Spike isn't."

"Yeah," Charley piped up. "He can talk to me."

Lizzie nodded, not trusting herself to be polite to this stupid woman.

"Talk?" Nadine snorted.

"Sign Language," Charley explained, his eyes lit up with excitement. "He's learned five or six words in the last two days. "Please, thank you, more, toilet, hungry, thirst—"

"We haven't been successful in teaching them anything."

"Bring him in. I'll show you." Charley's smile was irresistible.

Bill was grinning and Nadine's frown straightened. "Okay. Bring in the new one."

"I used up a lot of treats teaching him, but he's such a big man he needs the food anyway." Charley sliced up the rest of the carrots on his plate.

Lizzie knelt by Rachael and Saj. Let Charley do the talking; his boyish charm was the perfect response to the witch, Nadine. Rachael smiled at Lizzie, her joy with Saj was clear, like she'd been re-lit from within. Lizzie sat cross-legged watching them. Seeing Rachael's interaction with Saj, Lizzie felt guilty. *I don't play with him much.*

Saj giggled as Rachael jiggled his tummy, walking up his belly with the little toy man.

The guards brought Spike in. Charley showed off the words Spike knew, starting with hungry.

Spike signed, "No."

"Thirsty?" Charley asked.

Spike's hands hurried to sign, yes and please.

Charley handed him a glass of water.

Spike signed, "Thank you."

Lizzie glanced around the room. Charley had them spell-bound. Charley and Spike. Then Charley gave Spike a big hug and Spike hugged him back.

Charley backed away and said, "I love you, Spike." He signed it at the same time.

Spike's head cocked to the side like he did when he seemed to be considering. Then his hands, slower this time, formed a decent copy of Charley's, "I love you."

"There," Zach said, coming over to Spike and Charley. He put protective hands on both their shoulders. "See. Spike is family."

Bill nodded. "Nadine, I think—"

"Okay." Nadine stood abruptly. "Have their vehicle brought around, Mister Johnston. You may take your 'Dog-man.'"

Lizzie shook her head. The damn woman couldn't even call him by his name. *Oh, well, forgive her.* Everyone was smiling including the guards.

Then Lizzie saw a pistol in Nadine's hand. The severe face returned to a frown. "Rachael, take the baby out."

"What?" Lizzie demanded. "Rachael—" She could hear the hysteria in her own voice. Her heart pounded. "What are you doing, Nadine?"

"You're a bunch of children, taking a dangerous dog-man into the wilderness. There's no place for a small child. This baby is the light of the world. He is our hope. You will not take him. When you have found your father you may return and live near him."

Lizzie pleaded. "Nadine, please." The guards had guns out now, too.

"Lizzie," Nadine's voice lowered to that fake, kindly tone adults used to tell you how stupid you were. "He is not your child. You don't even think you can have children. You found him and almost immediately endangered his life by exposing him to drunkenness and debauchery."

"That wasn't how it happened." Lizzie fought for control. She glanced around for support. Her friends stood shocked. *Don't go Crazy Lizzie here.* If her limbs disobeyed her, she would give Nadine more ammunition. "I raised my little brother. We saved Saj."

"And we're saving him now. Do not let the sin of pride get in the way of choosing what is right for the child."

The door open and Bill came in. His eyes were wide and looking to Nadine for an explanation.

Nadine turned away from him. "Rachael. Take the baby to the nursery. You may stay with him."

Rachael stood frozen with indecision between Lizzie and Nadine.

Nadine gestured with her head. "Rachael," she said more forcefully. "Now."

"Wait," Lizzie pleaded. Saj was crying. Lizzie felt helpless. She did the only thing she could think of and threw her arms around Saj and Rachael. She hugged them both together, and slipped her cell phone into Rachael's pocket.

The guards took a step forward but Bill waved them off, letting Lizzie say goodbye.

Rachael's eyes leaked tears. "I'm sorry, Lizzie."

"Not your fault, Rachael." Lizzie hugged them both. "Take care of him like he's your own."

"Okay. Enough. Rachael, go. Bill, escort her out." Nadine barked orders, more comfortable being the cold commander, than BFFs. "Guards, take them out front."

They guards, Nadine close behind, marched them back the way they came. Lizzie's mind raced. Zach glowered. Nev was crying, and Charley clung to Spike like someone would take him away again. The Tank pulled up as they came out.

Nadine spoke. "Leave. If you wish to return after you find your father, and be a part of our community and our Plan, you will be welcomed and reunited with Saj. But if you attempt to steal him, we will shoot you on sight. Do not force our hand. The human race is counting on you children for its continuation. You are the light of the life. Make your decisions wisely."

"Fuck you. And your plan." Lizzie turned to the others. "Let's go."

"Follow the man on the motorcycle," Nadine said to Zach, ignoring Lizzie. "Your escort will make certain you do not get lost.

No one spoke as Zach drove, following the motorcycle. A Jeep filled with armed men drove behind them. They were guided back to I-84 South and then their escort stopped, waiting for them to disappear in the distance.

As soon as the Jeep disappeared, Lizzie barked, "Find a place to turn off."

Zach pulled off at a truck stop called Sage Travel Plaza. He turned the Tank off and sat staring straight ahead.

"Now what the fuck do we do?" Lizzie asked. She felt tears coming on. *Dammit. Be strong.* She blinked them back. "Saj is not going to be raised by any born-again birthers!"

"Lizz," Zach said.

His voice grated on Lizzie's nerves. "What?" she asked. "You don't fucking care?"

Zach blew up. "Fuck you, Lizzie. You think I don't care? Saj is part of my family, too. But we can't go waltzing into a machine gun nest and rescue him. We're three teen-agers, a kid and a dog-man."

"I gave Rachael my phone. She's gonna call or text. When she does..."

"If she does." Zach slammed his hands on the dashboard and this time it cracked. "But she won't. Saj's gone. She's not going to call."

"You don't know."

Zach opened the door and stepped down. "We're going to find a place to crash." His voice was measured, logical. "In the morning, when it's light, we head south. We find your dad. He's a vet, right? Maybe we bring him back and he helps us break Saj out. Okay?"

Lizzie refused to answer.

"We try to break him out now, somebody's gonna die. Maybe everybody. Okay?"

"Fuck you," Lizzie spit the words at him.

He slammed the door and strode toward a motel across the parking lot.

"Lizzie?"

She longed for Nev's calm comfort. "Boys?" She turned to them and flipped the seat up. "Follow Zach."

They hopped out and raced across the parking lot after him. Lizzie turned to Nev.

She looked tired and sad. "Zach's right this time, Lizzie."

"Whatever," Lizzie turned away hugging herself. "Go away."

Nev did. Then the tears came.

26

ZACH WAS RIGHT. BUT LIZZIE cared about Saj more than herself or her father. How could Zach possibly understand?

He frowned at her and turned the Tank around, driving on. He pulled into a motel parking lot. Everybody but Lizzie got out and headed inside.

No way Lizzie was going to let him think this was okay. When he back came out she said, "I'm sleeping in the Tank."

"Please don't do anything stupid, Lizzie," Zach said as he hooked his duffel bag over his shoulder.

As soon as Zach was gone she pulled the shotgun from its hiding place up inside the seat. *What the hell do I do now?* She grabbed one of the extra phones.

She texted her own number: **Rachael plz call me. U r a mom. Dont let them take Saj from me. Please.**

She wiped her tears away and lay in the backseat waiting. A long time passed. *Zach's right. Dad can help.* But he was at least a day or so away. *And can I trust him to help, or will he say the same thing as Zach and Nev?* There had to be something she could do. She took the gun and slipped out of the Tank. Lizzie scrambled across the parking lot and up the overpass. The street lights shone stark and bright against the dark sky. She ran across the freeway. There were lots of homes with cars in driveways.

While she walked she tucked the shotgun under her arm and pulled up a map of the area on her new phone. The converted school was there, north. She started checking cars. On the seventh try she found keys in the ignition. The car smelled awful but she ignored it. Lucky for her it was an automatic. And it had a car seat. Karma.

She got in and sat the shotgun in the passenger seat. She laughed a little too loud. "I got a shotgun riding shotgun." She turned the key and the engine purred.

It was a nice car. Lizzie slid it into drive and nudged the gas to get it rolling. When she got near the school she turned off the lights and found a place to park.

She wrapped her hand around the cold gun barrel and got out. The air was icy and the stars were bright. She snuck around the building hoping to be able to see the front of the school. The gate was finished and closed; there was a cement mixer parked nearby.

Lizzie didn't see any guards, but that didn't mean they weren't there. She set the phone to vibrate. She returned to the car, flipped the trunk latch and checked what kind of supplies she had at her disposal. Not much. A giant beach towel with a giraffe on it, a first aid kit, a tool box and jumper cables. She opened the tool box grabbing a big wrench with a rubber-coated handle and a roll of duct tape.

She wrapped up in the towel and tried to stay warm. Her eyes kept straying to the phone. *It's only been ten minutes.* Her fingers traced the scars on her arms.

Then the phone buzzed. "Shit." Her freezing fingers slid over the screen and she read. **Liz sorry 4 wait want to help u Saj needs u. Rach.**

"What do I say? Shit." **Rach thnxs im here. How 2 get 2 u? Liz.**

She rubbed her hands together.

1 guard sleeping mayb more outside end of building
Can you get out? I can come 2 u.
Mayb when?
Where ru? Which end of building?
Left side frm frnt by slide jungle gym
Im there 5 min brb.

Lizzie took the shotgun, the wrench and duct tape. On a whim she took the towel and rolled the wrench and duct tape in it. She pulled the car to the end of the alley near the front gate, then slipped from the car and left the keys in it.

She ran across the street and down the next alley with the blanketed tools under one arm and the shotgun in the other.

Out the other alley she headed down the street toward the school. The cinderblock wall was almost as high as her head here, but not as tall as near the gate. She lay the shotgun and towel on the top and pulled herself up with her freezing hands. It took all her strength to get her leg up over the wall and then she worked her way up and threw her other leg across. The cement tore into her stomach. She gritted her teeth and lowered herself to the ground on the other side. She slunk down behind a tree and pulled out the cell and texted: **Here by slide.**

She waited, pressing her cold hands against the warm welt on her scratched stomach.

When light comes on.
Locked?
No i unlocked. Ready?
Lizzie ran across to the building.
By door ready.

The light came on. Lizzie heard a male voice muttering. She pulled the door open and shoved the shotgun in front of her. "Be quiet or die," she hissed.

The guard spun, but his rifle pointed down.

"Put down the gun. Or I'll drop you." Lizzie watched his eyes. "That's my baby."

He set the gun on the floor. "What now?"

"Sit in that chair. Rachael, take this and tape him to the chair." She handed her the duct tape. Rachael set Saj down, pulled a long length of tape, and did as instructed.

Saj's eyes looked like he'd been crying, but when he saw Lizzie, he flapped his arms like he would take off. He had a pacifier in his mouth and was sucking on it. Must've been a gift from Rachael.

"Stay quiet, little man. Sissie's gonna take you away." She picked him up and hugged him. She handed him to Rachael. "You carry the baby. Whew. His diaper really is shitty!"

"Yeah. Should we change it?"

"No!" Lizzie hissed. "Later." She reached off another stretch of duct tape and wrapped it quickly around the man's mouth and neck. "Sorry."

Rachael tossed the strap of a diaper bag over her shoulder. "Let's go."

Rachael had been ready. Lizzie opened the door. There was no sign of movement outside. She gestured with her head. "Let's get to the wall and move alongside it."

"Here." Rachael handed Lizzie's phone back to her.

Lizzie shoved it in her other back pocket. "I've got a car on the other side of the wall. Across the street and down the alley. Can you drive?"

"Maybe."

"Okay. Take Saj and get in. Start it. I'm going to see what I can do to block the gate. Ready?"

Rachael nodded. "Yeah. Good luck."

Lizzie ran across the open parking lot and up to the wall. They slunk along the wall. *Please Saj, stay quiet.* When they got to the gate Lizzie motioned for Rachael to go. She pointed across the street to the alley and made a steering sign with her hands. When she was on her way, Lizzie pulled herself up into the cab of the cement mixer. The keys were inside.

"Thanks, Lady Luck." Her cell phone dug into her hip. She had no idea if she could even get it to move. "Clutch on the left. Brake in the middle. Gas on the right."

Run and trust they won't find you. She'd decided to sneak out and opened the door when lights came on at the schoolhouse and an alarm blew. "Damn it!" She turned the keys in the ignition. "Reverse is supposed to be easiest." She pushed in the clutch and pulled the gear shift knob into the R position. It groaned as she let out the clutch. It ground; she shoved the clutch back in and used both hands to jerk the thing into gear. She let out the clutch as gently as she could and pressed on the gas. The giant vehicle lurched backward and gained speed.

Lizzie felt a huge crunch. She knew she'd hit the new gate. She pressed the gas to the floor and the truck groaned in protest. It blocked the entire gate. She slid across the bench seat, shoving levers out of the way and threw the other door open. The truck spewed a dry gravel and sand mixture into the gateway.

She jumped to the ground and ran for the car. Rachael had started it and the door was open. She slid into the seat; Saj was still quiet in the car seat.

Lizzie stepped on the gas as she pulled the door shut. The car jumped forward, spitting gravel. "Shit. Take it easy, Lizzie." The phones poked painfully. "Rachael, keep an eye back there. Anyone coming?" She pulled the phones out of her back pockets and dumped them in the catch-all between the seats.

"Not yet. Wait. Someone on foot. Running after us. He's got a gun. Oh, shit!"

Lizzie shoved the accelerator to the floor, one eye in the mirror. She saw light burst upward and heard the rifle shot.

Where should she go? She saw a sign for I-84 and followed it. After a minute a movement in the rear view mirror caught her eye. A motorcycle had gotten through her cement-mixer mess. She kept the car going as fast as she could, taking turns that might lose him.

Lizzie's hands gripped the steering wheel. "Rachael, hand me the shotgun." She lifted it over the seat and set it comfortably close.

Ahead Lizzie saw a sign that said Single Lane bridge. She sped around the corner and saw headlights on the bridge coming toward her. "Shit." The truck stopped. "What the fuck?" There was a deer carcass on the roof.

Lizzie slammed on the brakes; the car slid sideways. The truck door opened and a man in camo with a rifle in his hand stepped out. "Oh, shit. Duke!"

Zach woke abruptly. He wasn't sure why. Nev still lay cradled in his arms. His hand rested on her chest. He couldn't hear anything. Maybe that was what woke him. He marveled at the warmth between his body and Nev's. Yesterday had sucked, but it had ended well. He kissed her cheek and whispered, "Thanks for not keeping me at arm's length." He lay awake listening to her breathe, matching his own breath to hers until he slipped back to sleep.

When he woke next Nev was shaking him. "Zach. Lizzie's gone."

"Aww, shit." He sat up glanced around, looking for his pants in the pre-dawn light. "Those people ain't messing around." Lizzie was busting his ass again. She was gonna get herself killed. Her self-centered self made him angry. "Get Spike and Charley in the truck. NO! Never mind. I need you to stay with the kids." Zach tied his shoes.

Nev knelt in front of him. "Zach." Her eyes filled with tears, but she fought them. "Don't let her get you killed. I need you. We need you."

Zach stood up and pulled Nev into a hug. "I want to stay with you, right here, right now." He let his breath out. "But I will come back." He kissed her and ran outside. "Stupid, stupid, stupid. Shoulda known she'd pull this shit." He jumped into the Tank and headed for the school.

He spun the GPS out of street view and studied it. There was a winding dirt road running near the school's playing field. Maybe he could get close without getting noticed. Nadine's last words came back to him. *"If you attempt to steal him, we'll shoot you on sight."* This was not the time for Crazy Lizzie to pull a stupid stunt.

An alarm blasted in the distance. Zach heard gunshots.

"Shit!" He stepped on the gas. The Tank groaned as the tires gripped the street. He swung left around the corner. The scene at the gate was chaos. Men with guns were running everywhere. No vehicles could get out. A large cement mixer blocked the gate.

The man on the motorcycle, their escort from the day before, revved his engine and took a run at the truck. Zach held his breath, expecting the motorcycle to somehow leap over the truck like a movie stunt. Instead at the last minute the rider slid the bike horizontally, clean under the truck and then spun back to vertical and raced off down the street. Probably chasing Lizzie. He pulled out from the curb to follow the motorcycle.

Zach drove halfway down the block. The cement mixer backed into the road. Zach swerved in behind a parked van and ducked. Vehicles filled with men and guns poured out of the compound.

The last vehicle out of the gate was a Jeep with Bill Johnston at the wheel. Zach let them have a good head start, and then followed the Jeep. They wound through city streets. He heard more shots in the distance. "Come on, Lizzie. Don't be stupid. Please."

The Jeep crossed an irrigation ditch and then pulled a hard right. The city had turned into countryside, tree-lined with small rural farms. Ahead all the vehicles and men lined up across the road. The Jeep pulled in and the men allowed it through.

Zach passed over the ditch and slowed down. He rolled the Tank to a stop at the row of men with guns, swung open the door, and stepped down. He walked toward the group, his hands upraised. "Take me to Bill Johnson, please."

One of the men stuck the barrel of a gun in Zach's gut. "Keep your hands over your head." He had a few missing teeth on one side of his mouth and a livid scar that seemed to match. His smile said he enjoyed the violence of playing army man.

The rest of the men split to let Zach through.

Bill turned away at Zach's approach, shaking his head.

Zach tried to sound annoyed. "I told her not to go. She was asleep, I assumed... She's a dumb, crazy girl. Please, let her go and I'll make sure she doesn't come back."

Bill gave Zach a sad look. "Go look. See what's left. Stupid girl. Four casualties today, such a waste of human lives."

The wall of men and guns stepped aside. A man's body lay next to a motorcycle face down, blood still red and liquid in the dust of the road.

Smoke was rising from below a rusty metal bridge. Zach's gut sank. He didn't want to move forward. But he had to know. There was a car at the bottom of the hill, its front end sunk in the water. Flames engulfed the interior and the back window. Bullet holes riddled the trunk. He could make out a body in the front seat, but the heat of the flames held everyone back. Bile rose to his throat. Zach's stomach contorted and yesterday's meal came up.

"Can't hack it, huh?" The guy with the missing teeth chuckled.

Zach spun on the asshole. The gun came up in his face, but Zach stood toe to toe with him, his glare locked onto the mock-soldier's eyes. But it wasn't worth it. Nev and Spike and Charley still needed him. Lizzie didn't. Lizzie never needed anyone. Zach turned back toward the Tank.

The gunman returned the barrel to Zach's back. Several guns cocked and leveled at him. He ignored them and kept walking. He half expected bullets to rip into him.

"No." Bill's voice was icy calm. "There has been enough death today. Enough lights have gone out."

Zach released the breath he had been holding and climbed into the cab. He eased the Tank onto the shoulder. When he was turned around he gunned it, tossing gravel back the way he'd come. "Shit! Shit! Shit!"

Tears streamed down his face. He wiped them away and tried to see the road ahead.

PART III

The Promised Land

27

THE SOUND OF THE HEATER kicking into high gear woke Mannie. Both his companions still slept. He pulled the Ranger uniform on. It smelled funky; he'd better get it washed soon. He snuck out and found a house attached to the back of the motel. In the kitchen there were some eggs in the fridge. He tossed together a quick scramble, grabbed some plates and salsa and then returned to the room. Jess brushed her hair and BeeGee sat playing with her cell phone.

"Here's some grub." Mannie offered the skillet around. "If anybody wants it."

The smell pulled them all to the table. They ate heartily. Mannie pushed back his chair. "Like to get an early start," he said, uncertain that they were free of pursuit.

They continued up the Devil's Highway into Utah. The mountains in the distance showed a distinct snow-line. So they would hit snow. Good thing they'd gotten chains. Mannie had always found it funny that most cars in the ditch when it snowed were 4X4s with overconfident drivers. For now the road continued straight, dry and long, with only a sign marking the crossover into Utah.

Monticello, with its pole buildings, Quonset huts and mini-storage, ended their trek on the Devil's Highway. They headed north on US 195 toward the Great Salt Lake.

Red rock formations swept higher, big and majestic into the stark winter sky. Snow covered most of the ground. Here and there scrub brush rose out of the skiff of snow. The red rocks formed impressive arches. They got out for a stretch at one—vivid like a giant had drilled a hole out of the ridges of the plateau. Beyond the red rocks, white-capped mountains peeked through.

Mannie's optical beauty circuits had shut down somewhere back near Green River. The country was stunning, but he wanted the drive to be done. The beauty that pulled him onward as fast as he could go was his daughter. Thoughts of potential redemption tangled with the possibility of rejection. Lizzie had every reason to hate him, but maybe in this fucked up universe, getting to know her was the silver lining.

They stopped as little as possible: Moab for gas, Wellington for lunch. Mannie felt worn out, but he wanted to get close to Salt Lake City by nightfall.

As dusk fell they pulled onto the Veteran's Highway I-15 near Provo. As they passed under the University exit to State 189, detour signs appeared on I-15. He ignored them and kept going until large orange pylons forced them off the road and toward downtown Provo. It reminded him of strategically placed damaged tanks that had forced a convoy of the road in Afghanistan.

"Maybe there's a bridge out?" Jess suggested.

"Maybe." He drove slow toward Provo, against the warnings in his gut. The memories of the concussions of explosives and the screams of friends dying were compelling. He wanted to forget that there was a big plastic bottle of vodka in the back. *Let go the ghosts.* Almost immediately they saw people, witless eyes stared at them. Dog-people. They scattered into the shadows as Rubi drove by.

Past the turnpike exit Mannie saw a portable building, like a guard house to a military base, complete with two men holding M-16 light machine guns. The older one, gray-hair, crew-cut and peaked cap neatly atop his head, looked like he'd been doing it his whole life. He stood with the practiced ease and erectness of a life-long military man.

Mannie slid Rubi to a stop next to him, noting the insignia and the name on his blue uniform. "Evening. Captain Foote?"

"Evening." He got Mannie's implied question. "Yes. I really am Captain Foote." His eyes narrowed in suspicion. "Where'd you get the Jeep, son?"

Mannie hated being called son. Something about the soft south-ern assumption of superiority. "Government issue, Sir. I'm a

Ranger at Amistad Reservoir.

"You're a long way from home." The Captain leaned in and looked over Jess and BeeGee.

"Yes, sir." Mannie tried to give him a pleasant smile. *Just answer his questions.*

"You on official business?"

Mannie hesitated "No, sir." *The truth would serve.*

"Are you ladies accompanying this man voluntarily?" The captain's rifle was where they could see it.

Jess gulped. "Yes, sir. He's my best friend's dad." She jerked her head at BeeGee. "We saved her from her drunken husband."

"Hold it." BeeGee glared at Jess. "I didn't need saving."

Mannie turned to look at her pleading with his eyes.

"But they didn't kidnap me neither," BeeGee continued with a wry chuckle. "I'm here of my own free will."

The Captain stepped back and the barrel of his rifle pointed down. "All right." His frown softened. "Where are you headed?"

"Salt Lake City, Captain." Mannie kept his voice respectful. "Is there a bridge out north?"

"A bridge?" The Captain looked for a moment like he wasn't going to answer, but he did. "No. We're bringing people into the city. We got a man with a plan. There's food and shelter and medicine. What's in Salt Lake City you're interested in?"

"My teenage daughter, sir." He ought to understand that. *Give him a little more.* "She's traveling from the Seattle area."

"That's a long trip." The Captain's frown returned.

"Yes, it is," Mannie agreed. "How can I get back to the highway?"

"I'm afraid you can't. You need to continue on this way." He pointed toward the city. "There'll be an escort in a minute. Once you get logged in, you can put in a travel request."

"Captain, with all due respect. I've done my service. I was in the first Gulf War and then Afghanistan. I am retired." Mannie set his jaw. "I have a seventeen-year-old daughter who is counting on me to meet her in Salt Lake." He slid Rubi into reverse. "I'm heading north."

"Not right now you aren't." The Captain placed his hands on the door as if he could stop Mannie with his strength. "We can't have people running loose, possibly spreading disease."

"I came through San Antonio," Mannie said in soft, measured

tones. "They've declared martial law." His hand slipped toward the Sig pistol. "Captain, I am going north. You don't want me going through your city, then I'll head back the way I came and avoid your roads. My daughter is 17 and I haven't seen her in 14 years. I thought she was dead. She thought I was dead. Are you going to shoot me?"

The older soldier eyed Mannie coldly, but the younger soldier behind him didn't seem nearly as cool. His hands were shaking. Mannie didn't think it was because of the winter weather. He had his gun pointed at Mannie, but the Captain was standing in the way.

"Don't play it this way, son."

"I'm not your son, *sir*. And despite your request, I am going to leave." Mannie pulled the 9mm Sig out to where the Captain could see it. "How do you want to play it?" Mannie stared him in the eyes. "Sir?"

They were at an impasse. The Captain seemed like the kind of man who couldn't stand to be weak. Mannie hoped he was not the kind to follow orders blindly or kill in cold blood.

The man's eyes narrowed, but he eased backward a bit. "You head back to the highway. Let the people know. If they're headed this way they're gonna get fed and taken care of but they have to give up some freedoms. Got it?" He barked like he was giving Mannie a set of orders that he expected to be followed.

Mannie nodded. Let him save face.

The young soldier hustled toward the older man. "But, Captain-"

"Yes, sir." Mannie switched hands with the pistol and backed away and drove sedately south, half expecting to hear shots ring out.

Jess let out her breath in a long sigh. "Jesus, almost pissed my pants."

He smiled at her. She had stayed calm and cool through the whole encounter. She handled her nerves better than with the fire. "You did just fine." He looked in the mirror. BeeGee was ghost-pale and sweating.

They drove the wrong way on the ramp, back to the highway. Then 4-wheeled it on the rugged shoulder around the orange pylons.

BeeGee broke her silence. "Randy was in the Army. He was a

ranger. But not the Lone Ranger." She gave a throaty laugh.

Mannie chuckled at BeeGee's laugh. "I wasn't a Ranger in the Army, but I ended up serving near the Rangers in the first Gulf War and Afghanistan."

"Randy was in both of those. Plus two tours of Iraq." BeeGee's voice got quiet. "That's when his drinking got bad."

"Yeah." Mannie knew that story too well.

BeeGee blurted, "He's headed north, following us. Randy is. He texted to say he's sorry. He can't live without me." BeeGee continued softly. "He says he's dry. I should text him to avoid Provo."

Mannie shook his head and gripped the steering wheel a little tighter. *Damn. One more thing to worry about.* He had Rubi back up to speed. The adrenaline from the encounter in Provo gave him the high he needed to push on.

His phone rang as they passed through American Fork. Jess and BeeGee were sleeping. He pulled it to his ear and hit the answer button. "Lizzie?

"Mr. Guerrero? This is Zach. If you're driving, you better pull over."

Mannie slammed on the brakes, waking both his passengers. "I'm stopped."

"Sir." The voice on the other end cracked. "Lizzie's dead. We ran into some trouble.

Mannie sat still. Zach was still talking, but Mannie didn't respond or really hear anything else he had to say. Eventually Zach stopped talking.

Jess reached a hand out to him. "Mannie?"

He turned to her and saw by the tears in her eyes she had heard everything. Mannie reached back and grabbed the plastic bottle BeeGee had stowed. He upended it down his throat. It burned like hell and then he went numb.

Lizzie stared as Duke strode toward her, his rifle pointed down. She picked up the shotgun and rolled the window down. She cocked it where Duke could see it and pointed it in his direction.

She heard the motorcycle behind her. Then it came into her rear view and skidded to a stop. The rider aimed a rifle, and the back window of Lizzie's 'loaner' car disappeared in a splash of glass. "Fuck! Get down, Rachael." Lizzie slunk down in the seat.

Saj cried; Rachael screamed, covering him with her body.

Duke raised his rifle; he pointed it at their car.

"We are so fucked." Lizzie saw the kickback as he fired, but nothing hit the car. In the rear view mirror she saw the man on the bike drop.

Duke ran toward them.

She sat up and gunned the car straight at him. Who knew how long before the motorcycle guy's friends arrived.

Duke's eyes got big. He tossed his gun down and raised his hands as he stepped out of her path. "Lizzie, I am not your enemy!"

"Damn it!" Lizzie slammed on the brakes. *Don't trust him.* She opened the door. She leveled the shotgun at him. "What the hell do you want, Duke?"

His eyes widened when she said his name. "Look, I know what a shit my brother was." He looked down. "I had to live with him. Whatever he did—I should have… I promised my father… We should have—."

"Shut the Hell up." Lizzie wanted to hate him, but she had no time. "There're more people like that guy behind us; they're going to kill us. Move your fucking truck."

"Wait. I have an idea."

Lizzie saw the wheels turning in his head. But he had tried to kill her. "I'm supposed to trust you?" Her habit of reacting against paranoia made her too trusting. Wasn't that what got her in trouble with C.J.? *But I don't want to live in fear.* "What's your idea?"

"Get in my truck and drive." Duke's face had an intensity that she recognized. "I'll make sure they don't follow you."

Lizzie hesitated; she wanted to trust him, her hate was wavering. And that made her question herself. "What about you?"

"There's a brown double-wide across the road and to the left. I'll meet you there. Please. Trust me."

I won't trust you. Not much. "Duke. You fuck with me, I'll kill you —dead like your brother."

He winced. She regretted saying it. She could see nothing of CJ in Duke. But she had to let him know she wasn't a scared little girl making empty threats. He nodded. They swapped keys.

Rachael already had Saj in her arms.

"Let's go," Lizzie ordered, running for Duke's truck.

Duke hauled gear out of the back of his truck. He left behind an impressive arsenal: guns, ammo and flares, along with things Lizzie didn't recognize.

He cut away the ropes holding the deer to the roof and hefted it onto his shoulders

Lizzie was glad to find this rig was an automatic, too. *Drivers Ed. would have been a good investment, Mama.* She stuck the keys in and cranked it up. Rachael was in the extended cab with Saj. "Buckle in!" she said, but didn't wait to be sure. The tires bit and she fishtailed then straightened out.

Damn good thing there were no other cars on the bridge.

She turned onto the dirt road Duke had suggested as an explosion echoed behind them.

Rachael's head jerked back at the sound. "Shouldn't we keep going?"

Lizzie didn't respond but when she reached the double-wide she stopped and pulled in front of the pole building. *Why am I trusting him?* "Get out and open the door. Please."

Rachael got out, but the door wouldn't budge. Lizzie jumped out to help and together they got it open.

She parked the truck inside and then Lizzie reached back for Saj who had settled into a fussy whine. She handed him to Rachael. "Do what you can to keep him quiet."

She reached in her back pocket for her cell phone. "Dammit."

"What is it, Lizzie?"

"My cell. I think it's in the car. It has my mom's last message and video of my little brother." Her gut twisted. She would never hear them again. Then a worse thought interceded. "Shit. My dad's number. And Zach's and Nev's. They don't even know I'm alive. I need that phone. I gotta go." She picked up the shotgun.

"Where?" A deep voice asked behind her.

Lizzie spun, jerking the shotgun up to defend them.

It was Duke; she let her breath escape and the shotgun drop. *Ten minutes ago he was going to kill me. Now I'm happy to see him?* His pants were soaked up to his thighs. "My phone. It's in the car." She headed for the door.

"Then it's toast." He dropped gear in the back of the truck and gripped her arm.

"What do you mean it's toast?" Lizzie demanded, jerking her

arm from his grasp.

"The car. I blew it up." He turned back toward the truck. "Let's go."

"Oh, god." Lizzie collapsed to the ground.

"Jesus," Duke sighed. "Come on. Get in."

"You destroyed my phone."

He stared at her. "I saved your life."

"Nobody knows I'm alive." Lizzie sat up on her haunches. "I need that phone."

"Here." Duke climbed out of the truck and knelt by her, offering his phone.

"I don't know their numbers." She stared at the dirty floor. Nothing mattered.

"Come on," Duke coaxed. "We're all alive." His voice softened. "Please, Lizzie. Get in. We don't know how long before they figure out you weren't in there."

"I'm going back." Lizzie stood.

Duke stood and stepped in front of her. "Don't be stupid."

Rachael climbed back into the cab. "Come on, Lizzie."

"Shut up, Rachael."

"Lizzie," Rachael pleaded. "Saj needs you. You're the only mom he's got."

Lizzie looked at Saj. His eyes were round as saucers, and his thumb was planted firmly in his mouth. He was her baby. They were right. But that didn't fill the hole in her heart where she knew she couldn't hear Jayce or Mama's voice again.

"Okay." Lizzie turned toward the truck. "All right. We need a car seat." She let Duke help her into the passenger seat. Rachael handed her Saj. She nestled her nose in his hair and hugged him. His usual squirminess was gone and he let her hold him tight.

"Let's get down the road a bit," Duke laughed grimly, "and we can go shopping." He shoved the shifter into reverse and spun around.

"Please. Drive slowly and carefully until then." Lizzie buckled herself into the passenger seat and put the little center lap belt around Saj.

"I will." Duke nodded and let up on the gas. "Thanks for waiting for me. There were a lot of cars, but nobody followed across the bridge. What do you know about those people?"

"What do I know about you?" Lizzie asked. "Why the hell did

you follow me across three states?"

Duke glared at her, but the corner of his mouth twitched and broke into a lopsided smile. "Fair enough. When I found C.J. dead and you ran, I wanted to kill you. I promised my dad I'd look after him. I wanted answers. Wanted you to pay." He rolled to the edge of an intersection. "North or south?"

"South. My dad's south."

He let the truck creep forward until they could see down the road toward the bridge. Nobody was in sight. He coasted out into the street and gently nudged the truck forward. Lizzie looked back, trying to make out anyone following them.

Duke pulled across the freeway.

Lizzie's heart pumped; she grabbed Duke's shoulder. "Hey, that was south."

"Yeah." His eyes met hers. "And it's the main drag. I'm going to drive alongside it until we're a ways away." He pointed at his GPS.

Duke drove. Rachael watched warily behind them and Lizzie watched Duke. "How'd you find me?"

Duke laughed. "Running into you back there? Pure dumb luck. But your friend in La Grande said more by not saying anything… You didn't cover your tracks and you stayed close to the main road. Then the guy at Guns and Buns told me you'd been through and said he didn't think you'd go far. That information cost me a buck."

"A buck?" Lizzie asked, incredulous.

"A deer. I'd bagged two. Now they're both gone. Oh, well. You're safe."

"Thanks for saving my life," Lizzie said softly. "Not sure I said it."

"Yeah." He flashed her a wry smile. "You're welcome."

28

LIZZIE HAD A CRICK IN her neck from looking over her shoulder. Duke's trick seemed to have worked; nobody followed them. She pulled her fingers away from her mouth. *Don't chew your nails.* She could hear Mama's exasperated voice. Duke pulled into a Wal-Mart. "Car seat?"

Inside Lizzie and Rachael searched for baby snacks, teething biscuits, bottled water, formula and baby food. She picked out a new car seat. Duke waited outside with a shotgun. Strange that this was a relief to her now.

After getting Saj settled into the new seat, they continued on, rejoining I-84 on the outskirts of Nampa. Lizzie kept glancing back, but no one seemed to be following.

Rachael's hand shot forward from the back seat. She jerked Duke's shoulder. "Hey, take this exit. Away from Boise."

Duke slammed the brakes and squirreled onto the off-ramp. "What the hell?"

"We don't want to go to Boise." Rachael's head shook. "They've got more people in Boise. Just like Caldwell. I bet they contacted them."

"Okay. Next time give me some warning." Duke tapped the GPS and a new map appeared. "Looks like a lot of back roads, but I expect they'll be emptier."

Rachael fed Saj, and Lizzie stared at the mountains—so close to Salt Lake City, to seeing her father, but still so far.

Soon Rachael and Saj had both fallen asleep but Lizzie was still staring out the window.

The silence was palpable and Duke said finally, "So, you want to tell me about C.J.?"

Lizzie shook her head.

"Fine," Duke said; his jaw tightened. "Not like I can't put it together. Girls don't shoot guys in the...*there* without a reason where I come from."

"Girls shoot guys a lot where you come from?"

He chopped off the laugh that escaped his mouth and they settled into silence again.

After a while, she said, "He was drinking. Stupid cheap beer. Whiskey."

Duke nodded, like he knew this story.

"He...wouldn't stop. I warned him. I begged him. I tried...before I pulled that trigger." There were tears in her eyes. "I never killed anything before, not even spiders." She wiped her eyes. "Sometimes I wish I'd let him. I'd rather have been raped than live with this for the rest of my life."

"Damn, Lizzie."

Lizzie dug the heels of her hands into her eyes as if she could drive out the image of CJ lying on her bathroom floor in a pool of blood. Strange. She hadn't been able to talk about it like this before. Not to the others. Was it her that was different or was it Duke?

They drove a way before Duke spoke again. "CJ was a stubborn, little fucker." He laughed bitterly. "When you wrote on his shirt..." He stared on down the road. "I didn't believe it at first. Then as I drove I thought maybe. Now, after meeting you and hearing your side of the story, I know I made the right call back there at the bridge."

Tiny white flakes floated to the ground, Lizzie stuck a hand out to catch the cold crystals. "Snow." They had pulled off for lunch where they could see the highway, but not be seen from it. For a second the snow raised her spirits, but the thought of her friends and father brought them back down.

"Thanks," Duke said as Rachael offered him a sandwich. He popped the cap off a beer and offered it to Rachael.

Rachael shook her head. "No, thanks. You got anything else?"

Duke dug in the back. "Coke? Mountain Dew. Maybe some others."

"Coke's fine." Rachael handed Lizzie a sandwich.

"None of it's really cold. Lizzie, beer?"

"I don't know." Lizzie shrugged and took it. "Looks dark." It didn't smell like Doug's piss beer. She sipped, tasting a thick, coffee-like flavor. "Not bad." The label said Double Chocolate Stout, somehow it didn't seem like a Duke kind of beer. "Chocolate!" Maybe she didn't know him as well as she thought. She swallowed another draught. It tasted good, she'd never drunk for the taste.

"Cheers." Duke smiled. His eyes twinkled at her over his sandwich.

"Cheers." Lizzie took another swig. "If we can get onto the Internet I can get a hold of someone by e-mail or Facebook. If there's Internet access."

"No Internet or phone service here. We'll have better luck in towns."

"Shit. Just my luck." She kicked herself for not memorizing phone numbers.

"Hey, Lizzie." Duke squeezed her shoulder. "We'll figure it out." The contact sent a shiver through Lizzie. He jerked his hand back. *No*, she wanted to say. *Hug me.* But she couldn't. She tried to offer a smile, but she was sure it came out as a grimace.

His eyes seemed sad and he looked away. "Well, let's hit the road." He picked up the empties and tossed them back in his truck. "Did you pick a spot in Salt Lake City to meet your dad?"

Lizzie got in the passenger seat. "Didn't figure it would be necessary. Shit."

An hour later they exited I-84 for Twin Falls, Idaho; Lizzie hoped there was power and cell service. But they found neither. They got gas by siphoning from a big van and raided a mini-mart for batteries and flashlights.

"Let's push on through to Utah," Duke suggested. "We get close to Ogden, there's a better chance for signal."

The consistently monotonous view of the road put Lizzie to sleep. She woke when the truck slowed down at a sign that said '900 No St.'

"Lizzie, I got signal." Duke handed her his phone.

"Lemme see if there's Internet." Her fingers were shaking. "No!" She jumped out of the truck, weaving around like the cell phone was a divining rod for signal instead of water. For a moment the Internet icon flashed. Her hand steadied as she pressed the Facebook icon. "Jessie, please have your phone listed." The screen went blank. **Cannot connect to network.** "Dammit."

Lizzie scanned the area. There was nothing nearby. She climbed back in the truck. "Can you keep driving and I'll tell you when to stop?"

"Can do." Duke said. The truck pulled forward, accelerating slowly.

Lizzie stared at the signal bars, willing them to increase. The original signal had disappeared. Part of her wanted to go back, but she knew she should go forward.

"You want me to take this exit?"

"Sure," Lizzie said. Probably wouldn't make any difference.

They pulled into a truck stop. Lizzie hopped out again and walked around trying to find a stronger signal. She spotted a ladder going up one of the metal tubes of the giant sign that lit up the snowy ground. She ran to it and started climbing.

"You sure that's a good idea?" Duke asked.

Lizzie glanced back at him. "Who knows?"

Rachael climbed out of the truck and set Saj down. He wandered around in the light of the gas sign.

Lizzie neared the top and got two bars of signal. She thumbed the Facebook app again and this time it opened.

Her fingers flew across the screen logging in. Then she waited. It took forever to load. She climbed up a few more steps but the signal went back to one bar. She climbed back down. When it loaded she went to Jess's profile. "Dammit." Jess had no number listed. Lizzie scrolled back to Jess' feed. The last comment was from before Lizzie's dad had picked her up.

Lizzie slid to Friends. "Zach? Come on. YES!" His number was listed. She double tapped on the phone number. It was ringing. It connected. *"The number you have dialed is no longer in service or is not connected to the network."*

"Update your number, Zach. Shit!" Her fingers ran through her hair: twisting, tugging, pulling. She typed into the *What's on your mind?* box. **Im alive. Call.** She hollered down to Duke. "What's your number?"

Duke repeated it slowly twice, while Lizzie typed it in. *No one's checking their feed.*

Who else could she reach? "Glen. What the hell is your last name?" She typed: **Glen La Grande, OR** into the search bar. Five choices showed up. Three had photos that were obviously not Glen. She clicked Glen number four. There was a phone number. She called and left a frantic message, not even knowing if she had the right Glen. Then she clicked on Glen number five. The profile said something about geek god. And there was an e-mail address. "Shit. Duke," she muttered, "you better have e-mail on this."

She clicked on the address and slid the keyboard out. A blank e-mail opened. She typed: **Its Lizzie. Please. Life and death! We got separated and I need Zach and Nevs #s!** Send.

The wind whipped her hair as she clung to the sign, staring at the phone. Down below, she heard Rachael and Duke speaking in low tones while Saj wandered around sucking his thumb. They must think she was losing it.

The phone buzzed—a reply with a phone number. She double-clicked it. The line picked up but all she heard was breathing.

"Glen?"

"Yeah," he whispered.

"Shit, are you sick?"

"I wish." Glen's breath wheezed out. "I'm hiding. People are looking for me."

"Shit, I bet that's my fault. I told the people in Caldwell about you. I'm sorry. We got interrogated."

"What people?" Glen's voice grew louder.

"I'll tell you later, please. My phones destroyed. Zach and Nev think I'm dead. And my dad. I need their numbers."

"Okay. But I want answers. Numbers on their way... now."

The phone buzzed. "Thanks, Glen."

"Gotta go. Don't call me," he hissed. "I'll call you back when I'm clear."

Could Glen handle the breeders? Could he take care of any-thing but computers? Still, he'd kept her and Zach at arm's length as long as he wanted. She cursed herself again for her flapping lips. Her fingers clicked through to Zach's number. "Come on answer, dammit. Please."

"What?" Zach sounded tired. "Who is this?"

"Zach, oh my god, I love you! I'm not dead. This is Lizzie. I'm not dead." She scrambled through all she had to say: how she'd rescued Saj and lost her phone.

"Whoa, Lizzie! LIZ! Shut up!" Zach shouted over her babbling. Lizzie stopped.

"Where are you? I saw a body. You scared the shit out of us, Lizzie."

"I'm sorry, Zach. It wasn't me. Saj and Rachael are safe, too."

"Oh, my God, Lizzie. I told your dad you were dead."

Her brain spun. "Give me his number."

"Okay." Zach's voice continued, calm again, "Just a minute."

Lizzie called down. "I need somebody to take down a number.

"Yeah?" Duke produced a pen and a piece of paper. "Repeat it. I'll write."

"Okay, here they are," Zach said.

Lizzie repeated the numbers. Duke wrote them down.

"Okay, thanks, Zach." Her heart was pounding.

"Wait. Lizzie. Where are you?"

"I don't know." She called to Duke. "Where are we?"

"Utah. Near Brigham City."

"Who the hell is that?" Zach had heard Duke's voice.

"Not important." She wasn't sure she could explain.

Zach made an frustrated sound, but didn't press her. "We came through there about 20 minutes ago."

"Where are you?"

"Ogden. The Hoagies Corner Conoco station. Liz, call your dad. I don't think he took the news so good."

Lizzie hung up, her hands shook as she dialed again. It kept ringing. Eventually voice-mail answered. "Dad. It's me. Lizzie. I'm not dead. Call me on this number." She ended the call and descended the ladder.

"What do you want to do?" asked Duke.

Lizzie collapsed into her seat. "Drive south."

Lizzie watched Duke staring at the roadway, speeding south, pushing triple digits on the speedometer. Snow fell outside. The new flakes stuck immediately to the frozen ground and the ice and snow from other recent weather. Why was he helping her? And more importantly why did she trust him? Her brain made the logical connection again—he didn't feel like C.J.

Glen called back and Lizzie gave him a thumbnail sketch of the last few days. He was hiding out in a janitor's closet with a bunch of computers monitoring the campus cameras. But no food. He was grumpy and hungry, but not that angry. He had planned for this contingency and made it look like he headed north when the campus was invaded. Maybe they would give up and move on.

About 15 minutes later, Duke and Lizzie pulled into the Hoagies Corner station. Lizzie jumped out before the truck stopped. Zach and Nev ran out to meet her, mashing her into one giant hug. Rachael and Saj, Charley and Spike came out, standing in the light dusting of snow. Everyone talked at once as they reunited.

Duke came around the side of the truck and the conversation died. Spike spotted him and dove for him, going for his throat. Rachael screamed.

Lizzie jumped on Spike's back. "NO, Spike. He's okay. Zach, help!" With Zach's help they pulled Spike off Duke. Charley was hugging Spike's leg. Saj howled.

Duke jerked his handgun out.

"Please, Duke, no! He's protecting me." Lizzie hollered. To Spike she spoke in a soothing voice, "Hey, big man. It's okay. Lizzie's okay."

Duke breathed heavy, his cheek bloodied and dripping where Spike had scraped him. "I'm okay." He wiped his cheek and glared at Spike. He got back in his truck without another word.

"Duke!? That's Duke?" Zach flipped out. "What are you doing with Duke? This is the guy hunting you down for revenge? Half the reason we left Bellingham. And now you are all cozy?"

Nev put a placating hand on his arm, but she looked as hurt and confused as Zach.

"It's not what you think." Lizzie blushed. "He saved our lives."

"You almost got me killed, Lizzie."

"What the hell are you talking about?"

Zach's phone rang. He glared at it and handed it to Lizzie.

Lizzie grabbed it. The screen said Jess. "Jess?"

"Oh, my god, Lizzie. We thought you were dead."

Her friend's voice made her happy. "I almost was." Lizzie laughed. "How's my dad?"

"Uh. He's sort of passed out. I don't think he'd had a drink in a really long time. Kind of overdid it when he heard."

Oh, god, Mama was right. "Where are you?" Lizzie asked.

"Just north of Provo, northbound on the highway." Jess gave her the mile marker number.

"Okay. We're on our way."

Lizzie helped Spike back into the Tank. She wanted to ride with Zach and Nev to explain, but she didn't want Duke to feel deserted. She gave Nev and Zach hugs. "Please don't judge me. At least not yet. We can talk. Right now, I'll ride with Duke."

"Whatever," Zach said and turned away.

It hurt to see Zach so angry with her.

Nev gave her another hug. "Let's go get your dad."

Lizzie nodded, knowing that if she spoke she would probably break out in tears. Saj and Rachael were already in the truck when she climbed in.

"You all right?" she asked Duke.

"Yeah." He dabbed his face with a red handkerchief. "Guess he owed me one. Sure is protective of you."

"Zach or Spike?"

"Both."

Zach pulled out and Duke shoved the truck into gear and followed him. They hit the freeway headed south.

"You okay to drive?" Lizzie asked. The snow spinning, flying at the windshield was hypnotic.

"Yeah, I'm not going to fall asleep."

Duke's eyes pulled away from Lizzie and returned to the road. What was he thinking? His scruffy beard made him look younger than she thought he was. He must be about 25. Would they have ever connected back in the day? Lizzie shook off the direction her brain was going.

"What you said back there. It wasn't the whole truth. When I saw you at the house, I wanted to hurt you. When I started following you from Bellingham... Well, my dad..." He stopped talking again and drove, staring ahead into the night. "Came a lot of miles with only my own thoughts for company."

"So when did you decide you didn't want to hurt me?"

He laughed, a quiet single chuckle. "When that guy had his gun pointed at you. If anybody was going to kill you, I was."

Lizzie couldn't decide how she felt, so she sat and pondered, watching the snowflakes spin. Duke wasn't the villain she imagined. But she hardly knew him. "So, what about you? What did you do before the uh…? What do we call it, the plague? Sounds stupid."

"I dunno. Plague sounds good to me. Pandemic sounds too quiet."

"Yeah, too quiet. That's it. 'The Quieting.' I didn't even know the word pandemic a year ago."

"Well, before the plague, 'The Quieting.'" He smiled over at her. "I took classes at Whatcom Community College. Wanted to be an electrical engineer, but we didn't have the money. My part-time job as an electrician's assistant got in the way of the classes. I was stupid." He smiled at her. "Not 'cause I couldn't do the schoolwork, but the pay was good for a poor kid, so I stopped going to classes." He sighed.

"I skipped a lot of classes for no good reason."

"Yeah, well, high school's free. After a while, the job sucked; I could hardly stand the guy I worked for. He was a friend of my dad's. Not that I liked my dad, either. He was a lot like C.J."

"I've never seen my dad. Not since I remember. Mom kicked him out when I was three." Lizzie couldn't believe she was telling him about her dad. She hadn't talked much about her dad with Zach or Nev or Jess. "I hope he's worth this trip. Better not be the asshole mom said he was." The trip had seemed like the most logical thing to do.

Duke glanced across at her. "I'm sure he's worth it."

"Weird thing is, if you hadn't scared me, the box might not have gotten smashed and I might not have found his number."

He tossed her a quizzical smile. "That is weird. I don't believe in religion or fate, but sometimes… Things like that make me wonder."

Lizzie saw headlights coming toward them through the softly falling snow. Her heart leapt. The road sign said the next exit was Bountiful. Lizzie smiled. She felt pretty bountiful. Now that she was almost with her father, she realized she wanted that more than anything.

They were driving on the wrong side of the highway. Zach's idea, of course. It made sense. Then they couldn't miss her dad and Jess.

"Oh, shit." Duke slammed on the brakes, the truck slid sideways, threatening to go over on its side. "Look at that."

29

ZACH STAYED AHEAD OF DUKE on the freeway. *What the Hell was up with Lizzie?* Hooking up with the brother of the guy she murdered? The guy had been "trying to kill her" last time Zach heard. Seemed like a pretty screwed up relationship.

He had really wanted to finish what Spike started.

Nev reached across and touched his thigh; he knew she sensed his frustration.

Headlights ahead of them shone in his eyes. He smiled. It had been his idea to drive on the wrong side of the highway so they wouldn't miss Mannie and Jess in the snow.

He let his foot off the gas as the lights got closer. Then the lights split into three sets.

"What the hell?" He rolled to a stop. He glanced in the rear view mirror. Duke's truck had stopped too. "I don't think that's Lizzie's dad."

The three sets of headlights surrounded the Tank. Each truck had guys with guns hanging off the roll bars. Nev's breath escaped slowly. "Nope. It looks like the official asshole welcoming party."

Spike growled and Charley whispered a reassurance to him, but the uncertainty in his voice did nothing to soothe Spike.

Zach saw red taillights in the rearview mirror. "Shit." *Turn tail and run, Duke. Take care of Lizzie."* Maybe they could get away.

"Step out with your hands up. Now." A balding redneck with a mullet fringe in Carhartts gestured with his gun.

Zach looked over at Nev. She nodded to him, set her jaw, and opened the door. *Guts.*

"Okay. We're coming out. We got a dog-man and a kid in the back. We're harmless. We don't want trouble."

The rednecks patted them down. Zach felt his phone and knife lifted from his pockets. Charley and Spike were herded out of the Tank.

Spike fought, sinking his teeth into one of the hicks. One of the men pistol-whipped him. Charley cried out as Spike stumbled into the snow.

"He doesn't know any better," Zach shouted.

"Spike, Charley. It's okay," Nev said in a strong soothing voice that even made Zach feel better. "Everything will be fine."

"Listen to the lady," said a grinning man with long blond hair, out of place in this crew. His appearance and his California accent were more surfer-dude than redneck. He ran his hand across Nev's shoulder and down toward her breast as he finished patting her down. Zach gritted his teeth.

"Hey!" Nev turned around and slapped the surfer dude. "Watch your fucking hand. You already got everything.

"What's the trouble?" the man with the mullet, the Bossman, demanded.

Nev sniffed. "He's reaching places he doesn't belong."

Bossman cuffed surfer-dude on the back of the head. "Don't mess." To Nev he said, "Turn around and be quiet."

Surfer-dude backed off, sulking.

"Jim, get these people burning at the stake." One of the men grabbed Zach's arm.

"What the fuck?" Zach asked, twisting out of the grip. The guns came back up.

The Bossman laughed. "Just a figure of speech. Need to keep you warm. You freeze to death we don't get paid."

Jim led them around a gas heater and handcuffed one to another into a circle. Then he turned the heater on and it got red hot. They could only get about four or five feet from it.

"Let's sit. Might be a little less hot," Zach suggested. They sat in a circle.

"What are you going to do with us?" Nev asked.

"Take you to *The City* tomorrow," the Bossman answered. "Collect our reward. Ain't gonna be much with only one girl and all this sausage, but there was three girls in the other group we collected tonight. So we'll have a good sum coming to us all told."

Nev whispered, "Jess? And Lizzie's dad?"

The Bossman had started walking away, but he came back. "You know 'em? Jess was the girl's name."

Zach shrugged.

The man grinned. "Well, you oughta see 'em tomorrow. They're probably already on their way into *The City*.

"Salt Lake City?" Nev asked.

"Nah. Provo. The only place in the country that's got things figured out."

"What's that mean?" Zach asked.

"You'll find out soon enough." Bossman placed three guards on the perimeter.

"Lizzie's still free," Nev whispered when they were alone

"Yeah, with a baby and a teenager and an asshole."

Lizzie looked where Duke pointed. Ahead of Zach's truck were three sets of headlights coming toward them.

"You said your Dad and your friend were in one rig, right?"

"Yeah." The lights formed a wall, foglights above and below the main beams. She couldn't see anything behind them and they lit up Zach's truck.

"I don't like this." He grimaced at her. Without waiting for input, he shoved the truck in reverse and spun in a one-eighty on the slick road.

Lizzie's stomach churned. "What are you doing? My dad's back there."

"I don't think that's your dad." He reached down below his seat and pulled out a rifle with a giant scope on it. "See what you can see, but I'm not taking chances."

"But Zach and Nev—"

"Will have to take care of themselves."

Lizzie looked behind them and squinted through the sight. Duke was right. "God damn it." Three big trucks had surrounded the Tank. Lots of young men with guns in the back. Zach and Nev were getting out of the truck with their hands in the air. One of the trucks pulled around and came after Duke's truck. "They're coming after us."

Rachael's groggy head came up. "What's going on?"

The engine in Duke's trucked groaned; they were really moving. Duke pushed it harder.

"Shit." Lizzie saw a second set of headlights pull away from the Tank. "Two."

"Describe the trucks."

Lizzie squinted. "I don't know. Big tires. Gun racks. Confederate flags probably. They're trucks and I couldn't see much, but they're full of guys with guns."

"Guys like me and my brother?" Duke asked.

"Yeah." Lizzie felt adrenaline rushing. "Hopefully more like you."

"Those big tires are not great for speed. Glad I got this truck with something other than mudding in mind."

She glanced away from the scope and looked into the back seat. Saj was slapping his hands on his car seat, happy and oblivious.

Rachael stared back at their pursuers, "Oh, God." She turned to Lizzie, her eyes and mouth wide open, her hands knuckled and white on the car seat.

Lizzie reached her hand to touch her shoulder. "We'll be all right, Rachael."

"Not planning on dying today." Duke hit a switch that turned off the headlights. The truck went dark, and so did the road. He took the next off-ramp.

"Don't we need the lights?"

"Moon's almost full." The off-ramp ended under an overpass. The rigs were coming up the freeway. Duke braked and slid to the right and slammed to a stop through the overpass. He grabbed the rifle from Lizzie and jumped out of the truck. "Drive."

"Okay," Lizzie said. *Where?* She climbed into the driver's seat, fastened her seatbelt and stepped on the gas enough to get around the corner, then she let it roll forward. Where was Duke?

She saw him jogging toward her, not too fast. She let the truck slow to a stop. Duke grabbed the door and jumped in the passenger seat. "Let's go. They went past."

"Uh, Duke. I don't really drive." The moonlight sparkled on the snow-covered road.

"You didn't wreck it last time. Drive thataway. Can you see?"

"Yeah. Well enough."

"All you need is well enough." He lifted the rifle and put his eye to the scope. "Get us out away from the freeway. I'll keep an eye out for them."

Lizzie drove. Everything was surreal. She had almost made it to her father. And now everything had gone to shit. She pulled off onto a road where they had a clear view of the freeway, and shut off the engine. "What now?" She looked at Duke.

"Call your friend." Duke handed her his phone.

"Good idea." She hit redial.

A male voice answered, "May I help you?"

"Dad?"

"I don't think so. Who is this?"

"Shit." Lizzie hung up. She scrolled up to her dad's number and pressed call. It rang.

"It's still me," the voice answered again, "Tell me who you are."

"Let me talk to my dad."

"This drunk spic? 'Fraid he's out cold. Drunken stupor." There were sounds of laughter in the background. "But you have a friend who wants to talk to you."

"Lizzie?" Jess choked off a sob. "Don't come."

"Jess?" Lizzie's voice edged toward hysteria. "Where are you? Are you safe?"

The male voice was back. "We're north of Salt Lake City. Mile marker 317. Come on down and hang out with your friends and family. In the morning we'll take you all into the city. For safety." The connection ended.

"Shit. Why'd all the assholes have to survive?"

"They're too mean to die," Duke said.

Lizzie dialed Glen, maybe he could help. "How are you?" she asked when he picked up.

"Starving." Glen sighed, his voice was a little louder than the last time. "Not that I couldn't lose a few pounds. These guys don't give up easy."

"I'm sorry. Look, Glen, I've got some more shit going down. Can you get access to Utah highway cameras too?"

"Yeah, I can get 'em. Where are you? What's up?"

"Bad guys. Things got worse instead of better."

"Yeah, I hear you." She could hear him breathing as a keyboard clacked. "Okay. I'm on the website. Exit number?"

"We took the exit north to Farmington. Don't know the exit number."

"322." Duke said.

"Exit 322. I think my dad's near mile marker 317 on Highway 15."

"Camera at 316.84. There are a number of vehicles in the distance. People standing around. It only updates every five minutes." His breathing stayed steady. "Nothing visible on the other cameras near there."

"Thanks. Glen." She sighed in disappointment.

"I'll keep the windows open and call you if anything changes."

"I owe you."

"Yeah, you do." He chuckled wryly. "I accept payment in Mountain Dew and information."

"Right. I'll pay when I can." Lizzie laughed. She closed her eyes and tried to calm herself. *Let me wake up and find out this is all a really, really bad dream.* Her fingers traced the scars on her arms.

"Lizzie." Duke's voice was gentle.

"Fuck you," she said, but only half-heartedly.

"Let's switch back." He scooted back toward the driver seat and Lizzie climbed over him numbly. "Those guys drove back south. Slower. One on each side of the highway. Spotlights." He backed up. "Luckily, they're lazy or incompetent or both. Let's head south by the side roads. Maybe we'll think of something on the way."

A light flashed above Nev's heart and her chest buzzed.

Zach's eyes bulged. She had a phone concealed in her cleavage. He was impressed considering she only wore an A-cup.

"Two phones." She grinned. Lizzie's obsessive collecting of cell phones had finally paid off. The men had taken away one phone from each of them and hadn't thought to look for a second.

Zach leaned toward her as she jerked his hand over so she could reach into her shirt. He kept watch to make sure none of the men were coming to check on them.

"It's Lizzie," Nev said. "She says hang tight."

"She better not try anything crazy."

"You know Lizzie." Nev tucked the phone into her pants'

pocket.

Zach smiled, enjoying her devious skills, but then he sobered. None of this would have happened if they stayed in Bellingham. The end of the world had been going so well. "Still glad you came?" he asked.

"Yeah." Nev held his hand to her face and kissed it. The cold of the hard cuffs connecting them bit into his wrist but he enjoyed the soft caress of her lips on his skin.

She examined the metal encircling her wrist. "I can get out of these, I think. Double jointed. 'member?"

Zach grinned. "I love you, Neveah."

Her lips formed a kiss and blew it. "Too bad our first experience with handcuffs wasn't under more pleasant circumstances."

A warm glow heated him more than the heater ever could.

Lizzie stood in the trees with Duke. The snow fell sparse and light. Rachael and Saj were safely stashed in a house away from the freeway. Duke had his rifle to his shoulder and squinted through the scope toward the highway.

She strained to see her friends through the trees; they were chained in a circle around a heater. "Okay. Do we need to go through the plan again?"

"Nope." Duke didn't take his eye from the scope. "But you still haven't told me what you're doing for a diversion."

"Wait and see," Lizzie said. The corners of his mouth twitched downward. He wasn't happy about her putting herself in danger. "They'll bite the bait. Trust me. They're not going to hurt me."

Duke grunted and brushed aside the snow accumulating on his eyebrows.

She rubbed her hands together to keep them warm. "I wish I had a frickin' cigarette."

"Me too." Duke took his eye away from his rifle scope and squinted at her. "No guns? You sure?"

"When you're in place I'll go."

He nodded. "All right. Be careful. And—"

"Don't do anything crazy?" Lizzie cut him off. "I am Crazy Lizzie. Crazy like a fox."

Duke laughed. "I was gonna say, good luck."

Half of her wanted to kiss him, but she said, "You, too. Now go."

Duke crouched and scuttled toward the freeway.

She sent a text to the phone Nev had responded on. **Now.** Then she pulled off her shoes and socks. Then her pants and underwear, and finally her shirt and bra joined the pile. She shivered.

You are crazy, Lizzie. She walked forward in the moonlight, not bothering to be stealthy. Rocks underfoot bit into the soles of her feet and so did the cold. She let the pain focus her.

The lights of the truck and radiant heater, with her friends sitting around it, came into view. She imagined being next to that heater, but it didn't help. So much for the power of the mind.

She walked briskly, her feet going numb. *Pretend you're drunk, stoned, or near-dead crazy.* She passed the guard with long, wavy blond hair sprinkled with snow. He was supposed to be watching. Nothing. So she kept walking. And walking. *Shit! I go streaking and nobody notices.*

"Hey, miss?" asked a puzzled voice behind her.

Bingo. *Keep walking, Lizzie.*

"Hey, come back here."

The wind had died or it would have been colder. Lizzie heard steps crunching in the snow. She let her neck go loose and she looked back at the fire and the guard without appearing to see anything. The guard walked toward her.

She kept her face blank and fearful. She ran clumsily a few paces. Dog-girl. Scared and confused. Her nipples hurt in the night cold. *This was a fucking bad idea.*

She made her eyes wide and wild as the man approached, and then turned and ran away down the highway. The sound of slow, deliberate pursuit came from behind. She ran across the lanes, trying not to skid on the icy asphalt. On the crunchy grass of the median she had better footing. She looked back to make sure he was following her. The ground wasn't slick but it was stony again. She felt the lumps of rocks underfoot, but not any pain—probably a bad sign.

"I won't hurt you, miss." His breath puffed in small clouds. "Please."

She slowed a little, letting him get closer. Then she stopped and looked uncertainly at the approaching guard, keeping up her ruse.

Behind him she saw that Zach, Nev and the others had disappeared. Mission accomplished! But she better give them more time.

"Are you okay? Come here, miss."

Lizzie cocked her head to the side like Spike did.

"I'm here to help you. I have a nice warm heater and a coat."
He coaxed her like an injured rabbit. His face showed genuine
concern. If he and his friends had not kidnapped her companions,
she might have been convinced.

More time. She rolled her eyes upward into her head and collapsed toward him. His arms caught her as she fell. Fainting was a
trick she'd learned in the psych ward to get out of things she didn't
want to do. This had not been part of the plan she'd told Zach or
Duke, but these people had her dad. Now she had gotten her
friends out of the jam, nothing else mattered.

30

ZACH SHOT AWAKE, ADRENALINE ANSWERING in his veins. Nev's phone buzzed glowing through the jeans on her hip.

"Okay, this is it," Nev said.

Zach tried to sense everything in every direction. Lizzie had said there would be a diversion. *What the hell was going to be the diversion?* "Nev?" he whispered. "Are you ready?"

"I hope so." Nev shrugged. "Never tried it with real cop cuffs." Nev twisted her hands inside the cuffs.

Zach watched her hands become slimmer as her thumb bent at an odd angle. She was free. Zach and Spike and Charley were still handcuffed together.

Nev gasped and her eyes widened. Zach followed her gaze. An ethereal shape passed on the edge of the freeway. It was Lizzie— her body clothed only in moonlight. *Shit, Lizzie, that is crazy.* It was crazy, but the guard stood and followed her.

"Let's go," Nev whispered. "Now."

Zach tore his eyes away. He held onto the loose cuff Nev had occupied, so it wouldn't make any noise. He motioned Charley to do the same. Nev led them, jogging toward the freeway. Zach, Spike, and Charley followed in an awkward three-legged-race stumble. Spike kept twisting to look at Lizzie and Zach had to tug hard on the cuffs to keep him going forward.

At the freeway a dark form detached from the shadows. They all stopped, frozen.

Then Zach recognized Duke. The handcuffs jerked Zach forward, as Spike launched at Duke.

"Spike," Zach hissed. "Not now."

Duke jumped backward, beckoning them to follow. They moved fast with Spike chasing Duke more than following him.

"It's okay, Spike," Charley soothed. "It's gonna be okay."

When they reached the tree line Duke stopped. He bent down and came up with guns. He handed Zach and Nev guns.

"What about Lizzie?" Zach hissed.

"She's gonna circle around and meet us at the house."

Zach nodded, reluctant to leave Lizzie behind without knowing she was away from danger. He spun all the way around, dragging Spike with him in a half circle.

Zach saw the guard carrying Lizzie draped over his arms. "Jesus fuck."

"What the hell is she doing?" Nev asked.

"Shit, Lizzie." Zach tugged at the handcuff chaining him to Spike.

Duke stared. "She really is crazy."

"Yeah." Zach gritted his teeth.

Duke's hands were white-knuckled on the barrel of the rifle. "There are only four of them."

Nev shook her head. "There are more coming. I overheard their leader talking about another crew meeting up with them at 4 a.m."

"Then we get out of here." Zach picked up Lizzie's clothes. "Figure something else out." A cell phone fell out of the pile and onto the ground. Zach retrieved it. On the screen was an unsent text intended for him. **Sorry 4 tricks. Gotta find my dad.** Zach read it aloud. "They have her dad, too."

"She thinks she can get to him," Duke said, "by being captured."

Zach sighed.

Yelling erupted behind them. Their escape had been discovered.

Zach said. "We're out of time."

"Okay, let's move." Duke led them at a hard pace through the trees and snow.

They broke out of the woods in a suburbia. Duke ran across a couple yards to one of the houses with a porch light on.

Rachael opened the door with Saj in her arms. She didn't protest as Nev took Saj and kissed his head.

Zach pulled the other handcuffed males to Nev and the baby,

checking him like a worried parent.

"You're with us now?" Zach turned a skeptical eye on Rachael. "That's convenient."

"I'm sorry," she said, casting her eyes down. "I didn't want to help them."

Zach's anger wavered. *Why am I pissed off at her?* Rachael shouldn't get the blame for the grudge he held against what those idiot Caldwell people had done. She had been as much a prisoner as Saj.

"Okay." He nodded once and said, "Now, how the Hell do I get these cuffs off!" He rattled his wrist at Duke.

Duke arched an eyebrow. "I'm supposed to know? I'm no criminal."

"I got Internet," Rachael said. "I'll see if I can figure it out."

"I got mine off." Charley grinned, holding up his hands. "Guess having little wrists helps."

They went inside the house and Rachael turned on a computer in the den. Zach's eyes swept the room. Spike jerked at the end of his tether and the cuff bit into Zach's wrist. Zach sighed. Of course he would end up literally chained to the hyper mutt.

"Dammit, Spike." Zach jerked his arm back toward himself, tugging Spike to a heel. "Charley, can you tell Spike to chill?"

Charley pulled Spike's hands toward him and made signs.

Rachael's fingers clacked at the keyboard. "Got it. There's a video."

She and Charley stared at the screen. Duke had disappeared to 'check the perimeter'. Zach sat on the couch. Spike had calmed down, but every time he exhaled he whined. Charley patted his leg and continued to distract him with sign language.

After watching the video over Rachael's shoulder and finding some bobby pins, Nev tinkered with the cuff between Zach and Spike. It took a few tries but eventually the cuff binding him to Spike popped open and he was free.

Zach picked up Saj and walked, the handcuff that had linked him to Nev still dangling from his wrist.

Nev followed him. "You okay, Zach?" Her hand touched his shoulder.

"No." He shrugged away from her. "Fucking pissed."

"Let me finish getting these bracelets off." Nev opened the door to a bathroom and flipped on the light. "Come on. The light's better in here."

"Thanks," he growled.

"Lizzie saved us." Nev poked and wiggled in the keyhole with the bobby pin. "Do you think she's in danger?"

"I don't know. The Boss guy didn't want us hurt. Just taken to their glorious *city*." He hugged Saj. "It's control. I don't want anybody telling me what to do. And I sure as hell know Lizzie doesn't want that." He gave a dry laugh. "But she set this up."

"Bingo," Nev said as the other handcuff released. Then she, quiet for a moment, searched his face. "Shouldn't we follow her?"

"As far as I am concerned, Lizzie made her bed and she can lie in it! You fucking bail her out." Immediately, Zach wished he could call back the words. "Nev-"

"Fuck you, Zach." Nev took Saj from his arms and stomped off.

The blond laid Lizzie down on something soft—a sleeping bag? She slipped her eyelids open, still playing unconscious. Her rescuer's eyes skipped back and forth from her breasts to her face. *Stupid jerk.* She opened her eyes, not caring about her ruse anymore.

His face twisted in embarrassment. "Are you okay?" he asked.

A rifle butt caught him in the gut and sent him flying backwards.

"Stupid shit." A mulleted man spat at Lizzie's captor. "You let them get away!"

"Fuck you, Carter."

He turned his glare down at Lizzie. She cowered at his feet, fig-leafing her arms, protecting her exposed parts.

"You let them get away for this, Travis?" His finger jabbed toward Lizzie.

"Hey!" Lizzie's anger gave her the presence of mind to pull the sleeping bag up over her shivering nakedness.

Travis lay a few feet away, groaning and clutching his stomach.

"I assume those were your friends," Carter said. "Well, I suppose a nice filled-out harlot like you might be worth a bit more. The males weren't going to bring us much and the one chick didn't have much of a figure." He leered down at her sleeping bag as if his eyes could bore right through it.

God, more breeders! The world's barely ended, you'd think people had other things on their minds. Lizzie met his eyes and held them. "Yes. They're my friends."

Carter's ugly mug split into a grin. "Well, I'll be a monkey's uncle. You traded yourself for them? If you wanted into *The City* so bad all you had to do was ask."

Lizzie shivered. "I don't want in *The City*, I want o see my dad. Fastest way, I figured, was to be brought in by you slavers."

"We're not slavers." His smile disappeared and the glare returned. "We're Collectors, collecting folks who need the safety of *The City*. Once you check in they don't keep you prisoner. People come and go. They need to have travel permits—for safety."

"Right. And I'm sure there is some benevolent, wise white-haired man who will let all us pretties know when it is safe to go back out into the big bad world. But lemme guess. It's not safe out here yet."

"Nope." Carter grinned. "We got the weather. The Utah Independents. The Crazies…

Lizzie yawned, as if bored. "I want clothes, a cigarette, a drink, and then some sleep—in that order." She jutted her chin out like a queen. If she was such a prize, he would treat her like one. Or so she hoped.

Carter stared at her for a long moment. He shook his arms out of the sleeves of his heavy black jacket.

She spied the Tank and pointed. "I have clothes in there."

"A cigarette and a drink? You old enough?"

"Are you?"

Carter chuckled handing her his coat. "What's your name?"

Lizzie slid her arms into the warm flannel-lined sleeves. It wasn't uncomfortable, but smelled of cigarettes and man. "I'm Lizzie."

He inclined his head. "Carter. Just Carter." He kicked snow at Travis who was starting to pick himself up off the ground. "Go fetch her bag of clothes." He asked Lizzie, "What's it look like?"

"It's a black duffle with Hello Kitty and Kiss patches."

A minute later Travis, still seething, dumped it at her feet.

Lizzie pulled out jeans, a tee, and a hoodie, dressing clumsily inside the sleeping bag. At the bottom of the duffel Lizzie spied a cell phone. She grabbed a baseball cap, scooping the phone into it as she shoved it in the belly pocket of the hoodie.

Once she was decent, and had warm socks and boots on, Carter motioned with his gun for her to get in the back of his truck.

"You'll be safe here." He tossed the sleeping bag next to her. He glared at Travis. "And warm—up off the ground. *The City* doesn't pay us for damaged goods."

Lizzie sat on the tailgate. Carter pulled a pack of cigarettes and popped one up. She slid the cigarette from the pack as he pulled an engraved Zippo out of his pocket and flicked it open. Lizzie stuck her cigarette in the flame and inhaled. Then she let it blow out of her mouth. She relished the dirty burn, but it didn't feel as good as it used to. It felt like ages since she had smoked and she realized she hadn't missed it. After that first drag, she stubbed it out.

"What do you mean by *The City*?" Lizzie slipped the cigarette in her pocket for later.

Carter raised an eyebrow. "Provo, but everybody calls it *The City*." He pulled a flask from his pocket and offered it to Lizzie.

"I've never been good at following rules, I don't think I'll make a very good citizen of this city." Lizzie accepted the flask.

Carter shrugged. "That's why some of us have to live on the outside as Collectors."

Lizzie raised the flask, "Cheers." She put it to her lips and then tipped it back. She grimaced at the burn in her throat and handed it back to Carter.

A 4X4 drove out of the dark, lights blinding as it rolled to a stop.

"Get some sleep," Carter said. "We'll be heading out in the morning." He strode toward the truck.

Lizzie unrolled the fresh sleeping bag he had tossed in the truck bed for her. She climbed inside the only privacy she was going to get. Under the cover of the downy shield, she pressed the power button on the phone and held it. She was rewarded with a flash of light, a logo and then a warning. "Plug in phone. Power level 0%." Then darkness. "Shit."

Mannie woke to a hand jostling him. Where was he?

"Wake up." Jess' voice came from behind him. "Mannie?"

"Jess?" He groaned. His blood pounded loud in his skull.

"I'm here, Mannie."

He let himself breathe. "What time is it?"

"It's four a.m. Lizzie's alive."

Lizzie's alive? Am I dreaming?

Jess' face held the hint of a smile.

"Really?" Had he heard her correctly? He didn't exactly trust his senses right now. He worked at rolling himself over.

"I talked to her. We were headed to meet her when some good old boys interrupted us." Jess lost the joy of the moment and now anger colored her voice.

Mannie got his legs over the edge of the bed and tried to stand. It was a bad move. His head throbbed and the room spun. "Jesus. What the hell was in that bottle?" He collapsed back, sitting on the bed, hands on his knees to stay vertical.

"Vodka," BeeGee said, chuckling sleepily. "You drank it all."

"Sorry."

"It's all good." BeeGee didn't bother to turn away from the wall. "You needed. I didn't."

Mannie took in his surroundings. They were in a small town jail. The three of them were in a cell with two beds and some chairs. A velvet painting of Elvis adorned the wall. An opaque shower curtain hung around when the stainless steel toilet was in use. Jess sat next to him on the edge of the bed covered with a pink frilly blanket. BeeGee lay on the other, a more sedate dark red.

"We're somewhere on the outskirts of Salt Lake City," Jess said, "awaiting transport into *The City.*"

"*The City?* Salt Lake?"

"Provo." Her face was grim and frustrated. "But they say, *The City* like it's some damned relic."

"The same people who stopped us at the roadblock?" Mannie watched Jess, her anger seemed so out of character he almost laughed. He held his own face tight. *Lizzie is alive.* Thinking the thought made everything okay. Even if they were locked in a jail.

"I think so. But the people who brought us here are like scouts or something. They call themselves Collectors."

"What do they collect?" Mannie knew the answer.

"Us. People. Young women seem to be their particular interest." Jess' face clouded.

Mannie put a hand on her arm. "Are you okay?" He was glad he hadn't laughed.

"Yeah," Jess shook off the darkness. "Just stupid. I drove right up to them and got out. Thought it was Lizzie."

"You did fine." Mannie smiled at her and then slumped back

down on his side. His hand throbbed, reminding him of the bite. "Shit. What day is it?"

"The twenty-sixth."

Mannie breathed a sigh of relief; he didn't need the next vaccine until day after tomorrow.

"A doctor came. He took off your bandage and redid it. I told him you needed the vaccine. He said he'd pass on the word." Jess seemed to sense his thoughts. "They're transporting us once the sun comes up.

Mannie nodded. "Okay."

"Lizzie knows we've been captured," Jess said softly.

Mannie turned to Jess; her voice sounded worried. "Is that bad?"

Jess looked tired, but holding herself together. She was tough, but he was pretty sure it was a thin sheen of strength. "You think she'll do something?"

"Yeah. We called her Crazy Lizzie in school…" Jess shrugged.

Mannie chuckled. *Blood will tell.* His Army buddies had tagged him *Poco Loco.*

"She'll probably get Zach to help her break us out."

"Randy will save me." BeeGee muttered and rolled over. "I'll be sorry if he kills you."

Mannie laughed again as Jess rolled her eyes. He tried to stand again, this time the room didn't move too much. The hangover faded to a fuzzy grogginess with a dull ache at the base of his brain stem as he paced. Regrets plagued his mind. After a while BeeGee sat up and started playing with her phone.

Their transport was delayed. The sun was well up. As much as he wanted to see her, Mannie hoped Lizzie was far away by now.

Jess leaned against the wall on the bed he'd slept on scratching words in a journal.

"You writing about me in there?"

"Maybe." She grinned up at him. "Some. Random thoughts mostly. Doodles. Trying to make sense of things." She tore the last sheet out and tossed it at the garbage can. It bounced off the edge and landed on the floor.

She scooched over to make room for him. He hesitated. Too exhausted to worry about what was appropriate, he lay down beside her and closed his eyes.

It seemed like he only had a moment of respite before the cell doors clanged open.

31

Mannie glared as a middle-aged man with a beer belly and a uniform loose everywhere else slid open the cell bars.

"You folks ready to go into *The City*?" The guard made it sound like he was taking them to Disneyland.

"We have some choice in the matter?" Mannie asked.

The guard, shook his head. "Nope. Sorry. I drive the bus."

Mannie stood up and stretched his knee. "You got a name?"

"Friends call me, Rocky." The man offered his hand.

Mannie paused and stared at the offered hand. "I'm Mannie." He shook it, startled by the surrealness of such a normal activity. *Not like they hadn't all been exposed.*

"Yeah." Rocky nodded. "I guess that makes sense."

Jess nudged BeeGee awake on the other bunk.

Rocky led them outside to a waiting van. Snowflakes floated down on the clean and pretty ground.

Inside the van, one man rode in the passenger seat, shotgun in hand. Two more young men with guns were in the back. They weren't an enemy Mannie was used to: civilians—realtors, accountants, gardeners. He thought about escaping, but with amateurs and guns things would go downhill fast. And he couldn't face any more ghosts.

Mannie stared northward and sighed. *So close.* He climbed in, nodding at the young men; they looked bored.

Jess climbed in and sat next to him, giving him a half smile.

BeeGee climbed in and Jess slid over until she was up against him. The ride was quiet.

Lizzie sat in the passenger side of the Tank as it bounced along toward Salt Lake City. Carter drove. Travis drove the boss's truck and the other truck followed behind.

Carter hadn't shut up since he finished his last Coke. "Lizzie, you really are kinda crazy, ain't ya? Kinda remind me of my daughter, God rest her soul." He sighed and shook cigarette ash out the window.

"Yeah."

"You know I really ain't a slaver. I worked it out in my head. You want to know what I figure?" He fumbled open the six-pack cooler, driving with his knee for a moment. "Damn, no more Coke."

Lizzie ignored him.

"It's like Lincoln said," he continued, even without a prompt. "*Most people do about the best they can with what they got any given moment.*' Or somethin' like that."

"It was Anne Frank."

"Yeah. Mebbe. I'm doin' right by people."

"Yourself included?" she spat.

"Why not?" He took another drag on his cigarette.

Her confidence was shaken in the light of the new day. She wondered if she really would find her dad in Provo, and once she did, how she would get away and find her friends again. What if they left without her? She realized she had been in such a rush to find her dad that she had left behind the people who were most important to her.

"Want some music?" Lizzie asked. "I can plug in my player." She held her breath and took the dead phone out of her pocket."

"Sure. But I doubt you'll have my kind of music, youngster."

"Try me." Lizzie's shoulders relaxed, as she plugged it into the cigarette lighter. He hadn't realized it was a phone—or maybe he didn't care. "I'm pretty eclectic."

"Waylon, Merle, Willie. Johnny Cash. You might have some of his stuff. That newer crap."

"Got 'em. Mom was into country and old rock. They're kinda all mixed in. You like Patsy? Emmylou?"

"Like 'em both." He sounded excited, like he hadn't expected to hear music again.

Lizzie slid through the music. "*Crazy.* Sort of my theme song."

He laughed and turned up the volume, belting out the chorus. The music put Carter in a better mood and she was able to flip back and forth, unnoticed, between the music and texting, as the phone charged.

She texted Zach. **Heading for provo. Where r u?**

Carter's phone rang, and Lizzie jumped, thinking it was her phone for a moment. He answered his phone, she made sure hers was on silent.

From Lizzie's side, the conversation consisted only of monosyllabic comments.

He took the next exit as he hung up the phone. He smiled at her. "A little detour. Keep us out of *The City* for a while…"

"My dad?"

"Already on the way."

"What?"

"On his way to *The City*. I got shit to take care of in Salt Lake."

Lizzie seethed. Behind them the others followed, taking the exit into Salt Lake City. The snow had thickened, coating the entire freeway white. No road crews anymore. She tried breathing gently like a counselor had suggested once. In deep, then out slow.

She forgot the music and the phone as they got further from her dad. Her mood became more foul. She slunk down low in the seat, refusing to look at Carter. They drove on in silence.

"Collectors ain't the only thing to worry about, you know."

He seemed disappointed when she didn't ask what he meant.

"There are people out there, call themselves the Utah Independents, they don't just *collect* young women. They're your slavers." He paused as if to let that sink in. "*The City*'s not all peaches and cream, but out here it's worse."

Lizzie texted one handed: **Not going to provo yet.**

Zach woke to full sun alone in a strange bed. He sighed deeply and shoved himself up. He found the others in the living room: Rachael playing blocks with Saj, Spike sleeping in the sun and Duke cleaning his guns. Duke nodded at Zach.

Nev's fingers tapped away on the computer. He crossed to her and hugged her from behind.

"Sorry," he whispered in her ear.

"I know." She turned her head and kissed his cheek. "Me too." Her words convicted him. She was sorry he'd been a jerk. But they also implied it would be okay.

"What'd you find?" Zach motioned to the computer.

"Nothing new." She shook her head. "It's like Utah is the dead zone. There's nothing happening. Not sure how I can explain it. No online activity. It's like someone's controlling the web. It's up, but nothing is originating from here. She pulled her chair back from the computer and turned to face him. "You wanna go for a run?" She jabbed him gently in the gut.

"Yeah, get some fresh air. Rachael, you okay with Saj?"

"Of course."

"Be back in a bit." Zach stared at Duke. *What a freaking weird world.* "Are you and Spike okay?"

Duke nodded. "I think so. I fed him some beef stick last night." He grinned. "That won him over. How about you?"

Zach shrugged. *You want to know if I have a grudge with you?* "I don't know."

Duke nodded. "Fair." He turned back to the guns.

Zach and Nev pulled on jackets and headed out into the cold.

They ran in silence for a while. Running cleared his head. Finding Lizzie's dad had been the whole plan. He wasn't sure what to do, but clearly they couldn't abandon Lizzie. They needed a new plan. If they rescued Lizzie and her dad was still a prisoner… She wouldn't leave without him. Their new plan would have to include getting Mannie and Jess.

"I tried sending texts to Jess' phone and Mannie's. Nothing back." Nev said.

They slowed to an easier pace, Zach puffed between words. "I guess we wait. Keep a low profile." They jogged on.

After a bit, Nev turned and continued to jog backwards. "I miss my folks. And my grandpa. And grandma. Can't hardly see how Lizzie could handle missing Jayce."

"Yeah, but she left Saj?" Zach shook his head. "I don't understand it."

"I don't get how she thinks she can break her dad out of *The City.*"

"The key word in that sentence is 'think.' Lizzie reacts; she doesn't think." Zach temper burned. "We need to take care of each other, but she keeps doing her own thing. She's so...so..." He stopped running, unable to talk and run like Nev. She stopped beside him.

"Selfish," Nev finished. "But as selfish as she was, she made sure we got out of there. Now we have to do the same for her."

He clenched his fists. "They got the Tank. Makes me feel naked."

"Then let's get another one. And we need weapons." Nev's lips tightened into a line. "I don't like guns. Never have. But last night when Duke handed one to me, it felt necessary."

"Duke seems well-stocked, but we should find you something your size."

They returned to the house hand in hand.

Carter drove with a scowl on his face. Something was going on and he had stopped being loquacious. He sat there stewing over something.

The sky darkened and Lizzie lost hope of seeing her dad today.

Carter barked, "Shut off the damn music."

She pulled some headphones out of the glove-box and slid them over her ears; Carter didn't argue.

Lizzie was no longer sure she wanted go into *The City* as a captive. If she could figure out a way to get them in an accident and pop the air bags, maybe she could run away.

The moon loomed large and low over the hills, glowing bright against the faded sky. The snow had eased off, only a few flakes, but it was deep on the freeway.

Before Lizzie could figure out how to enact her car crash plan, Carter's walkie-talkie spit static then voices; Lizzie jerked the headphones from her ears, so she could hear what was going on. She didn't like how worried Carter looked.

The walkie talkie speaker scratched, "Carter, we got trouble."

"On my way. Get reinforcements." He released the talk button.

"What?" Lizzie asked.

"Independents sighted near my home base." Carter gripped the steering wheel and the truck sped up. He didn't say another word until they pulled into "home base," the county jail.

Carter led her into a holding cell. He slid the door shut and hollered, "Clear."

Lizzie heard the bolts clunk into place. She glanced around. The cell had been modified from its former purpose, pink bedding, art on the wall, and a shower curtain around the toilet. There were a couple chairs and a pair of beds with a pile of reading material on one.

She lay down; she hadn't slept well. Self-doubts spun through her head as she lay there feeling queasy.

An old Rolling Stone magazine with Johnny Depp on the cover caught her eye. The thought of no more new music and no more new magazines made her sad. She tossed the pile onto the floor and crawled into the covers.

Carter had been dumb enough to leave her with her cell phone, and it was fully charged now. She pulled it out to text.

No signal. But there was an answer to her last text from Zach. **Okay. Waiting.**

Lizzie had done the right thing rescuing her friends. They were worth it, but letting herself get caught was making less and less sense. She'd hoped to be with her father by now. *Was he worth it?* The voice on the phone had said he was passed out drunk. She closed her eyes, tired emotionally and physically.

Zach, Duke and Nev talked strategy over lunch, cans of stew Rachael had found and heated up. They made a list of sporting goods shops in Salt Lake. They agreed to scout for vehicles and guns on the way.

Zach snorted. "Not like people have stickers on their doors that says 'Registered Gun Owners of America.'"

"Wait," Nev said. "That's it. I wonder if Glen can get us that info?" She was already dialing. "I bet it's on a computer somewhere."

"Good idea," Duke said.

"Yeah." Zach nodded. "Using your head."

Glen was still hiding, but no longer hungry. He'd stolen a case of army rations from the guys staking out his building. He ran some searches and e-mailed them a list of addresses of gun owners.

Duke mapped out a route on his laptop. "We'll look for a second vehicle as we go."

Zach scanned the streets as they drove. He was tired of driving in a vehicle crammed with people. Something smaller would do fine. He spotted a small white RAV4. "Stop. Back up. Down that street."

Duke whipped a u-turn, squirreling the tires.

Zach grabbed the oh-shit handle. "Thanks." It was a Toyota hybrid, not the big Highlander he'd had his heart set on in Bellingham, but the smaller RAV4. Ought to fit four comfortably. Hopefully it had a full charge. He hopped out. It was locked, of course. The dashboard alarm light was flashing. That was a good sign. He turned to Duke.

Duke shrugged. He reached into the bed of the truck and hefted a metal baseball bat. "Here. You might need a house key."

Zach caught it with his left hand, "Thanks." He strode to the house, swinging the bat loosely. He hit the doorbell. It echoed in the house.

He twisted the doorknob. The door opened. Zach pushed it gently. "Hello? Can I borrow your car?" Breaking in still nerved him up, but it came out as energy. He gripped the bat with both hands, holding it ready. There was a coat rack right inside the door with some key hooks full of assorted keys. In a dish on a little shelf lay a full ring of keys, including a Toyota key and a bunch of others. He pressed the unlock button and heard the vehicle chirp softly. "Bingo." He walked back outside.

"Always wanted to drive one of these." Duke opened the door and beckoned for Zach to get in. "And check out the engine."

"Yeah. Me too." Zach sat down wondering if Duke was humoring him. A button glowed green on the dashboard. Zach pushed it. There was a low hum and barely perceptible rumble. "So far, so good."

"You sure you don't want a gas-based one?" Duke smiled. "No need to save the planet, right?"

Zach wanted this car. "It'll do for now." He climbed in and played with the vehicle. Duke got in the other side. There was a red button on the dashboard. Looked like an aftermarket add-on. "What's this? The ejection seat?" Zach pressed it. Suddenly he heard engine noise, loud pistony engine sounds. The digital readout read V8 truck.

Duke was laughing. "It's a fake."

Zach pressed it again and again. VW Bug. Then Harley Davidson. Then Landspeeder. "Awesome." He grinned and left it humming.

His phone buzzed. Nev. He answered it. "Yeah?"

"Lizzie sent a text," Nev blurted. "Her dad and Jess are in some kind of trouble."

Zach sighed. "We're on our way."

At the safe-house he glanced around at the crew. He'd gotten another text, too. "They're not headed for Provo, some kind of delay. This is probably our last chance to get her back the easy way."

32

ZACH TURNED OFF THE WOOSHING Landspeeder sound and drove the RAV on silent. White always seemed like a stupid color for a car, especially a 4X4, but today in the snow it was good. He shut the lights off, too.

The snow had settled; the moon was full and bright. All was silent in the world. The tracks in the snow were visible, but only as a series of intertwining ruts, one filled with more snow than the other. The highway climbed gradually. Zach split the middle between the downslopes and the ditches, driving carefully.

Nev, Saj, Rachael and Charley waited in Duke's truck. Waiting while Zach, Duke, and Spike went on another damn fool's errand.

Spike's eyes scanned the snow, a smile on his face. In the backseat Duke checked the chambers of his small arsenal of guns for the umpteenth time. Click-clack. Click-clack.

"Duke? Is this a good idea?"

"Hell if I know. It makes as much sense as anything in this new world. You shoot a handgun before?"

Zach nodded. "Yeah."

"Here." Duke handed him a pistol.

Zach hefted it. Heavy. Solid. It reminded him of Gramps' war-issue .45. "Thanks. Hopefully we won't be needing it."

"Safety's on. Right by the thumb. Don't shoot your foot off."

Zach wound steadily up the mountain, silent as the wind outside. The perfect stealth vehicle.

"Spike?" Zach looked over at Spike, mesmerized by the snow. "When we stop. You stay. In car. Okay?"

Spike nodded.

Duke said, "Slow. My phone says we're near the pass."

A beam of light flashed ahead. "Duke. You see that?" Zach's eyes strained for more.

"What?"

"Up there," Zach said, "I saw a flashlight, I think." He took his foot off the gas and let the vehicle slow to a stop on its own. He pulled the emergency brake and took a deep breath.

Duke handed him two full magazines. "14 rounds each for the Smith & Wesson."

Zach pocketed them. He slid his hand up and turned off the door ajar light. "Okay. And?"

"Shotgun or rifle?"

"Rifle."

Duke handed him a rifle straight out of the Old West. "Big Boy. 45 Colt."

"That'll do." Zach smiled grimly. "I guess I'm growed up enough."

"I don't have extra holsters."

"I'll be all right." Zach turned back to Spike. "Spike. Stay. In the car. Okay?" He ripped open a bag of jerky and dumped it in his lap. *That ought to keep him busy.*

"Let's go."

Subdued light streamed into the cell. Lizzie blinked her eyes and forced herself up. Her stomach growled. She got out of bed and tugged the covers with her, shuffling to the door of the cell.

"Hey, Carter." No response. "Anybody out there? I'm hungry." She heard a boom followed by the small pop of firecrackers, and for a moment wondered what the celebration was. Then it hit her, those rat-a-tats weren't fireworks; they were gunfire.

"Shit." She envisioned herself starving, locked in the cell as the rest of the world went crazy around her.

Lizzie rattled the bars. "Hey! Anybody out there?" she yelled.

Hell of a place to die. Mama had always said things would get better. But they never did for her. *Mama had a way of not really living in the real world.*

Lizzie held out her cell phone and walked around the room, looking for signal. *Plenty of bars in here, but not the kind I need.*

From time to time she heard more gunfire, distant explosions and yelling.

Lizzie went through her pockets. She had 27 cents, a Band-Aid, the cigarette from last night and lint. "Looks like Crazy Lizzie fucked things up again." Nothing she could do but get back in bed and wait.

She should have waited. She should have let Zach and Nev and Duke help her, instead of being the stupid lone gun. She didn't even have a gun. As Zach would say, "Stupid. Stupid. Stupid."

Lizzie went to the garbage can, nothing in it. A scrunched up piece of paper lay beside it. She picked it up and straightened it out. There were drawings and words, names. Lizzie, Mannie, BeeGee, Zach… "Oh, my god. " Her father and Jess had been here. How long ago? Minutes before she'd arrived? Hours? She'd been so close. But close only counted in horse-shoes, hand grenades and slow dancing.

Lizzie's fingers traced the scars on her arm. How long ago since she'd cut herself? She could picture it happening. See the blood as the razor cut filled the line with red. It was another life. With all those other parts: Jerkwad, school, Chad.

Back then she had been afraid of the future. Now she feared the present.

The sun died on the horizon and the sound of gunfire died with it. The buzzing of the bare fluorescent corkscrew bulb above her head was the only sound—and the only light.

Lizzie lay back down and dozed fitfully.

The cell door slid open and into place with a metallic thud. Lizzie rolled out of the bed, groggy and looking for weapons.

Carter came through, tired, sweaty and dirty. "Come, if you're coming." His hair was disheveled; blood that didn't look like it was his stained his shirt.

"What happened?"

"Independents happened. They want us to stay south. Think we're honing in on their territory. The van carrying our last batch of folk is stranded. We need to get to 'em before the Independents do."

"Last batch?" Her heart stopped. "You mean my dad?"

"Yeah," Carter said over his shoulder as he headed outside. Lizzie ran after him. He climbed into the Tank again; someone had chained the tires. He started the engine. The familiar sound was a small comfort. She could have turned and run, but where would she go? And Carter was her best chance to find her dad. She got in and closed the door. He drove like a demon, tossing snow away before she even buckled her seat belt.

Her cellphone had full bars now. Lizzie sent a text to Zach and pinged him her location, not even trying to conceal it from Carter. He had other things to worry about.

"I thought I heard gunfire."

"That was gunfire. The Independents are getting gutsier as winter comes on."

The wind whipped the snow sideways.

"But why are they fighting you?"

"They think *The City* is cutting into their territory. Which it is. And *The City* saves people from the Independents."

Carter stopped talking and drove. The full moon shone through the clouds. The volume of snowfall increased the higher they climbed—smaller flakes, but lots more of them.

He took the winding curves at an insane speed but the chained tires bit into the icy snow and kept them on the road.

The road leveled out in front of them and there was a big passenger van with people huddled around it. Lizzie's eyes searched. Young men with guns, a dark haired woman, and... Her heart leaped. Jess! Then fell.

Where was her father? Carter pulled the Tank around the side of the van. Someone in khaki pants bent over the engine compartment. She had the door open and was running even before the Tank stopped.

"Dad?" Lizzie called. His head jerked upward, clunked against the hood. She heard a growl of anger. He turned, giving her a crooked smile, a reverse of the one she'd seen in the mirror for years. His arms opened as he limped toward her.

"Elizabeth." His voice, soft and warm, was even more comforting in person.

Lizzie dove into his arms. They fell into the snow. "Oh, Daddy." She buried her face in his warm chest. She heard his heartbeat, fast and strong. "I found you. You're alive."

"And so are you, my Elizabeth." His arms squeezed her tight.

For the first time in forever maybe, Lizzie realized she felt safe. Her brain said she wasn't, but her heart disagreed.

"Aww," Jess said above her. "Can I have a hug, too? When you stop blubbering?"

Lizzie smiled, holding her dad tight. "Yeah. Jess. Come get yours." Lizzie opened an arm, making room for Jess.

"Group hug," Jess hollered and fell toward them, knocking a fresh puff of icy powder in Lizzie's face.

Her father let out a muffled grunt.

Lizzie held them both with all her strength. Nothing else mattered. She had her dad and Jess for a bonus. Lizzie pulled back to look at him. Tears ran down his weather worn face. He reached a hand to cup her chin. She marveled in his smile.

Someone cleared their throat behind them. Carter's gruff, voice, softer than usual, said. "All right, this reunion's about the sweetest thing I've seen since before the goddamned plague hit, but if we don't get out of here, the Independents are likely to break things up. We need the van running."

His words brought Lizzie back into the moment. Carter jerked his head at a man holding a shotgun. "You keep watch." Then his head disappeared under the hood.

Lizzie, Jess and her father climbed into the van, all of them grinning and glowing.

Zach slipped into his brown jacket and pulled the gray hood of his sweatshirt out of the neck. "Would've been smart to get some white clothes."

"Oh, well." Duke zipped his black jacket. "Let's do this." He gestured toward a ditch on the side of the road.

Zach followed. They hunched low and jogged along the shallow indent. The snow was light and about a foot deep, piled up on each side of the ditch, offering a bit more cover.

They stopped a hundred yards away from the vehicles. Once they left the ditch, there was no cover but the vehicles themselves. *Damn.* Zach saw the Tank. *Assholes stole my truck!* His hands were cold, but he couldn't wear gloves and pull a trigger. Though he wondered if he would be able to do any better with frozen fingers.

Duke nudged his arm and motioned with his hands. *I'll go left. You go right.*

Zach nodded. He hustled around the van as quiet as he could. Two men with guns guarded the third under the hood. There were shadows huddled inside the van: Lizzie, Mannie and Jess. Seemed a little crowded for three people, so there were probably more guards inside.

Zach recognized the clothes of the man under the hood: Carter, the Bossman. He pressed the muzzle of his rifle to the man's neck. "Turn around really slow. We've got you covered."

The van door opened.

"Call off your dogs, Carter," Zach ordered, pointing the rifle at Carter's chest.

"Shit!" Carter turned to face him. "Stupid kid. This is all I need! Stand down, men."

Two men walked toward them with hands over their heads. Duke followed fanning his gun back and forth.

"Zach!" It was Lizzie's voice.

"Saving your ass again, sweetheart."

"Kid," Carter said, "put down the gun and let me get this van fixed. We're worried about bigger fish. You should be, too."

"Independents," Lizzie said.

Zach nodded, keeping his rifle pointed straight at the older man's gut. "We don't need your van. I'll be taking the Tank back. Besides, you can fix your van once we're gone."

"You'd leave me here to die from the cold or the Independents?"

"Not my problem." Zach shrugged.

Lizzie hopped out of the van. "Zach, he came back for me when he could have left…"

"Fucking enough, Lizzie," Zach growled. "Listen to me for once. This guy isn't some dog trapped inside a house. He has been doing his best to put us in cages. We'll go our way and let him go his."

A strong-looking, dark-skinned man in a uniform hopped down into the snow, quirking an eyebrow in amusement at Zach. The expression was one Lizzie had shot him any number of times. This could only be Mannie. "Kid knows what he's talking about, Elizabeth."

"Dad, this is Zach."

Zach nodded at Mannie. "Sir."

"Mannie, please." He patted down Carter and told him, "Get inside the van."

Carter glared, but got in.

Jess and a woman Lizzie called BeeGee joined them out in the snow along with two more Collectors from inside the van. Once they were disarmed, Mannie picked out his own gun and helped herd them all back inside the van.

Lizzie jingled keys she had lifted from Carter's pocket. "The Tank is back in service." She handed them to Zach.

Zach glanced around; the wind had gotten biting cold. "We have a hybrid parked a ways back. Who's going to drive what?" Zach glanced around at the new crew.

"You take Jess and BeeGee in the Tank; bet you miss it." Lizzie smiled. "Dad, Duke, and I will take the Hybrid."

"Yeah."

"Okay." Mannie motioned with the rifle in his hands. "You folks stay in the van. I'm going to walk backwards down the hill. If I see a door open before we're gone, and I shoot." With that he slammed the van door shut.

Zach climbed into the Tank. Jess and BeeGee climbed in the back. He pulled forward and turned it around. Then he rolled the window down, driving slowly. Lizzie and Duke walked alongside as he rolled, the snow crunching under the tires. Mannie did as he promised, keeping an eye on the van.

It felt good to be behind the wheel of the Tank again. He rapped his fingers on the cracked dashboard. He had Lizzie, Mannie, and Jess. In minutes he'd be back with Nev and everything would be fine. He was riding a high.

Lizzie's arm shot out, pointing. "What's that?"

Lights moving further down the highway caught Zach's eyes.

"Shit," Duke snarled, "That's my truck."

Zach leaned out the window. "God dammit. They've got Nev. And Saj and Charley!"

Lizzie spun around. "What do we do?"

Another truck spit snow behind Duke's truck. Zach sighed. "Surrender. Again. Shit."

When the trucks got close Zach could see the blond surfer dude, one hand on the steering wheel, one hand aiming a gun at Nev beside him in the passenger seat. Rachael cowered with Saj in the back seat. The trucks pulled to a stop and a window unrolled in the rear truck. Charley's head poked out, and Zach could see a couple other men bristling with guns behind him.

"I'm sorry, Lizzie," Charley called. "I was just keeping lookout."

"It's all right, Charley," Lizzie called. "Odds were long anyway. You okay?"

"Yeah. Just scared."

Blondie rolled down his window. "Everybody back to the van."

Zach could tell Lizzie was pissed.

"Fuck off, Travis," Lizzie glared at him.

Don't go ballistic now. Not while he has a gun on Nev.

Lizzie took a deep breath and turned to trudge back up the slope.

Zach sighed, releasing the brake and driving backward uphill. *They got us all but Spike.* He watched the white RAV, half expecting Spike to come out and run after them.

33

Lizzie stood in the biting wind. Her dad had his arms wrapped around her against the cold. The man with the shotgun stood close by.

A few more feet away, Carter and Travis argued.

Lizzie heard a low thrum sounded over the blasting snow and wind. Her father heard it, too. His eyes scanned the blinding white all around them. The rumble grew louder.

"Independents," the shotgun-toting guard growled. Men sprang into action.

"Scatter!" Carter hollered. His men headed in various directions, their weapons ready.

Lizzie's dad dragged her away from the road. The motors got louder. Snowmobiles. She stumbled, pushing herself to keep up with her dad. The lights cut through the darkness over their heads. Mannie lifted her off her feet and dumped her into a snowbank.

"Stay down," her dad said, his voice low and forceful. "Get under the trees."

Then he ran away from her as fast as he could. *Not again.* Tears stung her eyes.

One of the snowmobiles crested the rise, engine howling at an ear-piercing pitch. Shouts rang out, gunshots exploded and the sound died in the snowfall.

He wasn't deserting her, she reassured herself, but leading them away. The lights had him pinned, then he disappeared. The snowmobile dove down into the drifts, sliding, twisting, and pulled up short. Must be a cliff she couldn't see down there. *If he got himself killed now…*

The rider stood up, and swept a giant black flashlight across the snow. The flashlight swung toward her and she face-planted in the snow. She raised her head after a moment, icy trickles leaking down her cheeks. The rider holstered his light and spit snow in a broad curving turn.

As the snowmobile climbed the hill Lizzie slipped away. Her legs sank in up to her knees in a snow-drift. She slogged forward, glad she wasn't naked. Above her, loud angry voices echoed.

Lizzie glanced back to make certain no one followed on foot. She kept moving, but took a misstep into a hole as she twisted. The snow came up to greet her in slow motion. At least it was soft to fall into.

"Give me your hand."

Lizzie's heart jumped and continued pounding. "Shit, Dad," she muttered, "How the hell did you sneak up on me like that?"

"'Army training, sir,'" he whispered, smiling with his eyes, helping her regain her feet. "Let's get around where we can do something."

"With what? Our bare hands?"

"I don't know yet. Maybe we can sneak around behind the other trucks." He brushed some snow from her hair. "Sorry, I was a bit rough."

Lizzie nodded, biting her lip. "It's okay."

"Come on, let's get past the tree line," he said. "Easier to move and to hide."

Lizzie followed her father's footsteps through the deep snow. It was easier to move when someone else broke a path. Inside the trees the snow piled in places where it opened to the sky, but elsewhere the ground was bare.

They crept alongside the road under cover of the trees. Lizzie spotted the white RAV4 Zach and Duke had come in. Just knowing Duke as well as she did, she suspected there might be weapons inside and mimed "guns" to her dad. He nodded and pointed both fingers to his eyes and then away.

Even without army training, Lizzie understood: *Let's check it out.*

Another engine roared on the hillside above as Mannie led Lizzie to a spot they could make a run for the RAV. A big truck, diesel engine from the lup-a-lup sound of the engine, came into view. It pulled a long trailer behind it for the snowmobiles. A pack of barking dogs leaped from the bed of the truck.

Nobody else had gotten away. Her friends were all up on the hillside with arms raised in surrender. She stumbled after her father.

When they reached the place where the treeline curved closest to the RAV, he whispered, "This is as good as we're going to get. They'll be able to see us if they look. So, as fast as you can, get in, look for weapons, get out. Then we meet back here."

Lizzie nodded, catching her breath.

He paused, searching her face. "Lizzie—"

"I know, Dad." She bear-hugged him.

He said it anyway. "I love you, Elizabeth."

When they ran, she knew he was with her every step of the way. She reached the vehicle and jerked open the front door as he pulled open the back. Spike piled out on top of her.

Her father yanked Spike off her. Spike yelped.

"Dad, it's Spike. It's okay." His hot breath panted on her. In the distance dogs barked.

"Lizzie." Her father placed a shotgun in her hands, staring warily at Spike. "Here."

Her stomach flipped. The dogs had seen them and were running down the snow bank.

"Run," her father ordered.

Spike turned this way and that, he was scared. But he saw the dogs and Lizzie's reaction to them. There was understanding in his eyes. He lumbered uphill toward the dogs.

Lizzie froze. "Spike. Don't!"

For a moment he stopped, staring back at her, his eyes fathomless. He made the signs Charley had taught him. "Run." Spike gestured to himself then toward the dogs. "I run." Then he signed to Lizzie, "You hide." He turned and shuffled toward the dogs, hunkering down and growling at them. The dogs milled around, confused by the big man who did not act like a human.

Lizzie glanced back up the hill. Duke and Zach waved at her to run. Independents with guns were moving down the slope.

"Lizzie." Her father's urgent voice demanded her attention.

She couldn't tear her eyes away, even as he tugged her backward toward the tree line. Her eyes locked on Spike as the first dog lunged, then the pack followed, snarling and tearing. He had been the first person she had seen alive after everything went to hell. And now he was giving up that life for her.

Lights flashed across the snow and the rumble grew. The Collector in the van opened the door and jumped out. Zach turned to Duke. "Snowmobiles."

Duke nodded. "Independents?"

Nev grasped Zach's arm tight. "Shit. What do we do?"

"Hell if I know." Fear washed over him. He fought it—for Nev. He had to stay strong.

The Collectors scattered in a frenzy. Zach pulled Nev outside. Mannie and Lizzie had disappeared. They were on their own. Zach pushed Nev ahead and crept around the side of the van. Rachael and Jess followed, protecting the children between them. Duke brought up the rear.

A wall of snow flew at him as a snowmobile swerved to a stop. A gunman behind the driver aimed an AK-47 at them. The other two snowmobiles spun around the van, heading off in either direction.

The gunman with the Kalashnikov rifle pointed it in the air and squeezed off a quick burst. "Everybody freeze! NOW!"

Zach stopped. He put his hands up and the rest followed suit. The chilly wind buffeted them; they really would freeze.

The driver got off the snowmobile and took a shotgun out of a holster taped to the side of his snowmobile. "I want some answers and I'll hurt people to get them."

Zach felt sweat trickle down his armpits; a second ago he was freezing.

The driver continued. "I want to know how many Collectors were here before they scattered like a bunch of chicken shit pansies."

The gunman stayed mounted, covering them with an M-16, as the driver forced Zach to his knees with a kick.

Zach's knees burned in pain then the icy gravel bit into his jeans. *If only we hadn't been so stupid.*

The gunman pointed the shotgun at Zach's head.

"I'll talk," Nev yelled. She counted on her fingers slowly. "There were six I know for sure, and then a bunch more. Maybe ten."

The two other snowmobiles returned. The shotgun withdrew.

They hadn't caught Lizzie or Mannie. Zach breathed a sigh of relief.

The driver pulled his helmet off his head and set it on the snowmobile. He had a pock-marked face under a well-trimmed beard and a handlebar mustache. "Tell me about the rest."

The driver put his shotgun back in Zach's face. The chilly barrel caressed his cheek.

"Two more of our people," Nev blurted. "An old guy and a young girl."

"Let go." Lizzie pushed her father's arm away. "I'll run."

They were inside the trees again. An ear splitting whistle rang out behind them, once and then again. The snarling died down. Somebody had called off the dogs. Her father stopped. She fell against a tree to catch her breath.

He pulled her down into a crouch and then looked back they way they'd come. "I'm sorry about your friend," he whispered gently.

Lizzie's eyes searched, hoping to see Spike limping after them. But she knew he was gone.

Her father held her for a moment. Then he pulled back and placed his hands on the sides of her face. His eyes showed more sadness than Lizzie thought she had ever seen. He kissed her forehead.

She watched him as the sadness clicked out and anger replaced it.

"Okay," he said. "We want to get those guys that did it?"

Lizzie nodded.

"Okay. Focus. Tell me what you saw. How many people? Which sides?"

Lizzie closed her eyes, picturing the scene in her head. "Independents: three snowmobiles, four men. New truck, three men, five or six dogs." She gritted her teeth as she recited everything else she had seen. She surprised herself in the detail she remembered. But it was seared into her brain by the death of her friend. Because he *had* been her friend.

"Fits what I saw." Her father nodded, his hand brushed the hair away from her face.

"What's the plan, Cap'n?" Lizzie saluted him half-heartedly and wiped away the tears.

"Lieutenant. Not exactly a plan. I want to tell you to run that-away. Fast."

Lizzie bared her teeth. "My friends—no, my *family* is up there. You say we need a plan. *What. Is. It?*"

Her father sighed. "You move ahead of me that way, stay close to the road, but not too close. Keep your eyes peeled. Stay quiet. I'm sticking closer to the edge of the trees. I'll take them out if they follow you."

"Okay." She wrapped her arms around him awkwardly, the shotgun in her arms. "Daddy, I always loved you." His arms held her; the butt of his gun pressed against her back. "Always."

It looked to Lizzie like he wanted to tell her that everything was going to be fine. But he kept his mouth shut. *No guarantees.* She appreciated the honesty.

A pop-pop of gunfire set them both in motion. Lizzie slipped from tree to tree as quiet as she could be. She winced as a twig snapped under foot. Everything was surreal, like she was in a first-person-shooter, but there were no saves or resets. Despite the cold, her fingers were sweaty on the trigger. She wasn't sure she would be able to squeeze the trigger again, even if she had to. CJ's face bloomed, ashen and blood-spattered in her mind. *It's a game. Double points for shooting Independents.*

Lizzie stepped forward and angled toward the road. She couldn't see anything but trees. Everybody was here because of her. Why hadn't she let her father come up to Bellingham? But would he and Jess have ever have made it? At least this way she had seen him and told him she loved him. The others hadn't needed to come though. They could be kicking it back with the Hippies right now if it wasn't for her. She had to help them.

She picked her steps carefully, certain that she couldn't sneak up on an animal, but maybe on some redneck hunters. She leaned her back against a tree. The bark on the tree was thick and rough as she rested against it. Slowly she stuck her head around, staring at the ground ahead, planning her next step.

"Pssstt."

Lizzie spun. The shotgun rose. Her pulse raced.

It was Carter. A smirk graced his rugged face. His gun pointed skyward. He wasn't her enemy, right now.

She pointed her shotgun at his kneecaps.

"Nice. Where's your dad?" He stepped toward her and leaned his back against her tree.

Lizzie shrugged.

"You got a plan?" Carter asked softly.

"You got one?"

Carter shook his head. "Travis and Jim are trying to get behind 'em, so we can get them to surrender. Near as I can figure there are seven of them. We should be able to take 'em. That's about the extent of it."

"Okay." Lizzie motioned him forward with her shotgun. "My dad's behind me. If I stay between you and him, he probably won't shoot you."

"Good plan." Carter gave her an exhausted sigh. "Good luck, Lizzie."

"Thanks. You, too."

Carter walked ahead. No twigs cracked under his feet.

Lizzie slid around the tree, trying hard to see a sign of her father. Voices came from the road. She slipped forward and stopped with her back to another tree. She breathed, trying to be silent. When her heart stopped sounding like it would come out her ears she repeated the procedure on the next tree. Then the next.

As the voices got louder she heard arguing. No voices she recognized, but they were arguing about leaving with the people they had, her friends. She sped up the pace, until she was close enough to see the vehicles and the people.

She stopped and waited.

The waiting is the hardest part. She listened, intent for anything other than the wind. *Mama, if you can help me, now would be good.*

She glanced right. No sign of her dad. Then left. None of Carter either. What should she do now?

A single gunshot echoed. Lizzie gripped the rifle tight.

"We've got you surrounded," Travis yelled. "Two of you are hostages now."

Lizzie looked out from behind the tree. She could see the van, and the Independents with her friends, but no one else was visible.

"Carter," he hollered. "Demonstrate."

Lizzie heard a burst of gunfire to her left. Carter. Then more shots across the way and some to her right. Dad? She aimed her shotgun at the sky and fired. That she could do.

"We're coming in with your people as shields," Travis yelled. "Stand up, drop your weapons and raise your hands in the air. If you do not, we will shoot you immediately."

Lizzie saw people standing, their hands in the air. She walked toward the vehicles, her rifle out in front of her. By the time she got there, the Independents were disarmed.

Carter glanced smugly at Lizzie. "Nice work, Travis." He had his gun pointed at the circle of Independents.

"Thanks." Travis held two guns, a rifle jabbing one Independent in the side and the other, a pistol held at another's ear. Jim had two covered by his shotgun.

Lizzie breathed a sigh of relief. It was over.

A single shot rang out. Carter fell. Lizzie dropped her shotgun and dove toward him. His gun fell; blood, pouring from a ragged hole in his side, turned the white snow red. Lizzie stared helplessly. There was too much blood. She spun. Who had shot him?

34

Travis smiled at Lizzie. His smile chilled her to her core. Carter was dead by Travis' gun.

Travis was yelling. She barely registered the words. Something about him being in control now.

He tossed his rifle to the Independent he had been guarding. The man caught it and spun on the circle of Independents. He shot the one with the handlebar moustache. The body flew backwards; the head tilting at a crazy angle as more blood spewed into the snow.

Carter's eyes focused on her face. "Guess I get to see my daughter now." He chuckled and blood spit from his lips. "Hold onto your dad. He's lucky. So are you."

"Carter. You bastard." She pressed hard against the oozing hole in his side. She couldn't believe he was picking now to reveal he was a human being.

His left arm grabbed her hand and squeezed. Then his grip went limp.

The rest of the world returned. Travis screamed at someone to drop his gun and choose a side. Lizzie slid her hand onto Carter's rifle. Her breath froze; not daring to move, she twisted her head. Travis pointed his rifle at a kid, probably 15, one of his former partners in the Collectors. The remaining Independents stared, waiting. Jim and the Independents he'd come forward with were now all re-armed.

Lizzie realized she was watching a coup. Travis and the Independents had taken out their own leaders. Now they needed to control the rest or kill them.

The kid wasn't backing down. Neither he nor Travis. Too much testosterone. The young kid's gun bucked. Travis's fired. The kid went down; his rifle fired as he fell.

Lizzie aimed Carter's gun and shot at Travis. Lizzie heard more shots. People dove for cover. Snow flew in her face, exploding up from the ground.

She fired again. Something struck her in the arm. Travis spun. *I'm shot.* Slippery warmth oozed from her upper arm under her jacket. But it didn't hurt. Travis dove for the dirt. Lizzie propped the gun one-handed on Carter's body and squinted through the sight. She took another shot. Dirt spewed up from the snow like lava from a volcano. Another miss.

She wiped the sweat from her eyes, and searched for a target. Her right hand was numb. Blood flowed free from a wound on her arm where her oldest scars had once bled.

A cold piece of metal poked at her neck. "Toss the rifle away from you."

Lizzie froze. Cold metal pressed into her exposed skin. It felt like the size of a cannon, must be a shotgun barrel. The bathroom at home and the blood splattered over the white walls flashed in her head.

"Everybody else drop your weapons," Travis threatened behind her, "unless you want to see this little girl's brains blown out in the snow."

She tossed her gun out of reach. A hand grasped her and flipped her onto her back. A grim-faced man held the shotgun pointed straight at her torso, his sweaty hair plastered against his forehead. His face looked nervous, but his hands were rock steady. Travis stepped into her field of vision and his goon moved aside. Travis had blood soaking a through a rip in his shirt on the outside of his left arm. "You tried to kill me."

Had she hit him? She shrugged, playing it cool. "Well, you tried to kill me." She was glad she'd hit him. If it was even her shot that got him.

He shoved his pistol in a side holster and offered her his hand. "Looks like somebody got you."

Lizzie glanced down. Blood seeped from a small wound in her

arm. She twisted it, wincing as pain shot to her elbow up her arm to her heart. There was an exit hole on the other side. But there was more blood on her shirt. Had she gotten shot twice? She looked away as her body threatened to spin. Carter's body lay next to her. She saw the edge of something hard and black tucked under his belt. They had been so focused on taking weapons from the living, they had forgotten about the dead. Carter's jacket obscured it from their view, but it was within her reach. The only question was: *Could she get it fast enough?*

"I am in control now, things are gonna go my way." Travis bent closer. "Take my hand."

She took his hand with her injured left arm, pain screamed along the ravaged muscle fibers and her mind sharpened to a razor focus. As he yanked her upward, she screamed in pain. She swung her good hand down and whipped the snub-nosed revolver from Carter's body.

In an instant of cold clarity, she stood with Carter's handgun in Travis' face.

His eyes darted from hers to the gun and back.

"Travis, don't even fucking think about it. People are dead from not taking me seriously. You wanna be next?" Stars sparkled at the edge of her vision. "Put your hands up."

He did.

Lizzie kept the gun pointed at the middle of his face. She regretted shooting CJ. But she had learned a valuable lesson. She knew the truth. *If I need to, I will pull the trigger.* She wouldn't miss, not at this range.

Travis knew it, too; his Adam's apple bobbed as he shook.

She shoved the gun in the hollow of his throat. "Anybody want to follow this dipshit?"

The Independents in her field of vision glanced from one to the other. A rumbling rose behind them. Another snowmobile. Reinforcements?

Her father appeared beside her. He pulled Travis's handgun from the holster.

Her vision contracted. *Stay standing, Lizzie.*

Jess appeared with a rifle.

Lizzie saw Zach slip over to where the kid's body lay. He knelt with one knee up and picked up his rifle.

Mannie spoke, his voice loud and commanding. "Anybody else

want to die tonight? I don't." His eyes searched the crowd, begging for a calm, reasonable response.

Their guns were not going down. "Shit." Lizzie knew that everybody's trigger fingers were itchy. It would only take one, and then they would all die.

The rumble grew closer. Lights bounced across the snow. A huge man bulky in some sort of military armor rode the snowmobile standing up. He slid to a stop at the edge of the standoff, throwing snow. He jerked a large gun from the snowmobile. He pulled off his helmet and a giant braid fell. "Drop 'em." His big gun swept the Independents. The giant native man bellowed. "Drop the fucking guns. Now!" Their guns fell.

Then his gun pointed toward Lizzie and the rest as he backed up to a good vantage point. "I mean everybody!"

Lizzie heard guns fall, but she held hers to Travis's throat.

A squeal rose behind Lizzie until it became a word. "Randeeee!"

"BeeGee? Where are you?" The big man held his gun on Lizzie.

Lizzie felt the cold breeze. She stared back at him.

BeeGee came running out from behind the broken down truck, grabbing the rifle on the ground by Jess as she ran. "Randy Black-hawk. I knew you'd come."

"Which ones are the bad guys?" Randy asked.

BeeGee shrugged and pointed at Travis. "Him mostly. But them too." She hooked her head toward the Independents and continued to collect guns.

Blackhawk pulled his gun from Lizzie and grinned at her. "Pretty gutsy, girl."

"I'm Crazy Lizzie." Lizzie scrutinized him. "You're not an Independent?"

Blackhawk chuckled. "Always thought of myself as an Independent, but not one of them." His eyes swept the crowd. "I want everyone where I can see them."

"Move it," Lizzie ordered Travis. "Forward." He walked toward Blackhawk.

She searched for her father. He was standing funny with his fist pressed into his chest. She noticed there was blood on his shirt. Dizziness was coming. "Daddy?" *You can't die.* Her stomach contracted and she vomited bile into the snow and sank to her knees. Stars dotted the edge of her vision. She closed her eyes.

"You," Blackhawk growled.

Lizzie eyes shot open as her equilibrium left her. The last thing she saw as she fell into darkness was the deadly anger Blackhawk aimed at her father, along with his gun.

Zach took in the carnage on the ground. Carter lay in a bloody circle of snow. The kid who'd taken on Travis lay face up. Lizzie teetered as her eyes darted from her father to Blackhawk.

"You," Blackhawk said, staring an accusation at Mannie.

Then Lizzie fell. Zach ran to her, but stopped short as he saw Blackhawk's shotgun point toward Mannie. He froze. Wanting to scream. *No. Enough.* Nothing worked. *If Lizzie survives I'm going to have to tell her about her dead father.*

Mannie stumbled toward Lizzie. Blackhawk tracked him with the gun.

Zach stepped toward the gun and in between Mannie and Blackhawk. He saw BeeGee move.

Travis had stopped walking. Zach could see him gauging his chances. The surreality of the situation stole all sound. Zach couldn't get his mouth to say words.

BeeGee's hand touched Blackhawk's arm and the gun came down. "No," she said. "Not him."

Zach saw a curtain of darkness fall across Blackhawk's eyes and disappear as he nodded. Mannie was falling to his knees by Lizzie, holding his fist against his chest above his heart. Zach moved swiftly to help him down.

Mannie kissed Lizzie's cheek and then rolled to his back with a groan. His hand slipped from his wound as his eyes rolled into his head.

Zach applied pressure as blood began to flow through the hole in Mannie's shirt. He took the pistol from Lizzie's hand and pointed it at Travis. "Travis, don't move. Blackhawk?" His eyes found the big native's eyes, now calm. "Are we on the same side?" Zach saw Duke slipping around behind Blackhawk, a rifle ready in his hands.

Blackhawk glanced at BeeGee and she nodded. He looked back to Zach. "Yeah. Looks like it."

Duke's rifle moved to cover the Independents.

"Nev?" Zach hollered. "Jess?" The girls came out from behind the van with Charley and Saj. "First-aid training? Nev? Jess, grab a gun. Help Blackhawk and BeeGee. Rachael? I need you here. Your hand." Everybody moved.

Rachael knelt, Saj wide-eyed on her hip, and placed her hand next to Zach's. Zach moved it into place. "Press this hard." When Rachael was in place, Zach sidled over by the kid Travis had shot. He checked to see if there was any pulse. Nothing. There was a round hole in the middle of his chest. Zach felt like puking, but pulled away after closing the boy's eyelids. He picked the kid's rifle up again and turned his attention to the enemy.

Blackhawk, BeeGee, Jess and Duke had the Independents and the turncoat Collectors in a tight circle.

"The Collectors should have some handcuffs." Zach shoved the pistol in his jacket pocket and strode to the van. He pulled it open and found two pairs of handcuffs. He took them and put them on Travis, making sure they were tight enough to hurt. Then he handcuffed Jim through Travis' arms.

Blackhawk pulled a long knife from a sheath on his leg.

Oh, shit. Zach waited as Blackhawk approached the other prisoners. He pulled the man's shirt out as his knife moved in, cutting their shirts open and tearing them down to limit their mobility.

Zach was wet, but unwounded. He had dived behind the van, hauling Nev, Rachael and Saj with him. He knelt by Lizzie. Nev had tears on her cheeks.

"Lizzie's pulse is strong," Nev said through tight lips. "She's not losing a lot of blood."

Zach nodded, his eyes searching both Lizzie and her dad for any other wounds. Saj sobbed and wiggled. Zach replaced Rachael's hand with his on Mannie's chest. She stood and cooed at Saj, trying to keep him calm.

Mannie's shirt was soaked with blood. His breath sounded ragged, but steady. Zach released the pressure; blood did not flow. Zach didn't know if that was good or bad.

Jess knelt beside him, sobbing softly. "Are they going to be okay?"

"I don't know. Way past my level of nursing." Giving Gramps shots was all the experience he had. "We need to get them to a hospital."

A howl pulled his attention from the wounded. *Where the hell had Charley gone?* "Jess, keep an eye on Mannie. I'm going to get the RAV and check on Charley."

Zach jogged down the slope. Charley was hugging Spike, his head on his chest. Zach knelt, pulling Charley gently away from Spike's ravaged body. There was blood everywhere.

Zach shook his head, "Charley, I don't think… We can't…"

"No, you gotta save him." Charley's tears tore at Zach.

Spike's body shook as his eyes opened, searching. A whimper escaped his lips. Those eyes, so simple, so full of pain. Blood flowed from dozens of rips in his clothes and his flesh.

"Hey, dog man." Zach coughed, "You saved Lizzie. Good job." Zach ran his fingers through Spike's thick hair.

Charley sobbed, a howl in the emptiness.

Spike's hands raised up to Charley's face and made a sign *Good Job* and then dropped; his eyes slipped closed.

"Spike," Charley howled. "Don't go. Don't go away. Don't leave me." He laid his face on Spike's chest, ignoring the blood and wounds. His small arms reached around Spike, trying to hold him.

Zach's throat tightened. Of all the deaths he'd seen, Gramps' was the hardest to bear. Zach had cried then, but not since. Not even for his dad. But his cheeks were wet with tears for Spike and Charley. Spike was like a big kid. Zach wrapped his arms around Charley and pulled him up, holding him as much for himself as for Charley.

Charley let himself be held for a moment then squirmed out of Zach's grasp, pushing him away. He knelt again at Spike's side. His hand reached out tentatively to touch Spike's grizzled face.

Zach knelt down next to him.

Charley's face contorted, tears running down. His body shook, his breath came in short gasps. "We need to bury him."

"We need to leave." Zach glanced around. "Lizzie and her dad need a hospital.

"We need to bury him." Charley's eyes demanded.

Zach sighed. *Arguing with a 12-year-old.* He couldn't find the words to explain to this boy that taking the time to say goodbye to his beloved friend with a burial might mean that his other friends would die. So he simply said, "Rest in Peace, Spike. You were a good friend."

Zach hustled to the RAV. Charley stayed behind, weakly pushing snow over the still form of his friend.

35

Zach drove to the top as near as he could to the wounded. He hopped out and swung the back door open wide. "We need to get them to Provo." Zach refused to say *The City*. "It's about 30 minutes. I bet they have medical care. Can you get Charley to come?" Nev headed down the hill as Zach walked over to Blackhawk.

The big Native nodded in acknowledgement.

"Blackhawk? Can you get the snowmobiles on the trailer? And bring the prisoners. The people in Provo ought to appreciate the gear, don't you think?"

"Yeah." Blackhawk grinned.

They loaded the wounded carefully—Lizzie and Nev with Rachael driving the RAV. Jess with Zach in the Tank keeping an eye on Mannie's condition, with Charley with Saj in the back.

Further back Blackhawk drove the big beast of a truck pulling the trailer full of snowmobiles; with Duke and BeeGee guarding the Independents and renegade Collectors in the back.

Zach's eyes strayed to the white RAV Rachael was driving with Lizzie inside. His rag-tag, fugitive fleet following him on their way to Provo. He prayed that the truck Blackhawk drove and its contents were their ticket into Provo, rather than the eligible young women in their company.

What if something happens to Nev? What if they took her from him? Can't worry about that now. "Jess, where to?" Zach asked.

"We took an exit off I-15 that led us to a guard house."

Sure enough, when Zach saw University Parkway there were orange cones. He pulled onto the off-ramp. Plumes of smoke rose in the distance over Provo.

"As long as there're no Zombies we'll be fine." It didn't sound as funny as it had in his head, but Jess humored him with a hollow laugh.

At the guardhouse were half a dozen well-armed soldiers. They looked like real Army, not the impromptu paramilitary start-up in Idaho. He let the Tank roll to a stop a few feet short of the gate. The man without a rifle in his hands or a helmet on his head approached. "Who are you and where are you from?" His name patch said Benson.

The other soldiers splayed out around the vehicles.

"Zach Riley, Sedro-Woolley, Washington. We have wounded people. We need a doctor."

Benson swung his flashlight up, illuminating Mannie's face. He passed it across Zach and into the back seat.

"Please," Jess begged.

"I need a medic," Benson said into his mic, "or two, if possible."

Benson's walkie-talkie squawked, "Captain. Somebody IDing himself as Randall Blackhawk, U. S. Army Rangers, says he's bringing in Utah Independent prisoners and some renegade Collectors as gear to trade. Wounded coming in first."

"Check. Benson, out." Benson spoke into his radio mic, "Provo? Ambulance. Now."

His radio blew static and another voice replied, "Roger."

"The rest of you are going to have to wait." Benson motioned with his arm. "Pull over there."

Jess gasped in relief.

"Thank you, Sir." Zach moved the Tank. Soldiers helped Jess get Mannie onto a flat-board stretcher. Zach stepped down out of the cab and jogged back to the RAV.

A medic was checking Lizzie's pulse. "All right, let's move her." A second stretcher was coming, carried between two more soldiers.

Nev kissed Lizzie's forehead as the soldiers placed her on a stretcher. Zach stared at the blood on Lizzie's clothes. Maybe it wasn't all hers.

"Oh, god, Zach." Nev looked haggard as she fell into his arms.

The ambulance, siren wailing, drove into view.

Zach held Nev tight. None of the soldiers seemed overly interested in the women. "I hope we got them here in time."

The medics were pulling aside Mannie's and Lizzie's clothes, inspecting the wounds. The ambulance ground to a stop and the back doors popped open. Soldiers loaded both stretchers and then slammed the doors shut. One soldier slapped the door twice to indicate they were good to go and the ambulance sped off with siren howling. Zach closed his eyes and prayed. *Let them live.*

While the ambulance and medics had taken care of Lizzie and Mannie, Blackhawk had arrived. Benson oversaw the offloading of the prisoners. He had not questioned their status as prisoners or released any of them from their bonds, though it was clear he recognized some of the Collectors.

When he had sent them off, he turned his attention back to Zach and the others. "Everybody follow me." He led them into a building off the side of the road.

He took Zach into a small room and sat him down at a table. "I assume you can speak for the others." It was less a question and more an observation. Benson placed a small digital recorder on the table and said, "I need your statement. Start at the beginning."

Zach told Benson everything—almost: this time he did keep Glen out of it.

When Zach got to the part about the renegade Collectors and their interaction with the Utah Independents, Benson had him repeat and took prodigious notes. He asked for details and made some comment about passing on word to his superiors.

When Benson was satisfied, he released Zach and took him down the hall to his companions.

There were couches around the room and everyone laid out on them in various stages of consciousness. Charley was asleep in Rachael's arms. Duke snored on another couch. Nev was curled around Saj. Jess paced in the back of the room. She nodded at him, but didn't seem to want to talk. A bored-looking guard stood by the door.

There was food, army rations, but Zach was so hungry it didn't matter. He shoveled some peaches and crackers into his mouth, then lay down on the empty couch nearest Nev.

He didn't think he would fall asleep, but the next thing he noticed was waking to Nev's lips on his forehead. He turned to find hers with his own as he sat up. For a moment there was only the two of them and their lips. Her warmth surged through his body.

After a short but satisfying kiss, he pulled back, trying to read how things were by the look on her face. *How long did I sleep?* He had been tired—was still tired. Tired of running.

Nev raised her eyes to his. Her face was enigmatic. No answers.

"Lizzie?" he asked.

Nev's jaw tightened and she shook her head. "No word yet."

Zach sighed and pulled her into his arms. *Let it go. Everything's going to be fine. Maybe.* He held her close. "I'm glad you're safe."

Mannie woke to darkness. He was alive. He had been hit in the first hail of gunfire. But he hadn't let it stop him. Then he'd seen Lizzie take on Travis. He'd stood there, powerless, watching his daughter face death and win. But she was wounded in the side and the arm. Then Blackhawk had shown up and he'd watched her fall.

When Lizzie passed out he had tried to go to her. Blackhawk was going to hurt him, he could see it his eyes, but BeeGee had interceded for him and he'd fallen near Lizzie, kissed her on the forehead and then the blood left his head. The last face he had seen before the darkness came was Zach, Lizzie's friend, angry and scared.

Mannie explored his senses. He was strapped down. His shoulder throbbed. Alive. *But what about Lizzie?* He needed to know she was ok. There had been a lot of blood.

He struggled to raise his head. "Anybody there?" His voice came out in a whisper.

Jess came to him from a dark corner of the room. She looked weary, like she had been sitting up all night watching him. Her hand touched his forehead. "Rest, Mannie." She smiled.

"Lizzie?" Before Jess could answer, the world faded away.

A throb of pain in his chest brought Mannie aware. *Pain is good. Means I'm alive.* He opened his eyes slowly; the view screamed hospital. *Provo, I bet.*

He heard breathing—labored and fluttery. "Hello?"

The fluttery breath caught. "Daddy?"

"Elizabeth?" His heart pounded.

"I can't see you."

"I'm here," he said.

Jess's face appeared beside him. "The sleepyheads are awake." She smiled at him and pressed the button on the bed to raise him up.

The motor churned and his head lifted slowly. He closed his eyes as the ceiling spun.

"Open your eyes, silly," Jess commanded.

He did. Lizzie lay across from him. She grinned weakly.

"Daddy. You scared me."

"Scared myself." That was all he could get out. "I was afraid—" He lost sight of her as tears flooded his eyes.

Jess eased out of the chair beside his bed. "I'll give you two some time."

Mannie nodded. "Thanks, Jess."

"Daddy. I can hardly believe you're really here."

"It doesn't feel real yet to me either." The room spun a little. "Lizzie. I'm not perfect. I'm sorry."

"Stop saying you're sorry." Lizzie lay her head back. "I don't want you perfect. I want you here. I'm not perfect either. But I'd like to get to know you."

"I love you, Elizabeth." His eyes closed. "Now, we have time." He was exhausted. "See you in the morning." He felt himself drift out. He tried to hold his eyes open, seeing her smile as long as he could.

Lizzie let her head fall back against the pillow. Time. She had some now. She forced herself up and drank from the water glass on the nightstand. Jayce's calculator watch lay there along with one of the extra cell phones. Her eyes teared up. Mama and Jayce. She didn't have their voices anymore. But she had the memories. Maybe there were some in the house back in Bellingham—VHS tapes or something on the computer. *Mama, I'm sorry I broke my promise, but I'm glad I left the house.* She pulled the watch onto her wrist. *I miss you, Jayce.*

A knocked sounded on the door. Jess slipped in and closed it.

"Hey, girl. How are you?" She smoothed Lizzie's hair away from her face.

Lizzie smiled. "I'm hungry."

Jess laughed. "I'll tell the doctor you're awake. If he says you can eat, we'll get you some food." Jess kissed Lizzie's forehead. "Thanks."

"For what?"

"For making me part of your family."

Lizzie nodded and smiled. Jess walked out the door and Lizzie closed her eyes. She was so tired. Everything ached. Anytime she moved the wrong way it felt like a hot brand searing into her side.

A gray-haired doctor entered the room. He looked exhausted. "Good morning, Miss Gooden. Glad to see you're awake. I'm Dr. Wright. Your father woke up?"

"Yes." She felt warm and fuzzy and hoped it wasn't the drugs.

"Mr. Guerrero?" the doctor asked in a firm voice. Her dad didn't wake up, but the doctor didn't seem concerned. He checked her dad's chart and wrote something.

"Is he gonna be ok?" Lizzie asked.

"He'll be fine. We gave him the next rabies booster. He needs plenty of rest and time to recover." The doctor came back to Lizzie's bedside. "And I am happy to report you and your baby are fine too."

"My what?" Lizzie was confused. "You mean Saj?"

"No." He smiled. "Your unborn baby. I automatically run blood work. Your tests show you're pregnant.

"I'm pregnant? But that isn't possible." Her stomach spun in response.

"Did you have sex?"

"Yes, but—" *How could she have gotten pregnant? She and Zach had only had that one night.*

"Then it's possible."

She was silent, considering. Thoughts bounced off one another. *Having a baby? I'm not ready. Zach? Nev?* "Does anyone else know?"

The doctor shook his head. "No."

Lizzie touched her belly. "Thanks." There were bandages wrapped across it, but it didn't feel any different. "Can I eat?"

"Yes, you should. Food is on the way. Your friends take good care of you."

"Yes, they do." The warm feeling grew.

The doctor excused himself after writing notes on her chart.

Lizzie lay her head back and closed her eyes. There was a knock on the door.

"Jess, you better have food." Lizzie pushed the button to raise her head, instead of trying to sit up.

Zach brought in a covered tray. "I'm not Jess, but I do have food," he said, setting it on the rolling table and wheeling it close to her. "Sorry. I didn't fix it." He whipped off the lid.

There were mashed potatoes and gravy and a little cup of apple-sauce. She lifted a fork full with some potatoes dipped in the gravy to her lips. It was warm and real. "I'm sure it's not as good as yours."

"Thanks." Zach stared at her, a serious look on his face. "Lizzie?"

"Yeah?"

"Next time? Tell me what's going on, okay? Before you jump off the cliff?"

"I will. I'll tell you and Nev and Jess. And Dad." *God. If you only knew what cliff we already jumped off.*

"Everyone's waiting to see you. Charley wants to say good bye."

"Goodbye?" Lizzie's heart twisted.

"He's headed out with Blackhawk and BeeGee tomorrow." Zach sat down on the edge of her bed. "They're gonna try to help him find his grandpa."

"I don't understand. The City people are letting them leave?"

"Uh-huh. They've got a boatload of rules here. But they submitted the travel request and it got approved. We're safe, protected. No more running and fighting." His smile escaped.

Lizzie stared at him. "What the hell, Zach? We're staying? Were you going to tell me what's going on?"

"You don't have to stay, but I'm ready to quit traveling for a while. I think the worst is over. Duke and I've got job interviews tomorrow. Gonna be a Collectors here in The City."

"You and Duke? Collectors in The City? Jesus, Zach, how long have I been knocked out?"

"A couple days. Seems Carter and Travis were exceeding their orders. Collectors really are supposed to bring in people and gear without so much coercion."

"You really think it's safe here?"

He nodded.

Nothing is ever going to be safe. But Zach's boyish grin claimed otherwise. And with a baby on board, safety made sense.

How did she feel about Zach? And how did he feel about her? Well, if he was the last man on Earth, it wouldn't be a bad thing. But she was glad he wasn't. She was glad Nev was here, too. The rest of the thoughts were too complicated.

Her look must have made him uncomfortable because he shifted and cleared his throat. "I'll go get the others."

She smiled as he stood up and left to get the rest of her family.

Nev came through the door carrying a grinning, arm-flapping Saj. Lizzie felt warm inside. She put a hand on her bandaged belly as her father's eyes opened and a soft smile graced his weary face.

A new family for a new world. In more ways than one. She held out her hands for Saj. "Come to Sissie."

Lizzie's story continues...

STRAIGHT INTO
DARKNESS

A DESERTED LANDS NOVEL

ROBERT L. SLATER

Coming in 2015 from Rocket Tears Press

Go to www.desertedlands.com for more information, additional fiction and updates.

Acknowledgements

I would like to thank all of the students that I have had the honor of working with through the years. Also the many writers, teachers and librarians who inspired me, also a list to large too mention.

Most important, though, none of this would have been possible with the support of my partner, Elena; my kids: Cail, Tanner, Daen, Sheridan, Ian, Miranda; my family, immediate, extended and hyper-extended.

Other folks who have leant specific assistance and have not been mentioned heretofore include: Evelyn Nystrom, James Slater, Joannah Miley, Donald Drummond, Frank Slater, Christopher & Christine Perkins, Cory Skerry, Peter Rust, James Hagarty, Jesikah Sundin, Selah J Tay-song, Judy Penn, Christopher Key, Alice Acheson, Brendan Clark, Paul Hanson, Brenna Brister, Ivy Wright, Tsena Paulsen, Janet Godsoe, David Seltzer, Betsy Childs, Kathy Brown, Eddi and Katie Vulic. I am certain I have forgotten other helpful people, my sincerest apologies.

Places I wrote: Village Books & Book Fare, Green's Corner, Wood's Coffee, New York Pizza, Bellingham Public Libraries, Windward High School, Wilson Motors.

About the Author

Robert L. Slater is a teacher, author, playwright, singer/song-writer, actor, director who has been paid for all of the above jobs, but only one so far has proven capable of paying any bills much larger than the price of this novel. He lives and works in the northwest corner of Washington State near the Canadian border. You can find his music at www.robslater.com, more fiction at www.desertedlands.com and poetry at www.colleenaslater.com.

CPSIA information can be obtained at www.ICGtesting.com
Printed in the USA
LVOW12s0015060214

372463LV00002B/2/P